D1142411

PEARLS, GIRLS AND MONTY BODKIN
AND
BACHELORS ANONYMOUS

Monty Bodkin has returned to London after a year in Hollywood, leaving his secretary, Sandy Miller, quite heartbroken. Monty, however, is wooing Gertrude Butterwick, the English hockey international. Gertrude's father, hoping to prevent their betrothal, had made it a condition that Monty should first hold down a job for a year, and he is horrified at Monty's return. He does not know that Monty had blackmailed the film boss, Ivor Llewellyn, into giving him the job in Hollywood. Now Monty has returned to claim Gertrude's hand! But Mr Butterwick does not easily give in, and Monty's road to happiness proves to be riddled with pitfalls. . . .

*   *   *

Ivor Llewellyn, much-married founder of the Superba-Llewellyn Studios in Hollywood, is again a bachelor (for the sixth time). He is not renowned as a conversationalist with the fair sex, but proposals of marriage trip too lightly off his tongue. His friends at Bachelors Anonymous, alarmed about his imminent visit to London, arrange a bodyguard for him—one Joe Pickering, who manages to protect him from the formidable Vera Dalrymple, but who himself falls helplessly in love with a pretty London journalist, Sally Fitch. A reinforcement for the bodyguard arrives in the person of Ephraim Trout, an old friend of the reckless Ivor, but his assistance proves to be of very doubtful value.

PEARLS, GIRLS AND MONTY BODKIN

and

BACHELORS ANONYMOUS

*

P. G. WODEHOUSE

THE
COMPANION BOOK CLUB
LONDON AND SYDNEY

Pearls, Girls and Monty Bodkin, copyright © P. G. Wodehouse, 1972; *Bachelors Anonymous*, copyright © P. G. Wodehouse, 1973.

This edition, published in 1975 by
The Hamlyn Publishing Group Ltd,
is issued by arrangement with
Barrie & Jenkins Ltd.

*Made and printed in Great Britain
for the Companion Book Club
by Odhams (Watford) Ltd.*
060087186X
3.75/286

CONTENTS

*

PEARLS, GIRLS AND MONTY BODKIN

To Sheran with love

Chapter One

AS ALWAYS when the weather was not unusual the Californian sun shone brightly down on the Superba-Llewellyn motion picture studio at Llewellyn City. Silence had gripped the great building except for the footsteps of some supervisor hurrying back to resume his supervising or the occasional howl from the writer's ghetto as some author with a headache sought in vain to make sense of the story which had been handed to him for treatment. It was two-thirty of a summer afternoon, and this busy hive of industry generally tended to slacken off at that hour.

In the office bearing on its door the legend

ADVISER FOR PRODUCTIONS

and in smaller letters down in the left-hand corner the name

M. Bodkin

Sandy Miller, M. Bodkin's secretary, was waiting for her overlord to return from lunch.

Secretaries in Hollywood are either statuesque and haughty or small, pretty and vivacious. Sandy belonged to the latter class. But though a cheerful little soul as a general rule, as ready with a laugh as a television studio audience, at that moment she had allowed a frown to mar the smoothness of the alabaster brow which all Hollywood secretaries have to have. She was thinking, as she often did when in meditative mood, how much she loved M. (standing for Monty) Bodkin.

It had come on quite suddenly one afternoon when they were sharing a beef stew Bette Davis at the canteen, and had grown steadily through the months till now the urge to stroke his butter-coloured hair had become almost irresistible. And what was causing her to frown was the thought of how foolish it had been of her to allow herself to get into this condition with one whose heart was so plainly bestowed elsewhere. There was a photograph on his desk of a robust girl signed 'Love, Gertrude', and photographs endorsed like that cannot be ignored. They mean something. They have a message. This message had not escaped Sandy, particularly on the morning when she had caught him kissing the thing. (He had said he was blowing a speck of dust off the glass, but this explanation, though specious, had not convinced her.)

Who this Gertrude was she had not been informed, for M. Bodkin was reticent about his private affairs. Of her own she had concealed nothing from him. In the long afternoons when business was slack and there was the opportunity of exchanging confidences she had revealed the whole Sandy Miller Story—the childhood in the small Illinois town, the leisurely passage through high school, the lucky break when rich Uncle Alexander, doing the square thing by his god-daughter, had put her through secretarial college, the graduation from same, the various jobs, some good, some not so good, and finally the coming to Hollywood because she had always wanted to see what it was like there. And almost all she knew of Monty was that he had a good appetite and a freckle on his nose. It irritated her constantly.

He came in at this moment, greeted her with his customary cordiality, cast a loving glance at the robust girl on the desk and took a seat.

It is difficult to say offhand what ought to be the aspect of a production adviser at a prominent Hollywood studio. Of Monty you could only state that he did not look like one. His pleasant, somewhat ordinary face suggested amiability rather than astuteness. In the West End of London—say at the Drones Club in Dover Street, of which he was a popular member—you would have encountered him without surprise. In the executive building of the Superba-Llewellyn he seemed out of place. You felt he ought not to be there. Ivor Llewellyn, the president of the organization, had this feeling very strongly. There was an ornamental lake on the Superba-Llewellyn lot, and it was his opinion that his production adviser ought to be at the bottom of it with a stout brick attached to his neck. Though not as a rule a lavish man, he would gladly have supplied brick and string free of charge.

Refreshed by lunch, Monty was plainly in jovial mood. He nearly always was, and it was this unfailing euphoria of his that twisted the knife in Mr Llewellyn's bosom, he holding the view that a man who had chiselled his way into the Superba-Llewellyn as Monty had done ought at least to have the decency to behave as if his conscience were gnawing him.

'Sorry I'm late,' he said. 'I got entangled in some particularly adhesive spaghetti and have only just succeeded in hacking my way through to safety. Anything sensational happened in my absence?'

'No.'

'No earthquakes or other Acts of God?'

'No.'

'No trouble brewing in the writers' kraals? The natives not restless?'

'No.'

There had been an unwonted brusqueness in Sandy's monosyllabic replies, and Monty regarded her with concern. They gave him the impression that she had something on her mind. He was very fond of her—in a brotherly way, of course, to which even Gertrude Butterwick, always inclined to look squiggle-eyed at his female friends, could not have taken exception—and it pained him to think that anything was worrying her.

'You seem *distrait*, my poppet. Are you musing on something?'

It seemed to Sandy that at last an opportunity had presented itself for extracting confidences from this man of mystery. Never till now had their conversation taken a turn which provided her with such an admirable cue.

'If you really want to know,' she said, 'I was musing on you.'

'You were? I'm flattered.'

'I was trying to figure out what you were doing in Llewellyn City.'

'I'm a production adviser. See door.'

13

'Exactly. That's what puzzled me. At most studios, from what one hears, you have to be a nephew or a brother-in-law of the man up top to be given an important position like that. Yet here you are, no relation even by marriage, production advising away like a house on fire. And you told me you had had no previous experience.'

'That's good, don't you think? I bring a fresh mind to the job.'

'But how did you *get* the job?'

'I met Llewellyn on the boat coming over from England.'

'And I suppose he said "I like your face, my boy. Come and take charge of my productions"?'

'It amounted to that.'

'He must have liked your face very much.'

'Can you blame him? Of course there was another factor which was of assistance to me in the negotiations.'

'What was that?'

'Never mind.'

'But I do mind. What was it?'

'He had urgent need of something that was in my possession. In order to induce me to part with it he was obliged to meet my terms. That's how business deals are always conducted.'

'What was it he wanted?'

'If I tell you, will you promise to ask no more questions?'

'All right.'

'Sacred word?'

'Sacred word.'

'Very well. It was a mouse.'

'*What!*'

'That's what it was.'

'But I don't understand. How do you mean? Why did he want a mouse?'

'You promised not to ask any more questions.'

'But I didn't think you were going to say a mouse.'

'In this world we must be prepared for anybody to say anything.'

'But a *mouse*. Why?'

'The subject is closed.'

14

'You aren't going to explain?'

'Not a word. My lips are sealed, like those of a clam.'

Sandy's exasperation became too much for her. If she had had any more lethal weapon than a small notebook, she would have thrown it at him. She burst into a tidal wave of eloquence.

'Shall I tell you something that may be of interest? You make me sick. Here am I, trying to collect material for the Memoirs I shall be writing one of these days, and what ought to be the most interesting part of them, the time I spent working for the great Monty Bodkin in Hollywood, won't amount to a hill of beans because the great Monty Bodkin is one of those strong silent Englishmen who don't utter. They are generally described—correctly—as dumb bricks. All I shall be able to tell my public is that on the rare occasions when you did break your Trappist vows you talked as if you had a potato in your mouth.'

Monty started. The shaft had pierced his armour.

'A potato?'

'Large and boiled.'

'You're crazy.'

'All right. I'm just telling you.'

The discussion threatened to become heated. Monty, always the man of peace, raised a restraining hand.

'We mustn't brawl. Merely remarking that my enunciation is more like a silver bell than anything, ask anybody, I will tactfully divert the conversation to other topics, to take one at random. Pop Llewellyn. He was at the canteen.'

'Oh?'

'He was tucking into a pudding, or dessert as you would call it, of obvious richness, all cream and sugar and stuff.'

'Oh?'

'Shovelling it into himself like a starving Eskimo. I was sorry that our relations were not such as to make it possible for me to warn him it was adding pounds to his already impressive weight. I couldn't have done that, of course. He wouldn't have taken it kindly and would probably have bitten me in the leg.'

'Oh?'

'You do keep saying "Oh?", don't you? It's an odd thing about Llewellyn,' said Monty thoughtfully. 'I've been seeing him daily for a year, and you'd think I'd have got immune to him by this time, but whenever we meet my bones still turn to water and Dow Jones registers another sharp drop in my morale. I shuffle my feet. I twiddle my fingers. My pores open and I break into a cold sweat, if you will pardon the expression. Does he affect you in this way?'

'I've never met him.'

'You're lucky.'

'I once did some work for Mrs Llewellyn.'

'What's she like? Meek and crushed, I suppose?'

'Meek and crushed nothing. She's the boss. At her command he jumps through hoops and snaps lumps of sugar off his nose. It's like that Ben Bolt poem we used to learn in high school. "He weeps with delight when she gives him a smile and trembles with fear at her frown".'

'I used to recite that as a youngster.'

'It must have sounded wonderful.'

'I believe it did. But really you astound me. I can't imagine Llewellyn trembling with fear. To me he has always seemed like one of those unpleasant creatures in the Book of Revelation. She must be a very remarkable woman.'

'She is.'

'No doubt she is the motivating force behind this trip to Europe.'

'This what to where?'

'They are crossing the Atlantic shortly on a vacation.'

'Who told you that?'

'A fellow I met in the canteen who looked as if he might be a writer of additional dialogue or the man in charge of the wind machine. They'll be away for quite a while.'

'The old place won't seem the same to you.'

'It won't have to. I also am leaving.'

'What!'

You could have said that Monty's words had given Sandy a shock, and you would have been perfectly right. Her eyes had widened and her attractive jaw fallen a full inch. In her optimistic moments she had sometimes hoped that if their association continued uninterrupted, propinquity might do the work it is always supposed to do, causing the man she loved to forget the robust girl he had left behind him, but at this announcement the hope curled up and died.

Speech came from her in a gasp.

'You're quitting?'

'As of even date.'

'Going back to England?'

'That's right. And I shall want you to help me with my letter of resignation. So take pencil and notebook and let's get at it.'

Sandy was a girl of mettle. The dreams she had allowed herself to dream lay in ruins about her, but she spoke composedly.

'How far have you got?'

' "Dear Mr Llewellyn".'

'Good start.'

'So I thought. But now comes the part where I need your never-failing sympathy, encouragement and advice. The wording has to be just right.'

'I don't see why. From what you were telling me, he'll probably be delighted to get rid of you.'

'He will. I shall be surprised if he doesn't go dancing in the streets and ordering an ox to be roasted whole in the market place. But don't forget that sudden joy can be as dangerous as sudden anguish. Llewellyn is now loaded to the brim with that creamy pudding or dessert, and the announcement on a full stomach that I am leaving him, if not broken gently, might prove fatal.'

Chapter Two

THE SMOKING-ROOM of the Drones Club always started to fill up as the hour of lunch approached, and today a group of members had assembled there, like antelopes or whatever the fauna are that collect in gangs around water holes, in order to enjoy the pre-prandial aperitif. It was as the various beverages were brought in and distributed that a Whisky Sour, having taken the first lifegiving sip, said:

'Oh, I say, who do you think I met in Piccadilly last night?'

'Who?' enquired a Martini-with-small-onion-not-an-olive.

'Monty Bodkin.'

'Monty Bodkin? You couldn't have!'

'I did.'

'But he's in Hollywood.'

'He's back.'

'Oh, he's *back*?' said the Martini, relieved. 'I thought for a moment you must have seen his astral body or whatever they call it. I believe it often happens that way. A chap hands in his dinner pail in America or wherever it may be and looks in on a pal in London to report. It really was Monty, was it?'

'Looking bronzed and fit.'

'How long was he in Hollywood?'

'A year. His contract was for five years, but one was all he needed.'

'Why?'

'Why what?'

'Why did he only need one year?'

'Because that would satisfy the conditions laid down by her father.'

'Whose father?'

'Gertrude Butterwick's.'

'You couldn't make this a bit easier, could you?' asked a

Screwdriver with dark circles under his eyes. 'I was up rather late last night and am not feeling at my best this morning. Who, to start with, is Gertrude Butterwick?'

'The girl Monty's engaged to.'

'Reggie Tennyson's cousin,' said a well-informed Manhattan. 'Plays hockey.'

The Screwdriver winced. The sorrows he had been trying to drown on the previous night had been caused by a girl who played hockey. He had been rash enough to allow his fiancée to persuade him to referee a match in which she was taking part, and she had broken the engagement because on six occasions he had penalized her—unjustly, she maintained—for being offside.

'How do you mean, the conditions laid down by her father?' asked a puzzled Gimlet.

'Just that.'

'He laid down conditions?'

'Yes.'

'Her father did?'

'Yes.'

'Gertrude Butterwick's father?'

'Yes.'

'Sorry. I don't get it.'

'It's perfectly simple. I had it all from Monty last night over a Welsh rarebit and a bottle of the best. Extraordinarily interesting story, rather like Jacob and Rachel in the Bible, except that Jacob had to serve seven years to get Rachel, while Monty only had to serve one.'

The Screwdriver moaned faintly and passed a piece of ice over his forehead. The Whisky Sour proceeded.

'I think it was at a lunch or a dinner that he met Gertrude and decided that she was what the doctor ordered. Apparently she took the same view of him, because it wasn't more than a week or so before they became engaged. And then, just as it looked as if all they had to do was collect the bridesmaids, order the cake and sign up the Bishop and assistant clergy, along came the sleeve across the windpipe. Her father refused to give his consent to their union.'

The Gimlet was visibly moved, as were all those present except the Screwdriver, who was still busy with his ice.

'He did *what*?'

'Wouldn't give his consent.'

'But surely you don't have to have father's consent in these enlightened days?'

'You do if you're Gertrude Butterwick. She's a throwback to the Victorian age. She does what Daddy tells her.'

'Comes of playing hockey,' said the Screwdriver.

'Monty, of course, was as surprised, bewildered and taken aback as you are. He pleaded with her to ignore the memo from the front office and elope, but she would have none of it. Some nonsense about her father having a weak heart and it would kill him if his daughter disobeyed him.'

'Silly ass.'

'Indubitably. I have it from Reggie Tennyson that Pop Butterwick not only looks like a horse but is as strong as one. Still, there it was.'

'No daughter of mine shall ever be allowed to touch a hockey stick,' said the Screwdriver. 'I shall be very firm about this.'

'But why wouldn't her father give his consent?' asked a Comfort-on-the-rocks. 'Monty's got all the money in the world.'

'That,' said the Whisky Sour, 'was just the trouble. He was left the stuff by an aunt, and old Butterwick is one of those fellows who go into business at the age of sixteen and take a dim view of inherited money. He said Monty was a rich young waster and no daughter of his was going to marry him.'

'So that was that.'

'As it happened, no. Monty reasoned with the blister, who eventually relented to the extent of saying that if he proved himself by earning his living for a year, the wedding bells would ring out. So Monty got a job with the Superba-Llewellyn motion picture people at Llewellyn City, Southern California.'

It hurt the Screwdriver to move his head, but he did so in

order to cast a stern glance at the speaker. He resented a story sloppily told.

'You say "Monty got a job with the Superba-Llewellyn people" in that offhand way, as if it were the simplest thing in the world to get taken on by a motion picture organization, whereas everybody knows that if you aren't the illegitimate son of one of the principal shareholders, you haven't a hope. How did Monty worm his way in?'

The Whisky Sour guffawed amusedly.

'This is going to make you laugh.'

'Not me,' said the Screwdriver. 'Not this morning.'

'It all started on board the liner *Atlantic* en route for New York. Gertrude Butterwick was there because she was going to America with the All England women's hockey team. Monty was there because he wanted to be with Gertrude. Reggie Tennyson was there because the family were shipping him off to some office job in Canada. All straight so far?'

Those present agreed that up to this point they had followed him.

'And also among those sailing were Ivor Llewellyn, head of the Superba-Llewellyn, and his wife's sister Mabel Spence. That completes the cast of characters. You've got all that straight?'

'Yes.'

'Now here's where the plot thickens,' the Whisky Sour proceeded. 'All the above had come on board at Southampton with the exception of La Spence, who joined them at Cherbourg, having been in Paris whooping it up with Llewellyn's wife Grayce, and conceive Llewellyn's emotion when she told him she had brought with her a very valuable diamond thingummy, a purchase of Grayce's, and she, Grayce, wanted him, Llewellyn, to smuggle it through the New York Customs. It seems that she was a woman who held strong views on the foolishness of paying duty to the United States Government. They had more money already than was good for them, she used to say, and if you gave them any more they would only spend it. Am I making myself clear?'

His audience said that he was.

'This, as you can imagine, perturbed Llewellyn greatly. He had always had a horror of Customs inspectors. Even when his conscience was clear he shrank from the gaze of their fishy eyes. He quivered when they chewed gum at him. When they jerked silent thumbs at his cabin trunk, he opened it as if there was a body inside.'

The Comfort-on-the-rocks said he understood that feeling, and had started to tell what promised to be a long story about the time he had tried to smuggle in a hundred cigarettes at Folkestone, when the Whisky Sour continued his narrative.

'His impulse, of course, was to have nothing to do with the venture, but then the thought of what Grayce would have to say if he included himself out gave him pause. Customs inspectors terrified him, but not nearly so much as she did, and he had good reason for his tremors. In her professional days she had been one of the best-known panther women on the silver screen, and once a panther woman, always a panther woman. So he reached the conclusion that however unpleasant the alternative her wishes would have to be obeyed. But he didn't like the prospect.

'I'll bet he didn't.' said the Gimlet.

'The problem was—How to do the smuggling?'

'I'll bet it was.'

'That was what ruined his sleep at night.'

'I'll bet it did.'

'And then one afternoon Reggie pointed the way.'

'Reggie Tennyson?'

'Yes. I told you he was on board. In the days that had passed since the liner left Southampton he had become very matey with Mabel Spence, and she had confided in him all about Llewellyn's dilemma. And he went to Llewellyn and told him that the happy ending could be achieved quite simply by bringing Monty's mouse into the act. I must mention that in order to give her pleasure Monty had purchased at the ship's shop for Gertrude a brown plush Mickey Mouse whose head screwed off. You were supposed to put chocolates in it.'

The Screwdriver shuddered strongly. He was in no condition to hear such things as chocolates referred to.

'Monty and Gertrude had had one of those lovers' tiffs about something and she had returned the mouse to him, and Reggie pointed out to Llewellyn that it would be an easy task for him, Reggie, to insert the jewels in the mouse without telling Monty, and Monty would carry it ashore.'

'Neat,' said the Gimlet.

'Ingenious,' said the Comfort-on-the-rocks. 'And he got through all right?'

'Without a hitch. And then, of course, Llewellyn had to tell him about the jewels, and he saw that he had been handed a good thing on a plate with watercress round it. This, he perceived, was where he got a job that would carry him along nicely for the necessary year. And the long and short of it was that before they parted Llewellyn had given him a five-year contract as Adviser for Productions.'

'And he was reconciled to Gertrude Butterwick?'

'Oh, yes. He's giving her lunch today at Barribault's.'

The Screwdriver said it was a waste of money. Sooner or later, he predicted, Gertrude Butterwick would let him down, and he would be out the price of a lunch.

'What makes you say that?' asked the Whisky Sour.

'She plays hockey,' said the Screwdriver.

2

As Monty sat in the lobby of Barribault's world-famous hotel, his eyes constantly swivelling towards the revolving door through which Gertrude Butterwick would at any moment enter, his emotions, though coming under the general head of ecstatic, were nevertheless tinged with a certain uneasiness. Granted that he was on to a good thing and one which it would be a pleasure to push along, he could not but reflect that it was a year since he had seen Gertrude, and a year gave a girl plenty of time to think things over and change her mind, especially if she had a father who made no attempt to conceal that he was allergic to Bodkins and would certainly not have refrained from those parental cracks which can do so much to influence a devoted daughter.

23

True, she had agreed to this luncheon tryst without apparent hesitation, but had it been with the old fire and enthusiasm? That was what he was asking himself as he sat there, and that was what was preventing him from being in the frame of mind which the French call *bien être*. His spirits alternately rose and sank, and it was just as he had succeeded in raising them and convincing himself that his fears were groundless that there came through the door, which so far had revolved to admit only India Maharajahs and Texan millionaires, an elderly man with a face like a horse whom he had no difficulty in recognizing as Mr J. B. Butterwick of Butterwick, Price and Mandelbaum, Import and Export Merchants. And Mr Butterwick, advancing to where he was sitting, sniffed at him in a marked manner and uttered these appalling words:

'Good morning, Mr Bodkin. Gertrude will not be lunching with you today.'

One of the things which render his task so arduous for the teller of the tale of lovers long parted—sundered hearts as one might say—is that so often, just as he has got all set to start writing the big reunion scene, he finds that it is not going to take place owing to the failure to appear of one of the two principals. And if a mere chronicler in these circumstances has a feeling of bafflement and frustration, as though he had raced to catch a train on Saturday morning and found on arrival at the station that it was Sundays Only, how much more poignant must be the discomfiture of one who had been expecting to play a leading part in such a scene. The emotions of a young lover who has planned to lunch with the girl he adores and gets her father instead are more readily imagined than described. It is enough to say that Monty had them all and, had he not been seated in one of Barribault's deep arm-chairs, would have reeled and perhaps fallen.

Mr Butterwick was looking like a horse about to start in the two-thirty at Kempton Park or Catterick Bridge, and not a very attractive horse at that, but it was not this that caused Monty to gaze at him as if at a snake in his path. It was with difficulty that he found speech.

'What!' he cried.

'Not?' he added.

'Rot!' he concluded, summing up. 'Of course she will be lunching with me. We fixed it up last night over the telephone.'

'True,' said Mr Butterwick. 'But since then I have talked with her and made her see that it would be better if I took her place.'

The interpretation Monty placed on these words was that the old Gawd-help-us was expecting to touch him for a lunch, and his whole soul revolted at the idea. Mr Butterwick, however, reassured him.

'I do not mean at the luncheon table,' he said with a sketchy beginning of a wintry smile. 'You will, after you hear what I have to say, prefer to be alone, and in any case I am lunching at my usual health restaurant. I merely mean that as Gertrude is a sensitive girl and it would upset her to be compelled to give you pain, it would be better if I, and not she, broke the news to you.'

Monty could make nothing of this. Mr Butterwick had left his hat with the hat-check girl, but had it been on his head he would have accused him of talking through it.

'I don't get your drift,' he said.

'I will make myself clearer,' responded Mr. Butterwick. A less austere man might have said 'I will continue snowing'. 'I have decided that you and my daughter must not see each other again.'

Barribault's Hotel is solidly built, and there is no record of the ceiling of its lobby ever having fallen on a customer's head. This, however, was what for an instant Monty was convinced had occurred, and he was amazed that the Maharajahs and Texan millionaires dotted about at their little tables were taking it so calmly.

Then reason returned to its throne, and he fixed his companion with an incredulous eye.

'What!' he cried.

'Not?' he added.

'Great Scott!' he concluded. 'You mean you're giving me the old heave-ho?'

25

'The expression is new to me, but I gather its import. Yes, that is what I am doing.'

'But our agreement!'

'I am coming to that. Ouch!'

'It's no good saying Ouch. That's no answer.'

'I used the ejaculation,' said Mr. Butterwick with dignity, 'because my indigestion gave me a momentary twinge. I suffer from indigestion.'

Monty was aware of this, and the knowledge had always given him pleasure, though his gratification would have been increased if the malady had been bubonic plague.

'Well, all right,' he said, yielding the point. 'If you wish to say "Ouch", by all means do so. But, returning to the *res*, you promised that if I earned my living for a year, you would refrain from bunging a spanner into my union with Gertrude. I thought it silly at the time, and I still think it silly, but I said to myself that it was no use arguing about it and I buckled down to do it and fulfilled your conditions faithfully. For the past year I have held the post of Adviser on Productions at the Superba-Llewellyn motion picture studio at Llewellyn City, Southern California, and if that isn't earning my living, what is? Are you under the impression that the Superba-Llewellyn doesn't pay its production advisers? Each Friday I got my little envelope with a thousand dollars in it. And you have the nerve to assert that our agreement is null and void. At least you haven't actually asserted it, but you were just going to. Well really, J. B. Butterwick, if behaviour like yours is common form in the circles in which you move, heaven help the import and export business. Men with a higher standard than yours would undoubtedly describe it as welshing.'

'Have you finished, Mr Bodkin?'

'No.'

'Nevertheless, will you postpone any further observations and give me the opportunity to speak?'

'If you have anything to say.'

'I have plenty to say.'

'And provided it is not mere gibbering.'

26

'It is not. You claim that you have fulfilled the conditions of our agreement faithfully. I dispute this.'

'You aren't trying to suggest that I wasn't at Llewellyn City for a year? You're cuckoo, Butterwick. Drop a line to Miss Alexandra Miller at the studio and ask her. She'll tell you. She was my secretary. We were closeted together daily.'

'No, I am not trying to suggest that, Mr Bodkin. What I am saying is that your sojourn there, as far as our agreement is concerned, does not count.'

'Not count?'

'No. Because it was based on fraud. You obtained your position by means of . . . I was about to say a trick, but perhaps blackmail is a better word. You forced Mr Llewellyn to employ you by threatening, if he refused, to withhold from him the brown plush Mickey Mouse containing his wife's jewellery. Naturally, when I made our agreement I never considered the possibility of such behaviour on your part. I assumed that if you found employment, it would be through the ordinary channels through which young men do become employed. And so, as I say, your year at the Superba-Llewellyn studio does not count.'

He ceased, and once more Monty had the illusion that a large portion of Barribault's Hotel had parted from its moorings and fallen on his head. His manner, which had been belligerent, lost its fire and took on something of the embarrassment of a bag-snatcher at a railway terminus detected in the act of sneaking off with a suitcase. Mingled with this discomposure was unwilling awe. He had never suspected Mr Butterwick of being clairvoyant, but it had now become plain that he was equipped beyond the ordinary with psychometry and the sixth sense and all that sort of thing, and one cannot but admire these qualities in a man, however much you may think that wiser parents than his would have drowned him in a bucket at birth.

'How did you know that?' he asked feebly.

'From my daughter.'

'You mean to say she *told* you?'

'She tells me everything.'

27

Monty was appalled. That any girl should have behaved so recklessly seemed to him incredible. His normal attitude towards Gertrude had always been that the queen could do no wrong, but now he found himself in critical vein, and words that must inevitably have given offence—for no father likes to hear his daughter described as a halfwitted fathead—sprang to his lips.

He choked them back. They would have relieved him, but they would have been injudicious, for he had not altogether lost the hope that with the exercise of suavity and tact a peaceful settlement might be arrived at.

'Couldn't we talk this over?' he said.

Mr Butterwick said they were talking it over and that he would be glad if they could wind up the conversation as quickly as possible, as he was anxious to get to his health restaurant.

'I mean in an atmosphere of the utmost cordiality, the way statesmen do at places like Geneva. I will begin by conceding that in the matter of Llewellyn and the brown plush Mickey Mouse I did let myself get carried away a bit and acted in a manner calculated to draw raised eyebrows from the bar of public opinion, but all I could think of was that here was an admirable opportunity of bending Llewellyn to my will, so I bent him.'

'Disgraceful.'

'Quite, quite. Now that you have shown me with such wonderful clearness where I went off the rails, I can see that it wasn't the right thing to do, and I shall know better next time.'

'Next time? I do not understand you.'

'You will if you will listen attentively for about half a jiffy. What I would suggest is that you put me on appro for another year, and if at the end of it I can prove that during that year I have earned my living and you are satisfied that there has been no hanky panky about the way I've done it, you will give your consent to my scooping in the girl I love—in other words Gertrude,' said Monty, making his meaning clear. 'In short, that the Bishop and assistant clergy and the bridesmaids shall be encouraged to line up and do their stuff,' he added, making it clearer.

Mr Butterwick considered the suggestion frowningly. It was not to his way of thinking the ideal solution. He had hoped that the interview now in progress would have seen the end of any association between his daughter and this undesirable suitor, and the prospect of having him as a menace for another year was not an agreeable one. On the other hand, he was a fairminded man and recognized Monty's claims to consideration.

'Very well,' he said.

'Fine.'

'You will, of course, not see Gertrude.'

'If you insist.'

'I see no objections to occasional letters.'

'Splendid. So now all that remains is to think of a suitable job. I suppose you wouldn't have an opening in your office?'

Mr Butterwick said he would not.

'A pity. What actually do you do in the import and export business?'

'We import and export.'

'Yes, I thought that might be it. It would probably have suited me down to the ground. However, as you say you have nothing to offer me, I must look elsewhere. I shall have to think.'

'I will leave you to do so. Good morning, Mr Bodkin.'

'Eh? Oh, good morning, good morning,' said Monty.

He closed his eyes to assist thought, and shortly after he had done so a musical voice in his left ear said 'Hi', and looking up he saw that he had been joined by Alexandra (Sandy) Miller, the last person he had expected to see on this side of the Atlantic Ocean.

3

He mentioned this to her.

'Sandy,' he cried, 'What on earth are you doing here?'

'Lunching with you, I hope.'

'I mean——'

'Or are you waiting for someone? If not, take me into the grill-room and fill me up. I'm starving.'

'Cocktail?'

'No, thanks. Just Food. Oh, Monty, it really has made my day, running into you like this. I thought I should have to search London for you with bloodhounds. Are you surprised to see me?'

'Stunned. Why aren't you in Llewellyn City?'

'All shall be explained over the luncheon table. If I don't faint from malnutrition before I get there. But what luck!'

'Eh?'

'I took it for granted that you would be entertaining some lovely female.'

'Well, I am, aren't I?'

'Thank you, kind sir.'

'Not at all. Don't mention it.'

Monty had spoken with all his wonted cheerfulness. As they made their way to their table, he was conscious of a marked lightening of the spirits which Mr Butterwick had left at a low ebb. The agony of having Gertrude snatched from him was still there, but it had abated. Sandy might not be Gertrude, but she was unquestionably the next best thing. She was looking, he thought, particularly charming, and he was not surprised that as they passed his table a Texan millionaire had puckered up his lips as if about to whistle.

A waiter appeared and took dictation. When the order was completed, Monty repeated his question.

'What on earth are you doing in London?'

'That's where my employer is, and my place is at her side. If you mean Why did I come to London, the answer is simple. I'm pursuing the man I love.'

'I didn't know you loved a man.'

'I do. Like a ton of bricks.'

'And he's in London?'

'Yes, he's here.'

'Oh.'

For a moment Monty was aware of an odd depression. He felt a little aggrieved. His devotion to Gertrude Butterwick was wholehearted, and he had no intention of allowing it to waver, but it did seem to him that a girl who was lunching with a fellow showed a certain lack of tact when she informed the fellow that she loved another fellow, and like a ton of bricks at that. Then the primal jealousy of the male gave way to his natural goodness of heart. He told himself that anyone as attractive as Sandy could scarcely be expected not to have her admirers and, this being so, why shouldn't she confide about them to an old buddy.

'Nice chap?' he said.

'Very.'

'And you've found him?'

'Yes, I've found him.'

'Well, best of luck.'

'Thanks. Of course, there's a catch, as you might say. He's engaged to someone else.'

'That's bad.'

'It does present difficulties.'

'You'll overcome them.'

'You think so?'

'Sure of it. Just go on looking as you're looking now, and the thing's in the bag. Unless, of course, she's a sort of Helen of Troy.'

'Oh, she isn't. She's on the robust side.'

'You've met her?'

'No, but I've seen her photograph.'

'A gargoyle?'

'Very good looking, as a matter of fact. But the bossy type. A husband wouldn't be happy with her.'

'You must save him from her.'

'I'm going to try.'

'Well, I shall watch your progress with considerable interest.'

'Thanks.'

'But you haven't told me yet how you come to be here. Did you say something about an employer?'

'Yes, I'm working for Grayce Llewellyn.'

'Any relation to our Llewellyn?'

'His wife. You remember she was coming to Europe.'

31

'Of course, yes. But how did you get the job?'

'That was what I asked you about your job, if you recall, but you came over all strong and silent. I heard she wanted a social secretary and applied.'

'And what do you have to do?'

'The way it's worked out I'm a sort of lady's maid and general help, not to mention a masseuse. If there's anything to be done for her, I'm called on. For instance, I spent most of the morning rubbing Grayce's back, and this afternoon I've got to get a secretary for Llewellyn. Grayce is making him write the history of Superba-Llewellyn. What's the matter?'

'Matter?'

'You gave a sort of jump like a shrimp surprised while bathing. As if I'd said something full of significance and meaning. Did I?'

'You did, as a matter of fact. About Llewellyn wanting a secretary.'

'Why was that so sensational?'

Monty decided to reveal all, or nearly all.

'Because it sounds just the sort of thing I'm after,' he said. 'You see, I've got a bet on. Somebody has bet me I can't earn my living for a year, and I simply must win it.'

'But you've been earning your living for a year.'

'At Superba-Llewellyn, you mean. Yes, but that doesn't count. The opposition got me on a technicality, and I have to start all over again. Can you fix it for me?'

Sandy was regarding him with frank bewilderment.

'I don't see why not. It must be a big bet.'

'Very big.'

'Well, I'll do my best. I know you can drive a car.'

'Of course.'

'Grayce specified that.'

'Doesn't she drive?'

'No. Nor Llewellyn.'

'Haven't they a chauffeur?'

'No. It's one of Grayce's economies. She's a very economical woman. And there's another thing. Have you a lot of aristocratic relations?'

'Not one. Why?'

'It would weigh with Grayce. Well, I'll tell her you have, anyway. So if she asks you about your cousin the Duke, don't reply "My cousin the *what*?" Just say how much you're looking forward to your next week-end at the castle.'

'I will. It's awfully good of you, doing all this for me, Sandy.'

'Not at all, You will be nice company for me at Mellingham.'

'Where?'

'Mellingham Hall, the house Grayce has taken in the country. When we've finished our coffee, I'll go up and see her.'

'Up?'

'They've got a suite on the fourth floor. By the way, an amusing thought occurs to me. Shall I share it with you?'

'Do.'

'I was just thinking that Llewellyn's face would be well worth watching when he sees you and learns that you are going to be his constant companion.'

The coffee cup shook in Monty's grasp. He had overlooked this point.

'Oh, my God! The whole thing's off. He'll never consent to my being his secretary.'

'He will if Grayce tells him to,' said Sandy.

Chapter Three

SANDY'S ABSENCE from the table was not a long one. Returning at the end of perhaps ten minutes, she informed Monty that the preliminary negotiations had been conducted in an atmosphere of the utmost cordiality and escorted him to the suite on the fourth floor, whence, having introduced him, she discreetly withdrew, leaving him to face Mrs Ivor Llewellyn alone.

This he did with the rather sinking feeling customary with those who met her for the first time, for there was no mistaking the forcefulness of her personality, and he could well understand even as tough a specimen as his late employer snapping lumps of sugar off his nose at her behest. She was large, as all panther women were in the days when panther women were popular, and in the confined space of a hotel sitting-room seemed even larger. Her eyes were inclined to bulge a little, but people of her acquaintance had no objection to this provided they did not flash, for when they did it was as if lightning had struck an ammunition dump.

They were not flashing now. It was evident that Sandy had done her spadework well, for she was all amiability. Nevertheless, Monty was not at his ease. It so happened that her impact had been rendered still more overwhelming by the fact that she reminded him of the proprietress of his first kindergarten, whose iron discipline had done so much to embitter his formative years. The same suggestion of volcanic forces lurking behind a placid face. The same eye like Mars to threaten and command. The same unspoken promise of a juicy one over the knuckles with a ruler, should his behaviour call for it. The result of this was to cause him to miss her opening remarks.

When he was in shape to listen, she was speaking of Mr Llewellyn's forthcoming contribution to American letters.

And to his gratification she was speaking as though the matter of his own association with the venture had already been settled.

'Miss Miller tells me she has explained to you about my husband's book, and I am sure you will be able to give him the help we want. I see it as a great romance, the romance of a vast industry growing from practically nothing. When I first came to Hollywood, Llewellyn City was just a lot of shacks. If I told you what my salary was when I started, you wouldn't believe me. Just chickenfeed. And talking of salaries we won't be able to pay you a great deal.'

She named a figure which struck even Monty, a child in these matters, as not lavish. It was, however, definitely a salary and as such met the conditions laid down by J. B. Butterwick. Try to wriggle out of this J. B. Butterwick, he was saying to himself. He accepted the terms without criticism, and his hostess gave him an indulgent smile to indicate that he had said the right thing.

'Then that's settled,' she said briskly. 'I will leave you now. I have an appointment with my hairdresser. Don't go. Wait here. I want you to meet my husband. He has gone for a walk. I always like him to take a brisk walk at this time. He should be back quite soon.'

'And when——?'

'—do your duties begin? Not for a few weeks. We are going to Cannes before settling into our country house.'

'Miss Miller told me you had taken a country house.'

'A place called Mellingham Hall in Sussex. My daughter went there the day before yesterday to look it over. It is a lovely old house in a very quiet village, just right for my husband's work.'

'It sounds fine.'

'The very nicest people as neighbours—Lord Riverhead, Lord Woking, Sir Peregrine Voules. It makes such a difference, doesn't it?'

She left him, and he set himself to review the situation in depth. Thought was easier now that she was no longer there. But though he was glad that she had gone, her departure had this to be said against it, that he was now free to let his mind dwell on the impending reunion with Ivor Llewellyn. This he frankly viewed with concern. Sandy had said that if accepted by the female of the species he had nothing to fear from her mate, but his attitude towards the head of the Superba-Llewellyn studio had always been that of a nervous private of the line towards a short-tempered sergeant, and it required more than a verbal assurance to convince him that marriage, even to Grayce, had supplied the other with the sweetness and light which at Llewellyn City had been so lacking.

It was a moment for stiffening the sinews and summoning up the blood, as recommended by Shakespeare, and he was in the process of doing this, when a key clicked in the door, the door opened and Ivor Llewellyn lumbered in, paused on the threshold, mopped his forehead and stood gazing at him with something of the enthusiasm of one seeing the Taj Mahal by moonlight.

'Hullo there, Mr Bodkin,' he said.

Correction. A word as weak and inadequate as 'said' should never have been employed when such verbs as 'chanted', 'carolled' or even 'fluted' were at the chronicler's disposal. Mr Llewellyn's vocal delivery had been that of a turtle dove accosting another turtle dove of whom it was particularly fond, and he was now advancing with outstretched hand, plainly entranced by this meeting.

Monty stared, astounded. He had anticipated an encounter with something resembling a horror from outer space, and the horror from outer space had turned out to be one of the boys, as bubbling over with cheeriness and good will as if he had stepped from the pages of Charles Dickens. He could make nothing of this metamorphosis.

'Oh, hullo, Mr Llewellyn,' he said weakly.

The hand which had been moving towards him clasped his, and the other of the two with which Mr Llewellyn was equipped massaged his shoulder affectionately.

'Nice to see you again, Bodkin. I met my wife down in the lobby, and she tells me you are going to help me with this book of mine. Fine. Splendid. Capital. Listen, Bodkin, little

36

matter I want to take up with you. Can you lend me five hundred pounds?'

As one of the only two really moneyed members of the Drones Club—Oofy Prosser was the other—Monty had often been given the opportunity of coming to the rescue of financially embarrassed friends and acquaintances, and the urge of these to share his wealth had never occasioned him astonishment. But this was the first time a multi-millionaire had expressed a desire to get into his ribs, and he gazed at Mr Llewellyn with what the poet Keats would have called a wild surmise, his eyes widening to the dimension of regulation golf balls.

'Eh?' was all he could say, and he had some difficulty in saying that.

It is easy for a man endeavouring to float a loan to mistake bewilderment for hesitation. Mr Llewellyn did so, and the friendly exuberance of his manner became tinged with impatience.

'Come on, come on, come on. Don't just stand there. You must have got five hundred pounds. For a year at the studio you were drawing a thousand dollars a week. You can't have spent it all.'

Monty hastened to clear himself of the implied charge of being one of those thriftless young men who waste their substance on wine, women and song.

'No, no, I've got it.'

'And you'll let me have it?'

'Of course, of course.'

'Good boy, Bodkin. You have your cheque book with you?'

'Oh, yes.'

'Then no time like the present.'

While Monty was writing the cheque, Mr Llewellyn preserved a reverent silence, as if fearing lest the slightest interruption might be fatal to the success of the negotiations, but as soon as he had pocketed it he became his effervescent self again.

'Thank you, thank you, Bodkin. By the way, how *are* you? I forgot to ask.'

'I'm fine. How are *you*, Mr Llewellyn?'

'Not too good. Domestic trouble.'

'I'm sorry.'

'Not half as sorry as I am. Listen, Bodkin. It probably struck you as odd that a man of my wealth should be borrowing money, Peculiar, you said to yourself. The explanation can be given in a word, or rather two words. Joint account.'

'I beg your pardon?'

'My wife and I have a joint account. She started it shortly after you joined us at S-L.'

'Oh?' said Monty, and Mr Llewellyn frowned.

'You say "Oh?" Bodkin, in that light and airy tone of voice, apparently not recognizing the significance of those two words, the saddest in the language. What they mean is that I am not able to write a cheque for the smallest amount without having my wife ask "What the hell was *this* for?" and there is nothing that hampers and shackles a man more. I don't know if she told you that we were off for a few days to the south of France?'

'Yes. To Cannes, she said.'

'Exactly. You ever been to Cannes?'

'Fairly often. I met you there, if you remember.'

'So you did. Then you know that the facilities for gambling there are unexampled. Two Casinos, and Monte Carlo just around the corner. I'm devoted to gambling, Bodkin. Roulette is my game. I have a new system I want to try out. But if I drew a cheque on our London account and she asked me what it was for and I said "Playing roulette", she would . . . well, she would express herself very forcibly, in fact you might say the home would be in the melting pot. She disapproves of games of chance. It is not the winning she objects to, but she hates to lose, and of course, however sound your system, occasional losses are unavoidable from time to time. So, as I say, she has set her face against my having a little flutter at the tables, and when she sets her face against something there is nothing to be done about it.'

'I can imagine.'

'You're darned right you can imagine. And it's the same thing when she gets her face set *for* whatever it may be.'

38

'Mrs Llewellyn struck me as having a very strong personality.'

'Will of iron. Take this history of the Superba-Llewellyn she's making me write. I don't like it, Bodkin, I don't like it. How can you write the history of a motion-picture studio without leaving out all the best bits? If I were to reveal some of the things that went on at S-L in the early days, the things that give such a history grip and interest, I should have the police after me. But do you think I can make her see that? Not a hope. She insists that it must be done, so it will have to be done. It will make it better, of course, working with an old friend like you. What beats me is why you want the job. If I know Grayce, she isn't paying you much.'

'Not much.'

'She has an economical streak in her.'

'Yes, I noticed.'

'Then how come?'

If Monty hesitated, it was only for a moment. There was something about this new and improved Ivor Llewellyn that seemed to make the sharing of confidences with him almost obligatory.

In Llewellyn City he would never have dreamed of laying bare his personal affairs to him, but now everything was changed.

He told him all. He told him of his great love for Gertrude Butterwick, of her subservience to her father's edicts and of J. B. Butterwick's non-co-operative attitude, and Mr Llewellyn listened gravely and attentively.

'I'd think twice about getting married, if I were you,' he said as the recital came to an end.

Monty said he thought more than twice. As a matter of fact, he said, he thought about it all the time, and Mr Llewellyn said he had not got his meaning. What he was intending to convey, he said, was that the holy state was not a thing that prudent young men should jump into with a whoop and a holler as if they were going to the Cannes Casino with their pockets full of money, because there were snags attached to it which became visible only when it was too late. He had in

39

mind principally, he said, the joint account of which he had been speaking.

'From that to becoming a cipher in the home,' he assured Monty, 'is but a step. And one thing more. Let me impress it upon you with all the emphasis at my disposal that if you do get married, don't let it be to someone who has already got a blasted daughter.'

Monty said he would be careful not to do this.

'Wives boss you enough, especially if they started life as panther women, but step-daughters begin where they leave off. My step-daughter Mavis, Grayce's offspring by a former marriage, even bosses Grayce, and she treats me like what are those guys they have in Mexico, spoons or something they're called.'

'Peons?'

'That's right. She treats me like a peon. These modern girls! It comes of letting them go to college. That's where they pick it up. I pleaded with Grayce not to send Mavis to Vassar. She'll come back all starched up and thinking she's the queen of Sheba or someone. I said. No good. Wouldn't listen to me. But I mustn't bore you with my troubles. Thanks for that five hundred.'

'Not at all.'

'You couldn't make it a thousand, could you?'

'Of course.'

'I had an idea you were going to say that. You're all right, Bodkin.'

'Thank you, Mr Llewellyn.'

'Drop the Mister.'

'Thank you, Llewellyn.'

'Better still, make it Ivor.'

'Thank you, Ivor.'

'Or, rather, Jumbo. All my friends on the coast call me Jumbo.'

'Thank you, Jumbo.'

'Don't mention it, Bodkin.'

A beautiful friendship had begun between these two and already was functioning on all twelve cylinders.

Grayce was not a woman who took her hair lightly and casually. When she employed hairdressers to work on it, she saw to it that they earned their money. The afternoon was well advanced before she was at liberty to leave the premises of Antoine, scalp specialist, whither she had gone after parting from Monty, to join her daughter Mavis for tea. For the last two days Mavis had been down in Sussex, inspecting Mellingham Hall, and they had arranged to meet at one of those tea shoppes which are such a feature of the west end of London.

Mr Llewellyn, in speaking to Monty of this step-daughter who had come to him as part of the package deal when he and Grayce were joined in holy wedlock, had left no room for doubt as to her formidable qualities, and had not exaggerated them. She provided a striking example of what is so apt to happen when a panther man—her father had been one—marries a panther woman. What you are only too liable to get, should their union be blessed, is an offspring who might be described as super panther or panther plus. This, Mavis unquestionably was. Even Grayce quailed before her, and as for Ivor Llewellyn he was, as he had told Monty, a mere peon in her presence. She was a tall, handsome girl with a fine figure and as a rule he liked tall handsome girls with fine figures, but she had a habit, when he made an observation or expressed an opinion of any kind, of raising silent eyebrows at him, sometimes accompanying the gesture with an exasperated click of her tongue, and he found this wounding to the spirit.

'You're late, mother,' she said as Grayce entered the shoppe. 'I've been waiting hours.'

'I'm sorry, dear. I was engaging a secretary to help with the book about the studio. And after that I had to go to Antoine's and he kept me for ever. Shampoo and a set and a touch-up. How do you like it?'

'It might be worse.'

'Good.'

'But I don't see how. Why on earth did you go to a plumber like Antoine?'

'I was told he was the best man in London.'

'I've nothing against his morals, but he can't do hair.'

It was plain to Grayce that her child was in one of her moods. She exerted herself to soothe, and presently under the influence of tea and cakes with sugar on top of them something more like harmony prevailed. By the time of the first cigarette Mavis had become, for her, reasonably amiable.

'Well,' she said, 'I think the Mellingham place is going to be all right. I liked it.'

'I thought you would.'

'Kind of quiet, of course.'

'That's what I want. A real change from Benedict Canyon Drive.'

'It'll be that right enough. It's lonely, though. How far from Brighton?'

'About an hour in the car.'

'Who's going to drive the car if I'm not there?'

'Mr Bodkin. The secretary I've engaged. But surely you will be there?'

'I may have to go to some people in Shropshire. Friends of a girl I knew at Vassar. I've practically promised. How about neighbours?'

'Lord Riverhead would be the nearest. He's about six miles away.'

'It certainly is lonely. Have you given a thought to the possibility of burglars?'

'Burglars?'

'It seems to me made to order for them. I think I'll buy you a gun. And you ought to have a guard, like in Beverly Hills. You must hire a detective.'

'Oh, surely that's not necessary.'

'I think it is. Don't forget that that string of pearls of yours isn't really yours. By father's will they come to me when I marry, so I take a natural interest in their well-being, and I don't propose to put them at the disposal of every Tom, Dick or Harry who takes it into his head to drop in at Mellingham Hall with a black mask over his face. And it's no good saying that that sort of thing doesn't happen in England, because it does. An English porch-climber would probably say "Pardon me" before swatting you with his blackjack, but you'd get the treatment just the same. I'm going to phone a private eye and make an immediate appointment for you.'

And so it came about that half an hour later Grayce was sitting in the office of J. Sheringham Adair, private investigator, who conducted his business in a narrow dingy street only a short step from the tea shoppe. Mavis had chosen him from among his fellow sleuths because Adair came at the top of the list of investigators in the telephone directory, which went to prove that he had acted wisely in not using his real name, which was Twist. Chimp Twist his acquaintances called him, his features having a pronounced simian cast, and one employs the word acquaintances rather than friends, for of these he had few.

It was fortunate for the success of their first meeting that Grayce was a self-centred woman who never noticed much of her surroundings, for one more fastidious might have been discouraged by the conditions prevailing in the office and the appearance of its proprietor. Dust was present in large quantities, and not even the most indulgent critic would have claimed that Chimp was a feast for the beholder. His narrow eyes and little waxed moustache would alone have been enough to prevent him winning a beauty competition.

All that impressed itself on Grayce, however, was that he looked intelligent, and intelligence was what she had come for.

She opened the proceedings briskly.

'Mr Adair?'

'Yes, madam.'

'My daughter telephoned you just now.'

'Mrs Llewellyn?'

'That's right.'

'And what can I do for you, madam?' asked Chimp. He spoke with all the suavity and old-world courtesy at his command. A glance at Grayce had told him that here was money. A dress such as his visitor was wearing had obviously cost the earth.

'I'll come to the point right away.'

'Quite, madam.'

'It's about this pearl necklace of mine.'

Ears do not actually prick up unless they are a dog's, but Chimp's came very near doing so. Pearl necklace, egad. This began to look like a big deal. His professional services hitherto had mostly been required for the obtaining of the necessary evidence in divorce cases.

'It has been stolen?' he asked rather breathlessly.

'No, and I don't want it to be,' said Grayce. 'That's why I've come to you. I take it you have guards on your staff?'

'Guards, madam?'

'Keeping an eye on the wedding presents when there's a wedding and all that.'

'Ah, you mean skilled operatives specially assigned to the task of protecting property of value.'

'If you like to put it that way. Well, my daughter says I ought to have one.'

'Quite, madam. I have a very large and efficient organization,' said Chimp without a blush. His was essentially a one-man concern. 'I shall of course put the cream of it at your disposal. When is this wedding to take place?'

'What wedding?'

'I thought you mentioned a wedding.'

'I didn't do any such thing. I only said that about wedding presents as a kind of illustration. You'd best let me tell you this in my own way.'

'Quite, madam.'

'Well, I'm just over from the States, and I've brought along a very valuable pearl necklace.'

'Quite.'

'I don't know why you keep saying "Quite", but no doubt you have your reasons. At present it's at my bank. It could stay there, of course, and there wouldn't be any danger of anyone swiping it, but hell's bells I want to wear the damned thing. Where's the sense of having a fifty thousand dollar rope of pearls if nobody sees it? It's like that poem about jewels not being any more good to you than a cold in the head because they're under water. I don't know if you know it?'

Chimp did not. Catch him on poetry, and you caught him on his weak spot.

Except for a few improper limericks. England's great heritage of verse was a sealed book to him.

'One of those professors from UCLA came to dinner one night when I was wearing it and recited a bit of it. I can't remember just how it went, because I was eating asparagus at the time and you know you have to concentrate on that, but the general idea was that for all we know there's millions of dollars' worth of ice that nobody ever gets a sight of because it's hidden away under the sea somewhere. Yes, by golly,' said Grayce with sudden animation, 'I do remember how it went. Funny how these things come back to you. "A whole raft of gems of something something the something caves of ocean bear", he said, and what I'm driving at is that if I'm going to leave those pearls of mine at the bank, they might just as well be in a cave with the ocean on top of them. Am I right, or not?'

Perfectly correct, Chimp assured her. The value of pearls, if kept in banks, he agreed, was practically equivalent to that of the common cold.

'On the other hand I don't want any perfect strangers muscling in and getting away with them, so I shall need a guard.'

Chimp, on the point of saying 'Quite', said 'Yes, indeed.'

'A resident guard,' said Grayce. 'In Beverly Hills we had two, day and night shift, both with sawn-off shot guns. But then in Beverly Hills if you aren't surrounded with willing helpers, you're asking for it. I was arguing with my daughter about it being different here. I said Yes. She said No. She said there were plenty of crooks throwing their weight about in England, and I guess she was talking sense. So it'll be safest to have someone keeping an eye on the criminal classes, and he'll have to be in residence because I've taken this house in the country for the summer, miles away from anywhere. Can you supply someone good?'

Chimp had his answer to this. He would, he said, undertake the job himself.

45

'Not use one of your skilled operatives?'

'I should not feel justified in entrusting work of such importance to a subordinate, however efficient. Fifty thousand dollars you said your pearls were worth?'

'About that.'

'They must be singularly fine.'

'Quite. My God, you've got me doing it now.'

'Then it is certainly a job for me and not one of my staff. In what capacity would you suggest that I came to your house?'

'Would you mind pretending to be my husband's valet?'

'Not at all, madam. I have frequently impersonated a valet.'

'It'll mean shaving off your moustache.'

'I understand that, madam,' said Chimp, concealing the pang he felt and trying to give the impression of an artist eager to make any sacrifice for his art. He loved the little thing, but he was more than willing to part with it in return for admission to a house containing a fifty thousand dollar pearl necklace. He reminded himself, too, that waxed moustaches, though crushed to earth, will rise again. It just needed a little patience and top-dressing.

'You see,' said Grayce, 'it isn't only the necklace I want you to keep an eye on, it's my husband, and as his valet you'll be in a position to do that. You'll be able to watch his every move.'

Chimp started like a war horse at the sound of the trumpet.

'And obtain the necessary evidence?'

'What evidence?'

'Your husband is untrue to you? You are planning a divorce?'

He had said the wrong thing.

'Don't be a damned fool,' said Grayce. 'My husband wouldn't have the nerve to cheat on me if you brought him all the girls in the Christmas number of Playboy asleep on a chair.'

This was a disappointment to Chimp, for he knew that he was at his best when obtaining the necessary evidence, but Grayce continued to look so rich that he crushed down his natural chagrin and inquired why, if Mr Llewellyn was such a modern St Antony, she wanted an eye kept on him and his every move watched. In his experience there was only one reason for eye-keeping and move-watching.

'He's on a diet,' said Grayce. 'It was my daughter's suggestion. And I'm going to see that he sticks to it. No alcohol, no starchy foods. So search his room from time to time, and if you find he's hiding cakes and candy and all that, tell me immediately and I'll attend to it.'

She spoke with so much of the old panther woman spirit in her voice that Chimp, though not a sensitive man, gave an involuntary shudder. He could picture her attending to it.

'He's been putting on weight for years, and he was stout enough to start with. I had of course no means of knowing what he got up to at the studio canteen, but now it will be different. With you and me working together as a team we'll have him looking like Fred Astaire. Did I give you the address of this place I've taken in the country?'

'No, madam.'

'Mellingham Hall, Mellingham, Sussex. But don't come there till you hear from me, because we're going to the south of France for a spell. Cannes. You ever been to Cannes?'

Chimp said that he had not, and the impression he gave was that he would have preferred not to hear the name of that resort mentioned. This was because two acquaintances of his whom he disliked intensely were vacationing there, a Mr Molloy and his wife Dolly. Their paths in the past had crossed frequently, always with unpleasant results.

Having ushered Grayce courteously to the door and assured her that he would fly to her side the moment he received her summons, he sat down at his desk and resumed the study of the picture postcard he had been brooding on when she arrived. It presented a charming picture of the Croisette at Cannes; it was signed 'Soapy and Dolly', and it bore the words in a flowing feminine hand 'Having wonderful time. Glad you're not here'.

It was a comfort to him to feel that there was no danger of this uncongenial couple being at Mellingham Hall during his

47

Chapter Four

MONTY WAS WRITING a letter to Gertrude.

The intelligent reader will recall, though the vapid and irreflective reader may have forgotten, that Mr Butterwick, in outlining his conditions, had made the concession that a certain amount of correspondence would be permitted, and Monty had been swift to avail himself of this unexpected softening of the old buster's iron front. At half past eleven on the night of his arrival at Mellingham Hall he had retired to his room and taken pen in hand.

The letter, omitting the endearments customary in such communications, ran as follows:

'Well, here I am at the above address, starting on my second shot at earning my living for a year as insisted on by your fat-headed father, whose indigestion I hope, is not yielding to treatment. He has probably told you he won't let all the sweat of the brow I put in at Llewellyn City count, which, if you ask me, is about as low as you can get and if that's the way he treats contracts in his ruddy import and export business, all I can say is that he had better watch his step or he'll find himself on the losing end of a substantial legal action for breach of same. I may mention that opinion at the Drones Club is solid in condemning him as a twister and a crook.

'Fortunately I have been able to baffle his sinister schemes and ere long he's going to look sillier than he does already. He thought I wouldn't find a job, but I have. You remember Pop Llewellyn. He's in England now, and his wife is making him write the history of Superba-Llewellyn, and I have been engaged to help him with it. It's bound to take at least a year, and even a bunko artist like your father can't say this one doesn't count, as I am getting a regular salary.

'Talking of Llewellyn, this will give you a laugh. The first thing he did when we met was to greet me like a long-lost son and touch me for several hundred quid. You are perplexed. You raise your eyebrows. "But surely", you say, "Llewellyn is a man who wears thousand-dollar bills next to the skin winter and summer. Why does he borrow money?" The point is well taken, but there is a simple explanation. It seems that he and his wife have a joint account, and he can't draw a cheque without her approval. This made it awkward for him because they were on their way to Cannes and he wanted to play at the tables there, which she would never have allowed. So he touched me, and we are now as closely knit as ham and eggs. In other words he is no longer the Pop Llewellyn who was the menace when I was on the studio payroll but a bosom friend.

'Ma Llewellyn is a tough baby and her daughter, whom I have not yet met, is, according to the scuttlebut, even tougher. But we get along all right, She is all for the aristocracy, and has got the impression that I am related to half the titled families in England. So she isn't likely to fire me, so I am sitting pretty as Pop Llewellyn wouldn't get rid of me to please a dying grandmother. In short, it looks like a pretty bleak future for J. B. Butterwick. I've got him cold.

'Things at the moment are quiet at Mellingham Hall. There may be a lot of house parties later, but just now the only visitors are an American couple named Molloy, with whom the Llewellyns got matey at Cannes. I gather that Molloy has large interests in oil over in America. At first he talked of nothing else, but half-way through dinner tonight he suddenly cheesed it. I should imagine Mrs Molloy—he calls her Dolly—gave him a wifely frown because she thought he was boring everybody.

'Must stop now. Getting late. All my love. Remember me to your father and tell him I hope he chokes.'

2

Meanwhile, in a room further from the roof and considerably more ornate than the attics assigned to secretaries, Mr Molloy and his wife Dolly were preparing for bed. Mrs Molloy, clad in a dressing gown, had already rubbed off the baby oil with which she had coated her attractive face and was substituting for it the cream from an Elizabeth Arden jar for which a Cannes beautician had been looking everywhere since she had last paid him a visit, while Mr Molloy, in pyjamas, smoked the last cigarette of the day and between puffs gazed at her adoringly, for even when covered with cream she was the light of his existence. He often said he did not know how he could get along without her. This was particularly so when she was hitting Chimp Twist on the back of the head with the butt end of pistols.

They were a comely couple. Mr Molloy's resemblance to an American senator of the better sort inspired in those he met a confidence which was of the greatest help to him in his life-work of selling stock in non-existent oil wells. It was his modest boast that if he were allowed to wave his arms and really get going on the sales talk, he could unload Silver River oil shares on prospects hailing from even Aberdeen or New England.

The talents of Dolly, his wife, lay in another direction. Though occasionally deviating from her chosen profession if something unusually good presented itself, she was primarily a shoplifter of unique gifts, the quickness of whose hand never failed to deceive the eye. As Mr Molloy admiringly put it, her fingers just flickered, making the whole operation seem as simple and easy as taking sweets from a sleeping child.

Each respected the other's Art, which is recognized as being the firmest foundation for a happy marriage. If Soapy Molloy made a killing, nobody could be more eager to celebrate than Dolly, and he was the first to applaud when she returned from an afternoon at the stores with objects that would come in useful about the home.

Dolly's face was now free of cream. Its absence revealed her as a young woman of striking beauty, her eyes sparkling, her lips ruddier than the cherry, her whole appearance calculated to make a strong appeal to the discriminating male, though it is doubtful if somebody like the late John Knox would have approved of her much. She was smiling, as if at some secret

51

thought, and when she spoke there was a triumphant lilt in her voice.

'Well, here we are, honey. We're in.'

'I can't wait to get action.'

'You won't have to wait long. Mrs Llewellyn was telling me the neighbourhood is lousy with rich men you can sell oil stock to. Lord This, Lord That, dozens of them and all suckers. She doesn't know them at present, but if she's the woman I take her for she soon will.'

'Bring them on. I'm ready. I've been polishing up my sales talk.'

'Which was pretty good before. But it isn't only the neighbours.'

Loath though he was to say anything that would dampen her enthusiasm, Soapy felt compelled to point something out.

'If you're thinking of Llewellyn, forget it. I won't get a contribution from him.'

'I'd have thought he was just the sort you could have used in your business. Crawling with dough. He's the boss of a Hollywood studio, and what bosses of Hollywood studios pay themselves per annum ain't hay.'

'Sure. They get plenty. But he and his wife have a joint account. No, he didn't tell me so, but I can detect it with my sixth sense. There's a kind of man that always has a joint account with his wife. They have a sort of special look. Interesting Llewellyn in Silver River would be pie, but I'd also have to interest her, and she's not the right woman for that. She wouldn't take a chance, and there's no denying that investing in Silver River shares entails a certain risk.'

'I guess you could call it that.'

'It isn't as though there really was a Silver River oil well.'

'Perhaps there is. Somewhere.'

'Maybe. You never know.'

'Be quite a coincidence if there was.'

'It certainly would.'

'But actually I wasn't thinking of Llewellyn when I said that about our being in. What I had in mind were the fringe benefits.'

'I don't get you, sweetness.'

'Remember that rope of pearls of Mrs Llewellyn's? You saw it often enough at the Casino. It must be worth fifty thousand dollars at least. Fifty thousand smackers, honey, and no income tax to pay on it.'

A man of Soapy's dignity does not gape or goggle, no matter what the provocation, but as Dolly concluded her speech there came into his face the sort of look sometimes seen in that of a Senator who has just been astounded, nay stunned, by some statement on the part of a political opponent.

'You're planning to snitch it?' he gasped.

'That's right. I'm biding my time, that's the sort of girl I am. Any questions?'

'I don't like it, baby.'

'Why not?'

'You're going out of your line. It never pays.'

'Says who?'

'Says everybody who's studied the thing. Look at that time you got away with Mrs Prosser's ice. That didn't work out so well.'

Dolly winced. The episode to which he referred was one of which she did not care to be reminded. It had started out so promisingly and finished so deplorably. And she knew where to place the blame.

'And why didn't it work out well? Because you let that little weasel Chimp Twist get mixed up in it. You went and told him where the stuff was. You told him the house it was in and the room it was in and whereabouts to look.'

Soapy had the grace to blush.

'I thought he would help,' he said weakly.

'He did. He helped himself.'

There was a momentary silence.

'J. Sheringham Adair!' said Dolly bitterly.

'I've often wondered about that,' said Soapy, glad to divert the conversation from his own follies. 'Is Chimp really a private eye?'

'I suppose he has a licence, or he couldn't operate, but of course it's just a front. It gives him the chance of getting into people's houses and getting away with everything that isn't nailed down. Blackmail, too, I shouldn't wonder.'

'Well, there's one good thing,' said Soapy. 'We haven't got him breathing down our necks here.'

'No, there's that. So we go ahead about those pearls?'

'Sure, honey, sure. I'm still not too sold on the idea, but you're the boss.'

'That's the way to talk, sweetie. Trust to me. I know what I'm doing.'

A perfect harmony reigned in the room. It was still reigning when the door opened cautiously and Chimp Twist slid in, rather in the manner of one of Nature's more repulsive creatures wriggling under a flat stone.

3

'When gentlefolk meet,' says the Victorian book of etiquette, 'compliments are exchanged', and the absence of these on the present occasion was due to the fact that Soapy and Dolly had lost the breath with which to make them, while Chimp was busy closing the door in order to ensure the privacy which is so essential at a time like this. He had come to place a business proposition before these old associates of his and the negotiations would be delicate enough without outside interference.

His initial emotion, on realizing that Mellingham Hall, in addition to containing fifty thousand dollars'-worth of pearls, was housing a couple whom he knew to be as crooked as a pair of spiral staircases and as fond of pearls as he was, had been dismay. He feared their competition, or rather that of Dolly. Of Soapy's abilities, apart from a gift for selling worthless oil stock, he had the poorest opinion, but Dolly was a different matter. Dolly was a girl of sagacity and resource, and one who, if the circumstances called for physical action, looked upon the sky as the limit. The lump on his head had long since subsided, but he could still recall the sensation of being hit by that pistol of hers.

Dismay, however, never lasted long with Chimp. There was

54

no suggestion of uneasiness in his manner as he opened the conversation.

He was calm, cool and collected.

'Hello there, Soapy. Hello there, Dolly,' he said. 'Well, here we are again, all three of us, just like old times.'

Disregarding the opprobrious name which Dolly, recovering her breath, had called him, he continued.

'I must say it surprised me finding you here. I caught a glimpse of you as you were going into dinner, and I thought for a moment I was seeing things. Then I remembered that you had been at Cannes and the Llewellyns were there too, and you would naturally have made friends with anyone as rich as they are. It was Dolly who worked it, I suppose. I can just see her giving Llewellyn the eye. You're looking fine, Dolly. You always do. We may have had our little differences in the past, but I've never changed my opinion that you're the prettiest girl that ever swiped a silk camisole from the lingerie department when the store detective wasn't noticing. Soapy seems to have got a bit thin on the top since I saw him last. You want to watch that, Soapy, because if you go bald you'll look like nothing on earth. Not that you look like much even now. If you've ever been mistaken for a movie star, it can't have been lately.'

Soapy, too, had recovered his breath.

'What,' he asked tensely, 'are you doing here?'

'You rat,' added Dolly, seeming to find the sentence incomplete.

'I was coming to that,' said Chimp. 'I'm Mr Llewellyn's valet. Professional job. I've been engaged by Mrs Llewellyn to guard her pearl necklace. And you are here, I suppose, to try to pinch it.'

'And you're going to try to pinch it first,' said Dolly, eyeing him with dislike.

'The idea did occur to me.'

Dolly uttered a passionate cry.

'It's like some sort of fate. Every time I and Soapy get a chance to do a bit of business you come along and gum things up.'

Chimp seemed pained by her choice of words. His air was that of one who has been wounded by a friend.

'I'm not gumming things up. I'm here to help. I looked in to suggest that what we ought to do is pool our resources. Three heads are better than one, even if one of them's Soapy's.'

'What's wrong with my head?' Soapy demanded with some heat.

'Solid ivory,' said Chimp. 'And it doesn't even look nice.'

Normally such a critique would have caused Dolly to express herself with vigour and vehemence in defence of her mate, making full use of an extensive vocabulary, but she was a business woman. Chimp's proposition had given her the impression that he had some scheme or plan to put forward, and she did not want the conference to be diverted to side issues. Chimp was not a man she could ever be fond of, but she respected his ingenuity.

'How do you mean, pool our resources?'

'Go into partnership. Form a syndicate.'

'Work together, in other words.'

'It's the sensible thing to do.'

'And split the gross receipts?'

'Exactly.'

'And the divvying up would be?'

'Thirty per cent to you and Soapy, seventy to me.'

It was simply the thought that such a sound breaking the quiet hush of a house which had turned in for the night might cause comment that restrained the junior partners in the proposed enterprise from howling like indignant timber wolves. They had to content themselves with howling in an undertone.

'Seventy per to you?' Dolly hissed, and Soapy, who was given to homely phrases, begged the speaker not to make him laugh, as he had a sore lip. Each made it plain that he had not got the sympathy of his audience, Dolly going so far as to compare him to one of those unpleasant South American bats which devote so much of their time to sucking blood.

Chimp had expected some such reaction from his colleagues on the Board. He remained calm.

'Work it out for yourselves. Or, rather, you work it out,

Dolly, and then you can explain it to Soapy in words of one syllable. If you'll stop Soapy making noises like a sick dog, I'll explain. You're visitors here, aren't you?'

'So what?'

'I'll tell you what. Come and stay in our little country home, these Llewellyns said to you. Right?'

'Well?'

'Well, they don't expect you to stay for ever, do they? It won't be long before they're leaving railway guides around in your room with the early trains marked in red ink and telling you at breakfast how good the service to London is. And off you'll have to go. But me I'm a permanent official. No question of me having to leave. Long after you've said goodbye and thanks for a delightful visit I'll still be on the spot, waiting my chance to clean up. And I'll be bound to get a chance sooner or later. I'm a soft-hearted fool, really, giving you as much as thirty per cent. I wouldn't do it if we weren't old friends. So on second thoughts how about it?'

His eloquence was wasted. The glare Dolly cast at him might have been that of a basilisk at the top of its form.

'Nothing doing,' she said.

'You won't sit in?'

'For thirty per cent I wouldn't sit in on the theft of the Crown jewels.'

'You'll be sorry. So will Soapy.'

'Don't worry about us. Get out of here. The door's behind you.'

'All right, all right, I'm going. But you're doing yourself a great disservice. We might have made a good team.'

So saying, Chimp passed into the night, and Dolly suddenly remembered three more things she would have liked to call him.

Chapter Five

MONTY HAD FINISHED his letter, licked the gum and sealed the envelope, and he leaned back in his chair, a spent force. The communiqué had been set down as if it had been an uninterrupted effort with the golden words pouring out like syrup, but actually it had involved not a few false starts and revisions. It had always been so when he wrote to Gertrude because there was the backlash when she replied to be taken into consideration. She had a tendency to regard his letters as if she were a literary critic and they so many books sent to her for review, and this necessitated frequent pauses for thought. P's had to be minded and also Q's.

It was now quite late, but he did not go to bed. Instead, he continued to sit, and as he sat he found his thoughts turning to Gertrude. This would, of course, have been perfectly normal had they been tender loving thoughts, but such was far from being the case. A year ago loyalty would not have permitted him to question her claim to rank among the top ten angels in human form, but twelve months in Hollywood seemed to have done something to him, leaving him more captious, more censorious.

Her meek acceptance of her father's absurd stipulations with regard to their marriage had never pleased him. It now irritated him every time he thought of it. Would Juliet have behaved so to Romeo, he asked himself, or for the matter of that Cleopatra to Mark Antony? Of course not. Each would have given her nose a dab with the powder puff and been off to the nearest registry office with the man she loved, and if Daddy didn't like it, he could eat cake.

He smoked a pipe, and under the soothing influence of tobacco his thoughts became more charitable. Neither Juliet nor Cleopatra, he reminded himself, had had a father like

J. B. Butterwick. Crushed beneath the iron heel of a J. B. Butterwick, a daughter might excusably be converted into a mere automaton with no will of her own. Essentially fairminded, he recalled how he himself had grovelled to the man on the rare occasions when he had been invited to Sunday supper. It had been 'Yes, Mr Butterwick', 'You're quite right, Mr Butterwick' and 'How very true, Mr Butterwick' from start to finish. He could not have been less authoritative if he had been one of Mr Llewellyn's peons.

He had just decided that in consenting to this earn-your-living-for-a-year caper she was more to be pitied than censured, when his reverie was interrupted by the sound of footsteps outside the door, the sudden flinging open of the door and the unexpected incursion of Ivor Llewellyn in a purple dressing-gown.

'Hey, Bodkin,' said Ivor Llewellyn. 'You got any candy?'

Somewhat surprised by the question, Monty replied that he had not.

'Cake?'

'Sorry, No cake.'

'Even a cheese cracker would help,' said Mr Llewellyn wistfully, but here, too, Monty was obliged to fail him, and Mr Llewellyn sank on to the bed with the sort of sigh he might have heaved at the studio when signing the contract of a star whose agent had put her terms up.

'I thought it was too much to hope for,' he said. 'I was explaining my position to that little Miller girl who works for my wife, and she hadn't any candy either. And I'm a man who requires lots of nourishing food, Bodkin.' Said Mr Llewellyn, the gravity of his manner deepening. 'Do you remember me warning you against marrying anyone who had a blasted daughter? Well, I repeat that warning . . . in spades. Do you know what that step-daughter of mine has pulled on me? She's talked her mother into making me go on a diet.'

'You don't mean it!'

'What do you mean I don't mean it? Of course I mean it. She says I'm too fat. Would you call me fat?'

'Certainly not. Well-covered, perhaps.'

'My step-daughter says I'm obese.'

'She wants smacking.'

'Of course she does, but who's to smack her?'

'You have a point there. It would be difficult.'

'Very difficult. You ever tried to smack a Vassar girl?'

'Never.'

'Well, take it from me it can't be done. No, I'll just have to suffer. Do you recall that Bavarian cream at dinner?'

'Delicious.'

'I wasn't allowed to touch it. And those hot rolls. I wasn't allowed to touch them. I got diet bread. You ever eaten diet bread?'

'Not that I remember.'

'You'd remember all right if you had. Tastes like blotting paper.'

'Couldn't you have asserted yourself?'

'Married men don't assert themselves, not if they know what's good for them. I think I'll be going to bed, Bodkin. Doubt if I'll sleep, though, feeling all hollow the way I do. Good night, Bodkin.'

It was perhaps three minutes after his under-nourished visitor had left him that Monty was surprised to see the door opening again. He had not anticipated that his bedroom would become a sort of journey's end for all and sundry.

This time it was Sandy. She was carrying on its dish the remains of the Bavarian cream which had spoken so eloquently to Mr Llewellyn's soul at the dinner table.

2

When gentlefolks meet, as was stated earlier, compliments are exchanged, and Monty would have experienced no difficulty in finding one, for this second visitor, unlike her predecessor, was looking extremely attractive, but his whole attention was riveted on the Bavarian cream. And he was about to comment on this when she forestalled him with a pleased 'So you haven't gone to bed. Good', adding 'Come along' and motioning him to the door.

'Come along?' he said.

'Yes.'

'Where?'

'To Mr Llewellyn's room. To give him this.'

'That?'

'Yes. He wasn't allowed any at dinner.'

'So he was telling me.'

'You've seen him?'

'He's just left.'

'Social visit?'

'He came to ask if I'd got any candy.'

'Poor lamb. You hadn't, I suppose?'

'No.'

'Then this will be all the more welcome. Come along.'

'But what do you want me to do?'

'Lend me moral support and back up my story if we meet anyone.'

'Are we likely to meet anyone?'

'It's always possible.'

'What do we do if we do?'

'I tell them there was a mouse in my room and I drafted you to help me find a cat. Or would it be better to say I heard the nightingale and brought you along to listen to it?'

'Not so good.'

'No?'

'Definitely the mouse, if you ask me. But how will you explain the Bavarian cream?'

'Let's hope it won't be noticed.'

Monty was in thoughtful mood as they made their way down the stairs. A short while before he had been musing on Gertrude. He now mused on Sandy, and the new side of her character which she was showing him surprised him considerably. He had not suspected her of such versatility. It is one thing to take down letters in shorthand, with her skill at which he had long been familiar, and quite another to raid your employer's frigidaire for Bavarian cream after dark. He frankly admitted to himself that if he had been called upon to undertake such a task, his nerve would have failed him. And she

61

had done it, not for self, not for advancement, but simply from sheer womanly goodness of heart in order to oblige an unfortunate fellow-creature who needed Bavarian cream to ward off night-starvation.

Her altruism was a revelation to him. He had always been fond of her in that brotherly way of his, but it had never occurred to him to bother much about probing any hidden depths she might have. It now became apparent that brotherly affection was inadequate and would have to be fortified by respect and admiration, both of the deepest. His thoughts turning to this man she had said she loved, he hoped the fortunate fellow would prove to be worthy of her.

A soft knock on a door on the second floor produced Ivor Llewellyn. His face was gloomy, but at the sight of Sandy's burden it lit up as though it were being done in glorious Technicolor.

'What?' he gasped. 'What? What? What?'

'For you,' said Sandy. 'As you see, a spoon goes with it. And I'm off to bed.' Like a self-respecting Girl Guide she required no thanks for her day's good deed. It was enough to spread a little happiness as she passed by.

'Good night, all,' she said, and vanished with her customary abruptness.

Monty, starting to follow her, was arrested by the descent on his shoulder of a heavy hand.

'Don't go, Bodkin,' said Ivor Llewellyn, speaking a little thickly, for his mouth was full of Bavarian cream. 'Wanna word with you.'

He conducted Monty to a chair, dumped him into it, and stood over him, his attitude that of a father about to have a man-to-man talk with a favourite son. Monty received the impression that he was about to be informed of the facts of life and was on the point of saying that he already knew about the bees and the birds, when Mr Llewellyn proceeded.

'This girl of yours that you were shooting your head off about that day at Barribault's. Tell me about her. All I know is that her father says you can't get married till you've earned your living for a year. Silly idea.'

'Very.'

'Must be a damned fool.'

'He is.'

'Sort of man I wouldn't trust with a Western B picture, if I had him at Llewellyn City. He'd have the bad guy shooting the sheriff. Well, Bodkin, fill me in. What's the girl like?'

'You saw her on the boat.'

'I've forgotten her. And anyway I don't mean what's she like, I mean what's she *like*? What sort of girl is she?'

'The out-door type, I suppose you would call her.'

'Tip-toes through the tulips? That sort of thing?'

'Not so much tip-toes through the tulips, More energetic than that. Plays hockey.'

'Oh, a skater?'

'Not hockey on ice. English hockey. They play it on a field. She's very good at hockey. She's one of the All England women's team. That's how she came to be on that boat.'

'I remember her now. Big beefy girl. Large feet.'

Monty winced. He was familiar with his companion's reputation in Hollywood as man who called a spade a spade, and had he merely done that now, he would have had nothing to complain of. He had no objection to Mr Llewellyn describing spades as spades, but he keenly resented his reference to Gertrude Butterwick as a beefy girl with large feet.

'I wouldn't call her that,' he said coldly.

'I would,' said Mr Llewellyn. 'She reminded me of my first wife, who was a strong woman in vaudeville. Wore pink tights and lifted weights. I was a mere callow lad at the time, and she fascinated me. After she married me and retired from business she put on so much weight that she could hardly lift herself. It's the sort of thing that always happens with these muscular women. This girl of yours would go the same way, once she stopped playing hockey. But that's not why I'm warning you to kiss her goodbye and tie a can to her.'

'Are you warning me to kiss her goodbye and tie a can to her?' asked Monty, surprised.

'You bet I'm warning you to kiss her goodbye and tie a can to her. Never marry anyone who makes conditions and says

63

she won't sign on the dotted line unless you do something or other. Like when I was in Wales—I was born in Wales—and fell in love with the local school teacher. Do you know what she wanted me to do or she wouldn't marry me?'

'I was just wondering.'

'You'll never guess.'

'Probably not.'

'She said no contract until I'd got what she called a thorough grounding in English literature. That was the school marm in her coming out. English literature, you know what that means—Shakespeare, Milton and all those. See what I'm driving at, she made conditions.'

'So what did you do?'

'I spilled my guts studying English literature, and I was getting so that I could pretty well tell one of the damned poets from another, when I suddenly realized that I didn't want to marry her after all. To put it in a nutshell, I couldn't stand the sight of her. So I skipped out of town and came to America and got a job with Joe Fishbein, who was a big noise in pictures at that time, and one day discovered where he had buried the body, and of course after that I never looked back. I was like a son to him. So that sequence ended happily, but you can't rely on that sort of luck every time, and that is why I say to you, Bodkin, sever relations with this condition-making hockey-knocker of yours. You'll never regret it.'

'It wasn't she who made the conditions, it was her father.'

'Same thing. She agreed to them, didn't she? No, Bodkin, you don't want to go messing about with a dumb broad who lets her father tell her what to do and what not to do. The girl you ought to marry is that little Miller half-portion. There's a ministering angel if you want one. Brings me Bavarian cream at the risk of her life . . . well, practically. The imagination boggles at the thought of what Grayce would have done if she'd caught her.'

He paused, and Monty could see that his imagination was boggling. His own was in much the same condition. Mr Llewellyn's suggestion that he ought to marry Sandy had startled him as he had seldom been startled before.

'But she's in love with someone,' he said, feeling dizzy. 'She came to England because he was here.'

'Oh, I didn't know. She told you that, did she?'

'Yes, she told me herself.'

'You couldn't have misunderstood her?'

'No.'

'A pity. What sort of a fellow is he?'

'I haven't met him.'

'I'll make inquiries. We can't have a girl like that throwing herself away on some ghastly weed with side-whiskers. My God, for all we know he may be a movie actor. I'll certainly check up. What's the time?'

'I don't know.'

'Getting late, anyway. You ought to be in bed. Get the hell out of here, Bodkin. Good night.'

Monty withdrew, but he did not go to bed immediately. Having descended the stairs, he opened the front door and stood there listening to the nightingale of which Sandy had spoken. Its programme had been a long one, but it continued in fine voice. A few moments later it paused, possibly to clear its throat or to try to remember how the next song went, and all was still.

There is something very soothing in the atmosphere of an old country house in the small hours when all is still, but this is so only as long as all stays still. The whole effect is spoiled if, as you stand there soaking the old-world peace into your system, a form looms up in front of you and a voice, speaking abruptly, says 'Stick 'em up' and the muzzle of a .38 Colt Special is thrust against your solar plexus.

Happening to Monty at this juncture, it gave him quite a start. He stuck them up, as desired, and stood there speechless. An easy conversationalist as a general rule, he found it impossible to think of anything to say.

3

The speaker was a stalwart young woman shaped in a manner which made her look as if, when at her best, she could give the current champion stiff competition for the welterweight title. She had eyes like those of the Medusa of Greek mythology, one glance from whom was sufficient to convert those she met into blocks of stone, and the pistol in her hand added a great deal to these gifts of Nature. It had the unmistakable appearance of a pistol likely to go off at any moment.

Many girls in her position might have hesitated as to what to do next, but she had everything cut and dried.

'In there,' she said.

The 'there' of which she spoke was the familiar feature of the halls of all English country houses, the downstairs cupboard. Each of these is a sort of Sargasso Sea into which drift all the objects which over the ages have outgrown their usefulness and are no longer needed in the daily life of the home. The one to which Monty was being invited already contained, among other things, a cracked vase, a broken decanter, a lamp shade with a hole in it, several empty bottles, some galoshes and part of a rusty lawn mower. It was on the last named that he barked his shin as he entered, and his cry of agony might have drawn comment from the girl behind the gun, had she not been closing the door at the moment and turning the key in the lock, leaving the world, as the poet Gray would have said, to darkness and to him.

Monty had always been a great reader of novels of suspense, and he had often wondered what had been the emotions of the characters in them who kept getting locked up in cellars under the river by sinister men in Homburg hats and raincoats. He knew now how they had felt. True, in his present little nest there was no water dripping from the ceiling, but when you had said that, you had said everything. As he had suspected, the whole thing was most unpleasant. There was, for instance, the smell, to which the galoshes contributed largely.

Time passed, and as so often happens when a man has been standing for some minutes rigid and motionless Monty felt the urge to stretch. He stretched, accordingly, and dislodged from an upper shelf two bottles and the lamp shade with the hole in it. Their descent on his head caused him to leap back. He became involved with the lawn mower again, and the noise resulting from those activities came through loud and clear to the ears of Mr Llewellyn, who happened to be passing, giving him the momentary illusion that his heart, leaping into his mouth, had dislodged two of his front teeth.

Before this shock to his nervous system Mr Llewellyn had been what the compiler of a book of synonyms would have described as elated, flushed with success, exhilarated, exultant, exalted and in high spirits. He had taken the dish which had once contained Bavarian cream back to the kitchen, thus destroying all evidence of his crime, and he was returning to his room feeling like a trusted messenger who has carried important papers through the enemy lines.

The task had been a fearsome one, for his step-daughter Mavis had telephoned before dinner that she would be arriving late in her car, and the thought that he might meet her on the stairs with the dish in his hands had been a paralysing one.

Fortunately the disaster had not occurred, but he was still in a mood to jump at sudden noises. The noise of Monty's embroilment with the bottles, the lamp shade and the lawn mower had been very sudden, and he had jumped perhaps six inches. His initial impulse was to gallop up the stairs at a speed as rapid as his build would allow, but curiosity is an even stronger emotion than fear. Somebody was in that cupboard, and he had to ascertain who. Putting his lips to the door, he said:

'Hi.'

The effect of the word on Monty was much the same as that of the skirl of the Highland pipes on the girl in Cawnpore at the conclusion of the siege of that town during the Indian Mutiny. She had welcomed those skirling pipes with the utmost enthusiasm, and it was with equal enthusiasm that he greeted Mr Llewellyn's 'Hi'. Even when speaking in monosyllables the other's voice was a distinctive one, and he had no difficulty in recognizing it, and the knowledge that he had found a friend and sympathizer sent the red corpuscles racing through his veins as if he had drained a glass of one of those patent mixtures containing iron which tone up the system and impart a gentle glow. Wasting no time in speculation as to what his rescuer was doing there, he detached the lawn mower from his leg and the lamp shade from his hair, pressed his lips against the door, only of course on his side of it, and said:

'What ho!'

'Speak up,' said Mr Llewellyn. 'I can't hear you. What did you say?'

'Let me out.'

'No, you didn't. It was something quite different. Who is that?'

'Me. Bodkin.'

'Did you say Bodkin?'

'Yes.'

'The Bodkin I was talking to just now?'

'That's right. Monty Bodkin.'

'What are you doing in there? Fill me in, boy, fill me in.'

'I was put.'

'Who put you?'

'The burglar.'

'What burglar?'

'There's a girl burgling the house.'

'You don't say.'

'Yes, I do.'

'What sort of girl?'

'Most unpleasant type.'

'I ask,' said Mr Llewellyn, 'because we are expecting my step-daughter Mavis tonight, and she said she would be late.'

'I wish you would let me out.'

'Of course, my dear fellow, of course, certainly. Why didn't you ask me before? Now the first problem that confronts us is to find the key.'

'It's in the door.'

'So it is. Then everything is simple. Tell me,' said Mr Llewellyn, having performed what in a Superba-Llewellyn treatment would have been called 'Business with key' and watched Monty emerge like a cork out of a bottle, 'about this burglar of yours. Was she tall?'

'Tallish.'

'Blonde?'

'I couldn't see. There wasn't enough light.'

'But you were probably able to observe her eyes. Were they like a rattlesnake's?'

'Very like.'

'And her manner? Supercilious? Bossy? Domineering?'

'All three.'

'Abrupt, would you say?'

'The very word.'

'It must have been Mavis. I suppose she's gone up to see her mother.'

'At this time of night?'

'Well, she must have thought you were a burglar, or she wouldn't have locked you in the cupboard, and she would naturally want to tell her mother about it and get her to phone the police.'

'The police!'

'She's probably doing it now. If I were you, I'd go to bed.'

'I will.'

'They won't think of looking for you there. What actually happened?' asked Mr Llewellyn as they mounted the stairs.

'I was listening to the nightingale, and suddenly there she was.'

'And——'

'She said "Stick 'em up".'

'Upon which?'

'I stuck 'em. Then she put me in the cupboard.'

'Couldn't you have done something?'

'Such as?'

'Well, broken her neck or something.'

'No, because she had produced a whacking great pistol and was shoving it into my stomach.'

'She did that?'

'Just that.'

Mr Llewellyn clicked his tongue disapprovingly.

'The things they teach these girls at Vassar!' he said.

Mrs Grayce Llewellyn was one of those fortunate people who find it easy to drop off to sleep, and as a rule the sandman began his benevolent work on her as soon as she had plastered the night's mud pack on her face and got into bed. But there were things that could interfere with her slumbers, and one of these was the abrupt bursting into her room of her daughter Mavis—come, as Mr Llewellyn had predicted, to talk about burglars.

Mavis, true to form, had not bothered to knock on the door, and it had flown open with a bang, causing Grayce in her first waking moments to think that something had exploded. For an instant hot words trembled on her lips. Then she identified her visitor and this had a calming effect. Long experience had taught her that if you spoke hot words to Mavis, you got back others that were even hotter. Prudence made her opening speech a pacific one.

'Is that you, Mavis dear? You're very late.'

'My car broke down. I thought I'd never get here.'

'Are you staying long?'

'No, I'm off early tomorrow. Those people in Shropshire. I only came to pick up some things. And I'm leaving you this,' said Mavis, exhibiting the .38 Colt which had made such a powerful impression on Monty. 'My bet is that you'll find it comes in handy.'

Grayce regarded the weapon with repulsion. Panther women in times of crisis rely on personal magnetism rather than fire-arms, and objects like the one Mavis was laying on the bed made her nervous. She had never been at her ease with pistols since her first husband, giving her a preview of the role he was playing in his next picture, an epic of the West, had shot himself in the foot. The mud pack quivered on her face as she cried: 'Take it away! I don't want it.'

'That's what *you* think,' said Mavis. 'No home should be without one, especially a home like this, miles away from the nearest neighbour. I warned you that burglars would soon be pouring in. Well, they've started pouring.'

'What!'

'Found one in the hall on my arrival.'

'Good gracious!'

'But all's well. I locked him in the downstairs cupboard.'

'He'll suffocate!'

'Probably. And a good thing, too. Nasty-looking fellow with a hangdog expression and butter-coloured hair.'

'Butter-coloured hair!'

'It looked butter-coloured to me. It stood on end when I thrust the gat into his abdomen.'

'But didn't he say anything? Didn't he explain?'

'Not a word. He had no conversation. How do you mean explain?'

'That he was Mr Bodkin? It must have been Mr Bodkin. He has butter-coloured hair.'

'Who's Mr Bodkin?'

'Your step-father's secretary. I told you I was getting a secretary to help with that book about the studio.'

'So you did. I remember. Well, that'll teach him not to open front doors and stand looking out in the small hours. Naturally I thought the worst. But if you know all about him, I suppose he's all right. I'll leave you the gun, anyway. No knowing when it'll come in useful. You might want to shoot Jumbo with it.'

'I wish you would not call your step-father Jumbo.'

'Everybody else does. How is he getting on with that detective of yours?'

'He seems quite contented.'

'Doesn't suspect?'

'No. Mr Adair is a very competent valet.'

'These shamuses have to be able to do anything. What sort of a man is he?'

'Well, not much to look at.'

'But intelligent?'

'Oh, very.'

'And courageous?'

'I guess so. Don't detectives have to be?'

'You'd better give him the gun.'

'Won't he have one?'

71

'Probably two. An extra one for Sundays. So I can leave you with an easy mind.'

'Yes, But I wish you weren't going.'

'I've got to.'

'I don't see why. People you've never met.'

'Not all of them.'

On the words 'Not all of them' Mavis's voice had softened and a gentle glow had come into her eyes, which normally, if Mr Llewellyn was to be believed, had something of the austerity of a rattlesnake's. She now, though Monty would have said that such a thing was impossible, became definitely coy.

It would, perhaps, be too much to say that a girl with her strength of character giggled, but she certainly gave a short laugh and one of her feet traced an arabesque on the carpet.

'I've met Jimmy Ponder. You remember him at Cannes?'

'We saw so many people at Cannes.'

'But you must remember Jimmy.'

'Was he the one who wore glasses and made funny noises when he drank soup?'

'No, he was not the one who wore glasses and made funny noises when he drank soup,' said Mavis with some asperity. 'He is very good looking, more like a Greek god than anything, and he's crawling with money. He's a partner in one of those big jewellery firms.'

'Of course, yes. I remember now. Tiffany's, wasn't it?'

'No, not Tiffany's, one of the others. I've had a letter from him saying he's going to be at this Shropshire place.'

A mother can always read between the lines where her child is concerned.

It seemed to Grayce that she saw all.

'Darling, are you in love with him?'

'No argument about that. I go all crosseyed when I see him and my heart hammers like a bongo drum. But that doesn't mean that I'm going to plunge into matrimony till I'm quite certain it's the right move. I've had too many friends who've married Greek gods and spent the rest of their leisure time kicking themselves. I want a second opinion. That's why I'm going to get these people to invite you there. You can vet him. Give me the green light, and ho for the altar rails.'

'If he proposes, you should add, darling.'

'Oh, I'll see to that,' said Mavis.

Chapter Six

AND NOW FOR A PEEP into the home of Gertrude Butter-wick.

One of the first things a chronicler has to learn, if he is to be any real good at chronicling, is when to ease up and take a breather. Aristotle was all for sticking to pity and terror without a break, but he was wrong. It is a mistake to curdle the reader's blood all the time. Sequences of spine-chilling drama, with people telling other people to stick 'em up and prodding them in the stomach with pistols, should be punctuated with simple domestic scenes in which fathers are shown talking quietly to daughters and daughters equally quietly to fathers. Otherwise the mixture becomes too rich. It is with an agreeable sense of being on the right track that the present chronicler, leaving for a while the hectic world of Mellingham Hall, turns to 11 Croxted Road, West Dulwich, London SE21, and records the conversation at that address between J. B. Butterwick of Butterwick, Price and Mandelbaum, import and export, and his daughter Gertrude.

At the moment when we start allotting space to the sort of thing Chekhov would have liked, Gertrude was in the room she called her den, saying goodbye to a finely built young man in heather mixture tweeds. He was of rather gloomy aspect, seeming to derive little enjoyment from the photographs of school hockey groups that lined the walls.

'So that's that,' he said.

'I'm afraid so, Wilfred.'

'I see,' said the young man sombrely.

He took his departure, and he had scarcely left when Mr Butterwick appeared.

'Good evening, Gertrude, my dear.'

'Oh, hullo, Daddy. You're back early, aren't you.'

'Yes, I was suffering from indigestion, so I knocked off work and came home to see what Alka-Seltzer would do. I found this letter for you on the hall table.'

'Thank you, Daddy. It's from Monty.'

'Oh? Mr. Butterwick did his best to keep disapproval from creeping into the word, but not very successfully. He was aware that he had given permission for this correspondence, but that did not mean that he had to like it. 'By the way, who was the young man I met on the stairs?'

'Wilfred Chisholm. He's a friend of mine. We were playing in a mixed hockey game this afternoon, and he saw me home. He's an international.'

'A what?'

'He plays hockey for England.'

'Does he indeed? Well, I'll be going and finding that Alka-Seltzer.'

The door closed. Gertrude opened the letter, smiling gently as she did so. But the smile lasted only for the shortest of whiles. It was succeeded by a frown. The smiling lips became set. One foot tapped ominously on the carpet. As the Screwdriver at the Drones had learned to his cost, female hockey players are easily stirred, and Monty's *obiter dicta* on the subject of her father, though in his opinion erring on the side of moderation, had stirred her like a swizzle-stick.

Never one of those girls who wait weeks before answering a letter, she felt strongly that this one called for a reply by return of post. She rose and went to her desk, looking as she sometimes looked when a referee had penalized her for 'sticks'. Nobody seeing her face would have believed that it could ever have had a gentle smile on it. Her whole air was that of one about to compose what is technically known as a stinker. A moment later she was composing it.

Gertrude's attitude towards Monty had always borne a close resemblance to that of the school teacher in Wales towards the young Ivor Llewellyn. Educational is the word for which one is groping. Like the school teacher, she wanted a husband revised and edited to meet her specifications. Even when accepting his proposal of marriage she had told herself

75

that the Monty who was going to put on a morning coat and sponge-bag trousers and line up beside her at the altar rails would be a very different Monty from the one to whom she was plighting her troth.

It was as if he had been a play which she had written and was trying out on the road. When a play is out on the road before coming to London or Broadway, the words the author hears most often are 'It needs fixing'. Sometimes it is the manager who says this, sometimes a local critic, and occasionally the waiter at the hotel as he brings in breakfast. In Gertrude's case it was the inner voice which guided all her actions. 'He needs fixing', it said, and she agreed with it. Habits had to be changed, faults ironed out. And among the faults she was determined to correct was his practice of alluding to her father as a twister and a crook and expressing a hope that he would choke. She was a loving daughter, and sentiments like these jarred on her.

She was on her fourth sheet and going well, when Mr. Butterwick came in again, looking like a horse with a secret sorrow. His indigestion was still painful, and he had discovered that he had run out of Alka-Seltzer.

'Oh, are you busy, dear? I ought not to have interrupted you.'

'Come in, Daddy. I'm only answering Monty's letter.'

'So you were right; that letter was from Montrose. Is he in enjoyment of good health?'

'I imagine so. He seems quite cheerful. At present,' added Gertrude with a significant gnash of the teeth.

'Where is he now?'

'At a place called Mellingham Hall in a village called Mellingham in Sussex.'

'Idling his time away, no doubt?'

'Apparently not. He says he is working for Ivor Llewellyn, the motion picture man.'

'Again? After his disgraceful behaviour in the matter of the brown plush Mickey Mouse? It seems incredible.'

'It is odd.'

'Is Mr Llewellyn transferring his business to England?'

76

'No, he's over here on a vacation. He's writing a history of the studio and has engaged Monty as a secretary.'

'Him,' said Mr. Butterwick, wondering whether this form of employment, like Monty's previous career as a production adviser, might not be ruled out as contravening the articles of agreement. Reluctantly he was obliged to concede that, as there was no evidence that the young man had obtained the post by skulduggery and blackmail, this secretarial job would have to be considered a job within the meaning of the act, and looking at the shape of things to come he did not like them. Even a Montrose Bodkin might hold such a position for a year, and he shuddered to think of what would happen then.

Changing a distasteful subject, he said:

'Have you any Alka-Seltzer, Gertrude? My own supply has run out.'

'There's a bottle in my bathroom. I'll go and get it.'

'Thank you, my dear. It is just here that it seems to catch me,' said Mr. Butterwick, rubbing the neighbourhood of his third waistcoat button.

Left alone, he stood for some moments thinking how much he disapproved of Monty and how unjust it was that a reputable man like himself should be suffering these internal pangs while a young waster of the Montrose Bodkin type, with nothing to recommend him to thinking men's esteem, flourished like a green bay tree. Then his eye fell on the letter from Montrose Bodkin which Gertrude had taken with her to the desk for purposes of reference.

It cannot be insisted on too strongly that import and export merchants as a class do not read other people's letters. Few branches of commerce have a stricter code. Nevertheless, it must be stated that between Mr Butterwick's catching sight of this one and his leaping at it like a seal going after a slice of fish only a few seconds elapsed. It was bound, he felt, to contain passages relating to himself, and the urge to see what they were was too strong for him. In that disgraceful moment he forgot that he was an import and export merchant, and when Gertrude returned with the Alka-Seltzer she found him standing there with the letter in his hand. He had just got to the part where Monty described him as fat-headed and hoped that his indigestion was not yielding to treatment.

The great advantage to a father of having a daughter like Gertrude is that he never gets scenes and reproaches from her, no matter what his deviations from the done thing, she taking the view that whatever Daddy does must be right. If Ivor Llewellyn's step-daughter Mavis had caught Ivor Llewellyn perusing her private correspondence, the aftermath would have taken on something of the quality of one of those explosions in a London street which slay six. All Gertrude said was:

'Oh, you're reading Monty's letter?'

Mr Butterwick had the decency to look like a minor criminal caught picking a pocket.

'I was glancing at it,' he admitted.

'You can't have liked it.'

'I did not.'

'Nor did I. And I'm writing to tell him so.'

'I hope you will not mince your words.'

Gertrude assured him that mincing was the very last thing that would happen to her words.

She spoke with such quiet force that Mr Butterwick's heart leaped with sudden hope.

'Are you breaking the engagement?'

'Oh, no, not that.'

'Why not?' Mr. Butterwick demanded with heat. 'Why on earth do you want to marry a fellow like this Bodkin?'

'I promised.'

'Promises can be broken.'

'Not mine.'

'But you can't love him.'

'I'm quite fond of him.'

'And every day you must be meeting men who would give anything to marry you.'

The compliment plainly pleased Gertrude. A gratified smile softened the sternness of her face.

'Well, I wouldn't say that,' she said, 'but I did have two proposals this week.'

'Two?'

'One was Claude Witherspoon, which of course was too absurd for words. No girl would marry Claude except to win a substantial bet.'

Privately Mr Butterwick considered Claude Witherspoon a far more suitable match than the last of the Bodkins, but he prudently did not say so.

'The other was from a policeman.'

'A *what*?'

'Not an ordinary policeman. Wilfred was at Eton and Oxford, where of course he got a hockey blue. He's the son of Sir Wilberforce Chisholm, the Assistant Commissioner of Scotland Yard, and when he wanted to follow in his father's footsteps Sir Wilberforce insisted on him starting at the bottom and working his way up.'

'Very sensible. If I had a son, I'd start him in the packing room. Only way to learn the business.'

'Wilfred will be something big at Scotland Yard some day.'

'Unquestionably,' said Mr Butterwick, who was a firm believer in nepotism. 'Wilfred? Wilfred? Was he the young man I met on the stairs?'

'Yes.'

'A splendid young man he looked. Charming manners, too. He apologized most gracefully for treading on my toe.'

'Yes, Wilfred's a dear.'

'And he has asked you to marry him?'

'He was doing it just before you met him.'

'Well, why don't you?'

'How can I? I've promised to marry Monty.'

Mr Butterwick had no more to say. Against Gertrude's conscientiousness he knew that argument would be futile. Her late mother, he recalled, had been the same, always insisting that their position demanded that they entertain as dinner guests people whom, if left to himself, he would not have asked to dinner with a ten-foot pole. And what made it so ironical was that in matters where her ethical code was not involved his word was law to Gertrude. Nobody could have had a more dutiful daughter. It was simply that she suffered from elephantiasis of the conscience. In a mad moment she had become betrothed to Montrose Bodkin and conscience would see to it that she remained betrothed.

Unless . . .

Mr Butterwick, who had returned to his study, sat up with a jerk.

He had had an idea.

There was one thing which would render that betrothal null and void. To wit, the failure of Montrose Bodkin to hold his post with Ivor Llewellyn for a year. He knew nothing of Mr Llewellyn except that he was the head of a great industry, but a man cannot reach a position like that unless he is a man of intelligence. And a man of intelligence would surely be quick to appreciate sound reasoning. Suppose he were to ask Mr Llewellyn to lunch and over the luncheon table point out to him the rashness of employing a man like Montrose Bodkin as a secretary. Would not this cause him to relieve Montrose Bodkin of his portfolio?

It was certainly worth putting to the test. What, Mr Butterwick asked himself, had he to lose?

With import and export merchants to think is to act. Thirty seconds later he was at his writing table. A minute later he had assembled pen, writing paper and envelope.

'Dear Mr Llewellyn,' he wrote.

2

Ivor Llewellyn, who had been singing what he could remember of 'Happy Days Are Here Again,' broke off in the middle of a bar, to the relief of passing pedestrians and traffic.

'You ever been in prison, Bodkin?' he asked.

Monty said he had not. He was at the wheel of the Cadillac which Grayce had bought on arrival at Mellingham Hall, and he and Mr Llewellyn were driving to London, where, he gathered, the latter had a business appointment.

'I did a stretch once in my younger days,' said Mr Llewellyn.

'Drunk and disorderly and resisting the police. Not a pleasant experience.'

Monty said he imagined not.

'But worth it for the wonderful thrill it gives you when they let you out .You feel like a caged skylark which suddenly finds that somebody has left the cage door open. That's how I feel now. You are probably thinking to yourself that I am kind of peppy this morning.'

'I noticed that you were singing a good deal.'

'And I'll tell you why, I'm going to London to have lunch with a man, and what you must be wondering when I reveal that, is how I ever persuaded my wife to let me go. By using the little grey cells of my brain, Bodkin, that was how. I told her I had to see my lawyer. One of the advantages of being head of a motion picture studio is that you are always having to see your lawyer. Wives may look askance, but there's nothing they can do about it. You tell them that if you don't see your lawyer, a scandal will break which will rock the motion picture industry to its foundations and they're baffled.'

'Then you are not seeing your lawyer?'

'No, Bodkin, I am not. I had a letter from this man saying he wanted to confer with me on a matter of importance and would I meet him at his club, so I am meeting him at his club. I need scarcely tell you how I am looking forward to lunching with him there. I know these London clubs. Good solid fare. Soup as a starter, then game pie or roast beef and Yorkshire pudding, and some succulent dessert to finish up with. And, of course, cheese. You say you've noticed I've been singing a good deal. Can you wonder? Now is the winter of my discontent made glorious summer by this J. B. Butterwick. Odd how these things come back to you. I've remembered that bit since the time I was telling you about when I was getting a thorough grounding in English Literature in order to marry that school marm. Careful, man! You nearly had us in the ditch.'

And indeed Monty had given the wheel a dangerous twiddle, causing a meditative hen which had stepped into the road to take to itself the wings of the dove and disappear over the horizon. He was profoundly stirred. His was not a particularly quick mind, but even a slower thinker would have been able to recognize as sinister the fact that Gertrude's father had established communication with Mr Llewellyn.

There could be but one explanation of his desire to spend good money giving Ivor Llewellyn lunch. It was his intention to do all that human power could do to persuade him to make an immediate change of secretaries. How much better, he could hear him saying, if Mr Llewellyn were to employ to assist him in his monumental work some keen young fellow with horn-rimmed glasses and a thorough knowledge of typing and shorthand. Surely, my dear Mr Llewellyn, he would say, after the disgraceful way he behaved in the matter of the brown plush Mickey Mouse, Montrose Bodkin is the last person in whom you can have confidence. If you take my advice, my dear Mr Llewellyn, you will dismiss him without delay. Cast him into outer darkness, my dear Mr Llewellyn, where there is wailing and gnashing of teeth, and see that he stays there.

Such were the thoughts that flashed through Monty's mind as he gazed at his companion, who was now singing 'Love Me And The World Is Mine'. The remote possibility occurred to him that he might have heard the name incorrectly.

'Did you say J. B. Butterwick?' he gurgled.

'When?'

'When you were telling me about the letter.'

'What letter?'

'The one from the man you're going to lunch with. Was he J. B. Butterwick?'

'Still is, for all I know. That's how he signed the thing. He wrote from West Dulwich, wherever that may be.'

'It's a suburb of London.'

'Lots of suburbs around London?'

'Quite a few.'

'Well, good luck to them,' said Mr Llewellyn tolerantly. 'Do you know a song called "Barney Google"?'

'No.'

'Not many people do today. It's an old one.'

82

'But about this letter.'

'Came when my wife was out, fortunately. That's how I was able to describe it to her as a telephone call from my lawyer. It just shows how my circumstances have changed that I read it twice, every word, and clutched it to my bosom, as manna in the wilderness. If I had received a letter like that at Llewellyn City, perfect stranger asking me to lunch, I'd have instructed my secretary to write a curt note in reply telling the fellow to go boil his head, but in these hard times anyone who asks me to lunch gets V.I.P. treatment, especially if it's at a London club. I remember lunching at a club years ago on one of my visits to London, and it happened to be curry day. It was an experience I shall never forget. Chicken curry it was, and I had three helpings. Those were the days, Bodkin, those were the days.'

'They must have been.'

'They were.'

'But returning to the subject of J. B. Butterwick.'

'Do I gather from the quiver in your voice that the name is familiar to you?'

'He's the father of Gertrude Butterwick.'

'That may well be so, but I don't see that it gets us any further. Who the hell is Gertrude Butterwick?'

'I told you about her. The girl I'm engaged to.'

'Ah, yes, the one who tiptoes through the tulips.'

'I didn't say she tiptoed through the tulips. You did. As a matter of fact I don't believe she has ever tiptoed through any tulips.'

Mr Llewellyn's exuberance abated sufficiently to allow him to frown.

'One thing you will learn, Bodkin, as your association with me continues, is that I am seldom wrong. If I say a girl tiptoes through tulips, you can rest assured that that is what she does. Everything you have told me about this tomato points to the fact that ... Wait! Don't speak. Memory is returning. Yes, I have it. This Gertrude is the one whose father won't let her marry you unless you earn your living for a year.'

'Exactly. And he's asked you to lunch in the hope of talking you into giving me the sock in the eye on which his heart is set.'

'I don't follow you, Bodkin. Clarify the script.'

'He's going to try to persuade you to terminate my employment.'

'When you say "terminate my employment", do you mean give you the bum's rush?'

'Just that. His Machiavellian mind has got the whole thing worked out. He thinks, if you fire me, I haven't a hope of getting another job. He knows I'm rather hard to place.'

Mr Llewellyn snorted with such violence that for an instant Monty thought that something had gone wrong with the machinery of the car. He shook in every limb, and his face could not have registered wrath and disgust more accurately if he had been taking a screen test.

'Fire you?' he said, wrestling with feelings. 'Why, you're the only person in the world as it is at present constituted on whom I can rely for sympathy and understanding. Who else have I to tell my troubles to? Don't think I'm forgetting the signal services the Miller half-portion has rendered me. I'm not. That Bavarian cream. And last night she brought me the leg of a chicken and a piece of apple pie. But I can't *talk* to her. She oozes silently into my room like oil, delivers the nourishment and is off again as if she had a train to catch. You're different. You stay put, and you *listen*. Fire *you*? I wouldn't fire you if the President of the United States and his entire Cabinet fell on their knees and begged me to. If this son of a Butterwick thinks he can get to first base with me, he's very much mistaken. "Butterwick", I shall say to him—after I've had my lunch, of course—"You're a low hound, and you've as much chance of wheedling me into giving young Bodkin the pink slip as I have of getting my wife to let me eat a chocolate eclair. Drop dead, Butterwick", I shall say.'

'Thank you, Mr Llewellyn,' said Monty, much moved.

'How many times have I told you to call me Jumbo?' said Ivor Llewellyn.

It was with uplifted heart that Monty, having dropped his friend and benefactor at the Senior Conservative Club, went off to take his midday meal at the Drones. There he was interested to learn that a book on his chances of winning through to marriage had been started by his fellow member Oofy Prosser and that the current odds against were now a hundred to eight. Having invested a considerable sum at this figure, he returned to the Senior Conservative Club, and after a short wait Mr Llewellyn appeared.

But a very different Mr Llewellyn from the gay songster of the journey to London. Gone was the effervescence which had lent such zip to his rendition of 'Happy Days Are Here Again' and 'Love Me And The World Is Mine' and would have lent to 'Barney Google' if he could have remembered how it went. His face was sombre, his eyes dull and glazed. In response to Monty's courteous hope that he had enjoyed his lunch he uttered the sort of laugh sometimes described as hollow, sometimes as mirthless.

'I'm not a rabbit,' he said.

Monty could make nothing of this cryptic remark. He conceded that the head of the Superba-Llewellyn studio did not look like a rabbit—so little indeed that the fact that he was not one seemed hardly worth mentioning. His resemblance to a rabbit was even less marked than his similarity to a caged skylark.

'Did someone say you were?' he asked, groping.

'Butterwick appeared to think so. Carrots!' said Mr. Llewellyn morosely. 'Bran pudding. Lettuce. I ordered something which he told me was duck, and it turned out to be what they called mock duck, consisting almost entirely of nuts. Nuts to you, J. B. Butterwick, I ought to have said, only I was too polite. And the only alternative was those carrots and that bran pudding.'

Illumination came to Monty. He remembered his future father-in-law's peculiar views on what the human frame required to keep body and soul together. He himself had on one occasion experienced Mr Butterwick's hospitality, and the taste had lingered for days.

'Did he take you to that health food place of his?'

'He did, blister his insides.'

'He's a vegetarian.'

'He's a pain in the neck.'

Monty's spirits were soaring. He realized now that even after that encouraging speech in the car he had had doubts as to his employer's ability to withstand the subtle arguments which Gertrude's father would put forward in his effort to induce him to de-Bodkin himself. Had J. B. Butterwick provided the roast beef and Yorkshire pudding of Ivor Llewellyn's dreams, the latter, full to the brim and mellowed, might well have felt himself obliged to show his gratitude by falling in with his benefactor's every wish, especially if lunch had been followed by port and a good cigar. An Ivor Llewellyn, on the other hand, with only mock duck inside him would not have been easily swayed.

To make sure, he said:

'Did my name happen to come up in the course of lunch?'

'I wish you wouldn't call it lunch. It was a mockery.'

'A mock duckery.'

'Eh?'

'Nothing, nothing, just a passing thought. But was my name mentioned?'

'Ha!'

'It was?'

'He had lots to say about you. He kept urging me——'

'To kiss me goodbye and tie a can to me?'

'Precisely. I'll say this for him, that he didn't really start in on you till we'd finished lunch, if you can call it lunch. During the meal he was too busy chewing his food fifty times and what conversation there was was on neutral topics. But when we got back to his club he opened up. He said you were a worthless young waster and a lot of other things. Made my blood boil. "Butterwick", I said, "You have maligned a splendid young man whom I love like a son. Go into the silence, Butterwick, I'm not speaking to you. I wouldn't speak to you if your shirt was on fire. I regard you as a louse of the first water, and I hope that on your way back to West Dulwich you get run over by an omnibus".'

'Magnificent!'

86

'I could have put it stronger, but the man was my host. One has to be civil.'

'Of course, Jumbo. What you said was just right, Jumbo. You're a true friend, Jumbo. I don't know when I've met a truer, Jumbo,' said Monty.

During most of the journey home silence reigned in the car. It was plain to Monty that his companion was reliving the past, and tact forbade any interruption of his reverie. But as they turned into the road that led to Mellingham he gave another of his mirthless laughs.

'Ironical,' he said.

'I beg your pardon?' said Monty.

'At that club of Butterwick's I ran into a man I used to know in Hollywood. Fellow named Flannery. He was an agent then. He made his pile and came to London. He runs a night club.'

'Oh, yes?'

'We're sort of connected in a way. He married my third wife.'

'Really?'

'Yes, poor slob. And he's invited me to come to his night club any night, with friends, and the club will pick up the tab.'

'Free food!'

'And free drinks.'

'Wonderful!'

'But ironical,' said Mr Llewellyn with a sigh. 'Because with my wife watching me like a cop all the time, how am I to get away?'

3

Arriving at their destination, Mr Llewellyn left Monty to take the car to the garage, and trudged slowly upstairs to his bedroom, a prey to gloom. Chimp Twist was there, going about his duties.

'Good evening, sir,' said Chimp.

'Grrrh,' said Mr Llewellyn like a tiger of the jungle.

'I trust you had a pleasant day, sir.'

'Arrrh,' said Mr Llewellyn like another tiger.

'Madam left a message for you, sir. She wishes you to forward her wrist watch. She omitted to take it with her.'

'What are you talking about? Take it where?'

'To Shropshire, sir.'

'Shropshire?'

'Yes, sir. Madam received a telephone call from Miss Mavis shortly after you had left, urging her to join her immediately in Shropshire.'

'You mean she's *gone*?'

'Yes, sir. She expects to be away for several days.'

A long silence followed. Eventually Mr Llewellyn spoke.

'I do believe in fairies!' he said. 'Yessir, I do believe in fairies.'

4

Monty, returning to the house after putting the car away, found himself to his surprise confronted by an Ivor Llewellyn differing in every respect from the moody man so recently talking of things being ironical. In the brief interval of their separation the sun had apparently come smiling through in no uncertain manner.

'Hey, Bodkin,' said Mr Llewellyn. 'Remember me telling you that my friend Flannery had invited me to his night club, everything free including drinks?'

Monty's memory was not so treacherous that he had forgotten this.

'I also dwelt on my difficulty in taking advantage of his hospitality.'

'Mrs Llewellyn?'

'Mrs Llewellyn is correct. She would never have allowed it. But do you know what I have just learned from a reliable source?'

'I'm all agog.'

'You're what?'

'Agog.'

'Oh, agog. Well, I'll tell you. This reliable source has just informed me that Mrs Llewellyn has gone to Shropshire and will be away several days. Where is Shropshire?'

'Up north.'

'Not near here?'

'Good heavens, no. A train journey of three or four hours.'

'So no chance of her suddenly popping back?'

'None.'

'Then be prepared, Bodkin, to get the car out tomorrow after dinner, and ho for the open spaces. You will drive us to London. I use the word "us" because we shall be taking the Miller half-portion along. She deserves a treat, and she will be somebody for me to dance with. I have always been fond of dancing. Some years ago I took a course of lessons from Arthur Murray.'

'Best man in the business, they tell me.'

'He is.'

'You'll have a ball.'

'Nothing but, Bodkin, nothing but.'

It appeared, however, that there was one crumpled rose leaf.

It's a pity it won't be a fancy dress affair,' said Mr Llewellyn pensively. 'I have a Captain Kidd costume I would have liked to wear.'

Chapter Seven

THE BAND (Herman Zilch and his Twelve What-Nots), which had hitherto restricted itself to the more modern type of music, had begun to play one of those old-fashioned waltzes, and each saccharine note seemed to go through Monty's heart like a dagger. By an unfortunate coincidence Herman had selected a melody to which he—Monty, not Herman—had so often danced with his arm about the substantial waist of Gertrude Butterwick, and if that wasn't putting the frosting on the cake and rubbing salt into the wound, he—still Monty—would have been glad to know what was.

Earlier in the day he had been re-reading for the fourth time the letter he had received from Gertrude, and its every word had stung like a serpent and bitten like an adder. When a girl as strict a disciplinarian as she was writes chiding her betrothed, she chides. She had assured her father that there would be no verbal mincing, and she had fulfilled her promise . . . as Mr Llewellyn would have said, in spades. Short of beginning 'Sir' and ending 'Yrs faithfully' or being written throughout in the third person the missive had everything. Little wonder that Monty, giving it its first reading, had felt as if a powerful hand had struck him on the base of the skull with a cosh or blackjack.

He was alone at the table, for Mr Llewellyn was on the dance floor with Sandy, and had his mood been less sombre he might have derived entertainment from watching them. There was a piquant difference between their styles. Sandy moved like a feather in a gentle breeze, but it was plain that Arthur Murray had taught Mr Llewellyn dancing in a hurry —in such a hurry, indeed that he had omitted to tell him not to tread on his partner's feet.

Monty's pity for Sandy, however, was lost in pity for himself. Herman was singing the lyric now, and this constituted the last straw.

'We've drifted apart.'

'How true,' thought Monty.

'You've broken my heart.'

'Absolutely correct.'

'As I knew from the start it would be,' howled Herman. 'As I knew from the ster-art it would be.'

There was only one thing to do, Monty decided, and that was to reach for the bottle in the ice bucket and drink more of the champagne provided by Mr. Flannery, of which he had already drunk a good deal. He did so, and was surprised to find after the second glassful that his mental outlook had undergone a change. Where before he had been a mere toad beneath the harrow, under the influence of the generous fluid he had been converted into an up-and-coming toad which seethed with rebellion and intended to take a strong line with girls who did not mince their words when seated at their writing desks.

Gertrude, he told himself, needed a sharp corrective. Getting a bit above herself, he considered. Seemed to think she was everybody, he would have muttered if he had been in the habit of muttering when there was no one there to mutter to. It was his opinion that she ought to be thanking heaven fasting for a good man's love instead of going about the place ticking fellows off for expressing themselves in the most temperate way on the subject of her father.

In short, when Mr Llewellyn curvetted and Sandy limped back to the table, they found him in dangerous mood. Had Gertrude Butterwick been present, only the innate chivalry of an Old Etonian would have deterred him from plugging her in the eye.

Mr Llewellyn was in the best of spirits. Even now he did not look like a skylark, but he had all the animation of one. He would have got on well with Shelley.

'Nice place, this,' he said buoyantly. 'Class. Elegance. Refinement. What the French call *chic*.'

Monty could not endorse this opinion. In the days before

Gertrude had put her veto on them he had been something of a connoisseur of night clubs. He had not been obsessed by them as were some members of the Drones—the name of Oofy Prosser springs to the mind—but he had gone to enough of them to be able to distinguish between the respectable kind and the ones liable at any moment to have the police piling on the backs of their necks for selling alcoholic liquor after hours. To the experienced eye the garishness of the latter tells the story. The name helps, too. Your virtuous night club labels itself Ciro's or Les Ambassadeurs: the other sort prefer The Hot Cha-Cha, The Frozen Limits or The Mottled Oyster.

The one presided over by the husband of the third Mrs Ivor Llewellyn was called The Happy Prawn, and was definitely garish. Its decor appeared to have been the work of an intoxicated surrealist. It was dimly lit, always a bad sign. And Herman and his What-Nots were so obviously the dregs of Society that one wondered what they were doing outside Wormwood Scrubs.

It seemed to Monty that the shadow of the constabulary brooded over the place like a living presence.

He mentioned this to his host.

'Don't you think we ought to be leaving soon?' he said, and Mr Llewellyn looked at him in shocked amazement.

'Leaving?' he ejaculated as if he could not believe his ears, which as the result of his exertions on the dance floor were now a bright red. He was wearing a paper hat provided by the management, and in other ways was making plain his determination to be the life and soul of the party.

'It's very late.'

'Shank of the evening.'

'And drinks are still being served.'

'What's your objection to that?'

'I'm thinking of the police.'

Mr Llewellyn would have none of this defeatest outlook.

'Absurd. A level-headed man like Otto Flannery is bound to have squared the police. It would have been his first move on opening a night club.'

'You can't square English police.'

Mr Llewellyn looked more than ever as though there were a credibility gap between himself and his ears.

'Ridiculous. You're talking wildly, Bodkin. England's a civilized country, isn't it? Flannery is certain to have seen the right people. Pity he's not here tonight. I wanted to ask him how he was making out with that third wife of mine, and I hadn't time when I met him at Butterwick's club.'

'Satisfactorily, I hope,' said Monty, grateful for the princely hospitality which Mr Flannery had provided. The least he felt he could do in return was to wish him happiness in his married life.

Mr Llewellyn had doubts.

'I wonder,' he said. 'Gloria isn't an easy woman to get along with. Temperamental. It doesn't take much to bring her to the boil. Or usedn't to when I knew her. The merest suggestion that you didn't like a hat was enough to set her off. I remember one night we'd had some people in for Bridge, and when they'd left I happened to mention—quite casually, simply making conversation—that if she had bid me a club instead of a diamond in that last game, I'd have made my contract and won the rubber instead of going down three and losing the rubber. She went straight out to the kitchen, came back with a pail of water, and poured it all over me and the cat, who happened to be there. Did you know that a cat's tail becomes double the size when it gets wet?'

Monty said he did not. His had been in the main a sheltered life, and he could not remember having met any wet cats.

'A fact. Cookie was this cat's name, not that it affects the story in any way. And then there was that other time . . . What's the matter, young Miller? You're very quiet.'

It had indeed been quite a time since Sandy had spoken. She had been sitting there with a faraway look on her face. Nursing her wounds, Monty thought. She emerged with a start from her reverie.

'I was thinking,' she said. 'About those wives of yours.'

'What about them?'

'Mrs Llewellyn must be the fourth.'

'Fifth. You're overlooking Bernadine Friganza.'

'It seems rather a lot.'

'That's Hollywood. You sort of drift into it. There's nothing much to do after office hours, so you go out and get married.'

Monty said he supposed there was a sporting interest attached to the thing. Competition came into it. When you found yourself getting into the big figures, you tried for the record. And a most absorbing discussion of married life in Hollywood might have followed, had not a finely built young man wearing an Old Etonian tie stopped at the table and addressed himself to Monty.

'Why, hullo, Bodkin,' he said.

'Cheeser!' cried Monty.

He had not spoken immediately, for the passage of the years had caused him to forget the name of this old school-mate. It came back to him, and he uttered it in a tone made ringing by relief and champagne. It was with the utmost animation that he introduced him to Mr. Llewellyn and Sandy.

'Mr. Llewellyn, Mr Chisholm. Miss Miller, Mr Chisholm. Chap I was at school with,' he explained.

Mr Llewellyn's effusiveness rivalled his.

'Any chap who was at school with my friend Bodkin is a friend of mine. Sit down, Mr Chisholm, and have some champagne.'

'Sorry, sir, I don't drink.'

'Don't *drink*?' said Mr Llewellyn incredulously. 'What *do* you do when you come to a joint like this?'

'I dance. Would you care to, Miss Miller?'

He moved on to the dance floor with Sandy, and Mr Llewellyn followed him with a pitying eye.

'Sad to see a young man wasting his youth like that. Think what he misses. Bad for his health, too. Champagne has a nutritive value. If somebody had offered me some when I was his age, I would have leaped to play my part in the festivities, taking the stuff in a bucket if necessary. But he just stands there and says "I don't drink".'

'Perhaps he promised his mother he wouldn't.'

'It's possible. Mothers are peculiar. So are wives, for that

94

matter. Mine to take a case in point. Why does she go dashing off to Shropshire like that? Very fortunate she did, of course, but one seeks in vain for the reason.'

'Have you heard from Mrs Llewellyn?'

'Not a word.'

'You don't know when she'll be back?'

'Haven't a notion. She just goes off and leaves me with the burden of entertaining the Molloys.'

Except for a 'Good morning' at breakfast Monty had not noticed Mr Llewellyn doing much to entertain the Molloys, but it was not for him to criticize his employer.

'Who are they?' he asked. 'I was wondering how you come to know them.'

'We met them in Cannes. At the Casino. Which reminds me, Bodkin, I owe you a thousand pounds. I can't repay it immediately.'

'Oh, that's all right.'

'I rashly played chemmy instead of roulette, and lost a bundle.'

'I'm sorry.'

'Yes, it was a blow. I had half a mind to ask you if you could manage another couple of hundred.'

'Of course.'

'Thank you, Bodkin. You're a true friend.'

'That's what I called you when you took that splendid stand with J. B. Butterwick.'

'So you did. Both true friends and getting truer every minute,' said Mr Llewellyn, on whom the champagne with its nutritive value was beginning to have its effect. 'I'll tell you why I want that two hundred. It's essential to my well-being. Have you happened to see during your residence at Mellingham Hall a fellow who looks like a monkey suffering from an ingrowing toenail?'

'I know the man you mean.'

'His name's Adair, and he's my valet. I approached him on the matter of providing me with food, and he expressed his willingness to oblige, provided the thing was put on a business basis. He drives a hard bargain. We started our arrangement the day before yesterday, and he charged me five pounds for a Mars Bar.'

'Monstrous!'

'Shook me a good deal, I must confess.'

'The worst type of profiteering.'

'I suppose a critic with high moral standards would call it that. Still, one can't help feeling a sort of respect for a man who sees his opportunities and grasps them with vigour and decision. He would do well in Hollywood.'

The total abstainer Chisholm brought Sandy back to the table and again declined Mr Llewellyn's offer of refreshment. He must, he said, rejoin his friends.

'You're here with a party?'

'A sort of party,' said Chisholm mysteriously, and withdrew.

'Probably all teetotallers like himself,' said Mr Llewellyn. 'They tend to flock together. So you were at school with him, were you? Not the sort of young man I could ever make a true friend of. Not my type.'

'He's a dream of a dancer,' said Sandy. 'I've never known anyone who danced so well.'

Once again Monty had that curious feeling which had come upon him when he was lunching with this girl at Barribault's Hotel and she had been telling him about the man she was in love with, the feeling that she had shown a lack of tact. He had danced with her several times himself since coming to The Happy Prawn, and he resented her enthusiam for a rival performer.

He fought down his pique. With his usual fairmindedness he told himself that, his circumstances being what they were —engaged to Gertrude and all that—he had no right to expect to be top man in the life of a girl as much in demand as Sandy was bound to be. She was looking particularly attractive tonight. The female patrons of The Happy Prawn were for the most part hard of face and painted to the eyebrows. She was simple and wholesome, like a primrose among orchids he felt, for champagne brings out the poetry in a man.

But the depression her words had induced still lingered.

He was conscious of a Hamlet-like moodiness. He longed for home and bed.

'We really ought to be leaving,' he said.

Mr Llewellyn chuckled merrily.

'Bodkin thinks there's going to be a raid,' he told Sandy. 'Not a chance. Otto Flannery will have seen to that. A little palm-greasing here, a little palm-greasing there, and everything will have been satisfactorily arranged. In my younger days,' said Mr Llewellyn, becoming autobiographical, 'there wasn't this same wholesome give-and-take spirit. The cops had an unpleasant way of being zealous and uncompatible. As a young man I was frequently involved in police raids, and many is the fine I have paid to the clerk of the court next day. But I soon learned the lesson which ought to be taught in the schools, and that is that when a bunch of flatfeet burst in with their uncouth cry of "Everybody keep their seats, please," the thing to do is to iris out unobtrusively through the kitchen. Outside the kitchen there is always a yard where they put ash cans and so forth, and you just climb over the wall into the street and walk away to safety. I always adopted this policy. I am confident that Otto will have slipped the local Gestapo their cut and that we are in no danger of being the victims of zeal; nevertheless I lost no time after we were at our table in locating the door through which the waiters were coming and going with the food, which incidentally was excellent. When I write to Otto thanking him I must make a point of congratulating him on the outstanding merits of his chef. It's the door behind you, Bodkin, a mere step from where we sit, so I think I may say that even if the worst should happen. . .'

But what he thought he might say even if the worst should happen was lost to posterity, for at this moment the popping of corks and the musical activities of Herman Zilch and his What-Nots were overtopped by a stentorian voice speaking with something of the timbre of a drill sergeant of the Scots Guards addressing recruits.

'Everybody keep their seats, please,' it said.

'Everybody kindly keep his or her seat, please,' would

have been more in accordance with the principles laid down by Mr Fowler in his book on English usage, but the speaker got his meaning over, which is the great thing. With the exception of Ivor Llewellyn, Montrose Bodkin and Alexandra Miller, the patrons of The Happy Prawn froze where they sat like one patron.

2

It was no idle boast that Mr Llewellyn had made when he had spoken of his skill at irising out through kitchens. He was on the farther side of the door to which he had directed Monty's attention while the Voice was uttering the second syllable of the word 'everybody'. A man of his wide experience needed no more than the 'ev' to set him in motion. Like the daring young man on the flying trapeze, he flew through the air with the greatest of ease. Monty and Sandy followed close behind him.

It was plainly the kitchen into which they had penetrated, a long room full of smells and noises and men in white caps. These last paid little attention to their visitors beyond a cursory glance. Most of them had served under Otto Flannerys' banner when The Happy Prawn had been The Giddy Goat and before that The Oo-La-La, and police raids were no novelty to them. One white-capped man said to Monty as he whizzed by, 'Cops, Mac?' and when Monty replied in the affirmative wagged his head and said 'Well, that's how it goes', but apart from that the interest of the Kitchen Staff in the proceedings was tepid.

The yard and the dustbins were there, just as Mr Llewellyn had predicted. Monty seated himself on the nearest bin and drew a deep breath. After the stuffiness of The Happy Prawn the air seemed to him to rival the ozone advertised by Frinton, Skegness and other seashore resorts.

He would have been willing to sit breathing it into his lungs indefinitely, but Mr Llewellyn, the man of action, would not permit this.

'Don't sit there puffing like a stranded porpoise, Bodkin,' he said severely. 'We've got to get out of here before they start searching the joint. Gimme a leg-up over that wall.'

Monty gave him the leg-up, and paused for a space on top of the wall like Humpty Dumpty. In spite of his demand for haste he could not refrain from speaking a few words on the subject of Otto Flannery.

'I cannot understand it,' he said. 'I simply cannot understand it. Otto, when I knew him, was as shrewd a man as you could shake a stick at in a month of Sundays, and yet he omits to take the elementary precaution of sweetening the police. I can only suppose it to have been Gloria's doing. She always had a parsimonious streak in her. I can hear her saying "Why waste the money, Otto? You're having enough expense with this old night club as it is without bumping up the bank-rolls of a bunch of cops who've probably got large fortunes stashed away already. The odds are all against them busting in, so take a chance". And Otto foolishly let himself be persuaded. Gloria was like that with me when we were married. Grudged every dollar I spent on squaring the guys who had to be squared. I remember one time . . .'

At this point Mr Llewellyn suddenly overbalanced—he ought never to have gesticulated when speaking of his third wife—and fell on the other side of the wall. But any anxiety his companions might have had for his well-being was dispelled when his voice announced that he had sustained no damage from the descent beyond a slight abrasion of the left shinbone and would meet them at the car, which was parked in a neighbouring street.

It was as he prepared to help Sandy mount the wall that Monty became aware of footsteps approaching from the direction of the kitchen, and his heart gave a leap of the kind that used to excite such universal applause when Nijinsky did them in the Russian ballet. It so happened that this was his first encounter with the police, and his nervous system was not at its best.

His relief when a moment later the newcomer turned out to be only good old Cheeser was stupendous. He welcomed him with a glad cry.

'Cheeser!'

'Oh, there you are, Bodkin. I had an idea you might be.'

'We were just going to get over the wall.'

'So I supposed.'

'It seems to have been put there for the purpose.'

'Quite.'

'My goodness, Cheeser, I'm glad to see you. When I heard you coming, I nearly swooned.'

'You thought it was a cop?'

'Yes.'

'It was.'

This, Monty presumed, was a joke. It was not much of one, but he laughed civilly. There being no hurry now, he felt disposed to chat.

'You're looking very fit, Cheeser.'

'Thanks.'

'Put on a bit of weight, haven't you?'

'A pound or two.'

'Suits you.'

'Thanks.'

'What are you doing these days?'

'I'm a policeman.'

'What!'

'I am a member of the plain-clothes division of the Metropolitan Police Force. And you're arrested. Step this way, please.'

Monty stepped that way, stunned. If old Cheeser was really what he claimed to be, and if the old school spirit burned so feebly in him that he was prepared to arrest a chap who had been in the second cricket eleven with him, it seemed to him that there was nothing to do but step.

Sandy, womanlike, had other views. She took it that she had been included in the Chisholm invitation, but she had no intention of meekly accepting it. A situation like the present one brings out all the Joan of Arc and Boadicea in a girl of spirit. She was standing at the moment within easy reach of one of the smaller dustbins. Seizing this with a lissom pounce and swinging it as the third Mrs Llewellyn had swung her pail of water, she took advantage of the officer having turned his back to envelope his head and shoulders with its contents.

Nothing could have been more effective. It was a state of things which obviously could not last indefinitely, but for the moment Police Constable Chisholm was out of action. It took but that moment for her to scale the wall, on top of which she was joined by Monty. They dropped to the other side and ran on winged feet to the car.

Mr Llewellyn was leaning against it, smoking a cigar.

'So here you are at last,' he said. 'What kept you?'

Monty did not reply. He felt incapable of speech. Love had come to him this night. It had come to him several times before in the course of his career, notably when at the age of twelve he had been taken to the Drury Lane pantomime and had become enamoured of the Principal Girl, but these had been mere passing fancies. This was the real thing. If any man could fail to fall in love with a girl who had just exhibited such outstanding qualities as had Sandy, that man was not Montrose Bodkin.

3

By the time they were in the car and speeding homewards with Sandy asleep on the back seat, Mr Llewellyn, who had remembered how the song 'Barney Google' went, had begun to sing it. He had a pleasant baritone voice, though a little uncertain in the upper register, and at any other moment Monty would have been glad to listen and possibly, having memorized the words and music, to join in the chorus. But now his thoughts were devoted exclusively to the girl curled up on the seat behind him. His whole soul went out to her. How, he was asking himself, could he have been for so long oblivious to her splendid gifts of character and personality, so blind as not to have spotted that what he had mistaken for brotherly affection had really been, simply waiting to be uncorked, molten passion, the sort of thing in which the fifth Mrs Ivor Llewellyn had specialized when a panther woman on the silver screen?

After a while Mr Llewellyn, ceasing to sing, became conversational. Monty had given him a brief resumé of what had occurred in the yard outside the kitchen, and he spoke sternly of the part old Cheeser had played in the proceedings.

'I am shocked,' he said. 'If a man won't stretch a point on behalf of an old schoolmate, one wonders what the world is coming to. But that's the police all over. The sacred ties of friendship weigh nothing with them as long as they can get a word of commendation from their sergeant. However, let us not waste our breath condemning his iniquity. Let us rather turn to the magnificent behaviour of the Miller half-portion. What adroitness, Bodkin!'

'Yes.'

'What presence of mind!'

'Yes.'

'What was in the can?'

'Bottles.'

'They must have made that total abstainer wish he hadn't spoken.'

'Probably.'

'And after the can was empty she rammed it down on his head?'

'Yes.'

'Colossal! Sensational! One only wishes she had had a custard pie she could have thrown at him, but of course one can't have everything. Bodkin, you must marry that girl.'

'But she's in love with someone else.'

'Just thinks she is. That often happens in the first reel or two. Comes the dawn, and she finds it's Cary Grant she's in love with. You must cut this jerk out, Bodkin, just as Cary Grant always did. You can do it if you try. He's probably a . . . Good Lord,' said Mr Llewellyn. 'Well, fry me for an oyster.'

'Now what?'

'I've just remembered. Forget my own name next. Something I've been meaning to tell you all evening, only it slipped my mind. You recall that I was dancing with the half-portion?'

Monty said he did. It had not been a spectacle easy to forget.

'You had told me she loved another, and, if you recollect, I said I would check up, so that if he turned out to wear side whiskers or was a movie actor we could take steps through the proper channels.'

'Yes.'

'Well, I checked up and it's all right.'

'What is?'

'It.'

'I don't follow you.'

'It's you.'

'Who?'

'The man she loves.'

'Me?'

'Exactly. I asked her straight out, because I knew she regarded me as a father figure in whom she could confide. "Pint size", I said as we started to dance, "there's a lot of talk going around about you being starry-eyed about some man or other. Who is he? Fill me in". I said. Well, at first she talked some nonsense about it being none of my business, but eventually she came clean. "If you will stop treading on my feet and promise faithfully not to breathe a word to Monty, I'll tell you", she said. I couldn't see why she specified this, but I promised faithfully not to breathe a word to you, and then she said that you were the man she loved. Apparently she was just kidding you along with all that stuff about loving someone else. One sort of understands how she figured it out. She wanted to stimulate competition. By showing you you weren't the only onion in the stew she would get your attention, and that would be half the battle. After that it would just be a matter of giving you the works. Women are fond of tricks like that. That school marm of mine in Wales. I don't suppose I'd ever have thought of making my presence felt with her if it hadn't been for her always telling me what a swell guy the organist at her church was. It was only after she had told me for about the twenty-fifth time that he was a perfect gentleman and had mesmeric eyes that I felt something would have to be done about it. You *are* that way about the midget, aren't you? Yes, I can see you are, and after the way she dumped that can on the cop I'm not surprised. A girl who bonnets a policeman with an ash-can full of bottles is obviously good wife and mother timbre. So get an immediate move on, my boy, and heaven speed your wooing. Why are you gulping like a bullfrog?'

'I was thinking of Gertrude.'

'Who?'

'Gertrude Butterwick. I'm engaged to her.'

'I'd forgotten that.'

'I hadn't.'

'That *is* a difficulty.'

'It is.'

For perhaps half a mile there was silence in the car. Then Mr Llewellyn spoke.

'I see the solution.'

'You do?'

'Provided you can answer one question satisfactorily.'

'Yes?'

'It is this. Has she a contract?'

'A what?'

'Contract, dammit. You know what a contract is.'

'I didn't propose to her in writing, if that's what you mean.'

'Then you're sitting pretty. She can't sue. You just call her up on the phone and tell her it's all off.'

Monty was appalled.

'I can't do that.'

'Why not?'

'I couldn't.'

'I'll do it, if you like. What's her number?'

'No, no, no.'

'I don't get you, Bodkin. You baffle me. I wish you wouldn't make frivolous objections. You don't love her, do you?'

'No.'

'And you do love the half-portion?'

'Yes.'

'And love conquers all.'

'It doesn't conquer ringing up a girl you're engaged to and telling her it's all off.'

'I don't see it.'

Monty did not reply. He drove on through the night—now the quiet night, for his companion had fallen into a huffy silence. It was plain to him that nothing was to be gained by discussing the subject further. If Mr Llewellyn could regard the sacred word of an English gentleman so lightly, apparently completely unaware that there are things a chap can do and things a chap cannot do, driving on through the quiet night was about all that was left to a chap.

Chapter Eight

ON THE LAWN of the house in Shropshire to which she had been so abruptly summoned by a daughter in need of a mother's advice Grayce was walking with Mavis, deep in discussion of James Ponder. They had been having summit meetings for days on the same subject, and Mavis, whose temperament tended to be impatient, was saying with some peevishness that Grayce ought for heaven's sake to have been able to make up her mind about him by this time. It fortunately happened that Grayce had. She had come to a decision that morning. She spoke now at some length, but what she said could have been condensed into the words 'Go to it'. The impression James Ponder had made on her had been wholly favourable.

'You couldn't do better, dear.'

'I'm glad you think so.'

'He's charming.'

'He charms me.'

'Very fine family.'

'Grade A. One of his ancestors came over with William the Conqueror, or would have if he hadn't missed the boat. Some trouble about losing his passport.'

'It's a pity he won't succeed to the title.'

'No, there are about fifty-seven sons ahead of him.'

'And of course one is always taking a chance with someone as good-looking as that.'

'I'll risk it.'

'He may need some handling.'

'He'll get it.'

'Those photogenic men so often do,' said Grayce. She was thinking of Mavis's father, the first of her three husbands, who had been so photogenic that she had sometimes felt that it would require the united efforts of J. Edgar Hoover and a posse of his F.B.I. assistants to keep an adequate eye on him. 'You have to be prepared for anything.'

'I'll manage.'

'Yes, I think you will,' said Grayce. As they were walking side by side, it was Mavis's profile that presented itself to her most of the time, and that firm chin gave her confidence. It was not likely that much could go wrong matrimonially with a girl with a chin like that. She was filled with maternal pride. To Ivor Llewellyn Mavis might be the menace in the treatment, but the very qualities that made him quail were those which appealed to her. A panther woman likes to feel that her daughter has inherited the panther strain and is well able to cope with the handsomest of husbands. Marriage, she was aware, is a lottery, and Greek gods are not always to be relied on, but if James Ponder, having taken Mavis for his bride, were to stray from the straight and narrow path, he would know later on that he had been in a fight.

'I don't think you need have any uneasiness, dear.'

'I haven't.'

'So if he proposes?'

'When,' Mavis corrected. 'I am arranging it for after lunch. I've been avoiding him for the last few days, so I shall get him alone in one of these shady nooks they have here and ask him why he has been avoiding me. He will say he hasn't been avoiding me, and I shall say Yes, he has been avoiding me, and it hurt me, Jimmy, hurt me terribly, I thought we were such friends. And he will say this, and I shall say that, and I shall say that and he will say this, and in about five minutes by my stopwatch we ought to be fading out on the embrace. Any questions?'

'None, darling.'

'You like the script?'

'I love it.'

'Start shooting, you feel?'

'As soon as you can.'

They had seated themselves on a rustic bench at the end of the lawn, and Grayce, able now to see her daughter's eyes, found her confidence increased by the light of determination in them. It seemed to her unthinkable that James Ponder would be able to resist them, especially if filled, as no doubt they would be, with tears. James Ponder, she felt, was as good as on his honeymoon already.

It added to her gratification that she would now be able to go home. She had found her visit pleasant enough, but she never enjoyed being a guest and having no say in the running of the establishment. It cramped her not to be in command.

'Then as you don't need me any longer,' she said, 'I'll be leaving. There's a good train in the afternoon.'

'Stay on if you like. I know they'll be glad to have you.'

'No, I think I'll be getting back.'

'What's your hurry?'

'For one thing I want to see if your step-father is keeping to his diet.'

'You'll probably find him twice the size he was when you left. With you away, he must have been eating everything in sight.'

'He wouldn't have the nerve.'

'I don't know so much. Somebody may have been smuggling food in to him.'

'Nobody would dare.'

'How about the secretary bird? What did you say his name was?'

'Mr Bodkin. He would never do anything like that.'

'You consider him trustworthy?'

'I'm sure he is.'

'I'm not.'

'What do you mean?'

'I've been thinking a good deal about our Mr Bodkin since we met, and I wouldn't trust him as far as I could throw a medium-sized elephant. He's got a lot of explaining to do before he can sell me the idea that he's on the level. For one thing he's a sort of Houdini. How did he get out of that closet? I went to let him out, and he had gone. And I know I locked the door. No, it's no good saying it might have been the wind. Winds don't turn keys, and anyway there wasn't any wind. He picked the lock somehow, and anyone who could do that must have had a lot of practice. He's probably broken out of half the prison cells in England. I suppose you took him on without bothering to ask him for references?'

Remembering that this was precisely what had happened, Grayce did not answer the question. Instead she said:

'There can't be anything wrong with Mr Bodkin. He comes of a very good family. He's related to all sorts of prominent people.'

'Who told you that?'

'The Miller girl who works for me.'

'And who told her?'

'I suppose he did.'

'Exactly. I should imagine he was lying, but if it's true, it means he's one of those hard-up younger sons who hope to make their pile by working in with a gang of crooks.'

'Mavis!'

'It's no good saying Mavis. That's the way all the evidence points. Why had he opened the front door that night?'

'He may have been going for a walk.'

'At two in the morning?'

'It does seem odd.'

'I would call it a dead give-away. You'd better face it, mother. Guys like Bodkin are the scum of the earth. Mayfair men, the papers call them. They're so smooth—good looks, good clothes, good manners and all—that people let them into their homes without a suspicion that they're the advance guard of some mob or other, and once in they do the job they've been assigned to. Shall I tell you why Bodkin is a pleasant visitor? He's been instructed by his boss to work the inside stand.'

'I don't know what you mean.'

'Perfectly simple. He gets settled in, ingratiates himself with one and all; then, when he feels that zero hour has arrived, goes and stands at the front door and signals to his pals to come running. Do honest men come down in the middle of the night and open front doors? Of course they don't. In another minute, if I hadn't appeared, Brother Bodkin would have been imitating the cry of the brown owl or something as a tip-off to his associates that now was the time for all good men to come to the aid of the party. It's no use saying he wouldn't. The man who sneaks down and opens front doors at two in the morning is a man who you can bet your bottom dollar is all set to imitate the cry of the brown owl at the drop of a hat.'

Grayce was shaken. This eloquence was having its effect, as well it might, for Mavis had been on the debating team at Vassar and there was nothing you could teach her in the way of marshalling an argument and driving home a point. Just so had Demosthenes swayed his audiences in ancient Greece. For a moment she was trembling on the verge of conviction: then the thought of Monty's ancient lineage and long line of aristocratic kinsmen gave her strength.

'I don't believe it.'

'You'd better believe it.'

'Mr Bodkin is just an ordinary young man. There's nothing sinister about him.'

'That's why the gang brass hats gave him the assignment. It had to be someone who looked all right and inspired confidence. If you take my advice, you'll fire him the moment you get back.'

Again the thought of Monty's blue-blooded relatives fortified Grayce. It was her intention in due season to meet and fraternize with these, and she could hardly expect them to take to their bosoms a woman who fired him the moment she got back. Why, for all she knew he might number among them the very aristocrats she had come to Mellingham Hall to hob-nob with. A nice position she would be in if she dismissed a young man who was the apple of the respective eyes of Lord Riverhead, Lord Woking and Sir Peregrine Voules, Bart, all of whom, with their ladies, she was hoping to ply with strawberries and cream at garden parties. 'Most extraordinary' and 'Not cricket, what?' were the criticisms her conduct would elicit, and her invitations would be curtly refused.

'Well, I'll think it over,' she said.

The Molloys were dressing for dinner, Dolly prattling gaily, Soapy, who as a rule was never averse to what is known as kidding back and forth, strangely silent. He seemed *distrait*, and on his Shakespearian forehead—his hair, as Chimp Twist had told him, was beginning to recede a good deal in spite of patent remedies supplied to his wife free of charge by some of the best shops in London, Paris and New York—a frown had appeared.

Dolly, seeing it in the mirror, was concerned.

'Something on your mind, honey?'

Soapy stirred uncomfortably. He had hoped that question would not be asked.

'It's nothing.'

'Ah, come on, what is it?'

Soapy hesitated. He knew that Dolly was enjoying this quiet interlude at Mellingham Hall, and he hated to spoil her pleasure. He also knew that evasiveness would mean more probing, far into the night. He chose the lesser of the two evils.

'It's just that I feel we're wasting our time here.'

'Getting a nice rest.'

'I ought to be working.'

'That's the artist in you, sweetie. All artists get kind of nervous when they take time off.'

'I don't want time off.'

'It's what any doctor would advise. Got to watch your health. You need a holiday after all that hard work you put in at Cannes.'

'Cannes!' Soapy sighed. 'There's a place that calls out all the best in a man. Every time the Blue Train pulls in it's loaded to the roof with rich suckers just longing for a chance of parting with their money. You hardly need sales talk.'

'You certainly had a good season there this year.'

'I did clean up,' Soapy agreed, his gloom lightening a little. 'Remember that fellow I sold all those Silver River shares to?'

'I know the fellow you mean. I've forgotten his name.'

'Me, too.'

'Small clipped moustache.'

'That's right. I met him in the Casino bar.'

'And wove your spell''

'You bet I wove it, and I didn't even need to wave my hands. Now there's an instance of what I mean about Cannes. This guy was a big noise in one of the top jewellery firms and you'd think a man like that would have the sense not to buy oil shares from a stranger he was having a drink with in a bar, but no, that Riviera atmosphere was too much for him.'

'And your winning ways, sweetie.'

'But mostly the Cannes air. That's what saps the intelligence. I keep feeling I ought to go back there.'

'And leave those pearls?'

'They've left me. She's gone off on a toot somewhere and taken them with her. She may be away for weeks.'

'No, she got back this evening.'

'You're sure?'

'Sure I'm sure. I saw her.'

'Well, that's something.'

'She was in the car with that Bodkin guy. Met her at the station, I guess. I believe he's in love.'

'Who is?'

'Bodkin.'

'What makes you think that?'

'He looks like he was. Girl must have turned him down. Has he said anything to you?'

'Eh?'

'Do *listen*, honey. What's the matter with you? I said "Has he said anything to you about being turned down by a girl?".'

'No, why would he? No skin off my nose if his love-life blows a fuse.'

It would have amazed Monty if he had known that what was probably the most poignant love tragedy since Abelard and Heloise could be treated with such indifference, and even Dolly seemed shocked.

'That's a nice way to talk!'

'Eh?'

Dolly had heard enough. A wife's instinct told her that

something was being kept from her by her mate, and she intended to know what it was.

'Come clean, Soapy. There's something else on your mind besides being homesick for the Riviera. What's biting you?'

'It's nothing.'

'Yes, it is, and it's no good trying to kid me it isn't. I can tell.'

Her tone convinced Soapy that further reticence would be disastrous. Their married life had always been modelled on that of two love-birds, but even in such a union there come moments when the female love-bird explodes like a stick of dynamite. He shrank from saying what he was about to say, for he knew it would give offence, but he said it.

'Well, if you want to know, honey, I was sort of wondering if we hadn't goofed in not sitting in with Chimp on that pearls thing.'

He had been right about the offence. All the womanly indignation in Dolly blazed into life. Her eyes glowed and her fingers twitched as if they were reaching for a pistol with which to hit J. Sheringham Adair, private investigator, on the head.

'You're crazy!'

'Just an idea.'

'That little bacillus!'

'I thought I'd mention it.'

'Him and his thirty per cent!'

'I know, I know. I'm not saying thirty's much.'

'It's an insult.'

'All the same, you can't say Chimp isn't smart. What I mean is, he may have something up his sleeve about those pearls, and we'd look silly if he got in ahead of us. I think we ought to contact him again and make a deal.'

Dolly was experiencing the complex emotions which might have come to the Duke of Wellington at Waterloo if when he had said 'Up, Guards, and at 'em' he had been told by the Guards that they were not in the mood. She herself was resolution itself, but it was plain to her that her Soapy was weakening. She forced herself to speak calmly and quietly, as if to a fractious child.

'You mustn't talk that way, sweetness.'

'He may have a plan.'

'So have I a plan.'

Soapy brightened. A modest man, he knew himself to be not very gifted outside his lifework of selling non-existent oil stock, but he had a deep faith in his wife's ingenuity.

'You have?'

'Yessir, and it's a pippin.'

'Why haven't you sprung it?'

'I had to wait till she got back.'

'What is it?'

The sound of the gong broke in on their conference. Dolly rose and made for the door.

'I'll tell you later,' she said. 'No time now.'

3

It was in a mood of complete contentment that Grayce took her place at the head of the dinner table. She had had two cocktails, and these had had their usual beneficent effect, consolidating the conviction she had already formed that all was for the best in the best of all possible worlds.

It seemed to her that all things were working together for good. Doubts regarding Monty no longer troubled her. A brief talk with J. Sheringham Adair on her arrival had left her convinced that there had been no civil disobedience on her husband's part during her absence. And to apply to her felicity what Monty would have called the frosting on the cake there was the thought of what might be happening at this very moment in distant Shropshire.

Nothing had occurred by the time she had left to catch her train, for Mavis had decided that the tender scene she had outlined would go better with the assistance of artificial light and a low-necked dress. But it could not be long, she felt, before the telephone rang, bringing news that all was well, and the prospect of having James Ponder for a son-in-law electrified every red corpuscle in her system.

Until meeting him she had been a little apprehensive, for in spite of what Mavis had told her she had got him mixed up in her mind with the man at Cannes who had worn glasses and made a funny noise when drinking soup. But the first glance had been enough to dispel at least a portion of her fears. James Ponder's eyes were as lustrous as Mavis's, and not a lens to help him see with them. And at dinner the last of her misgivings had vanished. She had sat next to him, and though listening intently through the soup course could detect no trace of a funny noise. Where the man at Cannes had given a vivid impersonation of a mountain torrent rushing over pebbles, James Ponder had taken his nourishment with no sound effects whatsoever.

The more she saw of him, the deeper her thankfulness grew. Her child, who, girls being what they were nowadays, might so easily have brought in and laid on the mat a fiancé with a beard, long hair, sandals, no money and the most appalling family, had chosen for her mate the well-dressed nephew of an Earl who shaved twice a day, wore shoes made to order by the best bootmaker in London and was a partner in one of the great jewellery firms. My cup runneth over, she might have said, if she had been familiar with the expression.

All that was needed now was for the telephone to ring, and as dinner was nearing its end it did. It was placed, as is almost obligatory in an English country house, in the most inconvenient spot, out in the hall near the front door, and Grayce leaped to answer it. Mention was made earlier of Ivor Llewellyn's agility when making for the kitchen during police raids, but he was slow in comparison with his wife. A whirring sound, and she was gone.

Nothing would please the chronicler more at this point, while waiting for Grayce to return, than to be able to fill the hiatus with some of that bright and animated conversation which does so much to enliven the evening meal. All the ingredients were there. Mr Llewellyn, one would have said, must have had a fund of good stories to tell of life in Llewellyn City. Monty could have entertained with reminiscences of the Drones Club. Dolly and Soapy might have been expected to do their share by speaking of conditions in the business world of America.

It is regrettable, therefore, to have to report that silence, as the expression is, reigned. Mr Llewellyn was brooding on a recent interview with Chimp Twist, which had culminated in him being charged ten pounds for a pork pie. Monty was endeavouring to hit on a course of action which would free him from his honorable obligations to Gertrude Butterwick without hurting anybody's feelings. Dolly and Soapy were deep in thought, the former musing on her plan, the latter trying to make a guess at what that plan could be. It was to what virtually amounted to an assembly of waxworks that Grayce re-entered.

'That was Mavis,' she said.

'Oh?' said Mr Llewellyn morosely. He was still thinking of that pork pie.

'And I want you all to join me in drinking a toast.'

Here Mr Llewellyn, whose glass contained water, gave a short, unpleasant laugh.

'To Mavis and James.'

'Who's James?'

'James Ponder. You must remember James Ponder at Cannes.'

'Fellow with a small clipped moustache?'

'That's right. Mavis has just become engaged to him. She's bringing him down here the day after tomorrow. She can't get away before then.'

Chapter Nine

AS A GENERAL RULE after dinner Grayce liked a rubber or two of Bridge, for she was as ardent a player of that game as ever bid four spades on a hand containing the queen of that suit and three small ones, but tonight there was the letter of congratulation to Mavis to write, she having by no means said her say over the telephone, and she went to her room to write it. Monty, released from duty, also withdrew. He wanted to be alone with his thoughts. He did not expect them to be agreeable thoughts, but, such as they were, he wanted to be alone with them.

They were just as unpleasing as he had foreseen that they would be. He had once read a novel by Rosie M. Banks, the gifted authoress who had married his fellow member of the Drones, Bingo Little, and it still lingered in his memory. The title, *By Honour Bound*, had put him off a bit because his tastes lay more in the direction of tales with plenty of blood and lots of gangsters in them, but Bingo had practically forced the thing on him, and to his surprise it had impressed him profoundly. It was about a bloke called Aubrey Carruthers who had met a girl called Sonia Derringford on a P. & O. liner coming back from the East, and had fallen in love with her, and she had fallen in love with him, and they had clicked in the moonlight on the upper deck during the ship's fancy dress dance.

So far, so good, you would have said, because Sonia had laughing blue eyes and hair the colour of ripe wheat and could when amused utter a delicious rippling laugh, but there was a snag. Aubrey was engaged to a girl in England, and it was impossible for him to get out of it because he was in honour bound to her and no Carruthers had ever broken his word.

A dickens of a situation for a fellow to be in, Monty had

thought as he read, and he thought it all the more now that he was in a similar jam himself. In the book it had all ended happily, the girl in England getting killed in a motor accident, but no bookie would offer odds shorter than a hundred to eight on that happening in his own case, so he had to choose between giving the honour of the Bodkins a kick in the seat of the pants and getting along for the remainder of his life with a broken heart. It was enough to make anybody pensive.

Aubrey Carruthers, faced with the same choice, had spent a good deal of time pacing with tight lips and unseeing eyes, and one supposes that this is the usual form in circumstances like those, for it was what Monty had been doing since returning to his room.

Aubrey, however, had done his pacing on the deck of a liner with nothing to bump into. Monty, in sharp contradistinction, was operating in a small bedroom. It was not long, accordingly, before his shin collided with the wash-stand, and he was rubbing the wound preparatory to going on pacing, when somebody knocked on the door and limping to open it he saw Sandy.

Many men at such a moment would have frozen with amazement and stood silent and goggle-eyed. Monty was one of them.

It was left to Sandy to open the conversation, which she did with her customary 'Hi'.

Monty found speech. It was not much in the way of speech, but the best he could do for the time being. It is difficult for a young man who has been brooding for a considerable time on the girl he loves to become articulate when she suddenly pops up out of a trap at his bedroom door.

'Oh, hullo,' he said.

He was overcome by the poignancy of the situation. Here was a girl who had frankly admitted that in her opinion he was Prince Charming galloping up on his white horse and would have liked nothing better than to be folded in his embrace and hugged till her ribs squeaked, and here was he all eagerness to do the folding and hugging, and no chance of business resulting because the honour of the Bodkins said it mustn't.

Beat that for irony, he thought as he rubbed his shin. It was the sort of thing Thomas Hardy would have got a three-volume novel out of.

Sandy was as composed as always. If there burned within her searing passion of the type in which the fifth Mrs Ivor Llewellyn had specialized earlier in life on the silver screen, she gave no sign of it.

'Excuse informal visit,' she said. 'I know it's late.'

'No, no. Any time you're passing.'

'I felt I must see you. Why are you massaging your leg? Rheumatism?'

'I bumped my shin.'

'How did that happen?'

'I was pacing the floor.'

'Why?'

'Oh, I don't know.'

'You must have had a reason.'

'Actually, I was thinking.'

'Always a tricky thing to do. Well, here's some more food for thought for you. I'm worried about Mr Llewellyn.'

'Isn't he all right?'

'Far from it.'

'What's the matter with him?'

'I don't know, but it must be something serious. I looked in on him just now with the remains of the dessert we had for dinner, that creamy stuff, and he wasn't interested.'

'He refused it?' said Monty, amazed. He remembered the creamy stuff as particularly palatable, and it seemed to him incredible that Ivor Llewellyn had not jumped at it like a snowbound wayfarer in the Alps reaching for the St Bernard dog's keg of brandy.

Apparently this miracle had not taken place. Sandy shook her head.

'No, he accepted it, but in an absentminded sort of way and with a glassy look in his eye, as if he were feeling "Oh, what does creamy stuff matter now?". For all the enthusiasm he showed it might have been diet bread.'

Monty pursed his lips in a soundless whistle.

119

'I don't like that.'

'Nor did I.'

'Bad. Distinctly bad.'

'That's what I thought, too. Do you think it could be anything to do with his step-daughter getting engaged?'

'How do you mean?'

'Well, you know how devoted step-fathers get to their step-daughters. Look on them as real daughters. He may have been thinking how sad and empty the home would be without her. I happened to be looking at him when Mrs Llewellyn sprang the news, and there was no getting away from it that it had shaken him.'

'He registered dismay?'

'As if he had sat on a tin tack. I believe he's brooding on his loss.'

'The loss of Mavis?'

'Yes.'

She had touched on a subject on which Monty had inside information from an authoritative source. If Mr Llewellyn was a prey to melancholy, it was not the coming absence from home of his step-daughter Mavis that was depressing him.

'It can't be that,' he said. 'The girl gives him the willies. His attitude towards her is roughly that of a man confronted with a cobra.'

'How do you know?'

'He told me so in person. She's his main pain in the neck.'

Sandy laughed. She had, in Monty's opinion, a delicious rippling laugh, like Sonia Derringford, and he would have been glad to listen to it as often as she cared to let it ripple.

'Well, that rather rules out my theory, doesn't it. Have you met her?'

'I've met her.'

'When was that?'

Monty hesitated, dubious as to whether it was wise to tell her more. During his stay at the Superba-Llewellyn studio they had made a picture of Shakespeare's *Othello* and he remembered the disturbing effect Othello's recital of his misadventures had had on Desdemona. Were he to relate the

120

story of what had happened to him on that night of terror, Sandy, already a victim to his fatal charms, could scarcely fail to be plunged even more deeply into hopeless love than she was at present, and he did not want to cause the poor child unnecessary pain.

However, he related it.

'And then she held me up with a whacking great pistol and locked me in the downstairs cupboard,' he concluded.

'Golly.'

'Golly is correct.'

'I see what you mean about her. Not everybody's girl.'

'No.'

'Sort of takes after her mother.'

'And her father. Orlando Mulligan. He starred in those Epics of the West and was always shooting people. He used to walk slowly from one end of the street of the frontier town while the Bad Man walked slowly from the other, and then they both drew their guns and blazed away. Of course the Bad Man hadn't a hope. I can see Mavis carrying on in a similar manner. She'll probably plug James Ponder.'

'Very possibly. After the honeymoon.'

'Oh, yes, after the honeymoon.'

'Still, that's for Mr Ponder to worry about. Our job is to find out what's wrong with Mr Llewellyn. He may be sickening for something.'

'I'll go and ask him.'

'It would be a kindly act.'

'Will you come too?'

'Better not, I think. He's more likely to confide his symptoms to you if you're alone.'

The moment Mr Llewellyn's door opened in answer to his knock Monty could see that Sandy's gloomy critique of his condition had been in no way exaggerated. Not only did Mr Llewellyn appear to be sickening for something, but for something so serious as to occasion the greatest anxiety to his friends and well-wishers. He had the look of a man who was coming down with at least three of the exotic ailments which get written up in special numbers of *The Lancet*. Monty had seen dead fish on fishmongers' slabs with more sparkle and *joie de vivre*.

His disposition, too, had taken a turn for the worse. Staring from beneath lowered brows, he was more like the dreaded head of the Superba-Llewellyn studio than the carefree warbler who had so joyously rendered 'Happy Days Are Here Again' and 'Barney Google'. This was the Ivor Llewellyn whom J. B. Butterwick must have seen across the carrots and mock duck at his health restaurant.

'Well?' he said sourly. 'What do *you* want?'

Monty saw that suavity would be required. Not sure that a jolly all-pals-together smile might not add fuel to the already existing flames, he did not attempt one.

'Sorry to barge in like this,' he said. 'It's just that Sandy Miller told me she was in here a few minutes ago, and your aspect scared the pants off her. She came away convinced that your general health had taken the count of ten, and she sent me to make inquiries. Tell me where the pain is mainly. She's worried stiff.'

His words had the effect of bringing about a marked improvement in Mr Llewellyn's mood. He softened visibly and gave it as his opinion that the half-portion was okay.

'Heart in the right place, and I appreciate her sympathy. But a fat lot of use sympathy is to me. Bodkin, you see before you a broken man.'

'Oh, do I? Why's that?'

'Sit down and I'll tell you.'

Monty took a seat, and Mr Llewellyn, after remaining for a space in the Slough of Despond in which he was immersed, struggled to the surface and spoke.

'Bodkin, have you ever been tied to a barrel of gunpowder with a lighted candle on top of it?'

'Not that I remember. Why?'

'Because that's how it is with me. I watch that candle burning lower and lower, and I lie there waiting for the big bang. Nothing can save me. You know those pearls Mrs Llewellyn wears?'

Monty said he did. He might have added that nobody who

had broken bread at the same table as Grayce could have missed them.

'They were a present from Orlando Mulligan, her first husband.'

'Very handsome.'

'Yes, she was at that time. Younger then, of course.'

'I've often admired them.'

'They look all right, I agree. Remarkable considering they're Japanese cultured.'

'Japanese cultured?'

'They are phonies.'

'Phonies?'

'Fakes.'

'Fakes?'

'Make up your mind, Bodkin, whether you are a man or an echo in the Swiss mountains,' said Mr Llewellyn with a return of his earlier manner. 'Not that I wonder you're surprised. Grayce will be, too, when she finds out. And what's terrifying me is the thought of what she's going to say when she does.'

Monty was astounded. He remembered Orlando Mulligan as about as tough a guy as guys come, lightning-like on the draw and always able to rout any number of outlaws, but it was hard to believe that any guy could be tough enough to palm off an imitation rope of pearls on a woman like Grayce Llewellyn. Napoleon might have done it, but nobody except Napoleon, and he only when drunk with power and feeling particularly courageous.

'Do you mean,' he said, 'that Orlando Mulligan had the nerve to give her dud pearls? He must have been a man of steel and iron.'

Mr Llewellyn saw that there had been a misunderstanding, and hastened to put it right.

'No, they were genuine enough when he gave them to her. The substitution of the phonies was effected later.'

'Who by?'

'Me.'

'Good heavens!'

'Regrettable necessity. I was forced to do it when she started that joint account. I was drawing down eight hundred thousand dollars a year at the studio, but what good was it to me with Mrs Llewellyn keeping tab on every cheque I drew? I had somehow to get me a little nest egg that she didn't know about. So I thought of her pearls. I took them to be re-strung and had the switch made. But I little knew.'

'What did you little know?'

'About Mavis.'

'What about her?'

'When Orlando Mulligan handed in his dinner pail—cirrhosis of the liver—it was found that he had said in his will that the pearls were to go to Mavis when she married.'

'Aha!'

'Don't make animal cries, Bodkin. I'm in a highly nervous condition.'

'I'm sorry.'

'Too late to be sorry now. You made me bite my tongue.'

'I only meant to convey that I could understand you being worried.'

'Worried is a mild word. I'm paralysed. I don't think you have ever seen Mrs Llewellyn when she was really going good.'

'Not yet.'

'You will if you stick around awhile,' said Mr Llewellyn with a shudder. 'She ought to top all previous efforts. Of course I realized, when I switched those pearls, that I was taking a risk.'

'But it seemed a good idea at the time?'

'Exactly. The chances of anyone being crazy enough to marry Mavis were infinitesimal, I thought. I wouldn't have said it could be done.'

'Though she's by way of being a beauty, isn't she? I can't speak with authority, because it was pretty dark when we met, but that's what I've heard.'

Mr Llewellyn had to express grudging agreement with this.

'Yes, I suppose she might be called a dish, but what's beauty? Skin deep. It's the soul that counts.'

'How true.'

124

'And hers ought to be sent to the cleaner's to be thoroughly cleaned and pressed. When she finds out that her pearls are Japanese cultured, it'll bring out all the rattlesnake in her.'

'You don't think she may accept them as genuine, just as Mrs Llewellyn did?'

'When she's marrying a man who's a partner in a big jewellery firm and can spot a phoney pearl at fifty paces? Don't be an ass.'

'Ponder may not spill the beans.'

'Of course he'll spill the beans. You're talking like an idiot, Bodkin, and I wish you'd go away and stay away. You've got a bedroom of your own, haven't you? Do me a favour and go there. And if you trip on the carpet and fall downstairs and break your spine in three places, it'll be all right with me. Coming here and talking drip to a broken man. Get out, Bodkin. Your silly face nauseates me.'

Monty did not linger. He was sorry to go, for he had hoped to remain and continue to give friendly advice, but something in Mr Llewellyn's manner told him that his company was no longer desired.

2

A close observer, had one been looking in their direction as Grayce proposed her toast at the dinner table, would have noticed that the announcement of her daughter's betrothal had affected both Mr and Mrs Molloy far more powerfully than might have been expected in a couple to whom Mavis was a total stranger. Nor would such an observer have fallen into the error of supposing that they were elated by the news. In the look they exchanged consternation was manifest. So far from rejoicing that two loving hearts were to be joined together in holy wedlock they gave the impression that they would have been glad to learn that the owners of those hearts had gone down with cholera and were not expected to recover. Each had remembered simultaneously that James Ponder was the confiding investor to whom Soapy had sold those Silver River shares. The mention of Cannes and small clipped moustaches had been enough to refresh their respective memories. And the prospect of picking up the threads with James Ponder, who no doubt by this time had all the facts concerning Silver River in his possession, was not an agreeable one.

Of the two Soapy was the more particularly affected, for he was the one a justly indignant James Ponder would start to throttle on arrival. He put his apprehension into words as soon as they had reached their room and were able to go into conference.

'Now what?' he said, and Dolly agreed that that was the problem.

'It must be the same guy.'

'The name rings a bell.'

'He'll have had time to get all the dope on Silver River.'

'Plenty.'

'And he'll be here the day after tomorrow.'

'That's when.'

It is well established that the heart bowed down with weight of woe to weakest hope will cling. Soapy's did.

'Maybe he won't remember me,' he said.

'Talk sense, sweetie. Once seen, never forgotten, that map of yours. So dignified,' said Dolly with a touch of wifely pride. 'He could pick you out of any police line-up if he had cataracts in both eyes.'

'I'll duck out tomorrow.'

'Sure. And tonight we'll see how that plan of mine works. I hadn't meant to try it so soon. I wanted to mull it over some more. But that's not possible now. Still, I think it's the goods.'

Soapy, who, like Aubrey Carruthers, had been pacing up and down, halted abruptly. In competition with tonight's news bulletin the fact that Dolly had a plan had faded from his mind.

'Your plan?'

'I told you I had one.'

'But that was for getting the pearls. We can't mess about with them now. What we've got to think about is making our getaway before the Ponder guy clocks in.'

'I want those pearls.'

'Me, too.'

'I want them the worst way.'

'Same here. But——'

'Care to hear what I have in mind?'

'No harm in talking things over.'

'She's got them in her room.'

'And what do we do? Go in and bust her with a sandbag?'

The question was plainly satirical, but Dolly considered it gravely. 'We could, but my way's better. We bust a window on the ground floor—say one of the ones in the dining-room. Make it look like an outside job.'

'But——'

'Don't interrupt, sweetie. Keep listening. Then I go to her and tell her there's burglars in the house.'

'She'll probably get under the bed or lock herself in the bathroom.'

'A woman like that? She eats burglars alive. She'll come running out with me to catch this one and attend to him and while she's out you slide in and do your little bit. You won't have to hunt around. She's sure to have them in her jewel case. You just pick 'em up and leave.'

Soapy shook his head. He was thinking how sadly astray the best of women can go when they attempt anything practical.

'No good, honey.'

'What do you mean it's no good? It's a cinch. It'll be like finding money in the street.'

'And tomorrow?'

'What about tomorrow?'

'When the joint is full of cops asking us a million questions.'

'Why us?'

'Because I shall be the prime suspect.'

'Why will you be the prime suspect?'

'Because Ponder will put the finger on me.'

'He doesn't get here till the day after tomorrow.'

'We shall still be here the day after tomorrow. You don't suppose the cops are going to let us leave.'

'No, they won't let us leave, and I'll tell you why. Because we shall have left before they arrive. The minute we've got the stuff, we take the car and drive to London. And don't let me hear you murmur the words "road block", on account we'll be well away long before there's any road blocks. How long do you think it'll take to assemble the cops in an out-of-the-way place like this? It may be hours. We scrap the car outside London, and once we're in London we'll be as hard to find as a couple of needles in a haystack. Harder.'

Soapy did not speak. He could not. Love for his mate and admiration for her intellect held him dumb. He was asking himself how he could ever have doubted, when she told him she had formulated a plan of action, that that plan would be simple, effective, cast iron and, in a word, a ball of fire.

3

Night was well advanced towards dawn by the time Grayce had finished her letter to Mavis, taken a shower, covered her face with mud, put on pyjamas and got into bed. And she was just dropping off into the sleep which always came so easily to her, when the door opened swiftly and silently and her guest Mrs Molloy burst in with a finger on her lips like a member of a spy ring about to confer with another member of a spy ring. At the same time she uttered a 'Sh!' of such significance that Grayce instinctively lowered her voice.

'Mrs Molloy!'

'Sh!'

Grayce might have retorted that she *had* sh-ed and that if she sh-ed any further she could become inaudible, but thirst for knowledge overcame asperity.

'For the love of Pete, what's the matter? Is the house on fire?'

'Burglars!'

'What!'

'There's a burglar got in.'

'Well, I like his nerve,' said Grayce severely. An idea struck her. 'Was the front door open?'

'I haven't been down to see. Why?'

'Just wondering. My daughter says there's often someone in the house working the inside stand. He opens the front door and imitates the cry of the brown owl as a signal to his pals to come along. Let's hope this one's a solo worker. I'm not like my first husband, I can't take on a whole raft of desperados at the same time.'

'Your husband used to do that?'

'On the screen. He starred in Westerns. Orlando Mulligan.'

'Oh, is that who he was? I saw him in *The Sheriff of Painted Rock*.'

'You caught him at his best. There was talk of an Oscar. That was the year I got mine for *Passion in Paris*.'

'You were swell in *Passion in Paris*.'

'So they all said.'

'How much did it gross?'

'I forget, but it was colossal.'

'I bet it was.'

It occurred to both of them simultaneously that they had allowed themselves to wander from the main item on the agenda. Dolly said 'But about this burglar', and Grayce realized that precious minutes which should have been earmarked for the undoing of the criminal classes were being wasted in pleasant, but idle, chatter. She rose from the bed and looked about her for a weapon. Remembering that the pistol which Mavis had left was in the top drawer of the chest of drawers, she went there and took it out.

'Oh, goody,' said Dolly. 'You've got a gun.'

'Yes, but I don't know how to use it.'

'I do.'

'Then you take it. I've always been kind of allergic to pistols since Orlando shot himself.'

'You don't say!'

'In the toe. He was showing me how quick he was on the draw. You think this burglar's still there?'

'Why not? What would be his hurry? Come on, let's go.'

'Not with this mud on my face.'

'For heaven's sake you aren't going to meet the President, it's only a burglar.'

'Not even a burglar's going to see me looking like this. You go ahead with the gun, and I'll join you. I won't be long.'

'How long?'

'Five minutes.'

'Then I guess I'll wait.'

'And I guess you won't. We don't want this porch-climber sauntering around the place, filling his little sack with nobody to interrupt him. You've got the gun. Run along and tell him to reach for the ceiling.'

It was not the power of Grayce's personality that caused Dolly to fall in with her wishes, though this was considerable. What motivated her withdrawal from the room and her passage along the corridor to her own quarters was the thought of the disastrous effect any prolonged delay would have on her Soapy's nerves. Already he was suffering from the ailment known to the medical profession as the heeby-jeebies, and anything having the appearance of a hitch in the programme might lead to a total collapse.

It was imperative that a wifely pep talk be administered before the coldness of his feet, spreading upwards, rendered him incapable of active work.

Mud sticks. It took Grayce rather longer than the five minutes she had predicted to improve her appearance to the point where even the most fastidious burglar would be able to regard her without raising his eyebrows. Confident at last that she would be doing nothing to make the criminal classes wince, she came out of the bathroom and going to the bed pressed a button on the wall at the head of it. This caused a bell to ring in Chimp Twist's bedroom, shattering a dream he was having about leaving Mellingham Hall with pearls to the value of fifty thousand dollars in his pocket.

It was at his suggestion that the bell had been installed, and being a man who liked his sleep he now regretted that he had ever brought the matter up. Women, to his mind, ought never to be allowed to be in a position to rout a man out of bed in the middle of the night because they thought they had heard a noise. It was to terror arising from some such cause as this that he attributed this untimely summons, and he resented it. With a moody oath he put on a dressing gown, yawned several times and descended the stairs. If he had been acquainted with the works of the late Schopenhauer, he would have sealed with the stamp of his approval that philosopher's unflattering views on the female sex.

One glance at Grayce was enough to tell him that, whatever her emotions might be, terror was not one of them. Anything less timid he had rarely seen. The news that her home had been invaded by somebody not on her visiting list had brought to life all the latent flame in her and she was once more the human tigress who had won an Oscar for her sensational performance as Mimi the Apache queen in *Passion in Paris*. Her lips were set, her eyes aglow, and she had found an umbrella which she was swinging in a menacing manner. She would have been the first to admit that it was not the ideal weapon, but taken in conjunction with Mrs Molloy's Colt .38 it should be sufficient to convince this burglar that tonight was not his lucky night.

'Oh, there you are at last,' she said.

'I answered your summons with all the speed possible in the circumstances, Madam,' said Chimp with dignity. 'I was asleep.'

'So was I till Mrs Molloy came bursting into my room.'

'Mrs Molloy?' said Chimp, seeming to find the name significant.

'She came to tell me a burglar had got in.'

'Mrs Molloy,' Chimp muttered meditatively. 'She had seen him?'

'No, heard him.'

'Ha!'

'What are you going Ha about?'

'I merely intended to show my interest, madam.'

'Well, I wish you wouldn't,' said Grayce with a peevishness similar to that displayed by her husband towards Monty. 'She's gone down with the gun, and I'm just going to join her. I had one or two things to do before I left.'

'Was Mr Molloy with Mrs Molloy?'

'No.'

'Curious.'

'I suppose she didn't like to wake him.'

'Quite, madam.'

The meditative note was now plainly discernible in Chimp's voice. In any matter having to do with his old acquaintances the Molloys he was practically clairvoyant. Thoughts which would not have come to one who did not know them so well came readily to him, and he did not need a blueprint to tell him when funny business was afoot. It struck him now, as if some voice had whispered in his ear, that luring Grayce from her room in order that during her absence Soapy might sneak in and possess himself of the pearls was just the sort of scheme that would have presented itself to Dolly's active mind.

'If I might point something out, madam.'

'Point away.'

'You will be leaving your room unoccupied.'

'No I won't. You don't suppose I'm going to risk having this louse of a porch-climber give us the slip downstairs and come up here, do you? You'll be on guard. That's why I rang for you, Park yourself somewhere where you won't be seen and be ready to jump out like a leaping leopard when the time is ripe.'

'Quite, madam,' said Chimp, gratified that their minds had run on such parallel lines. 'I will conceal myself in the cupboard.'

The pep talk which Dolly had administered to Soapy had proved to be most effective, as her pep talks always did when she called on him to undertake some enterprise foreign to his normal line of endeavour. Beneath her soothing spell his doubts and fears had subsided, to be replaced by the spirit that wins to success. It was in confident mood that he made his way to Grayce's room.

'Keep the door ajar and your eyes skinned till you see her go downstairs,' Dolly had said, and he had fulfilled her instructions to the letter.

A momentary return of the heeby-jeebies had halted him on the threshold of the room, but he overcame it. The door was open. He stole in like one tip-toeing through tulips. He reached the dressing table, and as he did so Chimp Twist came out of his cupboard.

'Anything I can do for you, Mr Molloy?' Chimp asked, and Soapy uttered a stifled cry like a stepped-on cat suffering from laryngitis.

Chapter Ten

AS THE RESULT of her disturbed night Grayce slept late next day. You cannot pursue burglars with an umbrella at two in the morning without nature taking its toll. Dismissing Chimp with a drowsy wave of the hand on her return to her room, she climbed into bed and curled up. It was only after the morrow's luncheon gong had sounded that she was once more among those present.

At lunch she noted the absence from the table of Mr and Mrs Molloy and was informed by Sandy that Mr Molloy had been forced to leave by an urgent telephone call connected with his vast oil interests, the sort of thing that is always happening to these men with vast oil interests. Mrs Molloy, Sandy said, would be remaining. She had taken Mr Molloy to the station in the car.

Grayce received the news with no great regret. There was a bond between her and Dolly, for last night they had stood shoulder to shoulder like the boys of the Old Brigade, or would have so stood if they had been able to find the foe they were standing against, but she was not particularly fond of Soapy. She bore the loss of him, accordingly, with fortitude and, lunch concluded, went to the telephone to pour out to Mavis the tale of the burglary.

She had a good story to tell, and she told it well. Mavis was able without difficulty to grasp the main features of the drama. Her first observation on learning that thieves in the night had visited Mellingham Hall was a sharp 'Didn't I tell you? Didn't I warn you?'. This was followed immediately by an anxious query.

'The man didn't get away with my pearls, did he?'

Her use of the word 'my' cost Grayce a pang. It was not that she had forgotten that the pearls would soon be Mavis's

134

pearls, it was just that she disliked being reminded of it. A mother's love rendered her incapable of denying her child anything she desired, but she could not help thinking it was a pity the pearls fell into this category. She had worn them so long that she had come to look on them as her own property, and it was impossible not to think harsh thoughts of the late Orlando Mulligan in his capacity of testator.

Crushing down this unworthy sentiment, she said:

'No, dear, they are quite safe.'

A sigh of relief came over the telephone.

'That's good news. Not that anything's safe with that crook Bodkin in the house.'

'Don't be absurd, dear.'

'Who's being absurd? Isn't it obvious that he was the mastermind behind last night's song and dance? Did you hear the cry of the brown owl?'

'No, I did not.'

'Probably weren't listening.'

'I was asleep.'

'So you were, I was forgetting. But he must have made it. Was the front door open?'

'No. The man broke a window.'

'Bodkin put him up to that. It would of course look better if his buddy came in through a window. He had it all thought out. Avert suspicion by making it seem an outside job. These Mayfair men are smart. They know their groceries.'

Mother's Love Ordinaries took a sharp drop. As so often happened when she conversed with Mavis, Grayce was conscious of a sudden spasm of irritation. She had been similarly affected in her earlier days by directors who thought they knew everything. With an effort she contrived a light amused tone.

'You and Mr Bodkin!'

'Don't couple me with that king of the underworld!'

'You've really got a thing about poor Mr Bodkin, haven't you?'

'Rich Mr Bodkin he'll be if you give him the run of the home much longer. Though it depends of course on how his mob divvies up the loot. Would he be cut in on the gross receipts, do you think, or is he on a straight salary, the pie-faced young plug-ugly?'

Here Mavis did Monty an injustice, for he was not notice-ably piefaced. Sandy Miller, indeed, from the very start of their acquaintance had thought his features super. But it was on the other portion of the indictment that Grayce took her stand.

'Mr Bodkin is not a crook!'

'Want to bet?' said Mavis. 'Anyway, if he's as pure as the driven snow, if not purer, please take those pearls to the bank and have them put them in the safe with strong men with shot-guns watching over them. Goodbye, mother, I must rush. Jimmy is waiting to escort me to the links to shoot a hole or two of golf.'

Grayce hung up the receiver with an unnecessarily forceful bang. It irked her that, strong woman though she was, she was always unable to hold her own in debate with Mavis, a thing which Mr Llewellyn would have attributed to the sinister influence of Vassar. Let a girl go to college, he main-tained, and it was the end. You had no more chance of getting her to listen to reason than an extra in a mob scene would have of trying to impose his views on a ten-thousand-a-week director.

As regards Monty, her feelings varied from moment to moment. Under the spell of her daughter's eloquence it was difficult not to classify him as one of those characters whom the police are anxious to interrogate because they think they may be able to help them in their investigations, but, freed from that spell, the thought of all those titled relations of his made her strong again. She declined to believe that any man so closely connected with the flower of England's aristocracy, for which she had a respect amounting to reverence, could be guilty of such plebeian conduct as opening front doors and behaving like a brown owl. That sort of thing might be expected of cads and outsiders, but not of one whose name she presumed was in Debrett's Peerage, if only in small print among the Collateral Branches. It took her not more than a minute or two after hanging up the receiver to identify her daughter's views on Monty as apple sauce.

On one point, however, Mavis had been right. Those pearls unquestionably ought to be taken to the bank without delay, and she had the ideal man to take them, J. Sheringham Adair, private investigator, who as part of his professional duties was probably handling confidential missions of the sort all the time.'

She sent for him.

'Mr Adair.'

'Madam?'

'I hope you can drive a car.'

'Oh, yes, Madam.'

'Because I want you to take my pearls to the Sussex and Home Counties Bank in Brighton and give them to the manager to put in his safe.'

Only once in his life had Chimp experienced the thrill these words sent tingling through his weedy little body. That was when he had heard the foreman of the jury say 'Not guilty' when he had been expecting to be shipped to Dartmoor for a five-year stay. On that occasion he had come within an ace of bursting into song like the Cherubim and Seraphim, and he was conscious of a similar impulse now. It would not be too much to say that he felt like some watcher of the skies when a new planet swims into his ken, unlike stout Cortez when with eagle eye he stared at the Pacific.

If he had sung, the melody he would have selected would probably have been 'Now the labourer's task is o'er'. For days he had been straining his brain, trying to think of a way of vanishing unobtrusively from Mellingham Hall with the pearls as fellow-travellers, and now the thing had been handed to him on a plate with watercress round it. He was so moved that he found it difficult to speak.

However, he did so.

'Quite, Madam,' he said.

'I don't like being without them, but with burglars busting in every hour on the hour it's the only safe way. I had to do it in Beverly Hills.'

'I agree with you completely, Madam.'

'I did think that when I came here things would be different, but apparently you get as many bad guys in Sussex as you do over at home.'

'England's trend these days towards Americanization is very noticeable, Madam.'

'You're telling me! All right, I'll bring them down and you can get going. Tell the manager to guard them with his life.'

'Very good, Madam.'

2

It was a lovely day of blue skies and gentle breezes. Bees buzzed, birds tootled, and squirrels bustled to and fro, getting their sun-tan in the bright sunshine. In a word all Nature smiled, but not so broadly as did Chimp as he sauntered to the garage to smoke a cigarette. His artistic sense of what was fitting in a valet would not let him do this in the open air. He knew also that Dolly would be returning soon from the station, and he looked forward to tell her the news of the assignment he had just received. She would, he anticipated, have a series of conniption fits.

The antagonism between Chimp and the moon of Mr Molloy's delight was one of long standing. True, they had been partners in one or two profitable enterprises, for circumstances had sometimes made a partnership unavoidable, but for the most part they had been rivals and enemies, and anyone who was a business opponent of Dolly Molloy did well to watch his step. Opposition when money was at stake always brought to the fore the Lady Macbeth side of her character. Mention has been made of the occasion when she had hit Chimp on the back of the head with a pistol, and he had not forgotten the other occasion when she had discouraged his competition by quenching his thirst with a Mickey Finn, adding insult to injury by putting a lily in his hand as he lay apparently lifeless on the carpet. Sitting now on top of the world with a rainbow round his shoulder, he proposed to get a bit of his own back by taunting her after the manner of the villain in a novel of suspense who has got the hero in his power. There was nothing of generosity to a fallen foe about Chimp Twist. When he was in a position to rub it in, he rubbed it.

He had not been waiting long when Dolly drove up. She looked as attractive as she always did, but a physiognomist would have detected in the face beneath the perky hat signs of heaviness of heart. Mention has already been made of the buzzing bees, the tootling birds, the blue skies and the gentle breezes which lent such charm to the grounds of Mellingham Hall on this golden afternoon, and one might have expected that anyone in these grounds as of even date would have experienced a considerable uplifting of the soul. But Dolly's soul was far from being uplifted. For her the bees buzzed and the birds tootled in vain.

Last night's fiasco had dealt her a blow from which she had not yet recovered. She had been so sure the thing was in the bag and all that remained to be done was the spending of the money which Mr Whipple, the receiver of stolen goods with whom she did most of her business, would pay in return for Mrs Llewellyn's pearls.

The sight of Chimp added just that extra touch of anguish which Fate loves to supply when amusing itself at the expense of a girl in trouble. Her plan had come to nothing, Soapy had gone off leaving her with nobody on whose shoulder she could cry, and on top of all this she was going to have to talk to Chimp Twist, a thing she disliked doing even when in the sunniest of moods.

She made an effort to ignore his presence, but he was not a man easily ignored, especially when he had taunting to do. Like Apollyon in *Pilgrim's Progress*, he was straddling right across the way, and her only hope of avoiding conversation with him would have been to run over him in the car, a step which despite its obvious appeal she thought it would be unwise to take.

She did not waver in the view she had always held that there was no good Chimp but a dead Chimp, but she knew how fussy the police can be about these things.

She trod on the brake, and Chimp came to the window and

inserted head, shoulders and a repulsive grin through it, opening the exchanges with a breeziness that cut her like a knife.

'Hullo, Dolly, you look kind of washed out. That's what comes of keeping these late nights. Early to bed and early to rise, if you want to have that schoolgirl complexion. Been seeing Soapy off, they tell me.'

'Yes.'

'I thought he'd be taking a powder. Did he tell you about last night?'

'Yes.'

'Not so good, that plan of yours. I could have told you it wouldn't work. One of those things that look all right on paper, but don't amount to anything when you try them out. Back to the old drawing board, eh? All that's come of it is Soapy getting nervous prostration. I certainly got a giggle out of that. You should have seen his face when he saw me. The poor fish thought he had it made, little knowing that J. Sheringham Adair, the man who never sleeps, was watching his every move. His hair stood on end, what there is of it. Every time I see him he's lost a lot more, and the worst is yet to come. Have you ever reflected what it'll be like, going through life with a bald Soapy? Doesn't bear thinking of.'

With unerring accuracy he had touched on the topic most calculated to wound. The one dark spot in Dolly's happy life was the fear of Soapy losing his hair. She had tried lotion after lotion, but without success. Unable now to run him over in the car but feeling the urgent need to express herself, she thrust a shapely hand against Chimp's face, and had the satisfaction of seeing him stagger back, rubbing his nose, but he soon returned.

'Was that nice?' he asked reproachfully.

Dolly replied that from her viewpoint it had been. She only wished, she added, that she had a spanner or something at her disposal and had not been obliged merely to use her hand.

'You're a hell cat,' said Chimp.

'No comment.'

'You nearly broke my nose.'

'No comment.'

'One of these days that temper of yours is going to get you into trouble.'

'My temper's all right, so long as people who look as if they ought to be in the monkey house at the Zoo don't wise-crack about Soapy getting bald.'

'I only said——'

'I know what you said.'

'It was harmless pleasantry.'

Dolly, becoming anatomical, told him what he could do with his harmless pleasantries. When stirred, she was inclined to become a little coarse.

'Changing the subject,' she proceeded, 'will you kindly get out of my way. I want to put the car in the garage.'

It was Chimp's moment of triumph. He stopped rubbing his nose.

'Don't bother,' he said. 'I shall be using it very shortly. Mrs Llewellyn is sending me to Brighton to put her pearls in the bank.'

'What!'

Chimp stifled a yawn.

'Yes. I wonder if I shall get there with them. One never knows, does one. You're probably sorry now you didn't come in on that seventy-thirty deal. If we'd been partners, you'd have got your cut even though I had done all the work, because an agreement is an agreement and the word of J. Sheringham Adair is his bond. Now, you don't get a nickel and I'm laughing myself sick.'

It was unfortunate for Chimp that at this point he grinned again, possibly in order to give his auditor an ocular demonstration, for his merriment had the effect of inflaming Dolly to a recklessness of which, had more tact been exercised, she might not have been capable. She was animated by the same sentiment which made Samson pull down the temple pillars at Gaza.

'Don't get a nickel, don't I?' she cried, speaking from between clenched teeth. 'Nor do you. Would it interest you to hear what I'm going to do? I'm going to Mrs Llewellyn and tell her if she lets you go off with her pearls, she's crazy. "Mrs

Llewellyn", I shall say, "Can I have a moment of your valuable time? I want to put you hep about this J. Sheringham Adair you've got such trust in. He's a crook from Crooksville, and if you want to know how I know, I'm a crook, too, and Mister Sheringham by golly Adair has been associated with me in many of my enterprises". Then I shall supply full details, and if you expect, when you go indoors, to see Welcome on the mat, you'd better think again. I wouldn't put it past her to prod you in the ribs with a knife of Oriental design. It's the sort of thing she used to do on the screen to guys she didn't like. Or maybe she'll set the cat on you.'

It was shown earlier that Dolly had been wishing that she could have been more adequately armed for this interview, thinking wistfully in particular of the pistol of which on a former occasion she had made such excellent use, but she need have no regrets. She had achieved the same gratifying result with words. Beneath the impact of the pistol Chimp had reeled and tottered, but no more noticeably than he was reeling and tottering now. The only difference was that this time he had not got a lump on the back of his head.

It was some time before he was able to speak. When he did, there was incredulous horror in his voice.

'You mean you'd squeal on me?'

'That's right.'

'You can't do this.'

'Says who?'

'But it's not . . .' Chimp paused, searching for the *mot juste*. 'It's not ethical.'

'Whatever that means.'

'It means it's low. It isn't done. You can't do the dirty on a business competitor just to stop him from putting it over on you in a business deal.'

'Watch me.'

'And another thing. How long do you think you'll go on staying here once she knows all about you?'

'Who wants to stay on here? The main thing is that you won't. You'll be out on your ear before you know what's hit you.'

142

Chimp was silent for a while, thinking this over.

Then, for he was a man ready to make concessions if he had to, he said:

'That deal of ours. We'll call it sixty-forty.'

'No.'

'It's a good offer.'

'Not to me it isn't. I'm going to get those pearls myself.'

'That'll be the day.'

'Yessir, and it won't be long coming. Meanwhile, you be contacting Mrs Llewellyn and telling her you've got measles or fish poisoning or something, so much regret you can't go to Brighton for her.'

Chimp breathed a heavy breath. It was the breath of a beaten man.

'Understand?'

'I do.'

'Sounds like you were getting married and the minister had said to you "Dost thou?",' said Dolly merrily, and Chimp, who had been thinking how pleasant it would be to strangle her, changed his mind. Something lingering with boiling oil in it would be more in tune with his mood.

Generally on occasions like this the woman has the last word, but now it was Chimp who had it.

'I give Soapy two years,' he said. 'At the end of then his head will look like a new-born billiard ball.'

3

Chimp was not the only member of the Mellingham Hall household who was thinking hard thoughts of Dolly Molloy. In the study which had been placed at his disposal for the writing of his monumental work on the S-L studio Ivor Llewellyn was musing on her with equal warmth. He, too, would gladly have skinned her with a blunt knife and dipped her in boiling oil.

What caused his exasperation was not the fact that Grayce before retiring to rest had come to him, woken him up, filled him in, as he would have said, on the state of affairs, given him the Colt .38, and told him to go downstairs and spend the remainder of the night on a chair in the dining-room—in case, she explained, the marauder should come back. That would have been enough to sour a far more amiable disposition than his, but it was the thought that but for Mrs Molloy giving warning of his presence the excellent fellow might have got away with those Japanese cultured pearls that seared his soul as if he had backed into a red-hot radiator in the bathroom. He had not been so deeply stirred since the day when Weinstein Colossal had nipped in ahead of him and bought the motion picture rights of a best-selling novel for which he had been bargaining for weeks. An officious meddling interfering woman who hadn't the decency to mind her own business, he classified her as.

At this point in his meditations he dozed off. He had slept but fitfully in the dining-room chair. Grayce, entering, found him snoring and intruded on his slumbers with a powerful poke in the ribs, using her left hand for the purpose. In her right she was carrying her jewel case.

'Wah?' said Mr Llewellyn. 'Wah?'

'Wake up,' said Grayce. 'Sleeping!' she added. 'At a time like this.'

Mr Llewellyn was sufficiently removed from dreamland by now to be capable of resentment.

'One's lucky to get any sleep at all in this house. Dragging me out of bed in the middle of the night to sit on dining-room chairs.'

'We need not go into that.'

'Gave me a crick in the back.'

'I said we need not go into it. I don't know what to do,' said Grayce. 'I simply don't know what to do.'

A stronger man might have offered the suggestion that the thing for her to do was to get out of here and leave him to catch up with his sleep, but Mr Llewellyn, though resentful, was not quite capable of that. Now that he was awake he was able to recognize in his mate's demeanour the signs that indicated that something had upset her; and when Grayce was upset those who knew her best, her daughter Mavis always excepted, were careful to watch their words.

Quite mildly, accordingly, he said:

'What's your problem?'

'Adair has got a pain in his inside.'

Mr Llewellyn, though once more in possession of his faculties, found himself unequal to the intellectual pressure of the conversation.

'Who's got a what where?'

'Adair. A pain. He's doubled up with it.'

The name had registered with Mr Llewellyn, and it was perhaps natural that the dismay he felt was not excessive. The man who charges us five pounds for a bar of milk chocolate and ten pounds for a pork pie automatically forfeits our concern. We receive with indifference the news that his inside is not all it should be.

'Oh, is he?' he said.

'So he can't go to Brighton.'

Again Mr Llewellyn had the dreamlike feeling that he was missing the gist.

'Does he want to go to Brighton?'

'I was sending him to the bank with my pearls. It's the only sensible thing with all these burglars around.'

As she spoke, the telephone rang in the hall. She went out to answer it, leaving Mr Llewellyn staring at the jewel case she had left behind her. He was feeling relief comparable to that which had come to Chimp Twist when he had heard the foreman of the jury say 'Not guilty'. True, he had not emerged entirely from the soup which threatened to engulf him, but he had been granted a respite. Pearls taken to banks are beyond human reach, but now that, thanks to this merciful pain in his valet's interior, they were remaining on the premises, there was always the chance that another and more successful marauder might pay Mellingham Hall a visit. Slight, perhaps, but nevertheless something to hope for, and, as was emphasized earlier, hope is what the heart bowed down with weight of woe needs in its business.

He was thinking kindly thoughts of Chimp's gastric juices,

had certainly done the right thing at the right time, when the proprietor of those juices suddenly appeared at the open window and poked his head in. It surprised Mr Llewellyn considerably. When a man has been widely publicized as being doubled up with pain, one does not expect to find him strolling about and poking his head through windows.

He would probably have expressed his astonishment verbally, had not Chimp spoken first.

'Hey, cocky,' said Chimp. Now that he and Mr Llewellyn had got to know one another better he dropped, when they were alone, the rotund form of speech which he employed in conversation with Grayce. His business relations with Mr Llewellyn seemed to him to render formality unnecessary. 'Are you in the market for a snifter?'

If an underling had addressed him in this fashion at the S-L studio, Mr Llewellyn's way with him would have been a short one, but in the trying circumstances in which he now found himself he was loath to alienate anyone who mentioned the word 'snifter'. Deprived of alcoholic refreshment since that night at the Happy Prawn, he had panted for it as the hart pants for cooling streams when heated in the chase. He did not like Chimp's manner, but then nobody did. He replied most cordially that he was indeed in the market.

'Got a bot of champagne,' said Chimp. 'I can do you it for forty quid.'

It was perhaps only natural that Mr Llewellyn should have hesitated for a moment. Forty pounds a bottle was rather more than he was accustomed to pay for this wine and his little stock of ready money was shrinking. But he remembered how good champagne can taste, and as regards the money end of it he could always rely on his friend Bodkin's bottomless purse. A loan of another hundred or two would mean nothing to his friend Bodkin.

He put a tentative query.

'Small bottle?'

'Big bottle.'

'It's a deal.'

'I've taken it up to your room and stowed it away in the top

146

drawer of the chest of drawers along with your socks and handkerchiefs.'

'Ice?'

'In the bathroom.'

'Did anyone see you?'

'Nobody ever sees me. They call me The Shadow.'

Business concluded, Mr Llewellyn thought it only civil to inquire after the other's health.

'Feeling better?' he asked.

'Pardon?'

'I was told you were doubled up with pain.'

A cloud passed over Chimp's repulsive brow. He did not like to be reminded of that interview with Dolly.

'Oh, the pain. It comes and goes.'

'Always the way.'

'Right now I'm feeling fine.'

It occurred to Mr Llewellyn that he ought to be, after selling a bottle of champagne for forty pounds. However, he remained pacific.

'I get pains, too, sometimes.'

'You do?'

'Catch me right here.'

'They say bismuth is good.'

'Yes, I've heard that.'

One would have said that a delightful point of camaraderie had been reached between these two and one had been looking forward to further exchanges on these pleasant lines, but Chimp destroyed the harmony by striking a sordid note.

'Well, where are they?' he asked.

'Eh?'

'My forty smackers.'

'I'll pay you later.'

'Not me you won't. Cash down, or no bet.'

'But I have to get the money from my secret hiding place.'

'I'll wait.'

'And see my secret hiding place? No, sir.'

Chimp saw the justice of this. He, too, had had safe deposits which were not for the public eye.

'All right,' he said. 'I'll come back for the money. Have it ready.'

'I will.'

Left alone, Mr Llewellyn wandered to the window. From it one got an extensive view of the Hall grounds, including the drive. Up and down this, Monty was pacing with bent head and furrowed brow, as is customary with men who are brooding on their tangled love lives. The sight of him gave Mr Llewellyn one of those sudden inspirations which had so stunned his co-workers at conferences in Llewellyn City. He gave tongue.

'Hey, Bodkin. Cummere.'

Monty came there. He and Mr Llewellyn had parted last night on somewhat strained terms, but the voice uttering the summons had not been an unfriendly voice, and he assumed that bygones were to be regarded as bygones. Mr Llewellyn might have let the sun go down on his wrath, but daylight had apparently adjusted matters.

Moreover, even if hostile sentiments still burned in his bosom, these, Monty was convinced, would speedily cool off when he heard what he, Monty, had to say. Sandy that morning had outlined a course of action for the stricken man to follow which, if adopted, could not fail to be box-office. It was one of those simple, straightforward plans of campaign which occur only to minds like Sandy's, and Monty had no hesitation in classing it as brilliant. Mr Llewellyn had been baffled, he himself had been baffled, and probably Machiavelli would have been baffled if he had been there, but Sandy had found the way.

He inserted his head through the window, eager to impart the great news.

It was Mr Llewellyn, however, who spoke first.

'Got an idea, Bodkin.'

'So have I,' said Monty. 'Or, rather, so has Sandy, and you won't be far out in describing it as an inspiration. Her gentle heart has been much touched by your distress, and she has devoted considerable thought to trying to find a solution to your problems. This morning she got it. Look. You're wondering what you'll say when Mrs Llewellyn finds out those pearls are Japanese cultured and thinks that you made the switch.'

The day was warm, but a shiver passed through Mr Llewellyn's ample frame.

'I doubt if I'll say much. She'll do the talking.'

'But when she pauses for breath.'

'She probably won't.'

'Let us assume that she does. Do you know what you will do then? You will accuse her of making the switch herself, her idea being that as she's got to hand the pearls over to Mavis she could put herself ahead of the game by selling them and pouching the money. You know how fond she is of money. The beauty of this scheme is, of course, that she can't deny it. At least, she can, but denial won't do her any good.'

There was a long silence; to Monty a disappointing silence. He had anticipated from his companion something in the nature of three rousing cheers. And so far from bursting into applause he was looking as he had so often looked during conferences at the Superba-Llewellyn studio when somebody had been slow off the mark in saying 'Yes' to one of his suggestions.

At length he spoke.

'The half measure thought that up?'

'Yes, it was her own unaided work.'

'She ought to have her head examined.'

'You don't like it?' said Monty, taken aback.

'I don't want any piece of it. Who does she think I am? One of those dauntless death-defying guys who go into cages at the circus and look murderous man-eating monarchs of the jungle in the eye and make them wilt? I wouldn't have the nerve to talk to Grayce like that on the long-distance telephone. No, sir, not if I was in Paris, France, and she was in Honolulu.'

Monty preserved a prudent silence. There had been an instant when he had thought of saying 'Are you man or mouse, Llewellyn?', but he decided not to. Pleasant though their relations had been of late, he had never lost the awe with which the other had inspired him during his sojourn in Hollywood.

149

He had commented to Sandy on the resemblance, as seen by an employee at Llewellyn City, between this man and the less lovable fauna of the Book of Revelation, and he had always felt that there was no knowing when the similarity might not become noticeable again.

He said nothing, therefore, and Mr Llewellyn proceeded, now in more pacific vein.

'Don't get me wrong, Bodkin. I'm not saying the half portion's idea is a bad one for the right man, but I'm not the right man. Telling Grayce she switched those pearls calls for someone more the Orlando Mulligan type, though I doubt if even he would have been equal to it unless pickled to the gills, as he so often was. Where young pint size is at a disadvantage is in never having seen Grayce when she was really rolling. I've heard former husbands of hers say there has been nothing like it since the San Francisco earthquake of nineteen-six. Why, when we were doing *Passion in Paris* she used up three directors, two assistant directors and a script girl. Never themselves again. No, we give pint size an E for Effort, but we pigeonhole her treatment as unworkable and start shooting mine. I told you I had an idea. It is the fruit of long hours of intense thinking, but I have no hesitation in predicting that it will bring home the bacon. It is this. You take the jewel case, ostensibly to leave it with the bank, and on the way there you throw it into some convenient pond or river, where it will remain unseen till the cows come home. Or you might bury the damned thing.'

He paused, plainly satisfied that he had found a solution where all others had failed. He was so manifestly pleased with himself that Monty hardly liked to put a query which might offend by seeming a criticism of his brain-child. He nerved himself, however, to do so. He said:

'And then what?'

'I don't follow you, Bodkin.'

'You speak of cows coming home. What happens when I do?'

'I still don't dig you.'

'How do I explain? I start out with the jewel case. I come

back without it, and without a receipt from the bank. Won't Mrs Llewellyn ask why?'

Mr Llewellyn dismissed the dilemma with a careless wave of the hand. He had always prided himself on being a man who thought on his feet.

'Oh, that. You put up a story.'

'Er. . . . What story?'

'You say you were attacked by a gang of thugs. They held you up and swiped the jewel case.'

'How did they know I had it?'

'These thugs have their spies everywhere.'

Monty's mind was still not at ease.

'You think Mrs Llewellyn will believe that?'

'She can't disprove it.'

'There'll be trouble.'

'Isn't it there always?'

'As I see it from where I sit I shall be arrested and sent to choky.'

Mr Llewellyn waved away this objection with another of his careless gestures.

'Well, what do you care? You can't get more than a year or two, and they tell me prisons are more like country clubs these days. Concerts, lectures, movies. You'll enjoy it. And there's another thing. You've been beefing about how you can't slide out of your engagement to the hockey-knocker so that you can team up with the half portion. How long do you suppose the hockey-knocker is going to hold you to it when she hears you're in the calaboose? There isn't a chance she'll take up your option.'

A thrill passed through Monty from butter-coloured hair to shoe sole. He thought he had examined all the angles, but that one had escaped his notice. He gazed at Mr Llewellyn reverently. Satirists, he was thinking, were very funny at the expense of the men who ran the big motion picture studios, but it was to the latter that you had to go when you wanted hardheaded practical common sense. In a voice trembling with emotion he said:

'By Jove, I believe you're right.'

151

'I'm always right.'

'She wouldn't want to marry a convict.'

'She wouldn't marry one on a bet.'

'I'll do it.'

'That's my boy. That's the spirit we breed at old S-L.'

'Give me the jewel case. I'll go and get the car out,' said Monty, and Chimp, who had been approaching in his noiseless way with a view to receiving the forty pounds which Mr Llewellyn owed him for the champagne, halted and stood spellbound. He was thus in a position to hear Mr Llewellyn say 'No hurry, Let's run over the scenario first, to make sure it adds up right.'

Chimp had heard enough. Those words could have but one meaning. Monty had been entrusted with the job for which he himself had been the first choice and which but for Dolly's unethical behaviour he would even now have been carrying out.

Mr Llewellyn, commenting on Chimp at The Happy Prawn, had said of him that he was a man who could grasp his opportunities, and no critique could have been truer. When the chance of picking up money presented itself, he thought and acted like lightning. On the present occasion his strategy and tactics were complete in an incredibly short space of time.

He derived comfort from those last words of Mr Llewellyn, that there was no need for Monty to hurry in going to the garage, for it was imperative that he, Chimp, got there first. Monty, driving to Brighton, would make the journey in the Cadillac. The Cadillac, therefore, must be put out of action so that he would be compelled to use the station wagon. For while he, Chimp, though a small man, could never hope to hide successfully in a Cadillac, to lurk unobserved at the back of the station wagon would in the best and deepest sense of the words be duck soup.

Returning to the house and taking the stairs three at a time, he reached his room and found his gun. Then once more at express speed he proceeded to the garage to attend to the Cadillac.

Chapter Eleven

THE NAME OF THE CALLER on the telephone was strange to Grayce and she had to ask him to repeat it. She got it at last—it was Butterwick. It would have pleased her more if it had had a Lord in front of it, but she was a woman who always enjoyed a telephone conversation, and it was a nice change from having to talk to her husband, especially when he was half asleep.

'Oh, yes, Mr Butterwick?'

'Is that Mrs Llewellyn?'

'It is.'

'Atishoo!'

'I beg your pardon?'

'I have a cold.'

'Oh, I'm sorry.'

'I am somewhat subject to them.'

The day had started badly for Mr Butterwick. His cold, on the previous night a mere tickling in the throat, had so increased in virulence as to make it injudicious for him to go to the office, and when he was unable to go to the office melancholy marked him for its own. Like all importers and exporters, he counted that day lost on which he was not importing this or exporting that. An importer and exporter whose heart is in his work feels like the Prisoner of Chillon when he is kept at home with a cold in the head.

He might have borne up better if Gertrude had been there, but Gertrude had gone to a committee meeting of her hockey club, and in her absence it seemed impossible to find anything to do. A musician in his place could have played the piano or the electric guitar or the shawms or the cymbals or something, but he had never had a musical training. He could have read a good book, but there were none about nowadays. It really seemed as though he would be reduced to twiddling his fingers as recommended by the late Count Tolstoi as an alternative to smoking, when there suddenly flashed into his mind the thought of the letter Montrose Bodkin had written to his daughter Gertrude.

Owing to Gertrude having come back with the Alka-Seltzer when he was only giving the communication its first reading his recollection of its contents was a sketchy one, but he did remember that it had contained a passage alluding to Mrs Llewellyn as the Führer of the Llewellyn home, and if this was so he had of course made a mistake in approaching her husband with his anti-Bodkin propaganda. A lifetime in business had taught him always to go to the man—in this case the woman—up top.

He went to Gertrude's desk. Yes, there in its pigeon-hole was the letter. He took it out and found that his supposition had been perfectly correct. Monty's observations concerning himself caused a momentary wince, but he read the vile thing through and came on the lines he was looking for.

What Monty had written was more a hint of Mrs Llewellyn's position than an actual statement, but the lines were lines he could read between. 'Mrs Llewellyn is a tough baby'. 'A joint account, and he can't draw a cheque without her approval.' '. . . play at the tables, which she would never have allowed.' These were not words that conjured up a picture of a man who was master in his own house and ruled one and all with a rod of iron, they were words that convinced the reader that when it came to a clash of wills between him and his wife, Ivor Llewellyn curled up in a ball and said 'Yes, dear.'

But the passage that thrilled Mr Butterwick was the one near the end. 'She is all for the aristocracy and has got the impression that I am related to half the titled families in England.'

It was enough. It proved beyond possibility of doubt that Montrose Bodkin had done it again. Precisely as had happened before, the young human snake had wriggled his way into the Llewellyn circle by means of what he, the snake, would have described as rannygazoo. It was the sort of thing that made a decent-minded man ask himself what snakes were coming to these days.

'Related to half the titled families in England.' If Mr Butterwick had been given to colloquialisms, his comment on that would have taken the form of a sardonic 'I don't think'. He knew all about Monty's family. His father had been a solicitor with a small country-town practice, and the aunt who had left him her money had accumulated that money by marrying a Pittsburg millionaire on one of his visits to London, she being at that time in the chorus of a musical entertainment at the Adelphi theatre. Add her brother Lancelot, who got jugged for passing bad cheques the year Hot Ginger won the Cesarewitch, and the roster of Monty's connections was complete.

Only a short time before we have seen Mr Butterwick regretting that he had nothing to do. A congenial task had now presented itself to him. We all like exposing snakes, and it was with particular pleasure that he looked forward to exposing Monty. Ten minutes later—the necessity of sniffing at his Friar's Balsam caused a temporary delay—he was at the telephone in communication with Grayce.

Mr Butterwick was always inclined to be measured in his diction when telephoning.

'I believe, Mrs Llewellyn, you have in your employment a young man of the name of Bodkin.'

'I have, yes.'

'I feel I ought to warn you. . . . Atishoo.'

The receiver shook in Grayce's hand. That ominous word 'warn', coming so soon after her talk with Mavis, had touched a nerve. For an instant she wondered if this was the police speaking. Those weighty words might well have proceeded from Scotland Yard. With a quaver in her voice she asked:

'What was that you said?'

'I was *going* to say that I feel I ought to warn you that it would be unwise to repose trust in him.'

Grayce's uneasiness increased.

'Who are you?'

'A friend.'

'Whose? His?'

'No, yours.'

'Are you a Superintendent or something?'

'I am not attached to the police.'

'Oh,' said Grayce, relieved.

'I wish you well.'

'Good for you.'

'My name is Butterwick.'

Patience had never been one of Grayce's virtues.

'I know your name is Butterwick,' she said, checking an impulse to insert the adjective 'god-damned' between the 'your' and the 'name'. 'What I'm trying to figure out is how you got into the act. Do you know Bodkin?'

'He is engaged to be married—much against my will—to my daughter Gertrude.'

'Oh? And what do you mean, warn me?'

'It has come to my notice . . . It has been drawn to my attention . . . In fact, I have found out that he has ingratiated himself with you by pretending to have aristocratic connections. This is not the case.'

What virtually amounted to the scream of a soul in anguish came over the wire.

'You mean he *hasn't*?'

'Precisely.'

'My social secretary Miss Miller told me he had titled uncles and cousins in every nook and cranny of England.'

'She was misinformed, no doubt by him. His father was a solicitor, his aunt a chorus girl, and his Uncle Lancelot received an exemplary sentence for passing bad cheques. He has no other relatives.'

The gulp Grayce gave could be heard distinctly in West Dulwich.

'Well, the son of a . . .' she said. The final word was lost in the forceful replacement of the receiver.

Mr Butterwick returned to his Friar's Balsam, well pleased. Montrose Bodkin he was thinking would not hold down his present post for the twelve months essential for his marital plans. Mrs Llewellyn had not actually said so, but the trend of their exchanges had left him in no doubt that that young specialist in rannygazoo would soon be at liberty. Indeed, at this very moment he was in all probability being thrown out on his ear. Grayce had struck him as a woman who would resent being deceived and would not be slow to clothe her resentment in action. Gertrude, returning from her committee meeting a few minutes later, would have been delighted with the improvement in her father's general appearance since she had last seen him, had not her thoughts been otherwise occupied.

It was plain to see that these thoughts were not agreeable. Her eyes were flashing, her bosom heaving, her whole aspect that of a girl whose soul had been stirred up by an electric mixer. She looked as if she had been unjustly penalized for some infringement of the rules in the hockey match of the season.

'Father,' she said, too moved to employ her normal 'Daddy', 'I am not going to marry Montrose. I am going to marry Wilfred Chisholm.'

It is not easy to raise joyful eyes to heaven while sniffing Friar's Balsam, but Mr Butterwick managed it.

'My dear child! This is wonderful news. You could not have made me happier. But what led you to this decision?'

'I found out that Montrose was untrue to me.'

'I suspected as much.'

'He takes girls to low night clubs.'

'This comes as no surprise.'

'I met Wilfred as I was leaving our meeting, and he had a black eye. I asked him how he had got it, and he said it was during a raid on one of those night clubs. He was arresting a man he had been at school with, a man named Monty Bodkin . . .'

'Ha!'

'. . . whom he had found with a girl in the yard outside the kitchen.'

'Ho!'

'And he was just taking him into custody, when——'

'Montrose struck him?'

'No, but the girl emptied a dustbin full of bottles over his

157

head, and one of them blacked his eye. The girl and Montrose then escaped over the wall and Wilfred's sergeant was very angry with him for letting them go. Poor Wilfred was very upset about it, but he bucked up a good deal when I told him I would marry him. Have you a telegraph form?'

'I have some in my desk. You wish to telegraph to Montrose?'

'Precisely that,' said Gertrude, her teeth coming together with a click which sounded as if Spanish dancers were brushing up their castanet-playing in the vicinity.

2

Patrons of the cinema may recall a motion picture, which was put on the screen many years ago, though not by the Superba-Llewellyn Corporation, in which the hero, played by Maurice Chevalier, poses as a titled aristocrat and is revealed as the dealer in men's wear he really is. The reaction of the staff at the castle, taking musical form, ran as follows:

'Here is a joke, the great Maurice
Is not a Knight of the Golden Fleece:
The son of a gun is nothing but a tailor.'

It was bitterly ironic, thought Grayce, remembering this comedy, that she should have been amused by it, for now that she was in the same position as that impostor's hostess she could detect nothing humorous in her situation. She was, indeed, in an even worse case than the Duchesse, or whatever she was, in the picture, who had had to embarrass her only a son of a gun who was nothing but a tailor. Between such sons of guns and those who are members of gangs there is no comparison.

As she replaced the receiver and made her way back to the study, where Mr Llewellyn, his mind finally at rest, had dozed off again, she was at her most incandescent. The revelation of Monty's perfidy would alone have been enough to wake the fiend that slept in her, but what really put the frosting on the cake, as he himself would have expressed it, was the realization that Mavis had been right and was entitled to say 'I told you so', which she would unquestionably do not once but many times. There are girls, few perhaps but to be found if one searches carefully, who when their advice is ignored and disaster ensues, do not say 'I told you so'. Mavis was not of their number.

It was true, a consoling voice whispered in her ear, that disaster had not actually ensued. The jewel case was safe in the study with Mr Llewellyn watching over it, but the fact remained that against Mavis's warning she had continued to allow the serpent Bodkin to defile Mellingham Hall with his presence, and Mavis would undoubtedly make the most of it.

Her mood, accordingly, was not sunny as she entered the study. She came in like an avenging Fury, closing the door behind her with a bang that brought Mr Llewellyn out of slumberland with a jerk. He had been having a dream in which he was a spy and was being shot at sunrise, and the bang had synchronized neatly with the activities of the firing squad.

His initial emotion, after he had blinked perhaps fifteen times and regained possession of his senses, was indignation. It seemed to him that if a man was not to be allowed a moment in which to relax, things had come to a pretty pass. He did not, of course, say so, for one glance at Grayce was enough to tell him that the storm cone had been hoisted and that those who spoke to her, even on non-controversial subjects, did so at their own risk.

'Where is Mr Bodkin?' Grayce asked.

Relieved that so harmless a topic had been selected, he replied:

'He was in here a moment ago.'

A simple statement and one which he anticipated would not give offence, but it caused Grayce to gnash her teeth slightly.

'I did not ask where he had been. Where is he now?'

'Ah, that I couldn't say. I guess he must have started.'

'Started?'

'In the car.'

159

'In the car?'

'For Brighton.'

'Brighton?'

Here was Mr Llewellyn's opportunity to inquire, as he had inquired of Monty, if she supposed herself to be an echo in the Swiss mountains. He did not avail himself of it, and Grayce continued.

'So he went to Brighton, did he?'

Her manner took on the ponderousness which so many of her circle in Beverly Hills had resented.

'I engaged Mr Bodkin as your secretary. There was no understanding that he should go off on pleasure jaunts to the sea shore whenever he felt inclined.'

'It was not so much a pleasure jaunt——'

'No doubt he will return invigorated by the sea air, but that is not what I pay him a salary for. Brighton! The idea! Did he bother to ask your permission?'

Mr Llewellyn saw that she had formed a wrong conclusion. It was perhaps a natural mistake for her to have made, and rather amusing. He ventured on a light chuckle, and she asked him if he would mind not giggling like a half-witted hyena. He pleaded that it was rather funny that she should have said that.

'Yes, he had my permission. Matter of fact, I sent him to Brighton.'

'Might I ask why?'

'To oblige you. To do you a good turn. You wanted your pearls taken to the bank. Adair, who ought to have taken them, had this pain in his inside. So I told Bodkin to take them.'

There had been several occasions in the course of their married life when Grayce, conversing with her husband, had been compelled to register an assortment of mixed emotions, but she had seldom approached the high level of her present performance. If Mr Llewellyn had not happened to have closed his eyes, finding this restful, he would have been appalled.

Something seemed to have gone wrong with Grayce's vocal cords.

160

She gulped once or twice, and when she spoke it was almost in a whisper.

'You have let Bodkin go off with my pearls!'

'Sure.' It occurred to Mr Llewellyn that it would be a sound move to prepare her for the return of an empty-handed Monty. 'I hope he'll be safe.'

'Safe!'

'There's one thing I'm not quite easy in my mind about,' said Mr Llewellyn. He could not but feel that he was doing this extraordinarily well. Just the right note of anxiety in the voice. 'You're very apt these days to run into gangs of thugs on lonely country roads. I don't want to alarm you, but it's quite possible that young Bodkin on his way to the bank may get held up by hi-jackers. I ought to have thought of this when you were talking of sending Adair. Taking anything as valuable as those pearls to Brighton ought not to have been entrusted to one man. One should have had a lot of fellows with shot-guns, like they used to have on the Wells-Fargo Express. Hi-jacking's so easy if you only have one man. A pretty girl is standing at the side of the road with a broken-down car. She waves to Bodkin, probably with tears in her eyes. "Oh, sir, can you fix up my car for me. I can't get it to go. . . ." He says he'll have a look at it. "Probably the sprockets aren't running true with the differential gear," he says, or whatever. He gets out and *zowie* a gang of thugs come jumping out of the bushes, and next thing you know they're off with your jewel case. I don't say that's what's going to happen to Bodkin, quite possibly he'll get through all right, but I think you ought to be prepared.'

It was an appreciable time before Grayce replied to by far the longest speech her husband had ever been able to address to her. Her emotional upset had suddenly reached the point where fury gives place temporarily to a frozen calm. One sees the same kind of thing in hurricanes, which always take time off at Cape Hatteras to draw a deep breath preparatory to settling down to business. When she spoke, it was plain there had been on her part none of that willing suspension of disbelief of which dramatic critics so often speak.

'Talk sense,' she said curtly, giving in two words evidence that her disbelief had not come within a million miles of being suspended. 'If Bodkin dares to come back with a story like that, I shall send out a hurry call for every policeman in the country, telling them to come quick and bring their handcuffs, and if they care to use a little police brutality on Mister It-makes-me-sick-to-think-of-him Bodkin, it will be all right with me. Do you know who you handed those pearls over to, you moron? A crook. A Mayfair man, A gangster in good standing who was told by his gang to worm his way in here and get them. And if you want to know what my plans are at the moment. I'm going to go to my room to take three aspirins and lie down.'

And, so saying, Grayce went out, banging the door again.

3

Seated on a rustic bench on the lawn near the garage, Dolly was still a prey to gloom. The victory she had won over Chimp Twist had had its exhilaration, but it had been only momentary. She was a girl whom life had taught to face facts, and the existing facts, when faced, were not cheering. It was plain that her baffling of Chimp was not an end but a beginning. She was now confronted with that question that has chilled so many, the question 'Where do we go from here?'.

She might have found a readier answer to this query had her mind been full of plans and schemes waiting only to be put into operation, but the one which had failed so lamentably on the previous night had left her creative impulse exhausted. As she put it to herself, she had no more ideas than a rabbit, and everyone who has studied these animals knows how devoid they normally are of inspiration. And who could say what subtle plots the opposition might not be weaving? She did not like Chimp, she had never liked him, but she had a solid respect for his brains.

So she sat and mourned, and it was as she plumbed the very depths of despondency that Monty swam into her ken, complete with jewel case. He was swinging it jauntily, not actually singing Tra-la, but giving the distinct impression that he might do so at any moment. The effects of Mr Llewellyn's pep talk still lingered.

On Dolly the sight of what he carried acted like a double dose of one of those tonics which in addition to iron go in largely for Vitamins B and E. She recognized the jewel case as the one she had seen during chats with Grayce in the latter's bedroom, and a far less astute woman would have been able to divine what it was doing in Monty's possession. J. Sheringham Adair had been told to take it to the bank, and when J. Sheringham's unfortunate indisposition had ruled him out as a messenger the assignment had been given to Monty. Not only was this limpidly clear to her, but it had taken her only a few seconds to see how it was to be turned to her advantage.

She hailed Monty with the utmost enthusiasm, an enthusiasm which puzzled him a little, for their relations hitherto had been, if not exactly distant, at any rate on the formal side. That she should be so glad to see him was flattering, but he could not think what had caused this unusual exuberance. The theory that this was her customary form when her husband was not around he dismissed as unworthy. No, it was simply, he decided, that he was particularly fascinating today.

'Hello there, Mr Bodkin,' Dolly carolled. 'What lovely weather.'

'Hullo, Mrs Molloy. Yes, beautiful.'

'The sun!'

'Yes, I noticed the sun.'

'Are you off somewhere?'

'I am, as a matter of fact.'

'I thought so. You seemed to be headed for the garage.'

'Actually, I'm off to Brighton.'

'Oh really?'

'I'm taking something there.'

'You couldn't take me, too, could you? I want to go to Brighton to get a hair-do.'

Monty hesitated for a moment. He had not anticipated that he would be taking on passengers, and he was not sure how their society might affect his enterprise. Then he realized that it would be perfectly all right. While she was having her hair-do he could be sauntering along the pier and dropping the jewel case off the end of it into deep water. An even better hiding-place than the brook or river which Mr Llewellyn had suggested.

'Of course,' he said. 'But I ought to be starting pretty soon. Are you ready?'

'Just got to get my bag from my room. Won't take me a second. You don't mind waiting?'

'No, no, of course not.'

When Dolly returned, she was carrying her bag, and in the bag the .38 Colt, an indispensable property for the scene she had in mind.

She found Monty peering into the interior of the Cadillac. Whatever he was seeing there was plainly not to his taste.

'I say,' he said, 'I hate to break it to you, but something's gone wrong with this car. It won't start.'

'It was all right this morning.'

'Oh, were you out in it this morning?'

'I took my husband to the station.'

'Well, you won't take anyone to any stations now. I can't get a murmur out of it. I'm one of those fellows who are not bad at driving, but that lets me out. I don't know the first thing about the way the machine works.

'Me neither.'

'If there's a breakdown, I just sit and howl for the garage man.'

'Me, too.'

'And he tells me the exhaust box has been short-circuiting with the commutator, or whatever it may be, and I go on my way rejoicing, but still without the foggiest idea of what the hell he's been talking about, if you will pardon the word hell.'

'That's all right. I've heard it before.'

'In the matter currently under advisement I would say the ruddy car was in a trance of some kind.'

'Cataleptic?'

'If that's what it's called. It looks as if I'll have to go in the station wagon. Do you still want to come?'

'Sure. What's the matter with station wagons?'

Her cheerful acceptance of a state of affairs which might have occasioned peevishness in many women charmed Monty. His heart warmed to her. He saw that he was going to enjoy this trip to Brighton, for there are few things more pleasant than a tête à tête with a vivacious and intelligent female companion. He foresaw light sparkling conversation flowing between them like ginger ale out of a bottle.

And so it did for quite a while.

'Have you known the Llewellyns long?' he asked, as they drove off.

'Only a month or so. We met them in Cannes.'

'Oh, you've been to Cannes? Now there's a place I like.'

'Swell.'

'The sea. The mountains.'

'You betcher.'

'Did you play at the Casino at all?'

'Not much. We were there more on business. My husband has large oil interests, and he was establishing contacts. Seeing people, what I mean, and fixing up deals.'

'I've often wondered how you fix up a deal.'

'Oh, you talk a lot and wave your hands a lot.'

'Fine, provided you know what to say.'

'Yes, you have to know what to say.'

'Business,' said Monty thoughtfully, 'is a thing I've never been able to get the hang of. I know a man who makes an annual packet by importing and exporting, but what that actually consists of I haven't found out. I should imagine he ships half a dozen grand pianos to a bloke in West Africa, and the bloke in West Africa sends him apes, ivory and peacocks in exchange. Would that be it?'

'I shouldn't wonder. Your guess is as good as mine.'

'He then sends these to a bloke in Hawaii in return for a cargo of tuning-forks.'

'The bloke in Hawaii having more tuning-forks than he knows what to do with and wondering for weeks where he could get hold of a few apes and peacocks.'

'Exactly.'

'It's called Trade.'

'Yes, so I've heard.'

They were now passing through deserted country roads, but soon, Dolly realized, they would be coming to more populous regions where it would not be easy to operate unobserved. And so agreeable had each found the other's personality and so fraught with interest had their conversation been that it cost her a pang to think that her business interests would 'ere long compel her to produce the .38 Colt and order him to alight, leaving the jewel case behind him. By way of consolation she told herself that the more she postponed the painful scene the longer would be his walk back to Mellingham Hall, and it was only humane to make that walk as short as possible.

If what she contemplated were done, and it had to be done, then 'twere well, as Shakespeare would have put it, 'twere done quickly.

She reached in her bag and produced the Colt.

'Would you mind stopping a moment, Mr Bodkin?' she said.

The thought behind this request escaped Monty completely.

'Stop?' he said. 'Why? Do you want to pick a nosegay of wild flowers?'

'Not so much a nosegay of wild flowers,' said Dolly, 'as those pearls you've got there.'

It was as she spoke that he noticed that her shapely hand was advancing a hefty-looking firearm in the direction of his ribs, and he leaped in his seat as far as a sitting man can leap. Memories of Mavis flitted into his mind, and he found himself wondering dully if every member of the opposite sex whom he met was going to behave in this disturbing manner. Were they all, he asked himself, in the words of a song he had sometimes sung in his bath, pistol-packing Mommas, or was it just that he had bad luck in the women he associated with? Mrs Molloy was perhaps to be preferred to Mavis as a pistol-packer, for she had not locked him up in a smelly cupboard as had the future Mrs James Ponder, but only in that respect was there a preference. His opinion of her as a charming and entertaining companion for a jaunt through the countryside in an automobile had undergone a radical change. To say that he looked at her askance would be no exaggeration.

She, on her side, seemed to be feeling that her behaviour called for something in the nature of explanation and apology.

'You're probably thinking this all kind of rather strange and unusual,' she said, 'and I wouldn't do it if it wasn't absolutely necessary, because you're a good Joe and I like you, but business is business. It's what we were saying just now about Trade. You give me the jewel case, and I give you a nice country walk which'll do you all the good in the world.'

Monty had been perplexed in the extreme, but all things were now made clear to him.

'Good Lord!' he explained. 'You're a crook.'

'Well, we've all got to be something.'

'You ought to be ashamed of yourself. What's a nice girl like you doing shoving guns against people's waistcoats?'

'I get your point, and I quite agree that it's not the sort of thing that's done in the best sets, but listen, honey, we're just wasting time, chewing the fat like this. Leave me, I would be alone, as the fellow said. In other words, get out of the car.'

'Both of you get out of the car,' said Chimp Twist, appearing behind them as if shot out of a trap. 'And make it slippy, because I haven't got all day. And Dolly, drop the heater and leave that jewel case where it is, I don't want any unpleasantness.'

Nobody is so persuasive as the man behind the gun. The greatest orator in Chimp's position might have reasoned for hours and failed to convert his audience to his point of view, but Dolly and Monty fell in with his wishes with the minimum of delay. Silently they stood watching the car as it disappeared down the road. Only when it was out of sight did Dolly speak.

The word she uttered was so crisp and forceful that it raised the butter-coloured hair on Monty's head. Strong language was no novelty to him—he had once been present when somebody had slammed a car door on the finger of D'Arcy ('Stilton') Cheesewright of the Drones—but this particular ejaculation was new to him and it had the effect which things have on us when we hear them for the first time.

Even Dolly seemed conscious that she had expressed herself too freely.

'Sorry,' she said. 'It slipped out.'

'Quite all right.'

'If you knew how I'm feeling.'

'Not too bumps-a-daisy, I imagine.'

'I could yell and shriek and scream.'

'Go ahead if you want to.'

'You really are a good Joe,' said Dolly emotionally. 'Aren't you sore at me for holding you up that way?'

'Not a bit,' said Monty, 'and I'll tell you why. Can you keep a secret?'

'I doubt it.'

'Well, try to keep this one. Those pearls are fakes.'

'What!'

'Fakes. F for Ferdinand, A for Archibald, K for kidney trouble, and so on. They're cultured Japanese.'

'You're pulling my leg.'

'I wouldn't dream of it.'

'You mean they aren't valuable?'

'Barely worth the paper they're written on.'

'I can't believe it.'

'Of course you can't, but you will when you have heard all.'

It took some time for Dolly to hear all, and they had nearly reached Mellingham village before she was in possession of the full facts. It was perhaps characteristic of her that her first comment on Monty's narrative should have been a marked tribute to Mr Llewellyn for his sagacity in thinking up such an admirable scheme for adjusting his financial troubles.

'You'd never think he had the brains.'

'Oh, he's very shrewd really. I have a high opinion of Ivor Llewellyn's intelligence. I know of no man whom I would rather have at my side during a police raid on a night club. Good solid brains there.'

'I should think Mrs Llewellyn would spill them on the living-room carpet if she finds out what he's been up to.'

'How can she find out? The gentleman who was with us just now has gone off with the evidence. By the way, who was he?

He seemed to know you, and I had a sort of idea I had seen him before.'

'He's a guy of the name of Twist. Calls himself a detective. Mrs Llewellyn must have got him in to guard her pearls. He's been working as Mr Llewellyn's valet.'

'Oh my God! You don't mean he'll take them back to her?'

'Don't make me laugh. Anything Chimp Twist gets his hooks on goes out of circulation. And talking of laughing, a brief pause while I do it. When I think of Chimp trying to collect fifty thousand bones for a rope of pearls which turn out to be worth around ten dollars I feel like laughing my head off. And here we part, brother Bodkin,' said Dolly as they entered the little main street of Mellingham village. I've got to go to the post office to wire the good news to Soapy, and you will probably want to be getting along and having a chat with Mrs Llewellyn.'

Chapter Twelve

MR LLEWELLYN was feeling extraordinarily fit. He had not quite finished the bottle of champagne, but he had imbibed enough of it to put him at the top of his form. One remarkable result of his potations was that the fear with which Grayce inspired him had completely disappeared. Grayce (his thoughts ran) pooh. Less than the dust beneath his chariot wheels, if he remembered the quotation correctly from his school-marm days.

If she came into the room at this moment, he was convinced that he would look her in the eye and make her wilt with the easy nonchalance of one of those dauntless death-defying characters he had mentioned to Monty who had so calming an effect on murderous man-eating monarchs of the jungle.

The afternoon had reached the peak of its beauty. The skies were even bluer than before, the breezes even more gentle, and bees which had buzzed and birds which had tootled did so now with just that little extra vim and brio which makes all the difference. It would perhaps be too much to say that Mr Llewellyn, looking out of his bedroom window, felt the call of the wild, but it did occur to him that it would be rather nice to be out of doors. Having concealed the bottle beneath the bed, he made his way downstairs and into the open spaces. Shortly afterwards he was on the rustic bench on which Dolly Molloy had sat, where almost immediately his eyes closed in sleep.

He woke to find that he had been joined by Sandy. She was sitting beside him, and a glance at her profile told him that all was not well with her. She had the unmistakable air of a girl whom Fate had recently kicked in the teeth. As she turned her head, he saw that her eyes were dull, her face strained.

She reminded him of his fourth wife, who had looked like that whenever he told her a funny story.

'I'm sorry,' said Sandy. 'I didn't mean to wake you.'

'Had I dropped off for a moment? I had a tough night last night. Grayce made me sit up all night in a dining-room chair. What's the matter, half portion? You look kind of low.'

'I'm feeling low. I've just been fired.'

'Grayce fired you?'

'Yes.'

Mr Llewellyn frowned.

'Grayce is too fond of throwing her weight about. We shall have to correct that,' he said, or rather the champagne speaking in his voice. 'What was the trouble?'

'She found out that Monty hasn't any titled relations.'

'Well, why should he have? I haven't, and I venture to believe I'm as good as the next man.'

'But I told her he had. That was how I got him the job.'

'Ah,' said Mr Llewellyn, understanding. His wife's esteem for the aristocracy was no secret to him.

'So now I'll have to go back to America.'

'Well, what's wrong with America? Land of the free and home of the brave.'

'But Monty will stay on in England and I'll never see him again,' said Sandy, and the tears she had been trying to hold back burst their bonds. 'Don't pat my head,' she added.

'I will pat your head,' said Mr Llewellyn stoutly. 'If I can't pat your head when it needs patting, whose head can I pat? My heart bleeds for you, pint size, bleeds profusely. Not that I can see what all the fuss is about. What makes you think that if you go to America, Bodkin won't come after you?'

'Why should he? He doesn't love me.'

'Of course he loves you, you silly little sap.'

'What!'

'Told me so himself. Oh to clasp her in my arms and fade out with her on the embrace, he said, or words to that effect. And as I had already told him that you were crazy about him——'

'You didn't!'

171

'I certainly did. Men like to hear these things. It was as we were driving home from that night club.'

'You promised you wouldn't.'

'You can't go by what a man in my position promises. You don't really suppose, do you, that you can run a big studio successfully if you go about keeping your promises all the time? If you want me to keep a promise, have me put it in writing and take it to a public notary and get it stamped. And even after that you'll have my lawyers to deal with. But we mustn't wander from the point. What I was saying when you sidetracked me on to the subject of promises was that Bodkin regards you as the best thing that's happened since sliced bread and would give half his kingdom to have your slippers laid out beside his on the bedroom floor, and the only thing that's holding up the merger is the fact that he's tied up elsewhere.'

'He's engaged to a girl called Gertrude Butterwick.'

'I know all about her. Bodkin confided in me. She is the daughter of a J. B. Butterwick, a man who invites you to lunch and gives you carrots and mock duck, and a girl with a father like that cannot be anything but a pill of the first water. The sooner he gets out of it, the better.'

'How can he get out of it? He's much too honourable. *He* keeps his promises.'

'He's young yet. He'll know better when he's older.'

'He can't tell Gertrude Butterwick he loves me.'

'Why not? A couple of words on the telephone. But you needn't worry. He's bound to do something sooner or later that'll make the girl give him the air.'

'I wish I could think so.'

'You'd darned well better think so. We can't have you crying all over the place. As a matter of fact, between ourselves, he's working on a treatment this afternoon. He hopes to get sent to prison, which of course would solve everything neatly.'

'Prison!'

'He's gone off in the car with those fake pearls and will lose them somewhere on the journey. When he comes back without them and with a story about having been held up by hi-jackers, Mrs Llewellyn will undoubtedly have him put in the cooler. Matter of fact, she said as much when we were chatting just now. This will cause the Butterwick beasel to give him the bum's rush, and all will end happily. He won't get a long stretch, and you can go and see him on visiting days.'

For the last few minutes Mr Llewellyn had been articulating drowsily, and now he dozed off again. A man accustomed to getting his eight hours never holds up well after a wakeful night in a dining-room chair. He was dimly aware that his companion was speaking at some length, but machine guns would not have kept him awake.

When consciousness returned, he was alone and the air had the touch of chilliness which makes sitting in the open lose its charm. Feeling that his time would be better occupied in finishing the rest of the champagne, he went to his room and completed his work on the bottle. This done, he went downstairs with a heart for any fate. It was really remarkable how the elixir had changed his whole outlook. It will be remembered that Monty, enjoying Mr Flannery's hospitality at The Happy Prawn, had had the same experience. Evidently there is some magic property in the better brands of this wine that not only enlivens the body but braces up the soul.

He became aware that there was an unpleasant noise going on somewhere. Concentrating his faculties, he was able to pin it down as proceeding from the drawing-room and a moment later he had recognized it. Grayce was in there, rebuking someone.

It did not require deep thought to tell him who this someone was. Evidently it was his friend Bodkin who was on the receiving end, and as he realized this the champagne boiled in his veins and he frowned darkly. He could not have his friend Bodkin subjected to this sort of thing.

He opened the drawing-room door and strode in.

It was as he had supposed. Grayce was standing in the centre of the room looking like the Statue of Liberty and Monty was standing before her looking filleted, as well he might considering that this was his first introduction to the great emotional actress in one of her louder roles. He had anticipated that when he returned to the fold without the pearls and with what he knew was an inadequate explanation of their absence, a certain liveliness would ensue, but his imagination of the coming scene had fallen far short of the stark reality. His air in consequence was that of a man who has been trying to locate a leak in a gas pipe with a lighted candle.

Mr Llewellyn, on the other hand, was calm, cool and collected, as befitted one who had been assured by a quart of Bollinger that he was master in his own home and as such entitled to resent anything that disturbed the peace of it.

'What's all this?' he asked.

'Go away,' said Grayce.

'What do you mean, go away? I've only just come in. Hullo, Bodkin. Have a nice drive?'

'A very profitable drive,' said Grayce bitterly. 'He's got away with my pearls, as I told you he would.'

'Well, well.'

'Is that all you can say?'

'Nothing wrong with it, as far as I can see. If this house is not open for having "Well, well" said in it, I ought to have been informed.'

If Grayce had not known how impossible it was that her husband could have obtained the materials, she would have leaped to the conclusion that he had been drinking. As it was, she attributed his words to the slowness of intellect which had so often led her to address him as a moron. In spite of his success in the motion picture industry she had always held the view that if he had had an ounce more sense, he would have been halfwitted. All his other wives, oddly enough, had felt the same.

'It does not seem to interest you that I have lost a rope of pearls worth fifty thousand dollars.'

'Ha!'

'What did you say?'

'Just Ha.'

'Why did you say Ha?'

'Because I felt like saying Ha, and when I feel like saying

Ha, I say Ha. That's the sort of man I am. Bluff, frank, straightforward. No beating about the bush. What's all this nonsense about Bodkin pinching pearls?'

'Perhaps you would care to hear his story?'

'Capital, capital. Carry on, Bodkin.'

'It will be simpler if I tell it. He says that on the way to Brighton he was held up and robbed.'

'Precisely what I warned you might happen. Going to Brighton nowadays is like walking through Central Park at midnight; there are thugs behind every bush.'

Out in the hall the telephone rang.

'Answer that, Bodkin,' said Mr Llewellyn. 'If it's for me, say I'm out.'

'Stay where you are, Bodkin,' said Grayce.

Monty stayed where he was.

'The story Mr Bodkin tells,' said Grayce, 'is this. He was driving along, and suddenly Adair appeared from the back of the station wagon and held him up with a pistol.'

'Very good,' said Mr Llewellyn like a pleased literary critic. 'A very good story indeed. Adair? You mean that man of mine?'

'Yes.'

'Well, that clears everything up nicely. I never trusted that fellow. Obviously Bodkin is more to be pitied than censured. What can you do if a guy's holding you up with a gun? Yes, I call that an excellent story.'

'If one believed it.'

'Don't you believe it?'

'No, I do not.'

'You're hard to please. It sounds just right to me. Get out, half portion, we're in conference.'

The last words were addressed to Sandy, who had burst into the room waving a sheet of paper, a very different Sandy from the stricken girl who had wept at Mr Llewellyn's side on the rustic bench. Her eyes were sparkling, her nose twitching, her whole frame vibrating. She looked like a girl in a television commercial who has just been persuaded by a friend to try somebody's shampoo with all its locked-in goodness.

'Monty!' she cried.

Mr Llewellyn had a paternal fondness for Sandy, but he could not allow this sort of thing.

'You can't go rushing around shouting "Monty",' he said severely. 'If you have anything to communicate to Bodkin, send him an inter-office memo.'

'But there's a telegram for him. I've just been taking it down on the telephone.'

'Type it out in triplicate and deliver it later.'

'It's from Gertrude Butterwick, Monty. She's broken off the engagement.'

Monty came to life with a jerk that threatened to dislocate his spine. He seemed to expand like a flower watered by some kindly gardener. Such was his emotion that he quite forgot that he was in the presence of Mrs Ivor Llewellyn.

'Sandy!'

'I thought you'd be pleased.'

'"Pleased" doesn't express it by a mile and a quarter. Do you realize what this means? We can get married.'

'I can hardly wait.'

'I love you, Sandy.'

'Me, too. I mean I also. I mean I love *you*.'

'Oh joy, oh bliss!'

'Mr BODKIN!' said Grayce.

'Don't interrupt,' said Mr Llewellyn. 'Haven't you any respect for two young hearts entwined in Springtime? Well, this is certainly the happy ending. I had a feeling everything would come right in the last reel. Old-fashioned, yes, but it still sells tickets.'

The telephone rang in the hall.

'Answer that, Bodkin. No, I'll go myself. It may be the vicar wanting a subscription to the church organ fund, and feeling the way I do I'll be happy to oblige him.'

He went out, to return a moment later.

'For you, Grayce. Mavis. Fortunate to be alone,' he said as the door closed. 'Gives me a chance to have a word with you in private, pint size. Bodkin told me about that treatment you submitted, and I've been giving it a lot of thought and

176

I've come to the conclusion it's the goods. For some reason I was against it when he gave me the outline, but now I'm sold on it. I'm a strong man, and a strong man is never afraid to change his mind. When Grayce comes back, I shall say to her "Grayce" . . .'

He would have spoken further, but the door had flown open and Grayce was with them again. Her emotion, noticeable even before, had reached new heights. She came to the point without preamble.

'Mavis says James Ponder says my pearls are phonies!'

Mr Llewellyn's calm was monumental.

He stifled a yawn, and went so far as to flick a speck of dust from his coat sleeve.

'You hardly needed to be told that, did you?' he said mildly.

'What do you mean?'

'I was afraid he was bound to spot them. Even I could see they were Japanese cultured, and I'm no expert. If you had consulted me, I would have told you you couldn't get away with it.'

'What are you talking about? Are you suggesting that I——?'

'What other explanation is there? I know how your mind worked. You had to hand the things over to Mavis when she married, and you thought that if you couldn't have them, you might as well sell them and get the money. You said to yourself that Mavis would never know the difference. You couldn't have expected she would marry a man high up in the jewellery business. You couldn't have expected a girl like her would marry anyone. So you gave it the old college try, and it went wrong. It's like what a school-marm I once knew used to say about the best-laid plans of mice and men finishing up on the cutting-room floor. And now I suppose I've got to buy another rope of pearls, to keep Mavis quiet. Of course I'm quite willing to ante up to get you out of a jam, but let this be a lesson to you not to try to cut corners. Go, woman, and sin no more. I guess I'll lie down for a while and catch up with my sleep,' said Mr Llewellyn, as he made for the door.

'Come back!' shrieked Grayce, but he had gone. She

followed him out with flashing eyes, and silence like a poultice came to heal the blows of sound.

'What do you suppose Whistler's Mother will do to him?' said Monty, concerned. He was fond of Mr Llewellyn, and he feared for his well-being.

'I don't like to think,' said Sandy.

'He has the advantage in reach, but she must be a tough customer when it comes to infighting. Her footwork, too, is probably better than his.'

'I wonder why he married her.'

'He explained that. He was at a loose end, and it was something to do.'

There was a meditative pause. The thoughts of both of them were at the ringside.

'Did you ever see *Passion in Paris*?' said Monty.

'No. Did you?'

'No. But Llewellyn told me that in the course of the shooting she used up three directors, two assistant directors and a script girl. They were never themselves again.'

'Why a script girl?'

'I see her as an innocent bystander drawn into the hostilities against her will.'

There was another meditative pause.

'A timid little creature with spectacles, don't you think?'

'Who?'

'The script girl.'

'Why spectacles?'

'Why not spectacles?'

There was a third meditative pause.

'I hope all this hasn't discouraged you,' said Sandy.

'How do you mean?'

'This glimpse into married life. Because I won't be like Grayce.'

'You couldn't be.'

'I do think I'll make you happy, don't you?'

'Ecstatic.'

'I won't be bossy, like Gertrude.'

'How did you know Gertrude was bossy?'

'Feminine intuition. I don't like her.'

'You've not met her.'

'No, but I've read her telegram.'

'Good Lord, what with one thing and another I've not read it myself. What did it say?'

'Better not ask.'

'It might be wiser.'

'What I'm stressing is that I'm not the Gertrude type.'

'You're the sweetest, most wonderful thing this side of outer space.'

'That's the right spirit.'

The door opened. Mr Llewellyn appeared. He was yawning, but intact. His manner radiated cheerfulness.

'Well, kids,' he said. 'And how's love in Springtime?'

They assured him that love in Springtime was fine, and he said he was glad to hear it. He went to the sofa, removed his shoes and lay down with a grunt of contentment.

'Matter of fact,' he said, 'everything's fine. Grayce is getting a divorce.'

'What!'

'Pure routine. All my wives have done it. They come and go, they come and go. Ever seen a soiled glove? That's what they cast me off like sooner or later. Thank God,' added Mr Llewellyn piously.

'But what happened?' cried Sandy.

'Tell us all about it,' said Monty.

But deep breathing from the sofa told that Mr Llewellyn was beyond the reach of questions.

There was a fourth meditative pause.

'So long as he's happy, bless his heart,' said Sandy.

'He's happy all right.'

'Do you think he'll stop getting married now?'

Monty shook his head.

'Stop? You little know our Llewellyn. Rising to new heights of endeavour, he'll try for the record.'

And a snore from the sofa seemed to suggest that Mr Llewellyn endorsed this view.

BACHELORS
ANONYMOUS

Chapter One

MR EPHRAIM TROUT of Trout, Wapshott and Edelstein, one of the many legal firms employed by Ivor Llewellyn, head of the Superba-Llewellyn studio of Llewellyn City, Hollywood, was seeing Mr Llewellyn off at the Los Angeles air port.

The two men were friends of long standing. Mr Trout had handled all of Mr Llewellyn's five divorces, including his latest from Grayce, widow of Orlando Mulligan the Western star, and this formed a bond. There is nothing like a good divorce for breaking down the barriers between lawyer and client.

It gives them something to talk about.

'I shall miss you, I.L.,' Mr Trout was saying. 'The old place won't seem the same without you. But I feel you are wise in transferring your activities to London.'

Mr Llewellyn felt the same. He had not taken this step without giving it consideration. He was a man who, except when marrying, thought things over.

'The English end needs gingering up,' he said. 'A couple of sticks of dynamite under the seat of their pants will do those dreamers all the good in the world.'

'I was not thinking so much,' said Mr Trout, 'of the benefits which will no doubt accrue to the English end as of those which you yourself will derive from your London visit.'

'You get a good steak in London.'

'Nor had I steaks in mind. I feel that now that you are free from the insidious influence of Californian sunshine the urge to marry again will be diminished. It is that perpetual sunshine that causes imprudence.'

At the words 'marry again' Mr Llewellyn had shuddered strongly, like a blancmange in a high wind.

'Don't talk to me about marrying again. I've kicked the habit.'

'You think you have.'

'I'm sure of it. Listen, you know Grayce.'

'I do indeed.'

'And you know what it was like being married to her. She treated me like one of those things they have in Mexico, not tamales, something that sounds like spoon.'

'Peon?'

'That's right. Insisted on us having a joint account. Made me go on a diet. You ever eaten diet bread?'

Mr Trout said he had not. He was a man so thin and meagre that a course of diet bread might well have made him invisible.

'Well, don't. It tastes like blotting-paper. My sufferings were awful. If it hadn't been for an excellent young woman named Miller, now Mrs Montrose Bodkin, who at peril of her life sneaked me in an occasional bit of something I could get my teeth into, I doubt if I'd have survived. And now that Grayce has got a divorce I feel like a convict at San Quentin let out on parole after serving ten years for busting banks.'

'The relief must be great.'

'Colossal. Well, would such a convict go and bust another bank the moment he got out?'

'Not if he were wise.'

'Well, I'm wise.'

'But you're weak, I.L.'

'Weak? Me? Ask the boys at the studio if I'm weak.'

'Where women are concerned, only where women are concerned.'

'Oh, women.'

'You *will* propose to them. You are what I would call a compulsive proposer. It's your warm, generous nature, of course.'

'That and not knowing what to say to them after the first ten minutes. You can't just sit there.'

'That is why I welcome this opportunity of giving you a word of advice. You may have asked yourself why I, though working in the heart of Hollywood for more than twenty years, have never married.'

It had not occurred to Mr Llewellyn to ask himself this. Had he done so, he would have replied to himself that the solution of the mystery was that his old friend, though highly skilled in the practice of the law, was short on fascination. Mr Trout, in addition to being thin, had that dried-up look which so often comes to middle-aged lawyers. There was nothing dashing about him. He might have appealed to the comfortable motherly type of woman, but these are rare in Hollywood.

'The reason,' said Mr Trout, 'is that for many years I have belonged to a little circle whose members have decided that the celibate life is best. We call ourselves Bachelors Anonymous. It was Alcoholics Anonymous that gave the founding fathers the idea. Our methods are frankly borrowed from theirs. When one of us feels the urge to take a woman out to dinner becoming too strong for him, he seeks out the other members of the circle and tells them of his craving, and they reason with him. He pleads that just one dinner cannot do him any harm, but they know what that one dinner can lead to. They point out the inevitable results of that first downward step. Once yield to temptation, they say, and dinner will be followed by further dinners, lunches for two and tête-à-têtes in dimly lit boudoirs, until in morning coat and sponge-bag trousers he stands cowering beside his bride at the altar rails, racked with regret and remorse when it is too late. And gradually reason returns to its throne. Calm succeeds turmoil, and the madness passes. He leaves the company of his friends his old bachelor self again, resolved from now on to ignore scented letters of invitation, to refuse to talk on the telephone and to duck down a side street if he sees a female form approaching. Are you listening, I.L.?'

'I'm listening,' said Mr Llewellyn. He was definitely impressed. Twenty years of membership in Bachelors Anonymous had given Mr Trout a singular persuasiveness.

'There is unfortunately no London chapter of Bachelors Anonymous, or I would give you a letter to them. What you must do on arrival is to engage the services of some steady level-headed person in whom you can have confidence, who will take the place of my own little group when you feel a proposal coming on. A good lawyer, used to carrying out with discretion the commissions of clients, can find you one. There is a firm in Bedford Row—Nichols, Erridge and Trubshaw, with whom I have done a good deal of business over the years. I am sure they will be able to supply someone who will be a help to you. It won't be the same, of course, as having the whole of Bachelors Anonymous working for you, but better than nothing. And I do think you will need support. I spoke a moment ago of the Californian sunshine and its disastrous effects, and I was congratulating you on escaping from it, but the sun has been known to shine in England, so one must be prepared. Nichols, Erridge and Trubshaw. Don't forget.'

'I won't,' said Mr Llewellyn.

2

Leaving the air port, Mr Trout returned to Hollywood, where he lunched at the Brown Derby, as was his usual custom, his companions Fred Basset, Johnny Runcible and G. J. Flannery, all chartered members of Bachelors Anonymous.

Fred Basset, who was in real estate, had done a profitable deal that morning, as also had G. J. Flannery, who was an authors' agent, and there was an atmosphere of jollity at the table. Only Mr Trout sat silent, staring at his corned beef hash in a distrait manner, his thoughts elsewhere. It was behaviour bound to cause comment.

'You're very quiet today, E.T.,' said Fred Basset, and Mr Trout came to himself with a start.

'I'm sorry, F.B.,' he said. 'I'm worried.'

'That's bad. What about?'

'I've just been seeing Lewellyn off to London.'

'Nothing to worry you about that. He'll probably get there all right.'

'But what happens when he does?

'If I know him, he'll have a big dinner.'

'Alone? With a business acquaintance? Or,' said Mr Trout gravely, 'with some female companion?'

'Egad!' said Johnny Runcible.

'Yes, I see what you mean,' said G. J. Flannery, and a thoughtful silence fell.

These men were men who could face facts and draw conclusions. They knew that if someone has had five wives, it is futile to pretend that he is immune to the attractions of the other sex, and they saw with hideous clarity the perils confronting Ivor Llewellyn. What had been a carefree lunch party became a tense committee meeting. Brows were furrowed, lips tightened and eyes dark with concern. It was as if they were seeing Ivor Llewellyn about to step heedlessly into the Great Grimpen Mire which made Sherlock Holmes and Doctor Watson shudder so much.

'We can't be sure the worst will happen,' said Fred Basset at length. A man who peddles real estate always looks on the bright side. 'It may be all right. We must bear in mind that he has only just finished serving a long sentence as the husband of Grayce Mulligan. Surely a man who has had an experience like that will hesitate to put his head in the noose again.'

'He told me that when the subject of his re-marrying came up,' said Mr Trout, 'and he seemed to mean it.'

'If you ask me,' said G. J. Flannery, always inclined to take the pessimistic view, his nature having been soured by association with authors, 'it's more likely to work in just the opposite direction. After Grayce practically anyone will look good to him, and he will fall an easy prey to the first siren that comes along. Especially if he has had a drink or two. You know what he's like when he has had a couple.'

Brows became more furrowed, lips tighter and eyes darker. There was a tendency to reproach Mr Trout.

'You should have given him a word of warning, E.T.,' said Fred Basset.

'I gave him several words of warning,' said Mr Trout, stung. 'I did more. I told him of some lawyers I know in

London who will be able to supply him with someone who can to a certain extent take the place of Bachelors Anonymous.'

Fred Basset shook his head. Though enthusiastic when describing a desirable property to a prospective client, out of business hours he was a realist.

'Can an amateur take the place of Bachelors Anonymous?'

'I doubt it,' said G. J. Flannery.

'Me too,' said Johnny Runcible.

'It needs someone like you, E.T.,' said Fred Basset, 'someone accustomed to marshalling arguments and pleading a case. I suppose you couldn't go over to London?'

'Now that's an idea,' said G. J. Flannery.

It was one that had not occurred to Mr Trout, but, examining it, he saw its merits. A hasty conversation at an air port could scarcely be expected to have a permanent effect on a man of Ivor Llewellyn's marrying tendencies, but if he were to be in London, constantly at Ivor Llewellyn's side, in a position to add telling argument to telling argument, it would be very different. The thought of playing on Ivor Llewellyn as on a stringed instrument had a great appeal for him, and it so happened that business was slack at the moment and the affairs of Trout, Wapshott and Edelstein could safely be left in the hands of his partners. It was not as though they were in the middle of one of those *causes célèbres* where the head of the firm has to be at the wheel every minute.

'You're right, F.B.,' he said. 'Give me time to fix things up at the office, and I'll leave for London.'

'You couldn't leave at once?'

'I'm afraid not.'

'Then let's pray that you may not be too late.'

'Yes, let's,' said Johnny Runcible and G. J. Flannery.

3

Mr Llewellyn's plane was on its way. A complete absence of hijackers enabled it to reach New York, whence another plane took him to London, where at a party given in his honour by the Superba-Llewellyn branch of that city he made the acquaintance of a Miss Vera Dalrymple, who was opening shortly in a comedy entitled *Cousin Angela* by a young author of the name of Joseph Pickering.

She was a handsome brunette, as all his five wives had been, and it was not long before her undeniable good looks caused him temporarily to allow the wise words of Mr Trout to pass from his mind, such as it was. It was not till her play had been running nearly two weeks that he realized the advisability of establishing contact with Nichols, Erridge and Trubshaw of Bedford Row, W.C.1.

Chapter Two

ON THE STAGE of the Regal Theatre in London's Shaftesbury Avenue, Vera Dalrymple and a man in his fifties were rehearsing a scene from *Cousin Angela*, and anyone following the dialogue would have noted that Miss Dalrymple seemed to be getting all the good lines. And such a criticism would have been justified. The actor who was performing with her now had been known to complain that when you played a scene with Miss Dalrymple you might just as well be painted on the back drop.

In the stalls Joe Pickering was being interviewed by a girl so pretty that the first sight of her had affected his vocal chords. Her matter-of-fact briskness, however, had soon restored his composure, and they were now prattling away together like old friends. Her name, he gathered, was Sally Fitch, and she represented a weekly paper he had never heard of. Women's something, but Women's what he had forgotten.

Nature, when planning Joe Pickering, had had in mind something light-hearted and cheerful, and until the rehearsals of *Cousin Angela* had begun this was what he had been. But a sensitive young man whose first play has fallen into the hands of as exacting a star as Vera Dalrymple seldom retains those qualities for long. Quite early in their association the iron had entered into his soul, and with the opening a few days off he was feeling as he had often felt at the end of a strenuous boxing contest.

Sally, who had been probing into his methods of work, touched on another subject.

'Extraordinary how grim a theatre is in the daytime,' she said.

'Grim things go on in it,' said Joe with feeling.

'I wonder some mystery writer doesn't make it the setting

for a thriller. This stall I'm sitting in. The perfect place for finding a corpse underneath. A small corpse, of course. A midget, in fact, and one that had stunted its growth by cigarette-smoking in boyhood. His size enabled him to hide in the villain's Homburg hat and he overheard the villain plotting, but unfortunately he sneezed and was discovered and bumped off. I'll make you a present of the idea.'

'Thanks. Why did the heavy put the body under the seat?'

'He had to put it somewhere, and anyway that's up to you. I can't do all the work.'

In addition to being pretty she had, Joe thought, a charming voice. At least it charmed him, but not, apparently, everybody, for at this moment another voice spoke from the stage.

'For heaven's sake will you be quiet at the back there. It's impossible to rehearse with all this talking going on.'

'Oh, sorry,' said Joe. 'Sorry.'

'Who was that?' asked Sally, awed. 'God?'

'Vera Dalrymple.'

'Of course. I ought to have recognized her. I interviewed her once.'

'Please!' from the stage.

'Well, we don't seem to be wanted here,' said Sally. 'Let's go into the foyer. Tell me,' she went on, as the door closed behind them, 'what do you think of that gifted artiste? Off the record. Just between you and me.'

It was a question which Joe was well prepared to answer. He did so with the minimum of hesitation.

'Let's say that I think it possible her mother may love her.'

'But not you?'

'Not me.'

'Temperamental?'

'Very.'

'Bossy?'

'Most.'

'Disposition?'

'Fiendish.'

'But otherwise all right?'

'Not at all. She's a line-grabber.'

'A what?'

'She grabs other people's lines and throws the whole show out of balance. Take that bit they're doing now, it was supposed to be the man who was scoring. It linked up with something in the next act. The story depended on it. But a lot she cares about the story so long as she gets the laughs. I had to rewrite the scene a dozen times before she was satisfied that she had grabbed everything that was worth grabbing.'

'I've always heard she was a selfish star.'

'Ha!'

'But couldn't you have told her to go and drown herself in the Serpentine?'

'How could I? She's the boss. You wouldn't expect an Ethiopian slave to tell Cleopatra to go and drown in the Nile.'

'I wouldn't have taken you for an Ethiopian slave.'

'Only because I'm a bit blonder than the average Ethiopian.'

'Is she married?'

'Not that I know of.'

'I'm sorry for her husband, if and when.'

'Yes, one does feel a pang.'

'But we can't help his troubles. On with the interview.'

'Must we? I hate talking about myself.'

'I dare say, but you've got to when you're being interviewed.'

'I can't think why your paper wants an interview with me. I'm nobody much.'

'Well, we aren't much of a paper. And you've probably done something besides writing a play calculated to impress one and all. Have you a sideline? You box, don't you?'

'Who told you that?'

'My editress. She's a great boxing fan. She said you won the amateur championship the other day.'

'*An* amateur championship. Middleweight.'

'She was probably in a ringside seat.'

'Odd, her being interested in boxing. Does she perform herself?'

'I shouldn't wonder. Though I imagine past her best. And now let's have a word about Pickering the author.'

Joe shifted uneasily in his seat. He shrank from giving the floor to the totally uninteresting character she had mentioned.

'There's not much to say. I write as much as I can in the evenings after I leave the office.'

'So do I. What sort of office?'

'Solicitor's.'

'Rather dull. What made you choose that for a life work?'

'I didn't. I was supposed to be going to the Bar, but there was an upheaval in the family fortunes and I had to take a job.'

This silenced Sally for an unusual moment.

'Tough luck,' she said at length.

'It was something of a blow.'

'But how do you come to be able to attend rehearsals if you're in an office?'

'They let me out for the afternoon.'

'I see. Do you like office work?'

'Not much. It's a living, but I wish I had all day to write in.'

'Same here.'

'How's your writing coming along?'

'Not too badly. But I'm supposed to be interviewing *you*.'

'You're the one I'd like to hear about.'

'Oh, well, if you want the story of my life, you may as well have it. Clergyman's daughter in Worcestershire. Broke away from the reservation. Got various jobs. Spent a long time as secretary-companion to Letitia Carberry. Ever hear of her?'

'Not to my recollection.'

'Very active in connection with the Anti-Tobacco League.'

'Then I'm glad I never met her. I know the Carberry type. Fat and bullying everyone she came across.'

'On the contrary, slender and as sweet as pie. Not very intelligent.'

'I should imagine not, if she fired you.'

'What makes you think she fired me?'

'Well, here you are, aren't you, free from her evil influence.'

'The work got too hard for me and she decided to engage a male secretary. I could have stayed on as companion, but she suddenly took it into her head to go and settle in South

America, and I didn't want to leave England. Why South America, you ask? Probably because she had heard that a lot of smoking went on there and she hoped to spread the light. We parted on the best of terms. It was rather like a mother bidding farewell to a daughter, or at least an aunt bidding farewell to a niece, not that I've ever seen an aunt bidding farewell to a niece.'

'Much the same as an uncle bidding farewell to a nephew, I expect.'

'And I came to London and eventually landed my present job.'

'Happy ending?'

'Very. I love the little thing. And now for heaven's sake let's hear from you. I suppose this play means a lot to you—your first.'

'It means everything.'

'Well, good luck.'

'Thanks. Have you ever written a play?'

'Now don't get on to me again,' said Sally. 'Correct this impression that I came here to give you material for my biography.'

When she had gone, far too soon in his opinion, it occurred to Joe that it would be as well to make his peace with Miss Dalrymple. He intercepted her as she was leaving the theatre and asked her to lunch. The invitation was well received, but it appeared that she already had a luncheon engagement, with a Mr Llewellyn, a prominent figure in the motion picture world.

Chapter Three

ENTHRONED IN HIS BOX at the artists' entrance of the Regal Theatre, Mac the stage-doorkeeper was conscious of a feeling of depression. This was not because he wanted to smoke and was not allowed to but for a more altruistic reason. Beyond the door to his left the comedy *Cousin Angela* by Joseph Pickering was concluding its brief career, and this saddened Mac.

Not that its failure to entertain affected him personally. As he often said, what took place on the other side of that door made no difference to him. Triumph or disaster, socko or flop, he went on for ever like one of those permanent officials at the Foreign Office. But in the course of their short acquaintance he had become fond of the author of *Cousin Angela* and regretted that he had not enjoyed better luck. When he thought of some of the stinkers whose plays had run a year and more at the Regal since he first took office there, he could not but feel that Fate in allowing only sixteen performances to deserving Joe Pickering's brain child had shown poor judgement.

These thoughts were silent thoughts, for he had no one with whom to share them. His only companion was a middle-aged man who was propped up against the wall with his eyes closed and a dreamy smile on his face. One could not have said that the vine leaves were in this man's hair, for he had practically no hair, but it would have been plain to a far less able diagnostician than the keeper of the stage door that he was under the influence of what is technically known as the sauce. American, Mac put him down as, and he marvelled, as he had often done before, at the ability of the citizens of that great country to hoist so many and still remain perpendicular.

Obviously an exchange of thought—what Shakespeare would have called the marriage of true minds—was not to be expected with one so far below the surface, and Mac's meditations had turned to the prospects of a horse, shortly to run at Catterick Bridge, in whose prowess he had a financial interest, when there entered from the street someone younger and considerably more pleasing to the eye than his predecessor. He was indeed spectacularly good-looking—in the fragile ethereal Percy-Bysshe-Shelley way that goes straight to the hearts of women. His appeal to men was less marked, and Mac regarded him with a jaundiced eye.

He said:

'Mr Pickering here tonight, Mac?'

To which Mac replied:

'He's round in front'—which would not have been a bad description of the visitor propped against the wall, who was noticeably stout. Julius Caesar would have liked him.

The ethereal young man withdrew, and Mac returned to his reverie. But he was soon to resume his social life. The door leading to the stage opened, to admit Joe Pickering.

Things being as they were on the other side of that door, Mac did not venture on his usual smile of welcome. His face was suitably grave as he greeted him.

'Hullo, Mr Pickering.'

'Hullo, Mac. Just came to say good-bye.'

'Sorry to lose you, Mr Pickering. Too bad the show didn't click.'

'Yes, it was a disappointment.'

A snore proceeded from the man on the wall. Joe gave him a speculative glance.

'Blotto?' he said, lowering his voice.

'Sozzled,' said Mac with his Flaubert-like gift for finding the *mot juste*. 'He's waiting for Miss Dalrymple.'

'He'll be an entertaining playmate for her.'

'Ah.'

'Not that he hasn't got the right idea. I am about to go and get into a similar condition myself.'

'Now, Mr Pickering.'

'You don't approve of me drowning my sorrows?'

'I think you're taking this too hard, sir. Everyone has flops.'

'I hoped I'd be an exception.'

'Just got to make the best of it.'

'You preach contentment, do you? Like the butterfly.'

'Sir?'

'The toad beneath the harrow knows exactly where each tooth point goes. The butterfly upon the road preaches contentment to the toad. Kipling. All very well for you to talk. You're a happy rollicking stage-doorkeeper without a care in the world.'

'Yes, sir, but don't think I wouldn't have liked something better, if I could have got it. When I came out of the army, there weren't any cushy jobs going, only stage-doorkeeper, so I became a stage-doorkeeper. But you don't find me beefing about my lot. I'd rather be top man at the Bank of England or run a nice little pub somewhere, but I know when I'm well off.'

His eloquence moved Joe. He nodded understandingly.

'You've made your point, Mac, and I stand rebuked. I abandon the idea of drowning my sorrows. No more self-pity.'

'That's it. Stiff upper lip.'

A thoughtful silence fell. Mac broke it.

'You going out front, Mr Pickering?'

'No, I've seen all I want to of this particular drama. Why?'

'I was thinking that if you were going out front, you might run into Sir Jaklyn Warner, Baronet. He was in here just now, asking for you, and you know what a cadger he is. He wants to make a touch. I could see it in his eye. I should say he'd touched everybody in the West End of London since he started hanging round there. He even stung me for a bit the other day. Made me feel like one of a great big family.'

'One touch of Warner makes the whole world kin. He's certainly not one of our better baronets.'

'You can say that again, Mr Pickering. Jak Warner!' said Mac disgustedly, and the man supporting himself against the wall stirred like some Sleeping Beauty coming to life. 'If you want to know what I think of Jak Warner, he's a twister and a louse.'

The man detached himself from the wall. His eyes were now open and his face was stern. He spoke coldly.

'I heard what you said.'

A sharp 'Coo!' escaped Mac. It was as if he had been addressed by a statue or a corpse after rigor mortis had set in. Joe was equally taken aback. The last thing he had expected from this pie-eyed person was coherent speech.

'And,' the speaker continued, 'I am going to knock your block off. Jack Warner is a dear friend of mine. Well, when I say a dear friend, we haven't spoken to each other for three years, but that makes no difference. Anyone I hear aspersing his name, I knock his block off. It is a name at the mention of which men from one end of Hollywood to the other, including Culver City, bare their heads. If,' he added, 'they've got hats on.'

'He didn't mean that Jack Warner,' said Joe, the pacifist.

'You keep out of this.'

Joe persevered.

'You were speaking of hats and Hollywood,' he said. 'I suppose not many men wear hats there.'

'Very few.'

'The sun is never too hot. No danger of sunstroke.'

'Practically none.'

'But you get a nice tan.'

'Sure. Who's to stop you?'

Joe was relieved. It seemed to him that by cunningly turning the conversation to the weather conditions in Southern California he had averted an unpleasant brawl. Tact, he was thinking, that was what you needed in an emergency; tact and presence of mind.

'It must be wonderful in Hollywood,' he said. 'All those oranges and movie stars.'

With the best intentions he appeared to have chosen the wrong subject for his eulogy. The face of the inebriated friend of Jack Warner darkened, and his mouth twisted as if he had bitten into a bad oyster. His comment on Joe's words could only have been called curt.

'To hell with movie stars!'

'Quite,' said Joe hastily. 'Quite, quite.'

'The scum of the earth.'

'You're probably right.'

'I'm always right.'

'But the oranges. You like those?'

'To hell with them, too. No time to talk about oranges now. I've got to knock this guy's block off.'

And so saying the pie-eyed man approached the window of Mac's box and started to climb through it.

The situation, Joe saw, was one of delicacy, calling for adroit handling by a third party anxious to make sure that neither of the two contending parties did anything for which he would be sorry later. Mac was liable to get into trouble if he indulged in personal strife with visitors, and his opposite number could not fail to regret it if he went about knocking people's blocks off. With laudable promptitude he attached himself to the latter's garments and pulled. To gather him up and escort him to the street door and push him through it was a simple task. It was, he noticed, raining outside, but no doubt his charge would find a taxi before he got too wet. He returned to Mac with something of the feeling of a Boy Scout who has done his good deed for the day.

'Lord love a duck,' said Mac.

'Lord love a duck indeed.'

'You get all sorts.'

'You certainly do. Who was our guest?'

'Couldn't tell you. He gave his name, but I've forgotten it. Loo something.'

'From Hollywood, I gathered.'

'I don't know where he came from, but I wish he'd stayed there. Much obliged to you, Mr Pickering, for acting so prompt.'

'Don't give it another thought. Well, goodbye, Mac.'

'Goodbye, sir. Better luck next time.'

'If there is a next time.'

'Oh, there will be, Mr Pickering. One of these days the sun will come smiling through.'

'Well, I hope it hurries,' said Joe. 'If you meet it, tell it to get a move on.'

He went out into the street and started to walk to the modest flat which he called his home. The rain had stopped, but there were puddles which had to be avoided, and he had just stepped round one of these when a solid object bumped into him, causing him to stagger.

He clasped it in his arms. Tonight appeared to be his night for clasping his fellow human beings in his arms. A brief while before it had been Mr Loo something from Hollywood; now it was Sally Fitch. Some days had passed since their former meeting, but he had no difficulty in recognizing her.

2

'Good Lord!' he said. 'You!'

'Why, hullo,' said Sally.

'Pickering is the name, if you remember.'

'I hadn't forgotten. Thanks for catching me so adroitly.'

'Don't mention it. What were you doing? Practising rustic dances?'

'Staggering. My heel came off.'

'Oh, was that it?'

'I was walking peacefully along, minding my own business, and suddenly *wham*, no heel on right shoe. Interfered with navigation.'

'I can imagine.'

'There'll be a cab along in a minute. Meanwhile, let's have all your news. Been doing any boxing?'

'Not lately. I did think of plugging Vera Dalrymple in the eye, but I let it go.'

'I hope she hasn't ruined your play. How's it going?'

'It's gone.'

'Oh, no!'

'Came off tonight.'

'Oh, I *am* sorry. You must be feeling frightful.'

'I've been cheerier.'

'You seem cheery enough.'

'Just wearing the mask. I've sworn not to indulge in self-pity. After all, there have been lots of fellows worse off than me.'

'I suppose that's one way of looking at it.'

'Take the boy who stood on the burning deck whence all but he had fled. Can't have been pleasant for him.'

'Not very.'

'But I've never heard that he grumbled. And Napoleon. He suffered from chronic dyspepsia. Couldn't digest a thing. Every time he got up from dinner he felt as if a couple of wild cats were fighting for the wild cat welterweight championship inside him. And Waterloo on top of that.'

'And probably all he said was Oo la la.'

'I shouldn't wonder.'

'Or Zut.'

'Yes, possibly Zut.'

'And we could go on kidding like this indefinitely, but that doesn't alter the fact that I'm awfully sorry and think you're taking this awfully well.'

'Thanks. That means a lot to me.'

'I hope everything will get better soon.'

'I have it on excellent authority that the sun will shortly come smiling through. And now,' said Joe, 'I'll get you that cab.'

The cab rolled off, and he resumed his homeward journey. There was a letter lying on the floor as he came into the flat, and picking it up he recognized the handwriting of his friend Jerry Nichols, who worked for his father's legal firm of Nichols, Erridge and Trubshaw of 27 Bedford Row.

'Dear Joe,' wrote Jerry, 'If you can get your Simon Legrees to let you off for half an hour on Tuesday morning, come and see me. I think I may be able to put you on to something good. I specify Tuesday because haste is of the essence and I shall be away all Monday. Don't fail, as this good thing looks quite a good thing. Tuesday, remember, not Monday.'

Promising, Joe felt, very promising. Yet, oddly enough, his thoughts as he dropped off to sleep were not of Jerry Nichols but of Sally Fitch.

Chapter Four

DOTTED ABOUT LONDON in the less fashionable quarters of the town there loom here and there enormous houses which were built at a time when everybody had ten or eleven children, lots of money and vassals and serfs in comfortable profusion. No longer able to be used as private residences, principally because the serfs and vassals now know a thing or two and prefer to make their living elsewhere, some have become blocks of flats, others hostels for students and the younger wage-earners. Each of the latter has a communal living-room and dining-room and each resident his or her bedroom, and the general effect is of an informal and rather cosy club.

One of these younger wage-earners was Sally Fitch, and on the Sunday following the night on which her shoes had proved so untrustworthy she was in her room, discussing with her friend Mabel Potter the latter's marital problems.

Mabel was the secretary of Edgar Sampson the theatrical manager, but leaving shortly to get married, unless she decided to stay on after the honeymoon, and she wanted Sally's views on which course she ought to pursue. Charlie, it seemed, who made quite enough for two in a stockbroker's office, wished her to retire and concentrate on the home, but she wavered because she liked being a secretary.

'Sammy is awfully nice to work for, and you meet such interesting people in a place like that. There was a newspaper man in the day before yesterday who had delirium tremens right in front of my desk. Do you like your work, Sally?'

'I love it.'

'You must meet a lot of interesting people, too.'

'All the time. Have you ever seen an existentialist poet? Well worth a glance. The one I did offered me absinthe, not to mention a weekend at Bognor Regis. And on Tuesday I'm doing Ivor Llewellyn, the motion picture man. He ought to be good. The trouble with the job is that it's so ships-in-the-nightish.'

'How do you mean?'

'You meet someone you like, chat awhile, and part for ever. You never see them again.'

'Well, you can't expect celebrities to swear eternal friendship.'

'A paper like mine doesn't go in much for celebrities, though I suppose Ivor Llewellyn's one. Never heard of him myself. We get the lesser lights. I was thinking of Joe Pickering.'

'Who's he?'

'You see. The name means nothing to you. He had his first play on at the Regal and it flopped. I was awfully sorry for him. I ran into him again last night, but only for a minute. I suppose that's the last time I shall ever see him, and I've never met anyone I liked so much at first sight. We got on like long-lost brothers.'

'Good-looking?'

'Not a bit. He does a lot of boxing, and that's apt to impair the appearance. But I'll tell you something for your files, young Mabel. Looks aren't everything. A cauliflower ear doesn't matter if it covers a warm heart, which I could see Joe Pickering had. He hated being interviewed, but he remained perfectly courteous throughout, even when I was being most inquisitive about his private affairs.'

'Don't you feel awkward, butting in on perfect strangers and asking them about their religion and do they love their wives and what their favourite breakfast cereal is?'

'You get hardened, like a surgeon.'

'Sammy says interviewers ought to be drowned in a bucket. Oh well,' said Mabel, her interest in that branch of the literary world waning, 'carry on if you enjoy it. What do you think I ought to do? What would you do if you were me? About Charlie?'

'You can't go by what I'd do,' said Sally. 'I'm the meek, yielding type. I'd tell myself I had promised to honour and obey the poor fish, so why not get started. I suppose a lot depends on the man. Is Charlie one of those tough domineering characters who thump the desk and shout "Listen to me. Once and for all . . ."?'

'Oh no, he's not a bit like that. He says "Anything that will make you happy".'

'But he wants you to chuck your job?'

'Yes.'

'Then chuck it, honey, chuck it. A man like that is worth making a sacrifice for.'

'I think I will.'

'Do. It means, of course, that your life will lose a little in the way of entertainment, but what of it? I always say that when you've seen one Gentleman of the Press having delirium tremens, you've seen them all. Your Charlie sounds a pretty good egg. The unselfish type. Just the sort of man I'd like to marry myself.'

'Why don't you get married, Sally? You'd probably have the time of your life.'

'No one has asked me, not recently. I was once engaged, but it didn't jell.'

'You quarrelled? Misunderstanding, and both too proud to explain?' said Mabel, who read stories in women's papers like Sally's when not working or watching newspaper men have delirium tremens. 'Who was he? A curate?'

'Why a curate?'

'Your father was a vicar. You must have been up to your knees in curates. Or was it the doctor?'

'What makes you think that?'

'There couldn't have been a wide selection in a one-horse place like Much Middlefold. Was it——?'

'The landlord of the village pub? The odd-job man? The schoolmaster? No, it wasn't. It was a baronet, my girl, and a seventh baronet at that. Father used to coach a few assorted young men for Diplomatic Service exams and that sort of thing, and Jaklyn was one of them. So we met.'

'That's an odd name.'

'Family name. Handed down through the ages.'

'Did you break it off?'

'No, he did. He said it would be years before we could afford to get married, and it wasn't fair to ask me to wait.'

'Then he hadn't any money?'

'No, the sixth Bart had spent it all, backing losers.'

'Is he in London? Do you ever see him?'

'Who's asking questions now? Yes, he's in London, and I see him occasionally. We sometimes go to the theatre.'

'I suppose you've got over it all right?'

'Oh, completely.'

Mabel rose and stretched herself. She said she must be getting back to her room.

'Letters to write?'

'I don't write letters on my day off. The Sunday papers to read. There's a terrific murder in the *News of the World*.'

Left alone, Sally fell into a reverie. It was not often that she found herself thinking of Jak Warner these days, and now that Mabel's inquisitiveness had brought him back into her mind it was with some surprise that she realized that in stating so confidently that his spell had ceased to operate she had been in error. A good deal of the old affection, she discovered, still lingered. A man may not be an object of admiration to severe male critics like Mac the stage-doorkeeper, but if he combines singular good looks with a smooth tongue and a pathetic wistfulness, it is not easy for a warm-hearted girl to erase him entirely, particularly if she still sees him from time to time.

Magic moments of those days at Much Middlefold returned to her. Moonlight walks in the meadows. Kisses in the shadows. Drifting down the river in the old vicarage punt. By the time Mabel returned she had fallen into a mood which in anybody else she would have classified as mushy and getting deeper and deeper into that foolish condition.

Mabel's entry acted as a corrective. She had flung the door open with a violence that made the window rattle and was advancing into the room with wrought-up squeaks. She was waving a paper.

'Look at this, Sally!'

'Look at what?'

'It's about you.'

'What's about me?'

'Read this. Where my thumb is.'

Sally took the paper, and instantaneously the past with its moonlight walks and kisses vanished as if turned off with a switch. She had no need to call on Mabel's thumb for guidance. The moment she scanned the page her own name leaped at her.

'Golly!' she said, and Mabel's comment that she might well say 'Golly' was unquestionably justified.

If, the advertisement stated, Miss Sarah Fitch, formerly of Much Middlefold in the county of Worcestershire, will call at the offices of Nichols, Erridge, Trubshaw and Nichols, 27 Bedford Row, she will learn of something to her advantage; and if a girl was not entitled to say 'Golly' on reading that, it would be difficult to see what would entitle her to say 'Golly'.

Mabel's emotion had reached new heights.

'You know what that means, Sally. Somebody's left you a packet.'

Sally had begun to recover from the first dazed illusion that she had been hit over the head with something hard and heavy.

'They couldn't have.'

'They must have. It always means that when lawyers put in that bit about learning to advantage.'

'But it's impossible.'

'Why?'

'Who could have left me anything?'

Mabel had not read women's papers for nothing.

'Your grandfather,' she said with confidence. 'He disinherited your mother for marrying a clergyman when he had got it all lined up for her to marry the Earl of Something. It's happening all the time.'

'Not this time. My grandfather has always been particularly fond of my father.'

'Oh,' said Mabel, disappointed.

'And what's more he's still alive. I had a letter from him yesterday.'

'Oh,' said Mabel.

'And even if he wasn't, he wouldn't be leaving people

money. He hasn't a bean except his pension. If you ask me, it's probably a practical joke. It's the sort of thing some of the girls where I work would think funny.'

'But if it was that, they would have cut the thing out and shown it to you.'

'That's true.'

'Anyway, you'll go and see these Bedford Row people?'

'Oh, I'll *go*. I've enough curiosity for that. I'll go on Tuesday morning. I'm not seeing Mr Llewellyn till the evening.'

'Why not tomorrow?'

'I can't tomorrow. I'll be down at Valley Fields. My old Nanny lives there, and I've orders from home to go and see her every week. I missed last time, so I shall have to go twice this week. But don't worry. Nichols, Erridge, Trubshaw and Nichols will still be there on Tuesday.'

Chapter Five

AN EARLY HOUR on Tuesday found Joe Pickering on his way to see his friend Jerry Nichols.

He walked pensively and in a manner more suggestive of a somnambulist than of a vigorous young man in full control of his limbs. Pedestrians with whom he collided nursed bitter thoughts of him, but had they had the full facts at their disposal, they would have realized that he was more to be pitied than censured, for on waking on Sunday morning he had discovered that on the previous night he had fallen in love at what virtually amounted to first sight, and this naturally disturbed his mind and affected his steering.

His predicament was one he would never have permitted to the hero of any of the stories he wrote in the evening after the day's work at the office was done, for he was, though unsuccessful, an artist. Love at first sight, he felt austerely, was better left to those who catered for the Mabel Potters of this world—Rosie M. Banks, for instance, authoress of *Marvyn Keene, Clubman*, and Leila J. Pinkney (*Scent o' the Blossom* and *Heather o' the Hills*).

And yet it had unquestionably happened, however artistically wrong. He had met Sally Fitch only twice, but love, to quote Rosie M. Banks (*A Kiss at Twilight*, Chapter Three), had cast its silken fetters about him. The symptoms were unmistakable.

There is, of course, nothing to be said against love at first —or even second—sight, but if one is going to indulge in it, it is as well to know the name and address of the object of one's devotion. Sally's address was a sealed book to Joe, and though he remembered the Sally part, what followed after that he had completely forgotten. He had even forgotten the name of the paper for which she worked. And while it would no doubt have been possible for him to buy all the weeklies in London and read through them till he found the interview by Sally Whatever-her-name-was, it was more than likely that with his play such a failure the paper that employed her would not have bothered to print the interview.

It was in sombre mood, accordingly, that he arrived at the offices of Nichols, Erridge and Trubshaw. Fortunately his friend Jerry, an exuberant young man who always had cheerfulness enough for two, now seemed to be in even better spirits than usual. He gave the impression, one not shared by his visitor, that in his opinion everything was for the best in this best of all possible worlds. After preliminary greetings, marked for their warmth, he turned the conversation to the subject of his letter.

'Did anything about it strike you, Joe?'

'Only that it was very good of you to bother about me.'

'Nothing peculiar, I mean?'

'No. Was there anything?'

'It was headed Nichols, Erridge, Trubshaw and Nichols.'

'Well, isn't that the name of the firm?'

'Nichols, Erridge, Trubshaw *and* Nichols.'

Joe saw daylight, and his gloom noticeably diminished. He could rejoice in a friend's good fortune.

'Do you mean they've made you a partner?'

'Just that. About as junior as it's possible to be, but still a partner. Bigger salary, increased self-respect, admiration of my underlings, the lot.'

'Well, that's wonderful. Congratulations.'

'Thanks. And thanks for not saying "Why?". But I'll tell you why. I think my father felt that the firm ought to have someone who talked like a human being instead of in the legal patois affected by himself, Erridge and Trubshaw, in order to put nervous clients at their ease.'

'Putting anybody at their ease this morning?'

'Only you and a girl who wrote that she would be turning up. But don't let's talk of my triumphs. Let's get on to this Llewellyn thing.'

'The good thing you mentioned in your letter?'

'That's the one. Splendid opening it looks to me. Of course, it's a gamble. But what isn't?'

'Why is it a gamble?'

'Because it means quitting your job, which would put you in a bit of a hole if Llewellyn decided that you weren't the right man. There you would be without visible means of support, and it isn't easy to get visible means of support these days. I don't mind admitting that if I hadn't had a father who's one of London's most prosperous legal sharks, I'd have been hard put to it to secure my three square meals a day.'

'Could Llewellyn make up his mind in a week?'

'I imagine so. Why a week?'

'Because I'm in the middle of my annual fortnight's vacation, so wouldn't have to tender my resignation immediately.'

'That's good.'

'It solved the immediate problem. And now perhaps you'll tell me what Llewellyn wants and who the hell Llewellyn is.'

Jerry seemed surprised.

'Haven't you heard of Ivor Llewellyn?'

'Never.'

'The big motion picture man.'

'Of course, yes. I've seen the name on the screen at the beginning of films. "A Superba-Llewellwyn Production".'

'That's right.'

'But why does he want me, if he does want me? To do what?'

'To act as a sort of resident bodyguard, I gathered.'

'To guard him from what?'

'He didn't say. He became a bit coy when I approached that point. But if you go to 8 Enniston Gardens, where he lives, and say I sent you, I imagine he'll tell you.'

'Perhaps secret enemies are after him.'

'Possibly.'

'A man like that must have dozens.'

'Hundreds.'

'All wearing Homburg hats and raincoats.'

'And armed with Tommy guns. Though, if you ask me, he just wants someone on the spot to say "Yes" to him. Anyway, he'll pay a fat salary, so go and see him.'

'I will. And thanks, Jerry.'

'Not at all. I shall watch your future progress with considerable interest.'

'If it simply means saying "Yes", he couldn't get a better man.'

The inter-office communication buzzed. Jerry leaped to it.

'Yes, father? . . . Right away, father. . . . Expect me in half a jiffy, father. That was father, Joe. He wants to see me about something,' said Jerry, and disappeared at a speed that seemed to suggest that when the head of the firm sent for junior partners, he expected quick service.

Joe remained plunged in thought. He was by nature an optimist, and the slings and arrows of outrageous fortune which up to the present had played such a large part in his life had not completely crushed the hope that, as his friend Mac had said, the sun would one of these days come smiling through. And this Llewellyn opening seemed to him to indicate that this was just what the sun had decided to do.

Mr Llewellyn's reasons for requiring his services had still to be made clear. Possibly he wanted someone to dance before him as David danced before Saul, to entertain him with simple card tricks, or merely to be available to tell unwelcome callers that he was in conference, but, broadly speaking, he was plainly in need of a right-hand man, and in Joseph Pickering he would find that he had made the right selection. He saw himself so endearing himself to Mr Llewellyn, rendering himself so indispensable to Mr Llewellyn, that the latter would have no option but to bestow upon him one of the many lucrative jobs which were at the disposal of a magnate of his eminence. This would enable him, his finances placed on a sound basis, to marry the girl he loved and live happily ever afterwards.

He would first, of course, have to ascertain her name and where she lived, which might involve a certain amount of spadework, but this could be done with the aid of private detectives and bloodhounds.

Not a single flaw could he detect in the picture he had conjured up, and he closed his eyes, the better to enjoy it.

It was at this moment that the door opened noiselessly and Sally came in.

2

As Sally advanced into the room, she was feeling nervous, though she could not have explained why. Nothing to be nervous about, of course. Nichols and the rest of them had asked her to call, she had written to say she would be calling, and here she was. All perfectly straightforward. It was just that there is always something in a lawyer's office which gives the lay visitor the uncomfortable feeling that, though things are all right so far, he may at any moment be accused of soccage in fief or something of that sort and find it difficult to clear himself.

It did not make it easier for Sally that the particular lawyer she was visiting appeared to be asleep, worn out no doubt with toiling over the intricate case of Popjoy versus the Amalgamated Society of Woolworkers. But she was a courageous girl, so she said 'Good morning', and Joe leaped as if the simple words had been a red-hot poker applied to the seat of his trousers.

Springing up and turning, he enabled Sally to see his face, and her relief on discovering an old acquaintance, where she had anticipated an elderly stranger with a cold eye and a dry cough, was great. It did not occur to her to look on Joe's presence there as peculiar. He had told her he worked in a solicitor's office, and this was presumably it.

'Why, hullo,' she said.

Joe was for a moment speechless. For the first time in the past two weeks he found himself thinking kindly of Fate. In the matter of three-act comedies Fate might have let him down with a thud, but it had certainly given of its best now. The miracle of having found this girl, first crack out of the box as it were, stirred him to his depths, and he stared at her dumbly. When he recovered speech, it was of a very inferior quality. He said:

'Well, I'll be . . .'

'"Damned" is, I think, the word you are groping for. I suppose it *is* a coincidence.'

'It's the most amazing thing that has ever happened in the world's history.'

It was not in Joe to be dumb or even incoherent for long. He was a resilient young man, and already he had begun to recover, and was feeling his customary effervescent self again. It amazed him that he could ever have been a prey to depression. For him at this juncture the sun was not merely smiling, it was wearing a broad grin, like a Cheshire cat.

'Won't you . . . sit down, as we say in the theatre?' he said.

'Thank you. Had I better start by showing you my birth certificate?'

'Yes, do. People are always asking me if I have read any good birth certificates lately.'

'It proves that I am the Sarah Fitch——'

'Fitch! Of course. Fitch.'

'—formerly of Much Middlefold in the county of Worcestershire whom you've been advertising for.'

'And what's your address?'

'Where I'm living now, do you mean?'

'Exactly. Obviously you aren't in the county of Worcestershire, so you must be somewhere else—as it might be in the metropolis somewhere.'

'Oh, I see. I'm at one of those hostel places, 18 Laburnam Road, up Notting Hill way. Is it important?'

'Very,' said Joe. 'Very.'

He was relieved to know that there would now be no need for the detectives and bloodhounds whose services he had been planning to engage. Detectives and bloodhounds come high.

'Cigarette?' he said hospitably.

'Thanks,' said Sally, and laughed.

'What's the joke?' Joe asked.

'I was just thinking what Miss Carberry would say if she saw me now.'

'You look all right to me.'

'Yes, but I'm smoking.'

'Ah, yes, I remember you told me about her.'

'She caught me with a cigarette once and lectured me till I felt as if I had confessed to murder, arson, mutiny on the high seas and keeping a dog without a licence. So this is where you work,' said Sally, looking about her. 'Pretty snug.'

Joe coughed.

'I'm afraid I must advance a small correction. I don't work here. My overlords are Shoesmith, Shoesmith, Shoesmith and Shoesmith, who operate a bit farther east. I am just a waif washed up at the doorstep of Nichols, Erridge, Trubshaw and Nichols. They let me come in sometimes to get out of the cold when there's a snowstorm outside. As a matter of fact I looked in to see my friend Jerry Nichols. He was summoned to the presence of the big chief a moment ago, but ought to be back soon, and he, I fancy, is the man you want to see if you have important legal business. Have you important legal business? Not that I wish to pry into your affairs.'

'No, I noticed that. It's important to me all right. If I'm the Sarah Fitch they have been advertising for.'

'Bound to be. Birth certificate and everything.'

'And unquestionably formerly of Much Middlefold in the county of Worcestershire.'

'Ask me, the thing's a walkover. No contest. They will be dust beneath your chariot wheels. You must tell me all about it at lunch.'

'Lunch?'

'I forgot to mention that. You are lunching with me at Barribault's grill room at one o'clock. Unless you elect to put in what Shoesmith, Shoesmith, Shoesmith, Shoesmith, Erridge, Trubshaw and both the Nicholses would call a rebuttal.'

'No rebuttal,' said Sally. 'That'll be fine.' And squashed out her cigarette. She had been planning a roll and butter and a cup of coffee at some wayside tea shoppe, and, though she had never been to Barribault's world-famous restaurant, she knew its reputation.

'If I'm late,' she said, 'wait awhile.'

'Till the sands of the desert grow cold,' said Joe.

Jerry came back into the room. He had a relieved look, as if his interview with his father had turned out unexpectedly well. Mr Nichols senior was a perfectionist who, when his son's conduct called for rebuke, never hesitated to speak his mind.

'Oh, there you are, Jerry,' said Joe. 'How was Pop?'

'Very amiable. He only wanted to give me some instructions about a Miss Fitch in case she blew in.'

'This is Miss Fitch, if you mean the one who was formerly of Much Middlefold in the county of Worcestershire.'

'No, really?'

'Absolutely. Birth certificate and everything.'

'Good morning, Miss Fitch. I'm Mr Nichols.'

'Junior.'

'I'm one of the partners.'

'Junior,' added Joe, 'and if you had come in a day or two earlier, he wouldn't have even been that. A splendid fellow, nevertheless, in whom you can place every confidence. I know of no one I would rather show my birth certificate to. Well, as you will have lots to talk about, I'll leave you. Barribault's grill room at one o'clock, to refresh your memory, Miss Fitch. I'll book a table. Goodbye, Jerry,' said Joe, and was gone.

3

'That was Joe Pickering,' said Jerry.

'I know. I interviewed him for my paper.'

'A shame about his play, wasn't it.'

'Ruined by that Dalrymple woman.'

'Oh, really?'

'She pinched lines and upset balances.'

'Too bad.'

'That's not the way to win to success.'

'No,' said Jerry. 'And now—er——,' he added, feeling that, delightful though this exchange of views on the drama was, his father would have something to say if he caught him exchanging them, 'Shall we—er——?'

'Get down to what I suppose you would call the *res*? Yes, we ought to, oughtn't we? Why did you want me to come here?'

'It was with reference to the will of the late Miss Letitia Carberry.'

Sally gasped.

'*Late?*'

'I'm afraid so.'

'Oh, I *am* sorry. I was so fond of her, and she was always so kind to me. What was it?'

'Heart, I believe.'

'Oh, dear.'

'Would you like a glass of water?'

'No, thanks. I'm all right.'

There was a silence. Jerry was wishing that the task of breaking the distressing news had been placed in the hands of Alexander Erridge or B. J. Trubshaw. A tear was stealing down Sally's cheek, and crying women always made him feel as if he were wearing winter woollies during a heat wave. But he reminded himself that business was business and that he was a hard-headed partner in a prominent legal firm, and continued.

'Miss Carberry was a very wealthy woman.'

'I know. I used to have to write all the letters about her investments.'

'You were employed by her?'

'For two years, as a secretary.'

'And your relations were always friendly?'

'I was telling Mr Pickering that she was more like a sort of aunt than an employer.'

'Then that accounts for it.'

'It?'

'You *are* the daughter of the Reverend Herbert Fitch, vicar of Much Middlefold?'

'In the county of Worcestershire? I certainly am.'

'May I see that birth certificate for a moment?'

'Here it is.'

'Seems all in order, and as there must be dozens of people in Much Middlefold who will vouch for you, there doesn't appear to be any need for a lengthy . . . what's the word?'

'Quiz?'

'Yes, quiz. Though my father would have a fit if he knew I was conducting my investigations so——'

'Informally?'

'Yes, he's rather a man for taking several hours over things of this sort. So is Erridge for that matter, also Trubshaw. I prefer the simpler method—Who are you? What's your name? Can you prove it? You can? Then right ho, we know where we are.'

'It does you credit.'

'Saves time.'

'You aren't going to ask any questions?'

'None.'

'Well, I am. What did you mean by "it"?'

'I don't quite follow you.'

'I said Miss Carberry was like an aunt to me, and you said "Ah, that accounts for it."'

'I was alluding to the terms of Miss Carberry's will. The bulk of her fortune goes to the Anti-Tobacco League.'

'I can understand that.'

'But you are one of the minor beneficiaries.'

'So I do learn something to my advantage?'

'You do indeed, but there are strings attached to it. Tell me, Miss Fitch, are you a smoker?'

'I don't smoke much.'

'It was Miss Carberry's aim to stop you smoking at all, and she has left you this legacy on condition that you don't do it for two years. By which time, she says in her will, "she will have cured herself completely of the vile habit." I wouldn't knock off smoking myself for all the rice in China,' said Jerry, finally abandoning the conversational methods of Erridge, Trubshaw and his father, 'but you may think differently. Twenty-five thousand pounds is a lot of money.'

The room flickered about Sally. A shelf of legal volumes which Jerry had bought to impress visitors rocked as if in an earthquake, and Jerry himself had apparently been wafted back to the 1920s, for he seemed to have broken into the dance, popular in those days, known as the shimmy.

'Twenty-five thousand pounds!'

217

'A trifle to Miss Carberry. She probably couldn't think lower than that.'

Sally was still shaken. In a less pretty girl what she was doing would have been described as puffing.

'I wish you wouldn't say these things so suddenly. Couldn't you have led up to it by degrees or blown your horn or something?'

'I'm sorry. I thought you would prefer to get the gist without any of the whereases and hereinbefores you'd have got from Alexander Erridge or B. J. Trubshaw. They would have kept you in agonies of suspense for half an hour. My way, you get the drift immediately.'

'I'm not sure I really do. I can't believe it. Twenty-five thousand pounds!'

'And a very posh apartment at Fountain Court, Park Lane. Which, by the way, you will share with a Miss Daphne Dolby, a young lady from the Eagle Eye detective agency.'

Sally stiffened. The light died out of her eyes.

'Oh, no!' she cried.

'I told you there were strings attached to the legacy.'

'I don't want to share any apartments with any Dolbys.'

'Things being as they are, I'm afraid you've got to. I told you the bulk of Miss Carberry's fortune goes to the Anti-Tobacco League. So, if you break the clause about smoking, does your twenty-five thousand, and the Anti-Tobacco League have got their eyes fixed on it. They want to protect their interests, and how can this be done except by having somebody constantly at your side, spying out all your ways as the fellow said, watching to see that you don't sneak a quiet cigarette when you think nobody's looking? It's in the will. I imagine Erridge or Trubshaw, whichever of them it was who drew it up, pointed out to Miss Carberry that such an arrangement was only fair.'

'I don't call it fair.'

'The Anti-Tobacco League do.'

'A detective!'

'But not the sort of detective you're thinking of. You're picturing a hawkfaced female with piercing eyes and a sniffy disposition, who will make you feel it's only a matter of seconds before she slips the handcuffs on you and hauls you off to the jug. She's not like that at all. She's charming, and you'll like her. In a couple of days you'll be calling her Daffy.'

'All the same . . . You say it's in the will?'

'Plumb spang in the will.'

'Then I suppose I've no option.'

Chapter Six

OUTSIDE THE OFFICES of Nichols, Erridge and Trubshaw, now Nichols, Erridge, Trubshaw *and* Nichols, Sally paused for a moment in thought. In preparation for the interview she had put on her best dress, but though becoming it hardly seemed eye-knocking-out enough for the splendours of Barribault's Hotel, where standards were high. She looked at her watch. The morning was still young, and there would be plenty of time to go to the best place in London and buy something really glamorous. Her host had made a considerable impression on her, and she wanted to be a credit to him. Her identity established, Nichols, Erridge, Trubshaw and Nichols had advanced her a generous sum, so no obstacle stood in the way of her scattering purses of gold. She hailed a taxi.

When she came out of the best place in London with her purchase in her arms, the morning had aged a good deal, but not so much as to preclude a quick visit to Fountain Court. She was naturally curious to see her new home, and she had been given the key. She hailed another taxi.

Number 3A Fountain Court took her breath away. Jerry Nichols had described it as posh, and posh it most certainly was. In addition to her money Miss Carberry had had excellent taste. Everything was just right—the furniture, the curtains, the cushions, the rugs, the books, the pictures. To one accustomed to 18 Laburnam Road the effect was overwhelming, and she dropped into one of the luxurious chairs and tried to realize that all this magnificence was hers.

It was only after some time that a less agreeable thought intruded on her reverie, the recollection that with the magnificence went the constant company of an unknownMiss Daphne Dolby. She wondered with some trepidation what sort of a woman this Daphne Dolby would turn out to be, and was enabled almost immediately to discover at least what she looked like, for Miss Dolby entered through the door presumably leading to the sleeping quarters.

In spite of what Jerry had said, Sally had not been able to rid her mind of the picture of a female detective as something formidable and sinister, and seeing this one she was relieved. The newcomer might reveal herself later as the snake in this Garden of Eden, but she looked all right, very attractive, in fact. She was quite young, with a round pleasant face and brown eyes that had none of the piercing quality which one associates with members of her profession. Hers was quite an ordinary appearance, though a physiognomist would have seen in her mouth and chin evidence of determination and a strong will. They were not the mouth and chin of a weakling.

'Miss Fitch, I take it,' she said, 'and if you are going to say "Miss Dolby, I presume", you will be quite correct. Revisiting the old home?'

'Doing what?'

'Isn't this where you worked for Miss Carberry?'

'Oh, no, she bought it after I left her.'

'And kept it on although she'd gone to South America. What a thing it is to have money. How do you like it?'

'It's wonderful.'

'That's how it strikes me. I think we shall be pretty comfortable here. I hope my company won't spoil it for you. I know I'm a pest and a nuisance, but then those in my line of work so often are. I'll be as unobtrusive as I can.'

Sally, who liked nearly everybody, was now quite fond of her visitor. She replied with warmth.

'You aren't a pest and a nuisance at all. I shall enjoy having you here.'

'I believe you mean that.'

'Of course I do. Are you going to crawl about on the floor picking up small objects and putting them carefully away in an envelope?'

'I will if you want me to. Anything to oblige.'

'And you can tell me all about your cases.'

'They aren't very exciting.'

'No Maharajah's rubies and secret treaties?'

'It's quite a dull job really. Mostly leg-work. If your legs hold out, you're all right. And I don't do any of that now. I own the business.'

'How did you rise to such heights?'

'I had influence. My father was a Superintendent at Scotland Yard. When he had to retire, he founded this agency and worked it up into something big. I got him to take me on as an operative, which is how I come to know all about leg-work. I was promoted to a partnership. Father went off to the Channel Islands to grow tomatoes, and I became the boss. Just a story of local girl with lots of pull making good.'

'I wouldn't have thought the boss would have stooped to such a lowly job as watching over me. Sounds more like an assignment for one of the leg-workers.'

'That was Jerry Nichols's suggestion. He told me you would dislike having a female operative on the back of your neck. He was quite right. My female operatives are nice girls, but they have no conversation, while I, as you may have noticed, have plenty, which will make it fine for you in the long evenings.'

'I'm looking forward to it. Is this sort of arrangement usual?'

'I couldn't tell you. I've never come across it before. But you can see the idea. The Anti-Tobacco League want that twenty-five thousand if they can get it, and they haven't a chance of contesting the will, so they pin their hope on that smoking clause, Greedy pigs, not to be contented with what they've got, but there it is. Anyway, I wish you good luck.'

'Thank you. I'm glad you're on my side.'

Daphne Dolby became suddenly austere. The words seemed to have given offence.'

'I'm not on anybody's side.'

'Oh, sorry.'

'My sympathies are all with you,' Miss Dolby proceeded, softening. 'I wish you life, liberty and the pursuit of happiness, and I shall give three hearty cheers if you come through, but I'm like the referee in a football game. He can't take sides. He may want the boys in the pink shirts to clobber the lads in the green with purple stripes, but he doesn't allow that to affect his decisions. Same with me. I take my job religiously.'

'I see what you mean. Integrity.'

'Exactly. I may be rooting for you, but if I catch you smoking, don't think I won't denounce you. Duty first.'

'I understand. Thanks for the warning.'

'Not at all. What's that you've got there?'

'My new dress. I'm lunching at Barribault's.'

'Stepping high already? Quite right. Enjoy yourself while you've got it. I shall have a sandwich and coffee at the office. Unless the fellow I'm engaged to takes me out to lunch. I don't think he will. He never has the price. Too fond of backing losers, like his late father. Can I drop you at Barribault's? It's on my way.'

'No, thanks. I'm going back to my hostel.'

'Then I'll leave you. By the way, don't yield to temptation and have a cigarette while my eye isn't on you. I shall be asking you to breathe on me at unexpected intervals.'

'Breathe on you?'

'Routine precaution, just to make sure.'

'You're certainly thorough.'

'I pride myself on it,' said Miss Dolby.

2

Daphne Dolby's first port of call before going on to her office was number 5 Murphy Mews, which is situated in the seedier part of Chelsea and inhabited by some of the most dubious characters in London. A few may have hearts of gold, but the best that can be said for most of them is that they are not at the moment actually wanted by the police, though it is always a matter for speculation as to when the police may not feel a yearning for their society. One of these was Daphne's betrothed, Sir Jaklyn Warner. He had been living there for some weeks and would continue to live there as long as the rent-collector was prepared to accept charm of manner and glibness of speech as a substitute for cash.

Arriving at the battered front door of number 5, Daphne did not knock on it. Jaklyn, who always felt uneasy when people knocked on his door, had asked her not to. Placing two fingers of each hand on an upturned tongue, she emitted a shrill whistle, and Jaklyn appeared in his shirt sleeves with a glass in his hand.

'Oh, hullo, Daph,' he said. 'Thank God you've come.'

With those who had known them both it was a constant source of debate as to whether Jaklyn was or was not a more slippery character than his late father. Some said Yes, some said No, but it was agreed that it was a close thing, and the opinion of those who had suffered at their hands that the crookedness of each was such as to enable him to hide at will behind a spiral staircase was universally held. The only difference between the two was that the sixth Baronet had been bluff and hearty and had furthered his ends by slapping people on the back, while the seventh achieved his by looking wistful and pathetic.

He was doing so now.

'Daph,' he said, getting the tremolo into his voice which he found so effective in his dealings with women, 'I'm in a terrible hole.'

'Again?'

Over her glass Daphne fixed those clear eyes of hers on him. She had no illusions about the man she intended to marry. Theirs was not one of the great romances. She had become engaged to him because his bride would be Lady Warner, and he had become engaged to her because she had plenty of money.

She was waiting now for the inevitable moment when she would be given the opportunity of transferring a portion of that money from her possession to his.

'It's not my fault this time,' he said. 'I had this tip on a dead cert and the horse won all right, but there was an objection.'

'How much do you want?'

'Ten pounds.'

'That all?'

'Well, actually twenty.'

'I can manage that.'

'Thank God.'

'Merely remarking that after that disaster at Kempton Park you promised never to bet again.'

'I know, I know. But when you're given an absolutely sure thing.'

'Yes, no doubt you acted from the best motives. But I wish you were like the raven.'

'Raven? How do you mean? What raven?'

'The one who said "Nevermore".'

'Oh, yes, I see. Of course. Ha, ha. Good Lord, it must be fifteen years since I heard anyone mention that poem. My old guv'nor used to make me recite it as a kid when he got a bit bottled.'

'I'll bet you had him rolling in the aisles.'

The financial preliminaries concluded, Jaklyn was at his ease and in the mood for light conversation.

'Well, old girl,' he said. 'What's new?'

'My address for one thing. From now on you will find me at 3A Fountain Court, Park Lane. Make a note of it.'

'You're joking.'

'No. That's where I'll be.'

'Have you been left a fortune?'

'Somebody else has, and I shall be living with her. By the way, you must know her, because I saw you together at the theatre one night.' And, she added silently, I bet she paid for the tickets. 'Look in your little black book. You'll find her among the F's. Sally Fitch.'

'Sally *Fitch*? Good Lord.'

'You do know her?'

'I used to know her quite well. Her father was the vicar of a village in Worcestershire and did some cramming on the side. He coached me when I was trying for the Diplomatic Service. Sally Fitch! Well, for heaven's sake. But who on earth would be leaving her . . . did you say a fortune?'

'Figure of speech. But certainly not a windfall to be sneezed at. Twenty-five thousand pounds and this flat in Park Lane. I'm living there with her.'

'Why?'

'Because I've been hired to.'

'I don't understand.'

'You don't have to.'

'I can't see how you get into the act.'

'There are certain conditions attached to the legacy, and I'm there to see that she observes them.'

'What conditions?'

'Never mind. They've nothing to do with you. Well, I must be getting along. Heavy day at the office. All sorts of arrangements to make, now that I shall be away so much.'

She left Jaklyn in pensive mood. He was not a man to whom you could mention that a female of his acquaintance had acquired twenty-five thousand pounds and a flat in Park Lane without stirring his brain to activity. Even while his betrothed had been talking the thought had flashed into his mind that if he hurried round to Laburnam Road and asked Sally to marry him, he would have every chance of being successful. They had once been engaged, and surely some of the old affection must still be lingering. And he could picture his astonishment when, nestling in his arms, she informed him that there would be no need for them to live on bread and cheese and kisses as she was now an heiress.

Thus ran his thoughts, and he would have been out of Murphy's Mews and into a cab at lightning speed, had not there occurred at this juncture a sudden knocking on the front door.

It gave him pause. As he had told Daphne, when people knocked on his door he felt uneasy. Who this was, he could not say.

It might be the rent-collector, it might be the tailor to whom he was so deeply in debt or somebody hostile from the racing world. Whoever it was, he shrank from meeting him, and as these fellows had a nasty knack of waiting on the pavement outside in the hope of catching him sneaking out under the erroneous impression that the coast was clear, he reluctantly decided to abandon his journey to Laburnam Road and wait till his visitor had gone away.

Consoling himself with the thought that a letter would be equally as effective as a personal interview, he refilled his glass and sat down to write it.

He made it extremely passionate.

3

Sally, her toilet completed, was looking forward to lunch with mixed feelings. The new dress was all that she had expected of it, but she had a haunting fear that she was not going to be at her best. Excited by anticipation of the visit to Nichols, Erridge, Trubshaw and Nichols, she had slept badly on the previous night, and this had resulted in a tendency to yawn. It would be disastrous, she felt, if she yielded to this weakness at the luncheon table. Joe had struck her as an amiable young man, but even amiable young men resent it if the guest they are entertaining yawns at them all the time.

Hoping for the best, she made her way to the front door, and opening it found Mabel Potter playing truant on the other side, wriggling with eagerness to hear the latest news.

'Sally!' cried Mabel. 'I was afraid I had missed you. Are you off to see those lawyers?'

'I've been.'

'What happened? Did you learn of something to your advantage?'

'I certainly did,' said Sally.

She could not have asked for a more receptive audience. Mabel's favourite reading had always been the novels of the Rosie M. Banks and Leila J. Pinkney whose output so offended the artistic soul of Joe Pickering, and in those this sort of thing happened all the time. She would have considered it most unusual if an impecunious heroine had not been left a substantial legacy by someone.

The figure stunned her a little.

'Twenty-five thousand pounds!'

'And a flat.'

'Where?'

'Fountain Court, Park Lane.'

'Sounds terrific.'

'It is.'

'You've seen it?'

'I've just been there.'

'Come along and show me.'

'There's no time.'

'Of course there's time. I only want to look at it. It won't take five minutes.'

It was soon evident, however, that five minutes was an under-estimate. 3A Fountain Court fascinated Mabel. She flitted to and fro with squeaks of approval, while Sally, feeling drowsier than ever, sank into one of the deep armchairs and closed her eyes.

It was a disastrous move. When she opened them again, it was with a scream of dismay.

'Oh, heavens! It's two o'clock!'

Mabel Potter, reclining on a neighbouring settee with the air of one who has never been so comfortable in her life, nodded composedly.

'Yes, you had a nice sleep.'

'Why didn't you wake me?'

'It never occurred to me. I could see you were tired out, and no wonder after all this excitement. A good sleep was what you needed.'

'But I've missed my lunch.'

'Lots of doctors say that's a good thing. Charlie often skips lunch. He says it does wonders for him. Makes him bright in the afternoon.'

'He'll think I stood him up on purpose.'

'He? What he would that be?'

'A man named Pickering. He wrote a play and I interviewed him, and I met him again at the lawyers. He's a friend of one of the partners.'

'And you want to see him and explain?'

'And I don't know where he lives.'

'Well, for heaven's sake it's quite simple. You've only got to ask the partner he's a friend of. Ring him up.'

Sally relaxed. Not for the first time she found Mabel's

practical way of looking at things helpful. She supposed secretaries of theatrical managers had to be like that.

'Of course. He's bound to know, isn't he? But I must go to Barribault's first. He may still be there.'

'Pickering?'

'Yes.'

'When were you supposed to meet him?'

'One o'clock.'

'And it's now two fifteen. If he's still there after waiting an hour and a quarter, which'll be an hour and a half by the time you clock in, he must be something quite out of the ordinary.'

And it was as she spoke that it suddenly dawned on Sally that Joseph Pickering most definitely was.

Chapter Seven

JOE WAS NOT STILL THERE. There are limits to the staying powers of even the most enamoured, and he had eventually been compelled to recognize that this was just another of the slings and arrows and abandon his vigil.

The emotions of an ardent young man who has asked the girl he loves to lunch and has waited an eternity without the pleasure of her company are necessarily chaotic, and he had them all. On the whole bewilderment predominated. She had seemed so friendly, so eager to better their acquaintance. He found it incredible that she could simply have decided on reflection to have nothing more to do with him. But apparently she had, and all that was left to him was to accept the situation, dismiss her if possible from his mind and concentrate on this Llewellyn who, according to Jerry Nichols, was anxious to secure his services. He was now standing outside the door of 8 Enniston Gardens, the bell of which he had just rung.

The door opened, revealing a tall thin man with gentleman's gentleman stamped all over him. He was carrying a suitcase.

Joe said he had come to see Mr Llewellyn.

'Go right in. He's in there.'

'Perhaps you will lead the way?'

'Not me. I'm through.'

'You're leaving?'

'You're right, I'm leaving. Remarks I can put up with. Tantrums I don't object to. But throwing porridge at a man, that I will not have.'

And so saying the tall thin man passed on his way.

He left Joe a little uncertain as to how to proceed. His late companion's remarks had been brief, even terse, but he had said enough to establish beyond a doubt that behind the door which he had indicated with a jerk of the thumb there lurked something rather unusual in the way of prospective employers. He had an unpleasant feeling of being confronted with a situation to which he was unequal, like a nervous knight of King Arthur's court who, having undertaken to engage in personal combat with a fire-breathing dragon, finds that he has forgotten to bring his magic sword along with him. The years rolled away, and he was once more a boy of eleven, standing outside the study of the headmaster of his preparatory school, the latter having announced his wish to see Pickering there after morning prayers.

Rooted to the spot is a neat way of describing his position, and he might have remained so rooted indefinitely had not the door to which the man who disliked having porridge thrown at him had alluded suddenly flown open, the motive power behind it a large stout middle-aged individual with a bald head and a glare like a searchlight.

'Get out,' said this formidable apparition. 'I don't want any.'

Joe, though far from feeling at his ease, was able to say 'I beg your pardon?'

'Whatever it is you're selling. If it's magazine subscriptions to help you through college, I don't give a damn if you never see the inside of a blasted college. Bosher had no business to let you in. Wait there a moment and I'll ring for him to come and throw you out. Where the devil is Bosher?'

'Gone.'

'Gone?'

'With the wind.'

'You mean he's quit?'

'He said that was his intention. He had a suitcase with him.'

The news did not seem to depress the stout man.

'Well, easy come, easy go,' he said.

'He let me in,' said Joe, 'and didn't even start to announce me, so anxious was he to be off and away. I gathered that there had been a little friction.'

'He burned my breakfast cereal, and I threw it at him.'

'Ah, that would account for his peevishness. Many people dislike having breakfast cereal thrown at them. I for one.'

'And who are you?'

'My name is Joseph Pickering. You, I take it, are Mr Llewellyn. I was sent here by Nichols, Erridge, Trubshaw and Nichols. They said you wanted to see me. Which,' said Joe, 'you are now doing.'

A complete change had come over the stout householder. No longer glaring, he reached for Joe's hand and shook it.

'Oh, that's who you are, is it? Glad to meet you, Pickering.'

'Nice of you to say so.'

'I like the look of you. You give me the impression of being just the steady level-headed man I require.'

'That's good.'

'Couldn't be better. Sit down and I'll fill you in.'

It was almost with jauntiness that Joe accepted the invitation. The tremors which had oppressed him at the beginning of this interview had vanished as completely as had the recent Bosher, and he saw now that Mr Llewellyn was simply one of those lovable characters who readily explode but whose explosions, owing to their hearts being in the right place, are sound and fury signifying nothing. He had met them before, and he knew the type. They huffed and they puffed, but you just sat tight and waited till they blew over. As for throwing porridge at the breakfast table, that was a mere mannerism, easily overlooked by anyone broad-minded. He anticipated a happy association with his future employer.

At this point he noticed that his future employer was looking at him with an odd closeness.

'Hey!' said Mr Llewellyn.

'Yes?' said Joe.

'I've seen you before.'

'Really?'

'Where were you on the night of October the fifteenth?'

Joe winced. It was a night of which he did not care to be reminded, the night on which the comedy *Cousin Angela* had breathed its last.

'I was at the Regal Theatre.'

'In front?'

'Talking to the stage-doorkeeper.'

'I thought so. You're the fellow who gave me the bum's rush

232

when I wanted to knock the stage-door guy's block off. You attached yourself to the seat of my pants and slung me out.'

It was a severe shock to Joe, and had he not been sitting he would probably have reeled. His opalescent dreams of nestling into the position of Mr Llewellyn's right-hand man, no move made on the other's part without consulting him and a princely salary coming in every Friday, expired with a low gurgle. He was not unintelligent, and he knew that in this world a young man has the choice between two forms of self-expression when dealing with an elder whose patronage he is seeking. He can so ingratiate himself with him as to become his trusted confidant, or he can take him by the seat of the trousers and throw him out of stage doors. He cannot do both.

To his astonishment he saw only benevolence in his companion's gaze. If Mr Llewellyn was not looking at him like a fond father at a favourite son, he told himself that he knew less about fond fathers and the way they scrutinized favourite sons than he had supposed.

'Pickering,' said Mr Llewellyn, 'you little know what a signal service you were doing me when you acted as I have described. Your treatment of the script was just what was needed to make it box office.'

It seemed to Joe, though his grasp on the gist was necessarily insecure, that the thing to do was to smirk in a modest but self-satisfied way, as if, while gratified to think that he had been of service to Mr Llewellyn, he had only done what any man would have done. He did so, and Mr Llewellyn continued, 'Critics would call it a coincidence that you happened to be on the right spot at just the right moment, not that critics matter a damn. They all said that my *Two Hearts in Mozambique* was a bust, and it grossed twenty million. How did you come to be at the stage door that night?'

'It was the last night of my play. I had been saying goodbye to the company.'

'You wrote that play?'

'Yes.'

'I saw it three times. Kind of cute I thought it.'

A gush of affection for this discerning man swept through

Joe. The mild liking he had been feeling for him almost from the outset of these exchanges became intensified. Anybody who attributed kind of cuteness to *Cousin Angela* was a kindred soul.

'Oh, did you?' he said, beaming.

'With a little fixing it might make a good picture. I don't say great, I don't even say colossal, I just say good. It flopped, yes, but the practised eye like mine can see possibilities in the worst stage flop. We must talk about it later. Meanwhile I'll tell you why you did me such a signal service.'

'Oh, do,' said Joe.

Mr Llewellyn mused awhile.

'The essential thing for you to get into your nut,' he said, having clarified his thoughts, 'is that I am a man whom women find it impossible to resist.'

Joe said, tactfully, that he was not surprised to hear it. He had, he said, surmised as much the moment they met. Something in Mr Llewellyn's eyes he thought it was.

'There's something dominant about you. Like Napoleon.'

'Was he dominant?'

'Oh, very dominant.'

'That's how it's always been with me. The only exception was a school marm I knew when I was a young man in Wales. She refused to marry me until I had got a thorough grounding, as she called it, in English literature. Shakespeare, you know, and all those.'

'School teachers tend to bring shop into their love lives.'

'Yes, the wise man avoids them. But apart from her my batting average has been pretty darned good. Do you know how many times I have been married?'

'I couldn't tell you.'

'Five.'

'I'd call that good going.'

'Remarkable going. I have this unfortunate tendency to propose to them. There always comes a moment when I can't think of anything to say to keep the conversation from conking out, so I ask them to marry me.'

'Which of course they are eager to do.'

'Naturally.'

'I see your difficulty.'

'The problem is how to stop me proposing.'

'That's what you might call the nub.'

'And that's where you come in.'

'I don't understand.'

'You will. When I left Hollywood this time, my lawyer came to see me off. He had seen me through all my five divorces, and he was worried to think that at any moment he might be called on to see me through a sixth. He told me something I hadn't known before, which was that he belonged to a little group calling themselves Bachelors Anonymous and run on the same lines as Alcoholics Anonymous. If you follow me.'

'Yes, I follow you. When a member of Alcoholics Anonymous feels the impulse to have a drink, he collects the other members and they talk him out of it.'

'Exactly. And when a member of Bachelors Anonymous feels the impulse to propose to a woman, he collects the other members and they talk him out of *that*.'

'Ingenious.'

'Very ingenious. But where I'm concerned there's a catch.'

'I'm sorry to hear that. What is it?'

'I'm in England, and there's no branch of Bachelors Anonymous in England. So what my friend advised me to do was to go to a lawyers' firm he recommended and get them to supply me with a sensible level-headed individual who would take the place of Bachelors Anonymous's fellow members. Do you still follow me?'

'Like a bloodhound. You show signs of being about to ask someone to marry you, and this sensible level-headed individual tells you not to be a silly ass.'

'Precisely. No doubt he would put it even stronger and keep on putting it till he saw that he had convinced me and that the peril was past.'

'He would be able to tell that he had convinced you when he noticed that the dominant look had faded from your eyes.'

'So he would. I might have known that you were the man I wanted by the promptitude with which you acted that night at the theatre. You heard the stage-doorkeeper say I was waiting for Miss Dalrymple, and with your swift intuition you guessed that it was my intention to take her to supper. You knew how dangerous that would be, so you threw me out. It was raining, and you took it for granted that I would fall into a puddle. I did. I was soaked to the skin. Merely pausing to send Miss Dalrymple a telegram saying I had been called away on business, I went home to bed.'

'You were well out of it.'

'I was, and entirely owing to you. You're a one-man Bachelors Anonymous. You knew Miss Dalrymple, and it appalled you to think that I might be going to marry her.'

'No one marries Miss Dalrymple except over my dead body.'

'A very proper sentiment. Pickering, you're hired, and you will take up your duties immediately. You will move in here, of course. We will talk salary later, but I can tell you that it will be substantial. But for you I should now be an engaged man, and I've only just got rid of Grayce. Grayce,' said Mr Llewellyn, becoming reminiscent, 'was probably my all-time low in the way of wives, though many would say that it was a near thing between her and Bernadine Friganza. When I married her, she was known as the Empress of Stormy Emotion, and believe me the title was well-earned. In a single picture, *Passion in Paris*, she used up three directors, two assistant directors and a script girl, and her stormy emotion spilled over into the home.'

'She sounds rather like Vera Dalrymple.'

'And you saved me. How can I ever thank you, Pickering? What does Shakespeare say about a friend in need?'

'Probably something good.'

'I ought to know. When I was under the spell of that school marm, I absorbed Shakespeare till my eyes bubbled, though not knowing what the hell he was talking about half the time. Odd way of expressing himself he had. Take that bit where . . . My God! said Mr Llewellyn, breaking off.

'Now what?'

'I've just remembered that in that telegram I asked Vera Dalrymple to lunch today at Barribault's grill room.'

A sharp spasm of agony passed through Joe, causing him to

feel as if some unseen animal had bitten him in a tender spot. The words 'Barribault's grill room' could not be spoken in his presence without taking their toll.

'But it's all right,' said Mr Llewellyn, unexpectedly brightening. 'This makes a neat end to the whole unfortunate episode. A woman will overlook a man standing her up once, but not two days running. She'll be as mad as a wet hen and will write me off as a wash-out. What Shakespeare would call a consummation devoutly to be wished. Very satisfactory. Most satisfactory.'

His complacency offended Joe. He addressed himself to the task of wiping that silly smile off his face.

'How long have you known Miss Dalrymple?' he inquired.

'A couple of weeks. Why?'

'Because you seem to have got an erroneous grasp of her personality. You appear to think she will accept your abrupt disappearance from her life as just one of those things, perhaps dropping a silent tear but taking no further steps. Have you considered the possibility of her calling on you and setting about you with her umbrella? She may not be my dream girl, but she is a fine upstanding woman, fully capable of beating the tar out of you before you could say "Hullo there, good afternoon, lovely day, is it not.' It is a point to which I think you should give some attention.'

If he had expected to freeze Mr Llewellyn's blood and make his eyes like stars start from their spheres, as the motion picture magnate's school marm would have put it, he was disappointed. Mr Llewellyn remained calm, even smug.

'Naturally,' he said, 'I had not overlooked that possibility. But when you come to know me better, Pickering, you will realize that I have all the qualities of a great general. I look ahead, I form my plans. I develop my strategy. See that door?'

Joe saw the door.

'If Miss Dalrymple happens to drop in, I shall nip through it, leaving you to deal with her. And let me say, Pickering, that I place her in your hands with the utmost confidence that you will be able to wipe her off my visiting list. Ah,' said Mr Llewellyn as the door bell rang, 'this may or may not be the broad we have in mind, but a good general never takes chances, so, for the moment, goodbye.'

And he disappeared through the door like a diving duck, while Joe proceeded to follow his instructions with something of the emotions of a young lion-tamer about to enter the lion's cage and nervously conscious that he has only got as far as lesson three of the correspondence course which has been teaching him lion-taming. His relations with Miss Dalrymple had never been cordial, and there was every reason to suppose that he would find her now in an even less amiable mood than usual.

He need have had no tremors. It was not Vera Dalrymple who stood on the mat, but Sally Fitch. Sally was as conscientious in her way as Daphne Dolby was in hers. She had promised her editress to interview Ivor Llewellyn today, and the mere fact that she had been left twenty-five thousand pounds was not going to deter her.

Chapter Eight

IN THE COURSE of the last round of the amateur middle-weight boxing final Joe, hard pressed in a corner by an opponent who created the illusion of being all arms like an octopus, had thrown out a right hand purely at random and with little expectation of accomplishing anything constructive and, connecting with his adversary's chin, it had knocked the latter cold.

This had delighted Joe and his supporters, though—showing once again that one cannot please everybody—it had not brought the sunshine into the life of the opponent. For a long time it had been Joe's high spot, but it was now reduced to second place.

His emotions on beholding Sally, though somewhat similar, were much more powerful.

Not unnaturally, as has been shown, he had reached the conclusion that her failure to keep their luncheon appointment had been due to the fact that she had already had all the Joseph Pickering she required, but one look at her as she stood there told him how mistaken such a theory was. Her lips were parted, her eyes shining, her whole aspect that of a girl who has found the pot of gold at the end of the rainbow. If she was not glad to see him, he told himself that he did not know a girl who was glad to see a man when she met one.

'Can you ever forgive me?' she said.

He could answer that.

'Don't give it a thought,' he replied.

'I can explain, but I'm not sure the explanation doesn't make it worse.'

'No need to explain. I know what must have happened. You were on your way to Barribault's when you saw a little golden-haired girl in the process of being run over by a lorry. You rushed to the rescue and saved the child but got knocked over and have only just got away from the hospital. Am I right?'

'Not quite. I fell asleep.'

'You . . . What did you say you did?'

'I was tired after a bad night last night and like an idiot I sat down in a very comfortable chair and when I woke up it was two o'clock. I do hope you didn't wait long.'

'About an hour.'

'Oh, how perfectly awful!'

'Quite all right. An hour soon passes.'

'I feel like bowing my head in the dust.'

'No, really. I was quite happy. But if remorse is gnawing you, you can make amends.'

'How? Tell me how.'

'By dining with me tonight.'

'I'd love to.'

'Same place.'

'I'll be there.'

'About half-past seven?'

'Fine. And it's wonderful of you not to be frothing with fury.'

'Not at all. I quite understand. Got to get your sleep. It knits up the ravelled sleeve of care, as Mr Llewellyn's school marm would say.'

The allusion to the school marm was naturally lost on Sally, but she reacted powerfully to the mention of Mr Llewellyn's name.

'Mr Llewellyn! That reminds me. Now perhaps you will solve the mystery that's turning my hair grey. How on earth do you come to be at Mr Llewellyn's place?'

'Quite simple. I'm working for him.'

'What as?'

'General right-hand man.'

'But that's terrific. Then you've given up the solicitor job you didn't like?'

'As of today.'

'Well, that really is good news.'

'Yes, I'm pretty pleased about it.'

'What sort of a man is he?'

'Very amiable. Why? Have you come to interview him?'

'Yes, and I've heard he's a terror.'

'Nothing of the kind. He's a bit apt to throw porridge at people when the spirit moves him, but apart from that he's all sweetness and light. But here he comes now. You'll be able to judge for yourself.'

A moment before, the door which marked the line of Mr Llewellyn's retreat had opened just enough to allow him to put his ear to the crack and hear the voice of the visitor whose arrival had sent him into hiding. Satisfied that it was not that of Miss Vera Dalrymple, he now threw off all concealment and emerged.

'Oh there you are. Come on in,' said Joe hospitably. 'This is Miss Fitch, who wants to interview you.'

'I made an appointment,' said Sally.

'Sure, I remember. Let's get down to it. Pop off, Pickering.'

Joe was glad to do so. If he was to take up residence at 8 Enniston Gardens, it would be necessary to go back to his flat and pack a suitcase. His typewriter and the rest of his belongings could come on later.

'Don't forget tonight,' he said to Sally.

'I won't.'

Joe went out, his heart singing within him. When he returned, Sally had left and Mr Llewellyn was smoking a cigar with the unmistakable air of a man who has just been speaking at length on the subject of The Motion Picture—Whither?

'Nice girl,' he said.

He had broached a subject on which his young right-hand man felt himself entitled to speak with authority.

'Yes,' said Joe, giving the monosyllable a ringing emphasis which must have made his employer feel he was back with the boys at Llewellyn City. 'You speak sooth, I.L., if I may call you I.L. She is the most wonderful girl in the world. Did you notice her eyes? Terrific. Did you observe her mouth? Sensational. Did you get her voice? Like silver bells tinkling across a meadow in the moonlight. And as sweet and kind and lovable as she is beautiful. I'm giving her dinner tonight.'

'Is that so?' said Mr Llewellyn, starting.

'And I shall instruct her to pay no attention to the prices in the right-hand column, colossal though they are at Barribault's, for this, I.L., is an Occasion. Meanwhile I will be unpacking what I've brought for my simple needs. My bulkier belongings will be coming later. Where's my room? Capital,' said Joe, having been informed on this point. 'Did you happen to catch that little dimple in her left cheek? Earth has not anything to show more fair, as the poet Wordsworth said. You probably remember the passage from your school marm days.'

He left Mr Llewellyn looking as if he were taking a screen test and the director had told him to register uneasiness. He had conceived a warm affection for Joe, and it was impossible for one so imbued with the principles of Bachelors Anonymous as himself not to feel concern at this talk of dimples and silver bells tinkling in the moonlight.

It was precisely talk of this nature which would have made Ephraim Trout purse his lips and his colleagues on Bachelors Anonymous purse theirs. Fervently he wished that Mr Trout were here to advise him what steps to take in order to save Joseph Pickering from the peril that confronted him, and at this moment the telephone rang. He went to it, fortified by the reflection that if this were Vera Dalrymple calling to inquire what the hell, he could always hang up.

'Hello?' he said.

'Hello there, I.L.,' said a well-remembered voice.

The voice of Ephraim Trout.

2

Mr Llewellyn quivered from bald head to shoe sole. Direct answer to prayer frequently affects people in this manner.

'Eph,' he cried. 'Is that you?'

'Who else?' said Mr Trout.

'Where are you?'

'Here in London at the Dorchester. I was called over unexpectedly on business, and of course I got in touch with you right away. I naturally wanted to know how you were making out. Did you go to Nichols, Erridge and Trubshaw as I advised?'

'Sure I did, the first moment I got here,' said Mr Llewellyn, feeling it unnecessary to complicate things by mentioning his *passade* with Miss Vera Dalrymple. 'I saw young Nichols, the junior partner.'

'And he provided a bodyguard?'

'That's just what I want to talk to you about.'

'We must fix up a date.'

'Fix up a date nothing. Do it now.'

'I was going with a friend to that exhibition of first editions at Sotheby's.'

'Damn your friends and blast first editions and curse Sotheby's,' said Mr Llewellyn, who, when moved, always expressed himself forcibly. 'If you aren't here in twenty minutes, I'll take all my business away from you and give it to Jones, Jukes, Jenkinson and Jerningham.'

The threat was one Mr Trout could not ignore. Mr Llewellyn's business was extremely valuable to him, and Jones, aided and abetted by Jukes, Jenkinson and Jerningham, had been trying to get it away from him for years.

'I'll be there, I.L.,' he said, and in less than the specified time he was in a chair at 8 Enniston Gardens, and Mr Llewellyn was saying 'Listen', preparatory to cleansing his stuffed bosom of the perilous stuff that weighs upon the heart, as Shakespeare and the Welsh school marm would have phrased it, though Shakespeare ought to have known better than to put 'stuff' and 'stuffed' in the same sentence like that.

'Listen,' said Mr Llewellyn. 'I have a problem.'

'You aren't engaged to be married?' said Mr Trout in sudden alarm.

'Of course I'm not.'

Mr Trout could have criticized the use of the words 'Of course,' but he refrained.

'You relieve my mind,' he said. 'I had a dream about you the other night.'

'Never mind your dreams.'

243

'I dreamed I saw you coming out of the church with your sixth wife under an arch of crossed movie scripts, held by two rows of directors. But you say you aren't even engaged.'

'It's not myself I'm worrying about, it's Pickering.'

'Who's Pickering?'

'The man those lawyers sent me.'

'And you're worried about him? Don't you like him?'

'Yes, very much.'

'But he's no good for the job?'

'He's excellent for the job. But a complication has arisen.'

'Which is?'

'He's gone all haywire over a girl.'

'I don't wonder that that worries you. He sounds the very last man you ought to have around you in your delicate condition. Putting ideas into your head.'

'No, there you are wrong, Eph. No danger of that. I told you I wasn't worried about myself. My anxiety is all for Pickering.'

'Why? Is he your illegitimate son or something?'

'No, he's no relation, but I'm as fond of him as if he were. From our first meeting we have got along together like ham and eggs, and I don't want to see him ruining himself at the very outset of his career. He ought not to be dreaming of marriage at his age. He's much too young.'

'How old is he?'

'About twenty-five.'

'He'd be much too young if he were sixty-five.'

'So I wish you would talk to him.'

'I will.'

'You've had so much experience.'

'More than you could shake a stick at in a month of Sundays. We're used to these hot-headed young Romeos at Bachelors Anonymous.'

'They come to you, do they?'

'No, we generally go to them. Word reaches us that some young pipsqueak is contemplating matrimony, and we look him up. We regard him as an out-patient. And I may say that we are nearly always successful, though it sometimes happens, of course, that the madness has spread too far. Is the name Otis Bewstridge familiar to you?'

'Never heard it.'

'Heir to the Bewstridge Potato Chips millions. When we tried to dissuade him from marrying his fourth show girl, he blacked the eye of one of our members who was reasoning with him. But his was an exceptional case. Generally reasoning does what we want. Tell me about this Pickering. Is his case a severe one?'

'You bet your bottom affidavit it's a severe one. He raves about her eyes.'

'That's bad.'

'He says her voice is like silver bells tinkling across a meadow in the moonlight.'

'That's worse.'

'He also has much to say about the dimple in her left cheek.'

'I don't like the sound of that at all. You say there is no danger of you imbibing his views, but how are we to be certain? I shall take the earliest opportunity of talking to him like a Dutch uncle. Is this he?' asked Mr Trout as a fresh young voice raised in joyous song made itself heard from beyond the door. Mr Llewellyn said it was, and next moment Joe entered, looking like the jovial innkeeper in Act One of an old-fashioned comic opera

Seeing Mr Trout, he halted.

'Oh, sorry, I.L.,' he said. 'I didn't know you were in conference.'

'Just chewing the fat,' said Mr Llewellyn. 'This is my old friend Trout.'

In his present mood any old friend of Mr Llewellyn was an old friend of Joe's. Nothing could have been more cordial than his manner.

'How do you do?' he said. 'How do you do, Mr Trout? What a beautiful world it is, is it not?'

Mr Trout gave a short dry cough, as if to indicate that he had seen better in his time, but Joe was not to be discouraged.

'Full of love and joy and laughter,' he proceeded, flashing on the lawyer as sunny a smile as had ever been seen in the

S.W.7 postal division of London. 'It makes one want to sing and dance and turn handsprings, doesn't it?'

Another short cough seemed to suggest that Mr Trout was conscious of no urge in this direction.

'I'm off to get my hair trimmed. Can't take a girl to dinner looking like an English sheepdog,' said Joe, and with another smile as dazzling as its predecessor he floated from the room.

A weighty silence followed his departure. Mr Llewellyn broke it.

'See what I mean?'

Mr Trout said he did indeed. His face was very grave.

'Got it right up his nose,' said Mr Llewellyn.

'I have seldom seen a case where the symptoms were more clearly marked,' said Mr Trout. 'He is taking her to dinner.'

'That's what he's doing.'

'And getting his hair trimmed into the bargain.'

'You consider that bad?'

'Don't you?'

'I must say it struck me as sinister.'

'Nothing could be more so. The first thing one notices about these young fellows when they go down with the ailment is that they are always getting their hair trimmed. That and having a shampoo and manicure are the infallible signs that the case is serious. A man who has his hair trimmed and his hands manicured before taking a girl to dinner means business. But it's the dinner that does it, of course.'

'I proposed to Grayce at dinner,' said Mr Llewellyn, wincing at the recollection. 'It's the low lighting.'

'That and the music.'

'And the champagne. Pickering is sure to order champagne.'

'He must be stopped. I must call the boys together for an emergency meeting.'

'But aren't they all in California?'

'That's right, so they are. I was forgetting.'

'You could reason with him by yourself.'

'Hardly ever effective. It's the weight of mass argument that gets results. If only Fred Basset and Johnny Runcible and G. J. Flannery were here.'

'But they aren't, dammit, and he's taking the girl to Barribault's.'

'Why do you say that as if it were significant?'

'Because they have a blasted fiddler there who comes to your table and plays gooey love songs, the sort of stuff that makes a girl all sentimental and feeling that she wants to marry the nearest thing in sight. Let that guy get going around them, and there isn't a hope that she'll turn Pickering down.'

A look of resolution had come into Mr Trout's face. He was plainly a man who had reached a decision.

'That settles it,' he said.

'Settles what?'

'There is nothing to do but use Method B.'

'Method B?'

'It is not a course of action I am fond of, and we never use it except in particularly obstinate cases where verbal argument has failed and the subject is standing firm on his resolve to get his hair trimmed and take the girl to dinner. Should that happen, we fall back on Method B. We give him a Mickey Finn.'

It was plain from the quick lighting-up of Mr Llewellyn's face that Method B had his full approval. He was a man prone to sudden enthusiasms, and while they lasted he was entirely under their influence. Mr Trout had convinced him that the only life that held out any hope of happiness was that of the bachelor, and Joe's open partiality for Sally had appalled him. If ever a man needed to be saved from himself, he felt, it was Joseph Pickering.

'That would fix him,' he said, 'fix him good. When I first came to America, a man I met in a bar slipped a Mickey Finn into my drink, and I was out for hours. And when I came to, you could have paraded all the beautiful girls in New York in front of me and I wouldn't have given them a glance. I seemed to have lost the taste.'

The brightness of his face vanished. He spoke despondently.

'But we haven't got a Mickey Finn.'

'I have,' said Mr Trout, producing a white pellet from his vest pocket. 'I always carry a small supply. So do Fred Basset,

247

Johnny Runcible and G. J. Flannery. The subjects, especially when young, so often refuse to listen to reason and become violent. It was only by employing Method B that we were able to dissuade Otis Bewstridge from taking his showgirl to dinner. Drastic, you may say, but we of Bachelors Anonymous stop at nothing when duty calls. We regard ours as a holy cause.'

It was some time before Joe returned. His delay had been occasioned, he said, by the fact that in addition to the hair trim he had had a shampoo and a manicure. He took up the conversation where he had left off.

'I was speaking, if you remember, Mr Trout, of what a beautiful world this is. With your permission I would like to go deeper into this matter. What makes it so beautiful is that there are so many delightful people in it. Everywhere I went after I had left you I met a series of the most absolute corkers. Take the fellow who trimmed my hair. Many men are stand-offish with strangers, but this chap was affability itself. He never stopped talking. He told me the entire plot of a picture he had seen on his night off, and he held me spellbound. I wonder if it was one of yours, I.L. It was about——'

'Have a drink,' said Mr Llewellyn.

'Not a bad idea.'

'I'll fix it for you,' said Mr Trout.

3

Sally was sitting in the lobby at Barribault's, feeling sick. The Texas millionaires and Indian maharajahs grouped at the little tables around her noticed nothing untoward in her appearance, for her emotions did not show on the outside, but it was as though she had swallowed some nauseous draught and was finding it hard to bear up under the effects of it. She was seeing Joseph Pickering as he really was, and the revelation of his true nature was enough to appal any girl who had allowed herself to become fond of him.

Exactly when she had begun to be uneasy she could not have said, but it was probably when she had looked at her watch and seen that the hands pointed to ten minutes to eight.

Arriving punctually at seven-thirty, she had been a little surprised not to find Joe already there, but she had taken a seat without any misgivings, for with traffic conditions what they were a man might well be a minute or two behind time. But twenty minutes behind time was another matter.

Her first thought was that he must have had an accident. It was only much later that some evil imp seemed to whisper in her ear the revolting truth. He was not coming. He had never intended to come. This was his way of repaying her for her failure to keep their luncheon appointment.

It seemed incredible that he could have been so petty, yet what other explanation could there be? If he had had an accident, he would have telephoned. Even if the accident had been a serious one and he had been taken to hospital, a doctor or someone would have telephoned. No, he was deliberately standing her up, as Mr Llewellyn would have said, and it was not long before the sensation of nausea gave way to a boiling fury, and it was as Joseph Pickering Ordinaries, once quoted so high, had experienced a sharp drop and were down in the cellar with no takers, that she heard her name spoken and looking up saw Jaklyn Warner.

Jaklyn, though never fortunate enough to penetrate to the ornate grill room, was a frequent visitor to Barribault's lobby, for it seldom lacked the presence of one or two of his wealthier acquaintances who might be good for a small loan if approached with the right wistfulness. And he had never quite lost the hope that one of these nights some big-hearted reveller, mellowed by Barribault's cocktails, might invite him to come along and have a bite of dinner with him.

Tonight he had not seen anyone who looked like a promising prospect, but he had seen Sally, and he lost no time in joining her.

His eagerness to ascertain her reactions to that letter of his was naturally acute.

'Why, hullo, Sally,' he said. 'All alone?'

Sally's voice as she replied was bleak.

'Hullo, Jaklyn. Yes, I'm all alone.'

'I wish I could ask you to have dinner with me, but unfortunately I've come out without any money and they don't know me here, so I can't sign the bill.'

'I don't want any dinner. You can see me home, if you like. Not Laburnam Road. Fountain Court, Park Lane.'

'Yes, somebody told me you had moved.'

'I'm living there with another girl.'

'So whoever it was who told me said. Was it her you were waiting for?'

'No, she's gone to a dinner. Something to do with her old school.'

Jaklyn was relieved. He would have found a meeting with Daphne Dolby embarrassing. It is never agreeable for a man who is engaged to one girl and has just proposed to another to find himself in the company of both of them.

They walked the short distance to Fountain Court in silence. Years of studying other people's moods had made Jaklyn an expert on when to speak and when not to, and he could see that Sally was upset about something and not disposed for conversation. It was only when she had opened the door of number 3A and he had followed her into the living-room that he ventured on the question that was occupying his mind to the exclusion of all other thoughts and said:

'Sally.'

'Yes?'

'Er,' said Jaklyn.

He was not sure he liked the way she was looking at him. It seemed to him a speculative look, as if she were weighing him up, and he was a man who preferred not to be weighed up.

And indeed this was what Sally was doing. She had had no difficulty in interpreting that 'Er'. She was to be given the opportunity of putting the clock back and establishing their relations on what might be called the old Much Middlefold basis.

Had this occurred before Joe Pickering had revealed himself as the impossible character he really was, she would have had no hesitation in crushing Jaklyn's hopes with what Mr Trout would have called a *nolle prosequi*, but now she found herself wavering.

What turned the scale was that he was looking so particularly wistful. It was so obvious that all this while he had been eating his heart out for the one girl in his life and now could endure it no longer. Impossible not to be touched by such fidelity, especially when the man you had mistakenly supposed loved you as you had mistakenly supposed you loved him had turned out not so much to have feet of clay as to be clay all the way up. It was not a subject she liked to let her mind dwell on, but she did feel very definitely that a girl idiotic enough to give a thought to Joseph Pickering ought to be placed under some kind of restraint.

She came to a decision.

'I got your letter, Jaklyn.'

'And?'

'The answer is Yes. I'll marry you if you really want me.'

'*Want* you!' said Jaklyn, with fervour.

He had concentrated all his faculties on making this fervour as convincing as possible, but it now occurred to him that it would be judicious before going further to render quite clear his complete ignorance of the change in Sally's financial condition. There must be no suspicion on her part that he was in any way influenced by the fact of her having joined the ranks of the wealthy.

He proceeded to do so, regretting, for it would have been a neat way of putting it, that the popularity of the song of that title made it impossible for him to say that he could not give her anything but love.

'I'm afraid we shall be very poor, darling, but what of that? What's wrong with being poor if you love each other? It's fun. Everything becomes an adventure. The dreams, the plans, the obstacles that must be surmounted—the rich don't have any of that. They don't know how happy you can be in an attic. With a candle by the bed. When you blow out the candle, you make believe you're in a room in a castle with silk hangings and cupids dancing on the ceiling. Wonderful, wonderful!'

He thought for a moment of going on to the crust of bread for breakfast, but was not sure that that might not be overdoing it.

251

Even as it was, Sally showed herself unsympathetic to his poetic flight.

'We shan't be as hard-up as all that,' she said in her practical way. 'I've got twenty-five thousand pounds.'

'What?'

'And this flat.'

Jaklyn was stunned. He stared at Sally dumbly as she told her story. When she had finished, he conceded that this did make a difference as far as their scale of living was concerned, but maintained that it was essentially a triviality.

'After all,' he said. 'Money, what is it? Love is what matters.'

And on this admirable sentiment he took his leave.

4

Daphne Dolby returned shortly after he had left. She was in excellent spirits, having plainly enjoyed the reunion with the comrades of her girlhood.

'Where were you at school, Sally?' she asked.

'I was privately educated, as they say in the reference books.'

'There were times in my early days,' said Daphne, 'when I wished I had been, but I don't know. It wasn't so bad, looking back, and certainly the hellhounds I used to regard with loathing seem to have improved with age. I loved them all tonight. I'm giving lunch to some of them tomorrow. Care to come along?'

'I can't, I'm afraid. I'd have loved to, but I've got to go to Valley Fields and spend the day with an old nurse.'

'The Nanny of your childhood?'

'Yes.'

'I'm sorry for you. I know those old Nannies. Mine lives in Edinburgh, thank God. She——'

Daphne broke off. She sniffed. A stern look came into her face.

'Sally! You've been smoking!'

'Not me,' said Sally. 'My betrothed.'

'What! You aren't engaged?'

'I am.'

252

'You've kept it very dark. Since when?'

'It only happened tonight.'

'Who is he?'

'His name's Warner. Jaklyn Warner.'

The announcement caused a brief pause in the conversation. It is always disconcerting for a girl who is engaged to a man to be told by a friend that she, the friend, is also engaged to him. Daphne was less taken aback than most would have been, for she remembered that she had informed Jaklyn of Sally's legacy, and her knowledge of him told her that this was how, given that information, he might have been expected to act. Her illusions where he was concerned were few.

It was, accordingly, with perfect calm that she said:

'Oh, Jaklyn Warner, eh?'

'Do you know him?'

'I've seen him around.'

There was another pause.

'Of course he didn't know about this money of yours?' said Daphne.

'No.'

'Did you tell him?'

'It came out as we were talking. He was saying how hard up we should be, and I thought it would comfort him to mention it.'

'I'll bet he was astounded.'

'He did seem to be.'

'And overjoyed?'

'Not particularly. I don't think he thinks much about money.'

'No, pure spirit, that boy,' said Daphne.

5

There was a pensive look on Daphne's face as she sat in her bedroom after saying goodnight to Sally. Lightly though she had seemed to take the latter's revelation, it had shaken her not a little. It is disturbing for a girl who has been regarding her engagement as a stable thing, to be terminated by marriage whenever she feels inclined, to find that there is imminent danger of her betrothed making a sudden dash for liberty. Where everything was placid and leisurely rapid action becomes necessary, and nobody likes being hurried.

She blamed herself for yielding to over-confidence where Jaklyn was concerned. She had assumed too readily that he would feel that a fiancée with a prosperous business and always good for a loan would be something to cling to, and though she had had a marriage licence among her effects for some time, she had always been too busy to use it. She did not often do a foolish thing, but she saw that she had done one when relying on Jaklyn to stay where she had put him.

But she was not the girl to waste time in idle regrets. Long before she had switched off the light and climbed into bed she had found a solution to her problem, and next morning Jaklyn, finishing a late breakfast, was surprised by a familiar whistle at his door. Having ascertained by peeping round the window curtain that she was not a bookmaker or a tailor, he opened the door.

Her car was there, and in it, he saw, was a mysterious stranger.

This was an individual who as far as thews and sinews went could have been the village blacksmith or his twin brother, but in the matter of looks fell short of the standards of the lowest beauty contest. His was a face that could never have launched anything like a thousand ships, and something—possibly an elephant—appeared to have sat on it and squashed it. No one broadminded will allow himself to be prejudiced against a fellow-man because the latter has a squashed face, but this squashed face had in addition a grim and menacing look, such as is so often seen on the faces of actors playing bit parts in gangster films, and—possibly inadvertently—he gave the impression that it would take very little to give him offence. He was carrying in his hand a bunch of roses.

'I've come to take you for a ride, Jaklyn,' said Daphne brightly. 'You don't get nearly enough fresh air.'

Jaklyn, who had been eyeing her fellow-traveller with some alarm, relaxed. He had no objection to going for a spin in her car. A very agreeable way of passing the morning, and she would be morally bound to stand him lunch, possibly at one of those excellent hotels at Brighton where they understood lunch.

'That'll be fine,' he said. 'Who,' he added, lowering his voice, 'is the fellow with the face?'

'Cyril Pemberton, one of my operatives. He's coming with us.'

'Coming *with* us?'

'Yes, he's our witness. I meant to have told you before. We shall be stopping off at the registry office and getting married.'

'*Married!*'

'I've been so tied up at the office that I hadn't time to get around to it before.'

'But——'

'Now don't start arguing, dear,' said Daphne. 'Cyril has been looking forward so much to being a witness. He knows what prestige it will give him with the other operatives being chosen to be witness at the boss's wedding. He specially bought those lovely roses. And he has a very violent temper. I mean I don't know what he will do if you spoil his treat.'

Jaklyn did not spoil his treat.

Chapter Nine

IT WAS MR TROUT's healthy practice to take a brisk walk after lunch when the weather was fine. It tuned up his system and imparted a gentle glow. The day following his visit to Mr Llewellyn being adequately balmy, he set off down Park Lane and had reached the neighbourhood of Fountain Court when he observed approaching him the young man Pickering whose acquaintance he had made on the previous evening.

He greeted him with the utmost warmth, and so kindly and paternal was his manner that Joe, whose morale was at its lowest ebb, threw off perhaps five per cent of the gloom which was wrapping him as if in a garment and replied to his 'Ah, Mr Pickering' with an 'Oh, hullo, Mr Trout' which, though in many respects resembling a voice speaking from the tomb in a story by Edgar Allan Poe, was reasonably cordial.

'A lovely afternoon,' said Mr Trout. He felt no embarrassment at this encounter. Members of Bachelors Anonymous never felt embarrassment when meeting those in whose matrimonial plans they had interfered. To him Joe was just another out-patient who had come to him needing treatment, and this treatment he had given him. He experienced no more remorse at having introduced a Mickey Finn into his beverage than would a doctor who had prescribed for an invalid one of those medicines which nearly lift the top of the head off but effect a cure. 'Glad to see that you are restored to health, Mr Pickering,' he said. 'You had some sort of a fit or seizure yesterday. It alarmed me. It alarmed Mr Llewellyn. It alarmed both of us. And what are you doing in these parts?'

If Mr Trout had been a shade less kindly and paternal, Joe might have kept his private affairs to himself, but he was in the frame of mind when anyone really kind and paternal can extract confidences with the ease of a conjurer taking a rabbit or the flags of all nations out of a top hat. He told Mr Trout that he had been calling on a girl, and Mr Trout said 'Oh?' in a disapproving voice, as if he thought that that was no way for a young man to be employing his time when he might have been reading a good book. This talk of calling on girls, too, made him a little anxious. It seemed to suggest that his treatment of yesterday had not been as effective as he had supposed.

'The young lady of whom you were speaking last night?'

'Yes.'

'I trust you found her well?' said Mr Trout stiffly.

Joe gave a sharp yelp like that of some fiend in torment on whose sore toe another fiend in torment has trodden. The irony of the question had touched an exposed nerve.

'I didn't find her at all,' he said. 'She refused to see me.'

'Indeed? Why was that?'

'You remember I was to have taken her to dinner last night?'

'Ah yes. You had your hair trimmed.'

'And a shampoo and a manicure.'

'And then you had this fit or seizure. I begin to see. She went to the restaurant of your selection, but you did not.'

'Exactly. This must have given her a pretty low opinion of me, and I wanted to see her and explain. I went to the address she had given me, but they told me she had moved to Fountain Court or House or whatever the damned thing is called, so I've just been there.'

'And she would not see you?'

'No. She sent out word to that effect.'

'Then you are well out of it, my boy,' said Mr Trout, and went into his routine with the practised smoothness which years of membership in Bachelors Anonymous had given him. He never had to think and pick his words when holding forth on the drawbacks to marriage. The golden syllables came gushing out as if somebody had pressed a button. It was just the same with Fred Basset, Johnny Runcible, G. J. Flannery and all the other pillars of that benevolent group. As G. J. Flannery had once put it, they seemed to be inspired.

'Yes, Pickering, you are well out of it,' said Mr Trout. 'You have had a most merciful escape. Have you ever considered what marriage means? I do not refer to the ghastly ordeal of the actual service, with its bishops and assistant clergy, its bridesmaids and the influx of all the relations you have been trying to avoid for years, but to what comes after. And when I say that, I am not thinking of the speech you would be compelled to make at the wedding breakfast. That and the service that preceded it are merely temporary agonies, and a strong man can fortify himself with the thought that they will soon be over. But what of the aftermath, when you find that you are linked for life with someone who comes down to breakfast, puts her hands over your eyes and says "Guess Who"? From what you were saying about the dimple on this girl's left cheek I gather that she is not without physical allure, but can she drive a car? Somebody has got to drive the car and do the shopping while you are playing golf. Somebody has got to be able to fix a flat tyre. Letters, too. What guarantee have you that she will attend to the family correspondence, particularly the Christmas cards? Like so many young men,' said Mr Trout, 'you have allowed yourself to be ensnared by a pretty face, never asking yourself if the person you are hoping to marry is capable of making out your income tax return and can be relied on to shovel snow while you are curled up beside the fire with a novel of suspense. Yes,' said Mr Trout, warming to his subject, 'you are one of the lucky ones. If, as you say, she refuses to see or speak to you, you ought to be dancing sarabands and congratulating yourself on——'

'My God!' said Joe.

What had caused the ejaculation had been the passing of a cab in which was seated an extremely attractive girl with nice eyes and a dimple in her cheek—reading from right to left, Sally en route to Valley Fields to brighten the life of Miss Jane Priestley, her former Nanny. From London to Valley Fields was a journey of about six miles, and until today she had always made it by train from Victoria, but when a girl has twenty-five thousand pounds in or shortly to come into her bank account she can afford to be extravagant.

This explains the hired vehicle, and the fact that after travelling a short distance it was held up in a traffic jam explains why Joe, after standing congealed for a second or two, had time to leap into another hired vehicle which happened to be passing and shout into the driver's ear those words familiar to all readers of the right sort of book:

'Follow that car!'

The driver was a stout man with a walrus moustache, not that that matters, who when given instructions liked them to be quite clear, with no margin for error. He said:

'What car?'

'The one over there.'

'Which one?'

'The black one.'

'It's a cab.'

'Well, follow it.'

This delay had given Mr Trout time to join Joe in the cab, which he had been glad to do. Eloquent though he had been, he had still much wisdom to impart, and he was determined that Joe should get the benefit of it. But first there was a question to be put.

'Where are we going?' he asked.

It was the first intimation Joe had received that he had a travelling companion. In his perturbed state of mind he had failed to notice that there was a human form seated beside him. The discovery gave him no pleasure, but he was a young man who in all circumstances was polite to his elders.

'I don't know,' he said.

Mr Trout looked disapproving. He may even have clicked his tongue, but if this was the case the roar of London's traffic made the sound inaudible.

'Is it not a point,' he said, 'on which it would be well to come to a decision before starting on a journey?'

Joe saw that explanations would be necessary. He was not feeling as fond of Mr Trout as he had been some minutes earlier, before the latter had leaped uninvited into the seat at his side, but he supposed he was entitled to be taken into his confidence.

'That girl I was telling you about,' he replied. 'She's in that cab in front there.'

259

Mr Trout looked more disapproving than ever. He was thankful for the impulse which had made him join Joe.

'And you propose to pursue her and insist on a conference?'

'That's the idea.'

Mr Trout was shocked and hurt. Though not a conceited man, he knew that he was recognized by his colleagues in Bachelors Anonymous as in a class by himself in the matter of marshalling arguments against marriage. Fred Basset had often said so. So had Johnny Runcible and G. J. Flannery. It was galling to him, therefore, to find that his recent eloquence had had so little effect. This incandescent young man was plainly still as incandescent as he had been before a word was spoken.

'You were not impressed by my warning?' he said, not attempting to conceal the coldness in his voice. 'My efforts were wasted?'

'Your what?' said Joe.

'I spoke at some length on the folly of plunging into matrimony.'

'Oh, did you?'

'I did.'

'I'm sorry. I missed it.'

'Oh?'

'I was thinking of something else.'

'Oh?'

'You know how it is when you're thinking of something else.'

'Quite,' said Mr Trout icily.

He was deeply offended. He was not accustomed to mixing with deaf adders. Even Otis Bewstridge, though in the end becoming violent, had *listened*. For an instant he almost decided to withdraw from his mission and allow Joe to rush into ruin in the manner popularized by the Gadarene swine. Serve the misguided young fellow right, he felt. Then the never-say-die spirit which animated all members of Bachelors Anonymous asserted itself. It was as though he could hear Fred Basset, Johnny Runcible and G. J. Flannery urging him to have one more try.

'May I resume my remarks?' he said. 'I touched briefly on

the more obvious objections to marriage, and later I will go into them again, but at the moment what I would like to stress is what I may call the family peril inseparable from the wedded state. Most girls have families, and why should the object of your devotion be an exception? I very much doubt that you have bestowed your affection on an orphan with no brothers or uncles. You speak enthusiastically of the dimple in her left cheek, but are you aware that statistics show that eighty-seven point six of girls with dimples also have brothers who are always out of a job and have to be supported? And if not brothers, uncles. In practically every home, if you examine closely, you will find an Uncle George or an Uncle Willie with a taste for whisky and a distaste for work, whose expenses the young husband is compelled to defray. In the vast majority of cases the man who allows himself to be entrapped into matrimony is not so much settling down with the girl he loves as founding a Haven of Rest for the unemployed.'

He paused for breath, and Joe spoke.

'Now where on earth does she think she's going?' he said, once more making it plain that he had not been following his companion's observations with the attention they deserved.

In the course of the last twenty minutes they had passed through Clapham and Herne Hill and were entering a pleasantly wooded oasis, the Valley Fields to which Sally's former Nanny had retired to spend the evening of her days. She lived with her three cats in a semi-detached house called The Laurels in Burbage Road, and when not entertaining Sally, occupied herself by reading the Old Testament, from which she could quote freely, and thinking up ways of annoying her next-door neighbour. The latter's dog Percy had fallen into the habit, as dogs will, of chasing her cats, and she resented this keenly. The result had been one of those regrettable feuds from which even earthly Paradises like Valley Fields are not exempt.

Sally's cab was a fleeter vehicle than the one which chance had allotted to Joe, and despite the efforts of the driver with the walrus moustache she was inside The Laurels with the door closed behind her before Joe had entered the home stretch. Arriving, he leaped out, sped up the little front garden and rang the bell. The door opened, and Miss Priestley appeared.

If Joe had been in a less febrile frame of mind, he might have quailed at the sight of her, for like so many English Nannies, engaged for their skill at enforcing discipline rather than any physical charm, the aspect she presented was formidable to a degree. Very tall, very thin, and very stony about the eyes, she bore a distinct resemblance to Lady Macbeth, with a suggestion of one of those sinister housekeepers who figured so largely in the Gothic type of novel popular in Victorian days.

Joe, though she reminded him of a long-ago Nanny who had frequently spanked him with the back of a hair-brush, faced her without a tremor. He was far too preoccupied to allow himself to be disturbed by old memories.

'Good afternoon,' he said.

Miss Priestley had no comment to make on this.

'Can I come in?'

'Pardon?'

'Would you mind if I came in for a moment?'

'Why?'

'It's very urgent that I see the girl who arrived just now.'

His luck was not in. Sally's former Nanny might have been a friendly soul who would have been delighted to do all that was in her power to help a young man who was plainly in love, but in Miss Jane Priestley he had found the precise opposite of this admirable type. Her leading characteristic was a profound distrust of all men. She suspected their motives and eyed them askance. When they came ringing front-door bells and asking to see girls, she knew what they were after. Her eyes, stony enough to start with, became stonier. She said:

'What do you want with her? No good, I'll be bound. I know your sort. You go about seeking whom you may devour. Preying on innocent girls. Going to tell her you'll cover her with jewels. Repent ye,' said Miss Priestley, becoming biblical, 'for the Kingdom of Heaven is at hand. God shall smite thee, thou whited wall. Abstain from fleshly lusts which war against the soul.'

262

And so saying she went into the house, slamming the door behind her, and Joe tottered back to the cab.

Mr Trout was standing beside it, eager for details. He had been too far away to catch any of the dialogue, but he had interpreted without difficulty the general run of the scene he had just witnessed.

'Won't speak to you?' he said.

'No. Get in. We're going home.'

'You go,' said Mr Trout. 'I like the look of this place. I think I'll stroll around a while and go back by train.'

2

In stating that he liked the looks of Valley Fields Mr Trout had spoken nothing but the truth. He liked its tree-studded roads, its neat lawns and above all the flowers that bordered those lawns. It is estimated that more seeds are planted annually, more patent fertilisers bought and more greenfly rendered eligible for the obituary column in Valley Fields than in any other London suburb, and the floral display there in the summer months is always remarkable.

But when he gave him to understand that he merely proposed to stroll around, taking in the many charms of this sylvan spot, he deceived Joe Pickering. It was his intention, when he found himself alone, to proceed to The Laurels and ask to see Sally. The members of Bachelors Anonymous always liked to know that a case could be filed away as closed, and he wished to ascertain whether her avoidance of Joe was due to a temporary tiff which could be adjusted by a couple of kisses and the gift on the part of the latter of a box of chocolates or whether she had cast him off for ever. He was, moreover, actuated by simple inquisitiveness. As nosey a Parker as ever walked down Hollywood Boulevard, he wanted to see what the girl who had made such a deep impression on Joe looked like.

The moment the cab was out of sight, accordingly, he trotted to the front door and rang the bell.

It has been well said that the hour can always be relied on to produce the man. It now produced the woman. Miss

Priestley appeared, fresh from her triumph over Joe, and stood eyeing him with the cold intentness with which Jack Dempsey used to eye opponents across the ring. This was her first opportunity of seeing Mr Trout steadily and seeing him whole, but already she had decided that she did not feel drawn to him.

Mr Trout, unaware that suavity was going to get him nowhere, was at his suavist. Smiling a courtly smile which went through Miss Priestley like a dagger, he said:

'Good afternoon, madam.'

To this Miss Priestley made no reply.

'Could I speak to the young lady who arrived here just now?'

He could not have asked a more unfortunate question. For a moment, until he spoke, the châtelaine of The Laurels had supposed him to be another of the pests from one of those consumer research organizations which were always sending representatives to ask her what soap powder she used and what she spent on her weekly budget, but this brazen query revealed him as something far worse—a libertine to wit and, because older, worse than the first one.

'No you couldn't,' she said crisply. 'And you ought to be ashamed of yourself. At your age. Old enough to be her father.'

Mr Trout's courtly smile vanished as if it had been rubbed off by a squeegee.

'You wrong me, madam,' he hastened to say. 'I merely wish to——'

'Well, you aren't going to.'

'But, madam——'

'Get thou behind me, Satan.'

Many men would have felt at this point that the talks had reached a deadlock and that it would be impossible to find a formula agreeable to both parties, but Mr Trout was made of sterner stuff. His years of experience had taught him that all men—and this of course included women—have their price. A pound note, he estimated, would be Miss Priestley's. He felt for his wallet, produced one and pressed it into her hand.

'Perhaps this will induce you to lend a kindlier ear to my request,' he said archly, in fact almost roguishly, smiling another of those courtly smiles which, as we have seen, affected her so unpleasantly.

Miss Priestley looked dumbly at the revolting object. When a woman of high principles has nursed a girl through the storms and stresses of childhood and the moment the latter is grown up is asked to sell her for gold, her emotions are not easy to describe. Foremost among those of Sally's ex-Nanny was a wild regret that she had come out without her umbrella, for it would have soothed her a little to have been able to strike this smooth philanderer over the head with it.

Deprived of this form of therapy, all she could do was to hurl the bribe from her as if it had been a serpent and return to the house.

A pound note has many merits, too numerous to go into here, but it has the defect of not making a good missile. This one fell limply at Mr Trout's feet, and as he stooped to recover it a sudden breeze sprang up and lent it the wings of a dove. It leaped in one direction, frolicked in another. It was as if it had got the holiday spirit and was brushing up its country dances for the next dance around the maypole. It could not have been livelier if it had been told that it was going to be queen of the May.

Nor was Mr Trout any less agile. He was not one of those men who part lightly with anything in the shape of currency. He had once spent half an hour on his hands and knees trying with the aid of a walking-stick to retrieve a dollar bill which had gone to earth under a chest of drawers. The present crisis brought out all the huntsman in him. He wanted that pound note and was determined to get it. Wherever it went, he went, and when eventually it sailed over the fence into the next-door garden it seemed only natural to him to follow it. He would, he knew, be offending against the laws of trespass, but his blood was up and he didn't care.

The breeze had dropped and his quarry was lying inert on the little patch of grass outside the front door, an easy prey. Somewhat out of breath but thrilled by the prospect of the happy ending, he advanced on it with gleaming eyes and outstretched hands, and as he did so an odd sound as of someone gargling mouthwash in his rear made him turn. With a sinking heart he saw that he had been joined by a dog.

He stiffened, growing colder and colder from the feet upwards. He had never been at his ease with dogs, and this was a particularly formidable specimen of the species—the sort of dog that hangs about on street corners and barks out of the side of its mouth; a dog, more than probably, known to the police. He viewed it with concern, and the dog viewed him with open suspicion.

Percy was the dog's name, and mention was made earlier of his habit of chasing Miss Priestley's cats. But he was not a specialist who confined himself to this branch of industry. Postmen paled beneath their tan when they saw him, and representatives of consumer research firms were equally affected. His guiding rule in life was 'If it moves, bite it', and it was unfortunate, therefore, that at this moment Mr Trout should have moved. Abandoning the more prudent policy of standing rigid and hoping that he would be mistaken for a flowering shrub of some kind, he thrust forward a trembling hand, an action against which his best friends would have warned him, and said:

'Good dog. Good boy. Good old fellow.'

Percy's liveliest suspicions were confirmed. He had supposed himself to be up against a unit of organized crime, and how right, he felt, he had been. Panic had robbed Mr Trout's voice of its usual suavity. His 'Good dog' had sounded like a threat to take immediate aggressive steps, as had his 'Good boy', and his 'Good old fellow', and Percy had been left in no doubt that he was in the presence of a far more sinister character than any postman or consumer research man. He ranked Mr Trout even higher as a menace to the public weal than Miss Priestley's three cats, dangerous devils though they were.

He acted promptly, for he shared with Napoleon the belief that attack is the best form of defence. Without waiting for Mr Trout to start throwing the bombs of which his pockets were no doubt full he bit the outstretched hand with all the emphasis at his disposal, and Mr Trout uttered a howl which might well have been that of a dozen cats stepped on simultaneously by a dozen men in hobnailed boots. It had the effect of so startling Percy that he took to his heels and disappeared at some fifty m.p.h., while at the same time a woman came out of the house, plainly eager for explanations.

This was Mrs Amelia Bingham, the widow who owned the other half of the semi-detached house inhabited by Miss Priestley and her cats. Mr Trout, seeing her only dimly through the mist of unshed tears caused by Percy's prompt action, would not have been able to describe her, but she was what is generally termed a comfortable woman. A tendency to plumpness made it unlikely that she would ever become Miss Great Britain, or Miss London and Adjoining Suburbs, or even Miss Valley Fields, but she was beyond a question comfortable. She radiated an atmosphere of cosiness. Mr Trout had once got lost on a walking tour on a cold and rainy night and after hours of wandering had come upon an inn, its lights shining through the mists with their promise of warmth and comfort. His first sight of Amelia Bingham filled him with the same feelings he had had then.

Under normal conditions she smiled easily, but she was not smiling now. Knowing that Percy was at large, and hearing that awful cry, she feared the worst.

'Oh dear. Are you hurt?' she wailed, and ran to where Mr Trout was pirouetting like an Ouled Naïl dancer with his hand to his mouth.

'Madam,' said Mr Trout, removing the hand for a moment, 'I am.'

'Did Percy bite you?'

'If Percy is the name of that homicidal hound, he did.'

'He probably thought you were the postman.'

'If he cannot tell the difference between me and a letter-carrier,' said Mr Trout, who could be terribly bitter when moved, 'he ought to consult a good oculist.'

It was at this point that Amelia Bingham suggested that he should come into the house and have his wounds dressed, and he followed her there. He was still in the grip of the righteous wrath which animates men who have been bitten by dogs to

267

whom they have not done a thing except address them as good boys and good old fellows, but gradually resentment gave way to kindlier feelings. It was impossible not to be soothed by contact with this woman. Very soon conversation was proceeding in the most amicable manner. Amelia Bingham said that Percy was a naughty dog, and Mr Trout said he had already formed that opinion.

'You're American, aren't you?' said Amelia Bingham. 'I thought so. It was your saying "letter-carrier" instead of postman. Tell me if this hurts,' she said, referring to the iodine which she was applying to his hand.

Mr Trout, his good humour completely restored, assured her that it did not. He also complimented her on the skill with which she was applying the bandage, and she said she had had a lot of practice.

'Bandaging letter-carriers?'

'Not very often, because Percy usually goes for their trousers. I meant at the hospital. I'm a hospital nurse.'

'Ah, that would account for it.'

'This is my day off. We get one a week at St Swithin's. Whereabouts in America do you come from?'

'California,' said Mr Trout with the reverence that always came into his voice when he spoke that name. 'My home is in Hollywood.'

'Oh, are you in the movies?'

'No, I am a lawyer.'

Amelia Bingham uttered a pleased cry.

'Then you can tell me if the woman next door has any right to throw her snails into my garden.'

'None whatever. Legally, snails are wild animals.'

'What ought I to do?'

'Throw them back.'

Amelia Bingham said he had taken a great weight off her mind, and Mr Trout said he was happy to have been able to be of service to her. Their relations were becoming more cordial every moment.

'Is it nice there?' Amelia Bingham asked.

'Where?'

268

'In California.'

'Very nice. California is generally described as the jewel state of the Union. Bathed in eternal sunshine, cooled by gentle breezes, it affords the ideal dwelling place for the stalwart men and fair women who inhabit it. Its noble movie houses, its spreading orange groves——'

'How about the earthquakes?'

Mr Trout, who had been waving his hands emotionally, stopped with them in mid-air as abruptly as if he had heard a director say 'Cut'. He stared like one who is having a difficulty in believing his ears.

'I beg your pardon?'

'Didn't you have a bad one some time ago?'

'You are thinking of the San Francisco fire of 1906.'

'Oh, it was a fire, was it?'

'A fire,' said Mr Trout firmly. 'Earthquakes are absolutely unknown in California.'

'One always gets these things wrong. There,' said Amelia Bingham. 'That ought to hold if you don't wave it too much. And now you must let me give you a cup of tea. You would like a cup of tea, wouldn't you?'

'It would be extremely refreshing,' said Mr Trout.

It was over the meal that he first realized that strange things were happening to him this afternoon, strange emotions stirring within him. His whole outlook seemed to have changed. As he watched his hostess sip her tea and tucked into the superlative scones which, he learned, were of her own baking, he became more and more convinced that for the last twenty years he had been proceeding on entirely wrong lines. In supposing that the bachelor's was the ideal life he had been guilty of a gross error. More and more clearly as the scones disappeared into his interior he saw that what the sensible man wanted was a wife and a home with scones like these always at his disposal. He had, in a word, like Romeo, Joe Pickering and other notabilities, fallen in love at first sight, and if any thought of Fred Basset, Johnny Runcible and G. J. Flannery came into his mind, he dismissed it without a qualm.

It seems to be a law of Nature that when a confirmed

bachelor falls in love, he does it with a wholeheartedness beyond the scope of the ordinary man who has been scattering his affections hither and thither since he was so high. As a child of eight Mr Trout had once kissed a girl of six under the mistletoe at a Christmas party, but there his sex life had come to an abrupt halt, with the result that for forty years passion had been banking up inside him like water in a dam. Sooner or later the dam was bound to burst, and his meeting with Amelia Bingham had brought this about. Quite suddenly he found himself abandoning all the principles of a lifetime. No longer the silver-tongued denouncer of love at whom the personnel of Bachelors Anonymous pointed with pride, he yearned for Amelia Bingham as harts are said to yearn for waterbrooks. If somebody had happened to come along at this moment bearing a sprig of mistletoe, he would have kissed her under it without hesitation.

'Delicious,' he said, swallowing the last scone. 'You really baked these yourself?'

'And made the strawberry jam.'

'Amazing. You must allow me to make some return for your hospitality. Could I persuade you to dine with me tonight?'

'I should love it.'

'I am staying at the Dorchester. Shall we dine there? At about seven-thirty?'

'Splendid.'

'Don't bring Percy with you,' said Mr Trout. 'Ha, ha,' he added, to show that this was whimsical humour.

'Ha, ha,' said Amelia Bingham.

'Ho, ho,' said Mr Trout.

He made a mental note to get his hair trimmed and to have a manicure and a shampoo.

Chapter Ten

THE LATE AFTERNOON of the day on which love had come to Mr Trout found Ivor Llewellyn in the best of spirits. His intention of putting a stick of dynamite beneath the pants of his London employees had been amply fulfilled; the cook he had engaged was proving excellent; a transatlantic telephone call to the studio had assured him that all was going well there in his absence; and he had not heard a word from Vera Dalrymple. Providence, he felt, was going out of its way to make things pleasant for a good man.

It was the last item on this list that set the seal on his well-being. As the days went by, he had become more and more alive to the perils inseparable from association with Miss Dalrymple. Twice since their first meeting he had come within a hair's breadth of proposing marriage to her, and only the merest chance had averted disaster. Once a table-hopping friend of hers had interrupted him as the fatal words were trembling on his lips; on the other occasion he had been saved by a sudden attack of hiccups, giving him time to reflect while the waiter was patting him on the back.

But he knew that luck like this could not last if he continued to see her, and the fact that there had been no communication on her part put new heart into him. At their last dinner together he had been appalled to notice her close resemblance to the more recent of his wives, and the thought that she had ceased to be a menace was very comforting.

He had been musing thus for some little time, when the sound of the front-door bell broke in on his reverie. He rose and went to answer it. Doing so, he recognized, involved a risk, but it had to be taken, for it might be his friend Trout who had rung. He was particularly anxious to see Trout. Trout would support his view that in his dealings with Vera

Dalrymple he was proceeding on the right lines; and however confident he may be that he has outgeneralled a woman, a man likes to have reassurance on the point from a knowledgeable third party.

It was his friend Trout, but a very different Trout from the Trout of the previous night; a Trout glowing from head to foot and quite capable of doing buck-and-wing dances on the door mat. Even in repose he seemed on the verge of one of those soft-shoe Shuffle-off-to-Buffalo forms of self-expression which used to be so popular in American vaudeville. He twitched, and his feet pawed the carpet like those of some mettlesome steed.

These phenomena passed unnoticed by Mr Llewellyn. It is never easy to detect molten passion from outside, particularly if you are rather self-centred, as he was. Trout to him, whether a-glow or with his inner light turned off, was just Trout. He said he was glad to see him and hoped that he could dine with him, and Mr Trout said he already had a dinner date. Sherlock Holmes, had he been present, would have drawn conclusions from the tremor in his voice as he spoke, but it made no impression on Mr Llewellyn. If he thought anything about it, he merely assumed that Mr Trout was suffering from catarrh.

'I can only stop a minute,' said Mr Trout. 'I'm on my way to get my hair trimmed. I just looked in to have a word with young Pickering.'

'What about?'

'Oh, just something I have to tell him. Nice boy, Pickering. We spent the afternoon together.'

'Doing what?'

'Chasing girls in taxi cabs.'

'I thought you didn't go in for that sort of thing.'

'As a rule no, but Pickering made a point of it.'

'Damn fool. Playing with fire.'

'Would you say that?'

'Yes, I would say that. If that's the way he's going to carry on, he'll be married before he knows what's hit him.'

Mr Trout forbore to comment on this sentiment. Lawyers

learn to be diplomatic, and he could see that the subject had begun to annoy his friend.

'You didn't tell me if Pickering was in,' he said.

'No, he went out for a walk, looking like a rainy Sunday in Pittsburgh. Why he was looking like that he didn't explain.'

'It's his love life, I.L. It's come a stinker.'

'He doesn't know his luck.'

A spasm of pain passed over Mr Trout's face, as if he had been a curate compelled to listen to blasphemy from his vicar. Pursuing his policy of being diplomatic, he said nothing on the subject but in between two dance steps asked if Mr Llewellyn happened to know the name of the girl to whom Joe Pickering had given his heart.

'Sure,' said Mr Llewellyn. 'She interviewed me for her paper. It's Fitch. Did you ever hear a song of Cole Porter's—Mister and Mrs Fitch?'

'No.'

'Good song. I often sing it in my bath.'

'Indeed? I would like to hear it.'

'You must drop in some morning. About half-past nine would be the best time. Bring a raincoat, as I splash about a good deal. It's one of those songs that need putting over with gestures.'

Mr Llewellyn paused. Mr Trout had begun to float about the room like something out of Swan Lake, and Mr Llewellyn disapproved of this. He was apt to be a martinet in his dealings with his legal advisers, demanding that lawyers should behave like lawyers and leave eccentric dancing to the professionals. A man, he held, is either Fred Astaire or he is not Fred Astaire, and if he is not Fred Astaire he should not carry on like him. For the first time it struck him that there was an oddness in Mr Trout this evening, as if he on honeydew had fed and drunk the milk of Paradise, and he did not pay him a substantial annual retainer for doing that.

There was abruptness in his voice as he said:

'Why do you want the girl's name?'

'I shall be calling on her shortly, and I'd like to know who to ask for. She lives, I understand, at Fountain Court, Park

Lane. It is my intention to see her and effect a reconciliation between her and Pickering. I don't like the thought of two loving hearts being parted by a misunderstanding. Who do you think I am? Thomas Hardy?'

Mr Llewellyn was now definitely perplexed. He could make nothing of this. Mr Trout's diction was beautifully clear, leaving no possibility that he could have mistaken what he said, but his words did not appear to make sense. He would have scorched him with a rebuking glare if Mr Trout had stayed still long enough for it to reach its target, but had to content himself with projecting a rebuking glare in his general direction.

'Trout,' he said, 'have you had a couple?'

'Certainly not.'

'Then why are you talking this apple sauce about loving hearts? Last night——'

He did not complete the sentence. The telephone was ringing.

'Answer that, Trout,' said Mr Llewellyn. 'If it's for me, say I'm out.'

Mr Trout went to the instrument, and the first words he uttered caused Mr Llewellyn to stiffen from head to foot like a nymph surprised while bathing, for they were 'Good evening, madam', and they froze him to the marrow. Warmly he congratulated himself on his prudence in telling Mr Trout to answer the call. London, of course, was full of those who might be addressed as 'Madam', but he could think of only one. To only one, moreover, he had given his telephone number. He feared the worst. It appalled him to think how nearly he had come to kidding back and forth with Vera Dalrymple, a course which could not but have ended in disaster. He waited breathlessly for Mr Trout to say he was out.

'I am afraid,' said Mr Trout in his polished manner, 'that he is not at home at the moment, but he should be returning shortly, and I will not fail to give him your message. I am sure he will be delighted. Not at all,' said Mr Trout, apparently in answer to some expression of thanks at the other end. 'A pleasure. Good-bye, madam, good-bye. What lovely weather

274

we are having, are we not? A Miss Dalrymple,' he said, hanging up. 'She wants you to give her dinner the day after tomorrow. She will be calling for you at about seven-thirty.'

Mr Llewellyn was staring dumbly, as Tennyson's Lady of Shalott might have stared when the mirror cracked from side to side and the curse had come upon her. Indeed, if the Lady of Shalott had entered at this moment, he would have slapped her on the back and told her he knew just how she felt.

'And . . . you . . . told . . . her . . . you . . . were . . . sure . . . I . . . would . . . be . . . delighted!' he whispered.

Having said this, he was silent for a space, wrestling with his feelings. He was wondering how he had ever looked on Ephraim Trout as a friend and resolving, as soon as he could get around to it, to transfer his legal affairs from his hands and place them in those of Jones, Jukes, Jerningham and Jenkinson. Would Jones, he reasoned, have told Vera Dalrymple that he would be delighted to give her dinner? Would Jukes? Not a chance. Nor would Jenkinson and Jerningham. And this was a man who prided himself on belonging to Bachelors Anonymous. It was enough to make one ask oneself what things were coming to. It is not too much to say that Mr Llewellyn was stricken to the core.

Men who are stricken to the core react in one of two ways. They rave and curse—this was the method preferred by King Lear—all that Blow, winds, and crack your cheeks stuff—or a sort of frozen calm comes over them as if their circulation had been suspended. It was to the latter school that Mr Llewellyn belonged. He might become irritable over trifles, but in serious crises he was a block of ice. On the occasion when Weinstein-Colossal had stolen two of his best stars nobody could have guessed from his demeanour the volcanic fury that was surging within him. So now he said almost gently:

'You told her I would be delighted, did you? Do you realize that if I give this woman dinner, I shall almost certainly ask her to marry me?'

'And you couldn't do better,' said Mr Trout heartily. 'I have not had the pleasure of meeting her, but I assume that she is charming, and the thing that matters is to get married. Who was it described bachelors as wild asses of the desert? I forget, but he was right, and what future is there for a wild ass? Practically none. It just goes on being a wild ass until something happens to end its aimless existence, and nobody cares a damn when it's gone. You're crazy if you intend to go on being a lonely bachelor, not that I suppose one could actually call you a bachelor. Marriage is the only road to contentment and happiness. Think of the quiet home evenings, she busy knitting the tiny garments, you in the old armchair with your crossword puzzle. Think of the companionship, the feeling that you are never going to be alone again. Get married, I.L. Give this Dalrymple dinner tomorrow and over the meal attach yourself to her little hand and ask her to be yours. Excuse me,' said Mr Trout. 'I must be going. I have to get a shampoo and manicure in addition to the hair-trim.'

The effect of this eloquence on Mr Llewellyn was to add to the emotions of the Lady of Shalott those of Julius Caesar when stabbed by Brutus. We can put up with the knavish tricks of enemies—we may not like them, but we can endure them—but when we are betrayed by a friend we drain the bitter cup and no heeltaps. The one thing Mr Llewellyn had been sure he could rely on was the stability of the Trout doctrine. Whoever else might fail him, Trout was a solid rock. And here he was, mouthing these dreadful sentiments without, apparently, a qualm. He could not have been more horrified and in the depths if he had been a Tory member of Parliament and had heard his Leader expressing the opinion that there was a lot of sound sense in the works of Karl Marx, and the Communists were not such bad chaps if you got to know them.

We have said that in moments of crisis Mr Llewellyn always preserved an outward calm, but that was intended to apply only to ordinary crises. In one of this magnitude he could not be expected to keep dismay from showing in his appearance. When Mr Trout had left him, his trepidation was unmistakable. He sat motionless in his chair looking like something the cat had brought in. Even such a man, so faint, so spiritless, so dull, so dead in look, so woebegone, drew

276

Priam's curtain at the dead of night and would have told him half his Troy was burned.

It was thus that Joe, returning from his walk, found him, and it is greatly to his credit that one glance at that haggard face told him that his own troubles must be shelved for the time being and all his faculties concentrated on those of his employer.

'Good Lord,' he said. 'What's the matter?'

In broken accents Mr Llewellyn started to fill him in, as he would have put it, but the accents were not so broken as to render Joe incapable of following the scenario. Having the advantage of knowing Miss Dalrymple, he was able to appreciate without difficulty the emotions of anyone who found himself in danger of marrying her, and he would have clasped Mr Llewellyn's hand, had not the latter been waving it. Very clearly he saw that now was the time for all good men to come to the aid of the party.

'I don't like this,' he said.

'Well, you don't suppose *I* do,' said Mr Llewellyn.

'But what I don't understand is why you have to ask her to marry you. Surely there are other things you can talk about at dinner. The weather, books, the situation in China, the prospects of a general election.'

Mr Llewellyn uttered an impatient snort.

'I explained that to you very clearly the day we met, but I see that I shall have to do it again. The first thing you have to grasp is that I am a man of intense sensitiveness and spirituality. Got that into your nut? I can't hurt people's feelings. Do you understand that, or are you as big a damned fool as you look? Well then, I take her to dinner. At first everything's all right. We get through the soup, fish and whatever it may be without disaster because she's biding her time, and then we come to the coffee. Coffee's the danger spot. There is a pause in the conversation.'

'Why?'

'Because she's preparing to unmask her batteries. She is sitting with a sort of faraway look on her face. She heaves a sigh. She says what a lonely life hers is and how hollow success

277

is and how the applause of her public can never make up for not having a home. Upon which, I ask her to marry me. It's something to say. It's put me off coffee for life. All my marriages came about like that, even Bernadine Friganza, who wouldn't have recognized a home if you had brought her one on a plate with watercress around it.'

'And they never refuse you?'

'Of course not. Who would?'

Joe pondered. What with his sensitiveness and spirituality this man was plainly an object for concern. He could see but one solution of his problem.

'You mustn't take Vera Dalrymple to dinner.'

'How can I get out of it? She's calling for me the day after tomorrow at seven-thirty.'

'You mustn't be here.'

'Where else can I be?'

'In hospital.'

'In *what*?'

'Hospital. You'll be safe there.'

Again Mr Llewellyn snorted. If Joe had been making a suggestion at a studio conference, he could not have snorted more vehemently.

'And how do I get into a hospital? What do you propose that I shall do? Get run over by a taxi cab? Chew soap and pretend I'm having a fit?'

'Tell them you want a check-up. You probably need one anyway.'

The fire faded from Mr Llewellyn's eyes. The snort was silent on his lips. He regarded Joe with the admiration of a fond father whose infant son has spoken his first word.

'Pickering,' he said, 'I believe you've got something. She couldn't get at me in hospital.'

'Only on visiting days.'

'Between stated hours.'

'With nurses coming in and out all the time.'

'Exactly.'

'Watch out for the grapes, of course.'

'I don't get you.'

278

'She will bring you grapes. You don't want them to lead to anything.'

'I'll tell the doctor my doctor has forbidden them.'

'Because you're subject to appendicitis.'

'Exactly. Pickering, you're a marvel.'

'Awfully nice of you to say so.'

'And do you know what I'm going to do?'

'Keep off the grapes.'

'That of course, but in addition I'm going to make a picture of that play of yours. That's what I'm going to do. Presence of mind like yours deserves a rich reward.'

Chapter Eleven

IN ACCENTS AS BROKEN as those of Mr Llewellyn—on these emotional occasions it is rarely that an accent escapes unbroken—Joe expressed his gratitude and gratification, and Mr Llewellyn repeated the statement he had made at their first meeting, that *Cousin Angela*, while he did not expect it to be great, or even colossal, would make a good picture. It would, he pointed out, not be handicapped, as the play had been, by having Vera Dalrymple in it. Miss Dalrymple, he said, had dropped several hints that she was open to consider a Hollywood contract, but, he added, any time he let loose that sinister menace in the neighbourhood of Beverly Hills you could write him down as one who needed to have his head examined.

'And now to pack,' he said.

'Pack?' said Joe.

'A few necessaries—toothbrush, razor, shaving cream, pyjamas and a couple of Agatha Christies. I'm off to hospital.'

'But you can't just walk into a hospital. You have to be sent there by a doctor.'

'Where did you hear that?'

'Everybody knows it.'

'I didn't,' said Mr Llewellyn discontentedly. 'Do you mean I won't be able to get in till tomorrow? Then I'll have to go to a hotel for the night. I'm not going to stay here wondering when Vera Dalrymple will ring that front-door bell. I wouldn't sleep a wink.'

'She said she wasn't coming till the day after tomorrow.'

'Just her subtle cunning. Lulling me into a false security.'

It was with mixed feelings that Joe escorted his benefactor to the door. At one moment the realization that the waving of Mr Llewellyn's magic wand was about to place him in the sound financial position of which he had so often dreamed elated him; at the next he was cast into the depths by the thought that, however much money he made from the motion picture sale of *Cousin Angela*, the odds on his being able to share it with the girl he loved could scarcely be quoted at better than a hundred to eight. Indeed, taking into consideration her policy of refusing to speak to him, a shrewd turf accountant would probably make them even longer.

Sally's behaviour bewildered him. He could understand his non-appearance at the dinner table causing a certain annoyance, but the fact of her not giving him a chance to explain was beyond his comprehension. It piqued him, too, that such a splendid explanation should be going to waste. If there is one excuse for failing to keep a tryst that is beyond the reach of criticism, it is surely sudden illness.

That sudden illness perplexed Joe. His health had always been perfect, never more so than when Mr Trout was handing him the beaker. The reflection that in next to no time he would be seated opposite Sally in Barribault's grill room, with the lights down low and the fiddler of whom Mr Llewellyn disapproved so much straining at the leash and all ready to give of his best, had sent a shiver down his spine and filled him with what the French in their peculiar way call *bien être*. An unfortunate moment to be struck by lightning, as he apparently had been.

It was very quiet in the flat, and it was not long before the silence began to prey on Joe's nerves. A man whose spirits are as low as his yearns for companionship. A dog, even a dog like Mrs Bingham's Percy, might have helped, but 8 Enniston Gardens contained no dog. In a sudden flash of inspiration Joe thought of Jerry Nichols.

It was in not too sanguine a frame of mind that he went to the telephone and dialled his number. If Jerry had a defect, it was that his attitude towards the other sex was frivolous. He was not one of the Joe Pickerings, whose hearts when once bestowed are given for ever. He was one of those volatile young men who take on a wide field in the way of female society, and was apt to count that day lost when he did not entertain what he described as a popsy at the evening meal. The cocktail hour being now imminent, it was more than probable that his time would be spoken for.

And so it proved. In answer to Joe's invitation he was compelled to proclaim himself unavailable.

'Sorry, Joe. I've got a date.'

'Can't you put her off?'

'It isn't her, it's Father. He likes me to hob-nob with him once in a while, and tonight happens to be the while it's a once in.'

'Oh hell.'

'Why the dismay? Surely you can do without me for one night. Clench the teeth. It only needs willpower.'

'I want your advice about something.'

'Oh, that's different. I'm always eager to give advice. I'll tell you what I'll do. Father always goes to sleep after feeding owing to plentiful doses of old port and he dines on the stroke of dusk. I'll steal away and come and see you.'

Joe returned to his solitary brooding. He was soon obsessed with the idea that only through Jerry could his problem be solved. After all, he felt, a man so given to mingling with popsies must often have come up against a problem similar to his and would have been taught by experience how to handle it. By the time Mr Trout arrived Joe's mental attitude towards Jerry had become that of a disciple towards a sage or seer.

The advent of Mr Trout came on him as a surprise. He had not been warned that he would be calling, and he was not at all sure that he was glad to see him. He would have welcomed him with more pleasure if there had been in his demeanour a decent melancholy, for in his current mood the last thing he wanted to see about him was smiling faces, and a single glance told him that here was somebody who was sitting on a pink cloud with a rainbow round his shoulder. Mr Trout had not yet burst into song with a hey-nonny-nonny and a hot-cha-cha, but when you said that you had said everything.

'Oh, hullo,' he mumbled.

'Good evening, good evening, good evening,' said Mr Trout. He might have been one of a comedy duo billed as The Sunshine Boys, good dressers on and off. 'How lovely the world looks in the gloaming. London becomes a veritable fairyland. One is reminded of the words of the poet, which I have forgotten at the moment, but they are very beautiful. Is Llewellyn in?'

'No, he went out.'

'All for the best. I'm glad. Because I want to talk to you privately, Pickering. In the cab this afternoon I let fall some observations on the subject of love and marriage which I now regret.'

'Oh, did you?'

'I did, though apparently you were not listening. I expressed myself very strongly as disapproving of them. My views have since become radically altered. I am now wholeheartedly in their favour. It is love that makes the world go round, I am now convinced. I remember a song, popular many years ago, entitled "Love me and the world is mine". That's the spirit, Pickering, that's the spirit. An admirable sentiment.'

Joe was looking at him with a wild surmise. Had his diction not been so clear and his lower limbs so firm, he would, like Mr Llewellyn, have entertained doubts of his sobriety. As it was, he merely gaped, hoping that footnotes would be supplied later.

'Well, that's fine,' he said.

'"Fine" is the word, Pickering.'

'But you were saying that you had something private to talk to me about.'

'And I have, I have indeed. But in order to make my story intelligible to you I shall have to give an account of my life up to this afternoon. A brief account,' he added, seeing Joe wince. 'Just an outline.'

'Omitting childhood, boyhood and college days?'

'Precisely. The periods you mention are not of the essence. We move directly to my mature manhood.'

'That's good.'

'When I became a member of Bachelors Anonymous.'

'Alcoholics Anonymous?'

'*Bachelors* Anonymous. A little group of men whose aim in

life it is to avoid getting married. We strain every nerve to preserve our celibacy, and if we hear of a fellow-member weakening, we plead with him to be strong. We even have a song which we sing on these occasions. "Of all the ills with which we're cursed the married state is far the worst", it begins. I could sing it to you, if you wish.'

'Some other time, do you think?'

'Any time that suits you. It's a catchy little thing.'

'I'll bet.'

'Lyric by Johnny Runcible, music by G. J. Flannery.'

Joe stirred uneasily. Mr Trout had not given any formal promise not to sing, and there was no knowing when he might not do it. He shrank from having to listen on an empty stomach. To divert his companion's attention and prevent this becoming a musical evening he put a question.

'Has all this anything to do with me? It's all absorbingly interesting, but where do I come in?'

'I am about to tell you. But first I must reveal that I am no longer a member of Bachelors Anonymous. I cabled my resignation on my way here. I am afraid the boys will be terribly upset, but I had no option. As I told you, my views have undergone a radical change. It happened down at Valley Fields this afternoon. It was there that love found me, Pickering. I met a woman who taught me the meaning of passion.'

Joe's bewilderment increased. He could think of but one female resident of Valley Fields.

'Not the woman with X-ray eyes who talked about fleshly lusts and told me the Kingdom of Heaven was at hand?'

'I was too far off to hear what she told you, and in addition the cabman was telling me how wet weather always brings on his lumbago. But no, she was not the one. The divine creature to whom I allude is a Mrs Amelia Bingham who lives next door.'

Joe pursed his lips. He was shocked.

'*Mrs?* Trout,' he said severely, 'are you breaking up a home?'

'No, no, no, no, no.'

'Are you a modern Casanova?'

'Certainly not. Mrs Bingham is a widow. Her late husband fell overboard on a day excursion to Boulogne.'

There was a momentary silence while their thoughts dwelled on Mr Bingham, deceased.

'She bakes the most wonderful scones,' said Mr Trout.

'Oh?' said Joe.

'And her strawberry jam has to be tasted to be believed.'

'Oh?'

'You will notice that I have a bandage on my hand. Her dog bit me and she bound me up.'

'Oh?'

'With extraordinary skill. She is a hospital nurse.'

Joe rose once more to a point of order.

'All this may be so, but I don't see where I get into the act.'

'I beg your pardon?'

'What has all this got to do with me?'

'I am coming to that. I have merely been laying the foundation for my apology. What we call in the Law connecting up. If I had never met Mrs Bingham and ceased to be a member of Bachelors Anonymous, I should not have felt compelled to apologize to you.'

'What's all this about apologizing? Apologizing for what?'

'For putting that Mickey Finn in your highball yesterday.'

In one of her early novels Rosie M. Banks has a passage in which she described the reactions of Claude Delamere, the hero, on becoming aware that the girl to whom he was betrothed had not, as he had supposed, been deceiving him. (It was her brother from Australia he had seen her kissing.) He felt, she says, as if a blinding light had flashed upon him. It was much the same with Joe Pickering as he heard these words. But whereas Claude had been filled with a joy that threatened to unman him, he was as sore as a sunburned neck and as mad as a hornet. So intense was his righteous wrath that he could not speak, merely standing there making a noise like the death rattle of an expiring soda syphon, and Mr Trout proceeded.

'Yes, I do feel I owe you an apology, though I must claim to have had some excuse for acting as I did. You had spoken of the girl with the utmost enthusiasm, you were taking her to dinner, you had had a manicure and a shampoo. Naturally it seemed to a lifelong member of Bachelors Anonymous that there was no time to be lost and that only Method B would serve. I was actuated by motives of the purest altruism. I felt I had a mission to save you from yourself. I pictured you thanking me later with tears in your eyes. How could I know that I was going to meet Mrs Bingham and see the light? I can only say I'm sorry. But as a matter of fact no harm has been done. All you have to do is go to the girl and explain. You will probably have a good laugh together. Bless my soul,' said Mr Trout, looking at his watch. 'Is that the time? I must rush.' And he was gone.

But any shortage of Trouts was compensated for an hour later by the arrival of Jerry Nichols, who announced that his father had fallen asleep much more promptly than usual, thus enabling him to be at Joe's service with the minimum of delay.

'What seems to be the trouble?' he asked.

It did not take Joe long to inform him. The basic facts were readily tabulated. He loved a girl, and she would not speak to him. Jerry agreed that this was a disagreeable state of affairs.

'Who is this girl?'

'Sally Fitch. You've met her. She came to see you that day I was in your office about the Llewellyn job.'

'Oh, the heiress.'

'The what?'

'We had asked her to call because somebody had left her twenty-five thousand pounds.'

'What!'

'Didn't you know?'

'Of course I didn't. Good Lord, Jerry, do you think she thinks I do know and am after her for her money?'

'Impossible. Any girl with an ounce of sense could see that you aren't that sort of chap. Rugged honesty, that's you. It sticks out all over you. No, it must be something you've done. Have you done something?'

'Yes, but I can explain.'

'Tell me all.'

'I asked her to dinner and didn't show up. Naturally this would have annoyed her, but you'd think she would let me explain. But she won't.'

'Your explanation being——?'

'That just as I was starting out for the restaurant somebody gave me a Mickey Finn.'

'Somebody what?'

'Gave me a Mickey Finn. You know what a Mickey Finn is.'

A rather careworn look had come into Jerry's face. It was plain that he was having difficulty in becoming equal to the intellectual pressure of the conversation.

'I think you had better tell me the Pickering Story from the beginning, Joe. At the moment a bit abstruse it strikes me as.'

Joe told it to him from the beginning, and Jerry listened with growing understanding.

'You're quite right,' he said at its conclusion. 'You can certainly explain. I don't mind telling you that there have been times in my life when I've wished I had as good an explanation as that. We must call on this Fitch first thing tomorrow.'

'But she won't see me.'

'She'll see you all right. The lay-out is as follows. We go to her address, we ring the bell, the door is opened and we slide in, and there we are. I say "we" because I shall be at your side. You then tell her about the Mickey Finn. Good?'

'Perfect.'

'Not so good,' said Jerry. 'Because on seeing you crossing the threshold she would break into a spring and go and lock herself in the bathroom. Obviously you mustn't be there. I will go and see her and report to you if the All Clear has been blown. I say " if ", for we must never lose sight of the fact that the explanation of yours takes a lot of believing. It needs someone like myself to put it over.'

Chapter Twelve

AT TIMES WHEN one's affairs have become tangled, causing the brow to develop furrows and the soul to ask itself 'Where do we go from here?', it is always a comfort to place oneself in the hands of a recognized expert and allow him to carry on. Householders feel a new hope when something has gone wrong with the pipes and the plumber arrives, and the thought that Jerry, a man accustomed to coping with popsies since he was a slip of a boy, had taken over the difficult negotiations with Sally brought a new hope to Joe Pickering. It was in quite cheerful mood that he rose from the breakfast table next morning to answer the telephone. Before he had enlisted Jerry's aid his 'Hullo?' would have been a low faint 'Hullo?', almost a gurgle. Now it had quite a ring.

'Hoy!' said the telephone. 'Pickering?'

'Oh, hullo, Mr Llewellyn. Are you in the hospital?'

'Sure I'm in the hospital. St Swithin's.'

'Everything all right?'

'More or less. Hell of a lot of noise going on all the time. There's a contraption outside my room which keeps bellowing "Doctor Binns, Doctor Binns" every two minutes. What it wants Doctor Binns for I don't know. Probably to tell him a funny story. But that's not what I called up about. It suddenly occurred to me that the man Trout might come and ask you where I was. On no account tell him. The first thing he would do would be to run bleating to the Dalrymple pot of poison and spill the beans, and half an hour after that she would be round here with grapes and kind inquiries.'

'But he doesn't know where she lives.'

'He would find out. A man like Trout can find out anything. So don't breathe a word.'

'My lips are sealed.'

'Your hips are what?'

'Not hips, lips. I said they were sealed.'

'Keep them that way.'

A brief pause in the conversation took place at this point. A confused roaring noise, as of lions at feeding time, came over the wire. Then Mr Llewellyn spoke again.

'Pickering.'

'On the spot.'

'That was a girl in short skirts and a white thungummy on the back of her head who wanted a sample of my blood. I very soon told her where she got off. "I don't give samples of my blood to every Tom, Dick and Harry who comes asking for them," I said.'

'Only to personal friends?'

'Exactly. She didn't know which way to look. What were we talking about?'

'Mr Trout.'

'Don't call him Mister Trout. The hellhound Trout or Trout the traitor, if you like, but not a term of respect like Mister. Personally, it gives me a sinking feeling even to think of him. Ever hear of Benedict Arnold?'

'I've read about him.'

'Trout's name ought to have been that.'

'Don't you mean his name ought to have been Trout?'

'Do I?'

'I think so.'

'Perhaps you're right. But why you want to keep babbling on about a human gumboil like Trout I can't imagine.'

'Sorry.'

'What?'

'I said I was sorry.'

'Then don't do it again.'

'I won't. How do you like it in hospital?'

'Might be worse. All right for a visit, but I wouldn't live there if you gave me the place.'

'Nice nurse?'

'Ah, there you have said a mouthful, Pickering. I have a Grade A nurse.'

289

'Splendid.'

'The very word for her. Not one of your juvenile delinquents who bust in on you wanting samples of your blood, but a sensible comfortable middle-aged woman in her forties. We get on like a couple of sailors on shore leave. Well, go to hell now, Pickering; I'm expecting the doctor. Remember about Benedict Arnold Trout.'

'I won't forget.'

'Not a word if he comes inquiring as to my whereabouts.'

An old joke about them being at the wash flitted into Joe's mind, but he let it go. He was feeling better than he had been feeling, but not so much better as to allow him to indulge in light persiflage of that nature.

The upward trend in his spirits did not last. Despondency returned and grew, for the afternoon, though bringing callers of various descriptions including an optimist who hoped to sell richly bound and illustrated sets of Dumas on the easy payment system, did not bring Jerry Nichols. The evening was well advanced before he appeared.

'Well, you've taken your time,' said Joe.

Jerry dismissed the slur with a wave of the hand not unlike one of Mr Llewellyn's gestures when singing 'Mister and Mrs Fitch' in his bath.

'I came as soon as I could,' he said. 'I would have thought that you, being in the same line of business yourself until recently, would have been familiar with the iron discipline which prevails in a solicitor's office. If Father had caught me sneaking off before closing time, it would have made no difference that I was his son, I would have been marched off into a hollow square of clerks and office boys and had my buttons snipped off, or probably something even worse. You remember what happened to Danny Deever in the morning.'

Joe had to admit the justice of this. The head of Nichols, Erridge, Trubshaw and Nichols might take a nap after dinner now and then, but in the daytime his vigilance would have been that of the keenest-eyed type of lynx. He apologized, and Jerry begged him not to mention it. He was accustomed to being misjudged, he said. He would now, he added, proceed to make his report, a statement which brought Joe up in his chair as if a sharp instrument had come through his seat.

'Did you see her?'

'No.'

'Why not?'

'She wasn't there. A girl doesn't stay indoors all day. She has things to do which take her out from time to time. Let me tell you the whole story, omitting no detail however slight. I got to Fountain Court and rang the bell. All straight so far?' he said rather unnecessarily, and Joe said he had found no difficulty in following the narrative up to this point. Seeming pleased with his intelligence, Jerry resumed.

'The door was opened by a rather personable popsy, who proved to be a girl who lives with the Fitch. She informed me that the Fitch was at the hair stylist's having a permanent. "You had better look in later," she said. "There's a man called Trout waiting to see her." Well, I wasn't going to have that, of course. "Later be blowed," I said. "I have to see Miss Fitch on a matter of the utmost urgency, the nature of which I am not empowered to divulge. I'm jolly well coming in, and if Trout objects, I'll scatter him to the four winds." "Suit yourself," she said. "It's a free country," and she buzzed off, and I went on into the living-room where, as foreshadowed, I found Trout.'

'Trout', said Joe meditatively.

'That was the name.'

'I wonder what he wanted.'

'He told me that. His mission was the same as mine. He had come to tell Miss Fitch that he was the bloke who had given you that Mickey Finn which had caused your non-appearance at the dinner table.'

'My God!'

'Precisely. With your quick intelligence you have spotted that the coming clean of Trout is the one thing that was needed to extricate you from the soup in which you are wallowing. It gives verisimilitude to an otherwise bald and unconvincing narrative. I go to her and say "Hullo there, Miss Fitch, I'll bet you've been wondering why Joe asked you to dinner and didn't turn up. The matter is readily explained. Somebody gave him a Mickey Finn'', and it carries little or no conviction. But it's very different when Trout, tapping his chest, says "*I dun it.*" She swallows his story whole and asks for more.'

'Of course!'

'It's what we lawyers call the best evidence. The other sort is incompetent, irrelevant and immaterial and doesn't get you anywhere. I decided, accordingly, to come away and leave it to Trout to do the talking, though sorry not to see Miss Fitch again, for she had impressed me very favourably that time she came to my office. Nice girl.'

'How long does a permanent take?'

'I don't know. I've never had one. But I see what's in your mind. You're wondering if she'll be back by now. Probably, I should think.'

'Then I'll be moving along. And thanks for all you've done, Jerry.'

'A pleasure, old man, a pleasure. Not that I've done much. But, as I often say, it's the Boy Scout spirit that counts. Oh, one last word, Have you given any thought to what happens when you and she meet?'

'We talk things over, I suppose.'

'Talk things over be blowed. Don't waste time chatting. Get immediate action. Skip the red tape. Grab her, fold her in a close embrace and hug her till her ribs squeak. I have tried this policy on several occasions, and I have always found it to give the best results.'

2

London looked very beautiful to Joe as he drove to Fountain Court. Mr Trout had described it as a veritable fairyland, and he had been, Joe thought, pretty accurate. The streets were full of delightful-looking people with whom he was sure he would have got on splendidly if he had only had time to stop and fraternize. The dogs, too, taking the air on leashes. He would have liked, had speed not been so important, to have got out and passed the time of day with all of them and with the cats as well, if there had been any. He was, in a word, feeling in mid-season form and getting more so every minute.

As he drove, he mused on Mr Trout, and thought what a capital fellow he was. If that was the sort of man California produced, one could understand it being known as the Jewel State of the Union. A purist might shake his head at the old gentleman's practice of introducing foreign substances into people's drinks, but that was a negligible flaw in an otherwise saintly character, and how superbly he made amends when he considered the time had come for making them. Remorse gripped Joe as he thought how churlishly he had denied Mr Trout the pleasure of telling him all about his childhood, boyhood and college days and singing him the Bachelors Anonymous theme song.

It was Mr Trout who opened the door of 3A Fountain Court to him. One might have supposed that, having said his say, he would have left the premises, but Mr Trout was one of those men who do not leave premises. They stay on, waiting to see what is going to happen next.

They conversed in the hall.

'You've told her?' said Joe urgently.

Mr Trout said he had, and might have added that Joe could have guessed as much from his beaming countenance.

Pausing only to say 'At-a-boy', Joe asked how she had taken it.

'She wept.'

'*Wept?*'

'Tears of joy. She was overjoyed, Pickering. It was obvious that a great weight had been lifted from her mind and that the sun had—'

'Come smiling through?'

'The very phrase I was about to employ. It made me feel very happy, Pickering, to think that I had been instrumental in joining two sundered hearts together. Strange how one's views can change, as it were in a flash. It seems only yesterday, in fact it was only yesterday, that I thought the great thing with sundered hearts was to keep them sundered.'

'So you think everything's all right?'

'Everything is perfect. True, she is engaged to be married to somebody else, but she is extremely fond of you. It showed clearly in her manner.'

The effect of these words on Joe was somewhat similar to that which would have been produced by a blow on the bridge of the nose by a wet fish. His jaw fell. His eyes bulged. He tottered and might have fallen had he not clutched at the umbrella stand.

'Engaged to someone else?' he quavered.

'Yes. Owing, I gathered, to a regrettable misunderstanding. You asked her to lunch, and she was prevented by circumstances over which she had no control from putting in an appearance. When subsequently you asked her to dinner and in your turn did not put in an appearance, she assumed that you had done it to punish her, and being a girl of spirit she resented it. So when this man asked her to marry him, she accepted him by way of evening the score. The whole affair has in it something of the inevitability of Greek tragedy.'

'And it wouldn't have happened,' said Joe bitterly, removing a hand from the umbrella stand and waving it, 'if you didn't go about the place giving people Mickey Finns.'

A faint blush mantled Mr Trout's cheek.

'Yes,' he said, 'I suppose that is in a measure true. But you must remember that I thought I was acting in your best interests. And fortunately no harm has been done.'

'No harm?'

'I am convinced that you have only to fold her in a close embrace and she will forget all about this other man to whom she has rashly become affianced. Those tears of joy told the story. Fold her in a close embrace, and all will be well.'

Joe was impressed. Had this advice come solely from Mr Trout, he might have ignored it, reasoning that a veteran member of Bachelors Anonymous could scarcely be accepted as a fount of wisdom where feminine psychology was concerned. But Jerry Nichols had said the same thing, and Jerry was a man who knew. Any theory promulgated by him must have been tested a dozen times and proved correct.

The strong-arm methods favoured by both counsellors

might, of course, be resented, for he had no official knowledge that his love was returned. Nevertheless, he was resolved to put his fate to the touch to win or lose it all, as recommended by the poet Montrose. The phrase 'Nothing venture, nothing have' occurred to him. At the worst, if she drew herself to her full height and said 'Sir!' he would have kissed her and would have that memory to cheer him up in the long lonely winter evenings. Even if given time for only two or three kisses, he would be that much ahead of the game.

'Is she in there?' he said, indicating the door of the sitting-room.

'No,' said Mr Trout. 'When I had told my story, she went off in a cab.'

'What on earth for?'

'To see you, of course. Little knowing that you were on your way to see *her*. Quite an amusing little mix-up,' said Mr Trout.

And as he spoke a key clicked in the door.

3

A key clicking in a door is one of London's smaller sounds, not to be compared for volume to the thousand others which enliven life in that city, but the click of this one could not have arrested Joe's attention more immediately if it had been the explosion of a bomb. He quivered in every limb, and when the door opened and Sally entered he was about to leap forward and fold her in a close embrace, when she leaped forward and folded *him* in one, at the same time saying 'Oh, Joe, Joe, Joe!' It was plain that she, like Jerry, believed in skipping red tape and proceeding at once to the direct action which speaks so much louder than words.

'Oh, Joe!' said Sally.

'Oh, Sally!' said Joe.

'I've been feeling awful,' said Sally.

'Me, too,' said Joe. 'I wish I had a quid for every time I've thought of sticking my head in the gas oven.'

'Oh, Joe!' said Sally.

'Oh, Sally!' said Joe.

A man of more delicacy than Mr Trout would have withdrawn softly at this point, feeling that the tender scene was one that did not demand the presence of an audience, but Mr Trout's slowness at leaving premises was equalled by his reluctance to withdraw from tender scenes. He stood there drinking in this one with a benevolent smile.

It was a smile which conveyed only benevolence, but there was in his eyes anxiety and concern, for he was feeling that everything was not so simple as the two principals appeared to think. And when he heard Joe speaking enthusiastically of visits to registry offices and Sally falling in eagerly with the suggestion, he called attention to himself with one of those dry coughs in which lawyers specialize.

'Are we not forgetting something?' he said.

Joe started violently. He had had no notion that Mr Trout was among those present. He had supposed that on seeing Sally he would have realized that his company was not desired. But, as has been shown, it would have come as a surprise to him to learn that his company was ever not desired. He was as difficult to dislodge as a family spectre.

'Good Lord!' said Joe. 'Are you still here?'

'Still here,' Mr Trout assured him. 'And when you speak of immediate visits to registry offices with Miss Fitch, I think it is only fitting to remind you that she is engaged to be married to someone else.'

He had anticipated that the point he was raising would have a damping effect, and he was right. It did have a damping effect.

Joe blinked and released Sally, and Sally collapsed on the umbrella stand.

'Who is this fellow you're engaged to?' Joe demanded.

'Jaklyn Warner,' said Sally, and Joe had to rebuke her.

'No, this is serious, darling,' he said. 'Don't cloud the issue by being funny. Who are you really engaged to?'

'Jaklyn Warner.'

'But you can't be. You've never met him.'

'I've known him for years.'

'Then you must realize the utter impossibility of marrying him.'

'Who is this Mr Warner?' asked Mr Trout. 'Eh? Oh, I was not aware. Who is this Sir Jaklyn Warner?'

It was a question which Joe felt fully competent to answer.

'He is London's leading louse, a worm, a chiseller, a rat, a sponger, never done a stroke of work in his life, supports himself by borrowing money, which of course he never pays back.'

Mr Trout nodded sagely.

'I know the type. Young men like that abound in Hollywood. They live on cocktails and appetizers at parties to which they have not been invited. They roam the streets of Beverly Hills till they hear music and see a string of coloured lanterns, and then they go in and eat sausages on little sticks. I am surprised, Miss Fitch, that you should have plighted your troth to one of these.'

'I was engaged to him once before. When I lived in Worcestershire.'

'Well, that's no reason why you should make a habit of it,' said Joe severely. He was much moved. 'You must get in touch with him immediately and break the engagement.'

'Oh, I couldn't.'

'Why not?'

'He would be certain to cry, and I couldn't bear it.'

'A dilemma,' said Mr Trout. 'Definitely a dilemma.'

'But I see a way round it,' said Joe. 'Has he a telephone?'

'Yes.'

'Then it's perfectly simple. You just ring him up and say "Is that you, Jaklyn? I'm phoning to say it's all off. I'm marrying Joe Pickering." '

Mr Trout frowned, clicked his tongue and tut-tutted.

'I could not endorse that procedure.'

'Why not?'

'The party of the second part would bring an action for breach of promise.'

'Men don't bring actions for breach of promise.'

'Men of Sir Jaklyn Warner's stamp do.'

'That's true. I wouldn't put it past him.'

'They have no shame. And we do not want Miss Fitch to run the risk of being mulcted in substantial damages.'

'Then what do you suggest?'

'That I go and see this man. The situation is beyond the scope of a layman. It needs a practised lawyer.'

'I call that a splendid idea,' said Sally, and Joe, though his personal tastes ran more in the direction of knocking Jaklyn down and jumping on him with hobnailed boots, had to admit that it was reasonable.

'I have handled many similar cases in Hollywood. My clients have often complimented me on my gifts of persuasion. But we must of course not lose sight of the fact that in the matter under advisement we shall be facing difficulties. I cannot guarantee success. I gather from the luxuriousness of this flat that you are wealthy, Miss Fitch. When I was in the living-room I noticed a Corot over the mantelpiece which must be worth a considerable sum. This Warner will not resign his claims willingly. One can only do one's best. But I will go and see him.'

'Now?'

'At once.'

'I'll come with you.'

'No. I must be alone.'

'Then I'll wait in the street,' said Joe.

'I see no objection to that,' said Mr Trout.

'Tell me,' said Joe as they started their journey. 'How do you propose to conduct these negotiations?'

'Just as I have invariably conducted negotiations of this nature,' said Mr Trout. 'From what you tell me of this Warner he appears to be no different from the impecunious young men of Hollywood with their diet of dry Martinis and sausages on little sticks. I have always found them amenable to a money offer and I have no doubt Sir Jaklyn Warner will be the same.'

'You mean to buy him off?'

'Precisely.'

'H'm.'

'You have doubts?'

'I was only thinking it's going to cost a bit.'

'Money well spent.'

'Yes, of course. No argument about that. The catch is that I haven't any money. But if you'll chalk it up on the slate, I'll repay you later. I shall have some coming in soon.'

The visibility in the cab was not good, but Mr Trout's benevolent smile did much to light it up.

'My dear boy,' he said. 'You surely do not suppose that I am going to charge you a fee or ask to be reimbursed for any expenses I may be put to on this case. I would not dream of it. As the colloquial expression has it, this is on the house. A small compensation for getting your affairs into, I must admit, a certain disorder. No true Californian would think of sending in a bill for services rendered to two young lovers in what practically amounts to Springtime.'

It was a moment before emotion would allow Joe to speak, so moved was he by the nobility of these sentiments. When he did speak, it was to pay a marked tribute to California, which, he said, judging from its inhabitants, must be quite a place. Unless, of course, Mr Trout was unique.

'Tell me,' he said. 'Are there any more at home like you?'

'There are a few,' said Mr Trout, 'and better boys you never knew.'

He winced a little as he spoke. He was thinking of Fred Basset and Johnny Runcible and G. J. Flannery, and wondering if his defection from Bachelors Anonymous would mean the break-up of a friendship of twenty years.

Chapter Thirteen

THINGS WERE NOT GOING too well with Jacklyn Warner. In addition to being married, to which he greatly objected, he had a nasty hangover and he owed a bookmaker fifty pounds. This was the debt he had had in mind when he told his future bride that he owed twenty. He had lacked the nerve to reveal the full amount to her.

The bookmaker, moreover, was not one of those kindly bookmakers with hearts of gold who can sympathize with a fiscally embarrassed young man and allow his account to remain unsettled indefinitely. Informed by Jaklyn that there might be a long delay before payment could be made, he had drawn in his breath sharply and looked grave.

'Oh, I do hope there won't be, Sir J.,' he said. 'I know it's silly to be superstitious, but I can't help remembering that every single client of mine that's done me down over money has had an accident happen to him. Time after time I've seen it occur. Time after time after time. It's like some kind of fate. Only the other day there was a fellow with a ginger moustache called Witherspoon. Owed me fifty for Plumpton and pleaded the Gaming Act. Less than a week later, would you believe this, he was found unconscious in the street—must have got into some unpleasantness of some kind—and had to have six stitches. No, seven. I was forgetting the one over his left eye.'

This conversation had taken place at the house of the creditor, and Jaklyn had left his presence feeling like a nervous young member of Captain Kidd's pirate crew who has just been handed the black spot. Arriving at his Chelsea residence, he found Mr Trout knocking on the door and beginning to get tired of achieving no result.

'Sir Jaklyn Warner?' said Mr Trout.

Normally if a caller had asked this question Jaklyn would have replied in the negative, for he believed in taking no chances, but Mr Trout's aspect was so obviously that of one connected with the Law that he decided to risk it. He had prosperous relatives all over England, and one of them might quite easily have handed in his dinner pail, leaving him a bit of the right stuff, and this lawyer was here to tell him so.

'Yes,' he said. 'Who are you?'

'My name is Trout. Of the legal firm of Trout, Wapshott and Edelstein of Hollywood, California, in the United States of America.'

Jaklyn's hopes took a sharp rise. He remembered that his Uncle Eustace had left hurriedly for America at the time when he had been wanted by the police to assist them in their inquiries in the matter of a big long-firm swindle. He had always been fond of his nephew, and what more likely than that he should have fetched up in Hollywood, made a packet, perished of a surfeit of brandy smashes, and left that packet to that nephew. It was with a beating heart that Jaklyn put latch-key to door.

'Come in,' he said. 'Come right in.'

Following him over the threshold, Mr Trout was encouraged to observe the evidences of impecuniosity that met his eyes. A man with an abode as shabby as this, he felt, would surely be what he had called amenable to a money offer, and though he was prepared, if necessary, to spend cash lavishly on behalf of young lovers in what was practically Springtime, he hoped it would not be necessary. He had always been a man who liked to keep expenses down.

Taking a seat, he wasted no time on preambles.

'You are affianced,' he said, 'to my client, Miss Sarah Fitch.'

Another man in Jaklyn's position would no doubt have explained that owing to his having been the victim of what amounted to a shot-gun wedding, marriage to Sally was no longer in the sphere of practical politics, but his native prudence restrained him. The sixth sense which had stood him in good stead from boyhood told him that this lawyer

301

bloke's visit was somehow connected with money and that it would be rash to confide in him too freely.

'I am,' he said.

'Her father disapproves of the match.'

'He does, does he?'

'And he is prepared to pay you a reasonable sum if you will agree to consider it null and void.'

If Jaklyn felt that it was odd that Sally's father, a humble country vicar, should be in a position to scatter money about like this, he did not say so, feeling perhaps that the Reverend Fitch had won the Irish Sweep or backed a series of winners since he had last seen him. Nor did he protest, as some men would have done, that he had never been so insulted in his life. His thoughts riveted exclusively on the man with the ginger moustache and the seven stitches, he said:

'What do you call a reasonable sum?'

'Fifty pounds.'

'It's a deal.'

As Mr Trout had told Joe, this was not the first time he had had talks of this description with impecunious young men, but it was the first time an impecunious young man had reached a decision with such lightning speed, and it took his breath away. Fifty pounds had been what might be called his asking price, and he had taken it for granted that his mention of it would be the cue for the haggling to begin. Jaklyn's instantaneous acceptance of the offer gave him the feeling he had sometimes had when going downstairs in the dark and treading on empty space where he had supposed the last step to be.

His impulse on recovering his breath was to tell Jaklyn what a good man thought of him, but he had a dinner date with the woman he loved, and though she had warned him that she might be a little late in getting away from her hospital, he did not dare to spend time rebuking young men so lost to shame that censure would be wasted on them. He paid Jaklyn fifty pounds, and left in silence. And he had not gone far before emotional breathing made itself heard and Joe emerged from the shadows.

'Well?' said Joe. 'Did it go off all right?'

The anxiety in his voice amused Mr Trout. It seemed to him bizarre that his young friend should be entertaining any uncertainty as to the success of a mission entrusted to Ephraim Trout of Trout, Wapshott and Edelstein. He replied that it had gone off with the greatest smoothness. He had, as expected, swayed Jaklyn Warner like a reed, bending him to his will with eloquence which there was no withstanding. Warner could see from the firmness of his manner that argument would be futile and that no nonsense would be stood.

Joe gave him a worshipping look.

'Trout, you're a marvel!'

'One does one's best, Pickering.'

'It's a knack, I suppose, this ability of yours to look people in the eye and make them wilt?'

'I would prefer to call it a gift.'

'You're probably right. Anyway, thanks again. I wish there was something I could do for you.'

'There is. You can give me a word of advice.'

'What's your problem?'

'I am dining tonight with Mrs Bingham, and I would like you to brief me as to the advisability of proposing marriage to her.'

Joe in his uplifted mood was feeling that the world would be a better place if everybody started proposing to everyone. He said it struck him as a splendid idea.

'You do not think it would be too soon?'

'How do you mean?'

'An exhibition of masculine impetuosity might frighten her.'

'I doubt it.'

'I have not known her long.'

'Incompetent, immaterial and irrelevant. Women like a dashing man.'

'Is that so?'

'Why, it's only a year or two since man used to snatch women up on their saddle bows and ride off with them. And the women loved it. A pity you can't do that.'

'A great pity.'

'But nowadays, of course, they expect you to propose. The great thing is not to do it over the soup. Wait for the coffee. Where are you dining?'

'At the Dorchester.'

'I'll drop you there.'

'Very good of you. Why not over the soup?'

'Not romantic.'

'Of course, of course, of course. I might have made a grave blunder. Thank you, Pickering.'

'Not at all. Go to it, Trout, and heaven speed your wooing.'

It was in the spirit of the Polish gentleman in the song who sang 'Ding dong, ding dong, ding dong I hurry along, for it is my wedding morning' that Joe, having deposited Mr Trout at his destination, took the cab on to Fountain Court. If you wanted to be finnicky about it, it was not actually his wedding morning, but this made no difference to his euphoria. Admitted by Sally to number 3A, he folded her in a close embrace, waltzed her four times round the room and informed her that this was the maddest merriest day of all the glad new year because the dark menace of Sir Jaklyn Warner, Bart, had ceased to operate.

'Everything is fixed up,' he said. 'No wedding bells for you.'

'I know,' said Sally. 'He's married already.'

Once more Joe found himself gripped by that peculiar feeling of having been struck on the bridge of the nose by a wet fish. He relaxed the folded embrace and stared incredulously.

'He's *what*? Who told you that?'

'Daphne. She's the one he married. She told me just after you and Mr Trout had left.'

'Who's Daphne?'

'Daphne Dolby. She lives with me.'

'Oh, the personable popsy,' said Joe, recalling Jerry Nichols's remarks.

'She is personable,' said Sally, 'but that's not why Jaklyn married her. I think I had better explain.'

'If you don't want me to have a dizzy spell.'

'It's quite simple really.'

'To a brain like yours, perhaps, not to mine.'

'Daphne was engaged to Jaklyn.'

'One of those easy to please girls?'

'She was all set on becoming Lady Warner.'

'Oh, I see.'

'So when I told her I was engaged to him, it naturally made her think a bit. She decided she had to move quickly, or she would lose him, because I was a much better bet from Jaklyn's point of view than she was. I had just been left twenty-five thousand pounds.'

'Yes. Jerry Nichols told me about that.'

'Great added attraction, twenty-five thousand pounds. So she took him to the registry office and made him marry her.'

'Yes, I get the picture now. She sounds like quite a girl.'

'She is.'

'We must have her to dinner some night when we are in our little home'.

'And it will be a very little home, I'm afraid.'

'Meaning what?'

'That's all we shall be able to afford. Oh, Joe,' said Sally, 'I've made the most awful fool of myself. I'm the world's worst half-wit.'

Chapter Fourteen

JOE FROWNED.

'You are speaking of the woman I love,' he said stiffly.

Sally continued in the depths.

'But will you after you hear what I've done?'

'Will I what?'

'Love me.'

'Certainly I will. Love conquers all, as Trout would say. Oh, by the way! Trout.'

'What about him?'

'We've got to be very careful what we say to Trout. He must never know about Jaklyn being married. He thinks his triumph over him was due entirely to his eloquence and the force of his personality. It would give his self-esteem a nasty sock on the jaw if he learned the awful truth.'

'I don't see why we should be fussy about Trout's feelings. He nearly ruined our lives.'

'But with the best intentions.'

'As it is, he's probably ruined mine.'

'How do you figure that out?'

'All through him I may have lost you.'

'What gives you the idea that you may have lost your Pickering?'

Sally gulped. The moment had come for confession, and confession was as unpleasant to her as it is to most people.

'How much does money matter to you, Joe?'

'Very little. Dross, I sometimes call it.'

'Would you still want me if I hadn't any?'

'Don't ask foolish questions.'

'You would?'

'Of course I would.'

'Well, that's a relief. Because I haven't.'

There are observations, popularly known as conversation-stoppers, which are calculated to cast a hushed silence on the most animated dialogue. One might have supposed that this would have been one of them, but Joe, though startled, received the news with equanimity. The truth was that in spite of Jerry Nichols's assurances he had not been able to overcome a certain uneasiness at the thought of the wide gap between Sally's finances and his own. Pure though his motives were in seeking to make her his bride, he had had the uncomfortable feeling that people who did not know those motives might place him in the Jaklyn Warner class. Thanks to Mr Llewellyn, that modern Santa Claus, this uneasiness had ceased to trouble him. He was able to speak with perfect calmness.

'You haven't any money?'

'No.'

'But what's become of it all? You can't have spent twenty-five thousand pounds on chocolates and ice cream since last Tuesday.'

Sally smiled politely, but it was a painful smile. Confession was still to come, and she hated it more than ever.

'Did Mr Nichols tell you about my legacy?'

'Not in any detail. I happened to mention to him that I loved you, and he said "Oh, the heiress", adding that somebody had left you a packet.'

'Yes, Miss Carberry. I told you about her.'

'The anti-tobacco woman you once worked for.'

'Yes. She left me the money on condition that I didn't smoke. And Daphne Dolby was to live with me to see that I didn't. If she caught me smoking, it was all to go to the Anti-Tobacco League. So I was careful not to smoke.'

'Very prudent. Very sensible. But I feel there is more to come.'

'There is. Tonight I did. I had a cigarette.'

'With the Dolby prowling and prowling around like the troops of Midian!'

'She wasn't prowling around. That's the whole point. She went out about five minutes after you and Mr Trout left. She forgot to take her cigarette case with her. It was lying on that little table there. It caught my eye, and suddenly I felt I would die if I didn't have a smoke. It was all Trout's fault.'

'That's the part where I don't quite follow you. I don't see how Trout comes into it.'

'It was the way he talked. Don't you remember? All that stuff about being unable to guarantee success because we must not lose sight of the fact that in the matter under advisement we should be facing difficulties. He made it sound as if he hadn't a hope.'

'Lawyers always talk that way. You should hear Shoesmith of Shoesmith, Shoesmith, Shoesmith, and Shoesmith. It's their native caution. Building for the future, as you might put it. If the thing's a flop, they can say "I warned you that this might happen." If it's a success, you will think how wonderful they must be to have brought it off against all the odds.'

'Well, I didn't know that, so he left me a quivering mass of nerves—'

'But looking terrific.'

'—and I was just wondering how I could pull myself together and shake off this awful feeling of depression, when my eye fell on Daphne's cigarette case.'

'And you reached for it?'

'I reached for it.'

Joe nodded understandingly.

'Just what any girl would have done in your place. And the Dolby remembered her case and came back to get it and found you blowing smoke rings?'

'Yes.'

'I thought as much. I am a playwright, and we playwrights have a sort of sixth sense. Well, when I say I'm a playwright, *Cousin Angela* did have sixteen performances. Many a dramatist has to be content with opening on Friday and closing on the following Saturday. And talking of *Cousin Angela*. . .'

'She was as hard as nails about it.'

'Talking of *Cousin Angela*. . .'

'You might think that as we had become friends she would

have pretended not to notice, but when it has anything to do with her job she has no friends.'

'Very praiseworthy. But I was about to speak of *Cousin Angela*. I have a bit of news which may bring the roses back to your cheeks. Llewellyn is going to do it as a picture.'

He was right about the roses. They returned just as predicted. Sally emitted what in any popsy less personable would have been a squeal.

'You might have told me before,' she said reproachfully.

'Slipped my mind.'

'I've been going through hell.'

'Good for the adrenal glands.'

'How much?'

'We haven't talked terms yet.'

'But these studios always pay the earth, don't they?'

'Invariably.'

'We shall be rich without my money.'

'Modestly bloated.'

'And no danger of your feelings being hurt because I paid the bills.'

'The husband always ought to have the money. Ask any husband.'

'Yes. Otherwise it offends his *amour propre*.'

'My God. French and everything. I'm getting a gifted wife. You must have been on many a day excursion to Boulogne.'

'I did go once.'

'You didn't happen to run into a man named Bingham, did you?'

'Not that I remember.'

'You would have remembered if you had. He fell overboard. You would have noticed. Well, excuse me for a moment.'

'Where are you going?'

'Only to the telephone. I thought I ought to ring Llewellyn up and ask him how he's getting on. He's in hospital.'

'Is he ill?'

'No. Merely hiding from Vera Dalrymple. I'll explain later.'

From her knowledge of Ivor Llewellyn, gathered at the

time when she had interviewed him for her paper, Sally would have supposed that any telephone conversation in which he took part would have been of considerable duration. She had thought of him as a man always with plenty to say and not averse to the sound of his own voice. But this telephone conversation terminated almost before it had begun. Joe said 'I.L.? Pickering,' and that was all he said. And after listening for not more than a minute he hung up and came away from the instrument, Mr Llewellyn having apparently replaced the receiver at the other end.

It perplexed Sally. Then she saw Joe's face, and perplexity was succeeded by dismay.

'Joe!' she cried. 'What is it?' and he smiled the ghost of a twisted smile, the smile of a man whose world has collapsed beneath him but who knows that he must show himself one of the bull-dog breed whose upper lips never unstiffen.

'Do you want it broken gently?'

'No!'

'It'll be a shock.'

'I don't care.'

'Well, I'm sorry to say Llewellyn has fired me and isn't going to do the play.'

Sally did not swoon, but looking back later she wondered how she had managed to avoid doing so. The floor heaved like an ocean swell, and Joe became for a moment two Joes, both flickering. It seemed an age before she could speak, and when she did she could only say 'But why?'

Joe replied that Mr Llewellyn had not told him why.

'All he said was "Pickering, eh? Just the man I wanted to contact. You're fired, Pickering, and if you think I'm going to make a picture of your damned play, you're mistaken." '

'Nothing else?'

'Only instructions to remove my blasted belongings from 8 Enniston Gardens without delay.'

'But what had you done to him?'

'Not a thing.'

'Had he seemed hostile?'

'On the contrary, my stock was particularly high with him.

He wanted to avoid Vera Dalrymple, who had phoned to say she was coming to call, and I suggested that he should go to hospital. His gratitude was touching.'

'Well, I don't understand it.'

'I do. It's the jinx that's been following me around for weeks, making everything I do go wrong.'

'Not everything. You found me.'

'But we can't get married.'

'Why can't we get married? Try to stop me.'

'What'll we live on?'

'I've got a job.'

'I haven't.'

'You'll get one.'

'Who says so?'

'I say so. We'll be all right. All it needs is prudence and economy. And now go and get your things, and then you can take me out to dinner at Barribault's. You owe me a dinner at Barribault's.'

Joe, as he reached journey's end, was feeling somewhat, if only a little, better. Agony though it was to be parted from Sally even for a moment, there was something, he felt, to be said for being alone and free from interruptions. He had much on his mind, and the solitude of 8 Enniston Gardens allowed him to think.

One of his subjects for thought was of course the mystery of the sudden animosity of Ivor Llewellyn, which, as Sherlock Holmes would have said, undoubtedly presented certain features of interest. For when a man has thanked you—and in broken accents, at that—for showing him the way out of an unpleasant dilemma, you do not expect him five minutes later, or practically five minutes later, to start treating you like a leper who has tried to borrow from him.

But in these bustling times one is seldom permitted to remain uninterrupted for long. Scarcely had Joe set the little grey cells to work on the Case of the Inexplicably Annoyed Motion Picture Magnate than the telephone rang. With a sigh and wishing that he had someone, as Mr. Llewellyn always had, to whom he could say 'Answer that. If it's for me, say I'm out,' he reached for the receiver, and a familiar voice spoke.

'Joe?'

'Oh, hullo, Jerry.'

'I'm phoning to ask if everything went off all right. I must say I didn't expect to find you at Enniston Gardens. I thought you would have been at Fountain Court.'

'I'm going back there.'

'Did things go according to plan?'

'Yes.'

'You followed my advice?'

'Yes.'

'Close embrace?'

'Yes.'

'Till ribs squeaked?'

'Yes.'

'Result, complete reconciliation?'

'Yes.'

'You don't sound very ecstatic.'

'I've got a spot of Llewellyn trouble.'

'Is that all?'

'It's enough for me.'

'Don't let it get you down. These things always iron themselves out. It's like when my father starts throwing his weight about. We just sit tight and let him rave, knowing that he will eventually come off the boil and resume his place in the comity of nations. And now I must leave you, Joe. In fact, I must rush. I'm putting on the nose-bag with a popsy.'

Jerry withdrew, but the truth of the old saying that if you particularly want to be left undisturbed to brood over your problems the telephone is sure to ring was exemplified once more a moment later. This time it was Mr Trout.

'Pickering? A hearty good evening to you, Pickering. Glad to find you in, Pickering. You might have been out, and I want a word with you.'

Even though separated from him by a length of wire Joe had no difficulty in diagnosing the speaker's mental state. Mr Trout's voice was the voice of one who, putting his fate to the touch to win or lose it all, has found himself a winner. Its volume made that plain. No man, Joe felt, to whom the adored object had handed the pink slip could so nearly have fractured his ear drum, and forgetting his own troubles for the moment he rejoiced in the other's good fortune. Mr Trout might be the sort of man whose morning post was never without its quota of attractive offers from lunatic asylums, but he wished him well.

'I gather from your manner,' he said, 'that you have offered your heart with good results. Over the coffee?'

'No, Pickering, over the oysters. I couldn't wait for the coffee. Swallowing my fifth oyster, I snatched her up on my saddle bow, ha ha, and carried her off. We are going to have coffee after I have finished telephoning. I was hoping to get Llewellyn.'

'He's in hospital.'

'So Amelia told me. She was his nurse. But he is not in hospital. I phoned St Swithin's, but he had gone.'

'Gone?'

'Leaving no trace. Some trouble about somebody wanting a sample of his blood. One supposes that he is on his way to Enniston Gardens. Well, if he comes, I want you to tell him about me and Amelia. Tell him tactfully, for it will be a shock.'

'Why?'

'Because, as she was leaving the hospital, he asked her to marry him.'

'You don't say!'

'On the contrary I do say. And she told him she would think it over. Think it over! Ha,' said Mr. Trout. 'I didn't give her much chance to think it over. I must have electrified her.'

Joe gave him an admiring look, its effect, of course, largely diminished by the fact that they were talking on the telephone.

'I told you women liked a dashing man.'

'How right you were.'

'You and Errol Flynn, not much to choose between you.'

'I suppose not.'

'Give my respects to the future Mrs Trout.'

'I will.'

It now needed only Mr Llewellyn to make the little circle of Joe's intimates complete, and shortly after Joe had said goodbye to Mr Trout the roster was filled. There was the sound of a turning key, and Mr Llewellyn walked in, looking a little ruffled, as if he had just escaped from a hospital against the wishes of its staff. His hair was disordered, and he had omitted to put on a tie.

Even to an unobservant eye it would have been apparent that he was not one of Joe's admirers. In the look he gave him as he entered there was something of the open dislike which a resident of India exhibits when he comes to take his morning bath and finds a cobra in the bath tub. Not even at the nurse who had wanted to take a sample of his blood had he directed a more formidable glare.

'Oh, it's you,' he said.

Joe conceded this.

'What are you doing here? I told you to get out.'

Joe said he had been collecting his belongings.

'As instructed,' he added. He spoke curtly, for since their talk on the telephone he had not been well pleased with his former employer, deprecating his habit of firing good men simply, apparently, to gratify a passing whim.

'And do you know why I told you to get out?'

'I've been trying to think.'

'I'll tell you.'

Mr Lewellyn had swelled like a bull-frog, and his glare had intensified in animosity. A sense of grievance often has this effect.

'Because you officiously insisted on my going to that damned hospital, when you must have known what would be the result if I did. This afternoon the inevitable happened. I asked my nurse to marry me. She said she would think it over. One can scarcely suppose that having thought it over she will not say Yes. No woman I've ever asked to marry me has not said Yes. There is something irresistible about me. Tomorrow, therefore, I shall be engaged, and from there to being married is but a step. I'm not saying anything against Amelia Bingham, she's a very good sort, but I don't want to be married, and thanks to you I shall be. And you wonder why I've fired you. Why are you grinning like a halfwitted ape?'

He was referring to the gentle smile which had appeared on Joe's face as he heard the name Amelia Bingham.

'May I say a word?' said Joe.

'No.'

'It's just that—'

'I don't want to hear it.'

'It's simply—'

The telephone rang.

'Answer that,' said Mr Llewellyn. 'If it's for me, say I'm out.'

Joe, though half inclined to say 'Answer it your ruddy self', did as directed, and was surprised to hear the voice of that great lover Mr Trout. He had thought Mr Trout would be otherwise occupied.

'Pickering?'

'Yes.'

'Is Llewellyn there?'

'Just come in.'

'Have you told him?'

'Not yet.'

'Let me speak to him. It will come as a shock to the poor fellow to hear that I have won Amelia from him, but he only has himself to blame. The idea of letting her think it over. You don't win a woman that way. The way to win a woman—'

'I know. Saddle bow stuff.'

'Exactly.'

Joe handed the receiver to Mr Llewellyn.

'Trout,' he said.

Watching Mr Llewellyn as he telephoned, Joe was not surprised to see his face light up shortly after he had addressed Mr Trout as Benedict Arnold and asked him if he had sold any good forts lately. His share of the conversation after that was mostly gasps and gurgles, but it was soon evident that

315

good relations had once more been established between him and his old friend. When he replaced the receiver, his face wore the expression which one notices on the faces of those who have been saved from the scaffold at the eleventh hour, and his voice when he spoke had so much of the carolling skylark in it that Percy Bysshe Shelley, had he been present, would have been fully justified in saying 'Hail to thee, blithe spirit'.

'Don't tell me miracles are no longer box office,' he chanted. 'How wrong I was in supposing that my guardian angel was asleep at the switch. Do you know what?'

'Yes.'

'Amelia Bingham is going to marry Trout.'

'Yes. That's what I was trying to tell you.'

'It's colossal!'

'Yes.'

'It's sensational.'

'Yes.'

'Don't be so damned calm about it, Pickering. You don't seem to realize what this means to me. Would you care to have a rough scenario of my future plans? I shall return immediately to California, where I shall become a member of Bachelors Anonymous. Trout is giving me a letter to a friend of his named Runcible, and he assures me the boys will welcome me with open arms. Gosh, I feel like a million dollars!'

Joe laughed one of those hollow, mirthless ones.

'I dare say you do,' he said, 'but I don't.'

'What's the matter with you?'

'You aren't going to do my play as a picture.'

'Who says so?'

'You said so.'

'Hell's bells,' said Mr Llewellyn, astounded. 'You surely don't believe everything the top man of a motion picture studio tells you? I remember now, I was feeling a little sore with you at the time, and I expressed myself with the generous strength which is so characteristic of me, but you don't have to pay any attention to that. Of course I'm going to do your play. We've only to settle terms. How about two hundred and fifty thousand dollars?'

Joe rose from six to eight inches into the air with a hoarse cry, and Mr Llewellyn misread his emotion. He had so often heard stars cry hoarsely like that in response to an offer. Coming from Joe, who was not a star, it piqued him.

'Dammit,' he said, 'you can't expect top prices for your first picture. Two hundred and fifty thousand isn't at all bad, ask anyone. Take it or leave it.'

'I'll take it,' said Joe.

'Good. Come and have some dinner.'

'I was giving my fiancée dinner.'

'I'll come along,' said Mr Llewellyn, who knew the pleasure his company was bound to add to a meal.

It was as at Joe's suggestion he completed the writing and signing of a rough form of contract that the doorbell rang, and his torso and both his chins shook in sudden alarm.

'Vera Dalrymple!' he gasped.

Joe did not share his tremors. There had been a time when he had trembled with fear at the lady in question's frown, but with that contract in his pocket and the air vibrant with wedding bells he felt more than equal to a dozen Vera Dalrymples.

'Leave her to me, I.L.,' he said. 'Go and hide in the bathroom or under your bed or somewhere. I'll attend to her.'

And with a firm step he strode to the door.